JOHN O'E

TIPPING POINT:
OPLAN 5015

BOOK III OF TIPPING POINT

Printed in the United States of America

First printing: April, 2022

Dedicated to President Zelensky, the Ukrainian soldiers, and the valiant people of Ukraine.

Other books by John O'Brien

A New World Series

A New World: Chaos

A New World: Return

A New World: Sanctuary

A New World: Taken

A New World: Awakening

A New World: Dissension

A New World: Takedown

A New World: Conspiracy

A New World: Reckoning

A New World: Storm

Companion Books

A New World: Untold Stories

A New World: Untold Stories II

The Third Wave: Eidolon

Ares Virus

Ares Virus: Arctic Storm

Ares Virus: White Horse

Ares Virus: Phoenix Rising

Red Team

Red Team: Strigoi

Red Team: Lycan

Red Team: Cartel Part One

Red Team: Cartel Part Two

A Shrouded World

A Shrouded World: Whistlers

A Shrouded World: Atlantis

A Shrouded World: Convergence

A Shrouded World: Valhalla

A Shrouded World: Asabron

A Shrouded World: Bitfrost

A Shrouded World: Hvergelmir

A Shrouded World: Asgard

Lifting the Veil

Lifting the Veil: Fallen

Lifting the Veil: Winter

Lifting the Veil: Emergence

Lifting the Veil: Risen

Tipping Point

Tipping Point: Opening Shots

Tipping Point: Escalation

Tipping Point: OPLAN 5015

Author's Note

I want to take a moment here to acknowledge the people of Ukraine, to whom this book is dedicated to. We here talk of struggles with gas prices and inflation, but that is nothing compared with what the populace there is having to deal with on a daily basis. I truly hope they withstand the storm and evict the invaders so can start to rebuild, coming out stronger on the other end.

Now, I will admit to hoping that President Zelensky might actually read the book. I mean, who knows. But, in all seriousness, my thoughts are constantly with the hardships that all of Ukraine is having to endure. Take a moment as you go about your daily life to send positive thoughts their way.

I have to also confess that I was plenty upset about Russia's invasion. Part of that comes from a selfish place. The future of the story circulating in my mind had included a Russian invasion of Ukraine. When the Russian units crossed the border, I saw a part of my story vanish in the wind. However, that part of my tale went very differently than what is actually transpiring in that war torn country, and I'm thankful for it. Go Ukraine!

* * * * * *

Okay, so I believe I said there would be three books, but that was going to be it. Yeah, well, so, that didn't happen. I don't know how these stories get away from me, but it's probably better that you don't trust it when I say how many books a series will hold. Right now, it's definitely going to be four, but I don't dare say that will be it. There's still a lot of story crammed into my head and I'm not sure how many books it will take to tell it.

Okay, so, does anyone else hear Idiocracy every time when writing or hearing "I'm not sure?" Yes? No? Well, maybe it's just me, then. Let's just slide on past that and continue on.

So, there is so much technology, both upcoming and in

operation, that I chose not to mention some as a way of simplifying things. I don't want this to end up as some kind of manual, dry and full of technical writings. Perhaps it's too late for that.

One example would be the digital radio frequency memory jammers which receives a signal, stores it, and then replicates it before retransmitting. It's sent out as the same signal, therefore fooling radar systems into thinking it's a valid return. As much as I wanted to get into the intricacies of modern warfare, again, I felt that too much of it would render this as more of a manual rather than a story.

Another aspect that I took for ease of understanding was the use of the western rank structure for their associated counterparts in the Chinese and Taiwanese militaries. There are so many moving parts inside my head, that I'm not sure I could keep up with different naming structures. I'm barely keeping afloat as it is.

I would also like to mention that the orders given in the combat situations have also been simplified. They are generally much more specific as to who the order is for, as well as the order itself.

So, I'm going to mention here that it's very difficult to come up with different descriptions for similar combat scenarios. Given the long-range, beyond visual engagements inherent in today's warfare, those seem to mostly play out in similar ways. I found myself drowning in monotony when faced with writing the various engagements. It was hard not to just write the same thing over and over again and I agonized to somehow make them different. I don't know if I was successful in that or not, but know that I tried. It feels like there should be some sort of emoji following that sentence, perhaps like a smiley face or something.

Well, there's really not much more to say. This book didn't advance the timeline of the story much as I found myself spending a lot of time focusing on one engagement. You'll see what I mean. I hope you like this next segment. That's the most important thing for a storyteller, that it's enjoyed and can transport a reader into a different universe for a while. I hope that's what I've been able to do.

Thank you for taking the chance with this and my other books. I can't tell you just how much I appreciate it. So, without further ado, let's get to turning some pages.

John

Cast of Characters

US Personnel

Presidential Cabinet

Jake Chamberlain, *Secretary of the Navy*

Tom Collier, *CIA Director*

Elizabeth Hague, *Ambassador to the United Nations*

Imraham Patel, *CDC Director*

Aaron MacCulloch, *Secretary of Defense*

Bill Reiser, *NSA Director*

Joan Richardson, *Homeland Security Director*

Fred Stevenson, *Secretary of State*

Frank Winslow, *President of the United States*

Joint Chiefs of Staff

Phil Dawson, *General, USAF—Joint Chiefs of Staff Chairman*

Kevin Loughlin, *General, US Army—Joint Chiefs of Staff Vice Chairman*

Tony Anderson, *General, US Army—Army Chief of Staff*

Duke Calloway, *General, US Marines—Commandant of the Marines*

Brian Durant, *Admiral, USN—Chief of Naval Operations*

Mike Williams, *General, USAF—Air Force Chief of Staff*

US Naval Personnel

Jerry Ackland, *Commander, USN—Captain of the USS Texas*

David Avelar, *Commander, USN—Captain of the USS* Topeka

Peter Baird, *Commander, USN—Captain of the USS* Cheyenne

Charlie Blackwell, *Vice Admiral, USN—Third Fleet Commander*

Kyle Blaine, *Lieutenant, USN—F-35C Pilot*

Shawn Brickline, *Admiral, USN—Pacific Theatre Commander (USPACCOM)*

Jeff Brown, *Commander, USN—Captain of the USS* Connecticut

Alex Buchanan, *Captain, USN—Indo-Pacific Watch Commander*

Ralph Burrows, *Captain, USN—Captain of the USS* Abraham Lincoln

Chip Calhoun, *Rear Admiral, USN—Carrier Strike Group 5/Task force 70 Commander*

Alan Cook, *Commander, USN—Captain of the USS* Springfield

Bryce Crawford, *Admiral, USN—Commander of the Pacific Fleet (COMPACFLT)*

Jeff Dunmar, *Commander, USN—Captain of the USS* Seawolf

Sam Enquist, *Lieutenant (j.g.), USN—F/A-18F Electronic Warfare Officer (EWO)*

Ed Fablis, *Rear Admiral, USN—Carrier Strike Group 9 Commander*

Scott Gambino, *Commander, USN—Captain of the USS* Ohio

John Garner, *Captain, USN—Captain of the USS* Theodore Roosevelt

Steve Gettins, *Rear Admiral, USN—Carrier Strike Group 1 Commander*

Matt Goldman, *Lieutenant, USN—F/A-18F Pilot*

Myles Ingram, *Commander, USN—Captain of the USS* Howard

Tom Jenson, *Lt. Commander, USN—Executive Officer of the USS* Howard

Zach Keene, *Lieutenant (j.g.), USN—F/A18-F Electronic Warfare Officer (EWO)*

Tyson Kelley, *Captain, USN—Captain of the USS* Ronald Reagan

Carlos Lopez, *Lieutenant, USN—P-8 Pilot*

Ryan Malone, *Lt. Commander, USN—Executive Officer of the USS* Springfield

Brent Martin, *Commander, USN—P-8 Combat Information Officer*

Ben Meyer, *Commander, USN—Captain of the USS* Illinois

James Munford, *Lt. Commander, USN—Executive Officer of the USS* Texas

Michael Prescott, *Rear Admiral, USN—Carrier Strike Group 11 Commander*

Carl Sandburg, *Rear Admiral, USN—Carrier Strike Group 3 Commander*

Kurt Schwarz, *Captain, USN—Captain of the USS* Nimitz

Nathan Simmons, *Commander, USN—Captain of the USS* Preble

Patrick Sims, *Commander, USN—Captain of the USS* Columbus

Mike Stone, *Commander, USN—VFA-137 Squadron Commander*

Chris Thompson, *Lieutenant, USN—F/A-18F Pilot*

Warren Tillson, *Vice Admiral, USN—Seventh Fleet Commander*

Chris Walkins, *Captain, USN—Captain of the USS* Carl Vinson

Tony Wallins, *Lt. Commander, USN—Executive Officer of the USS* Preble

Charles Wilcutt, *Lt. Commander, USN—Executive Officer of the USS* Cheyenne

Joe Wright, *Commander, USN—Captain of the USS* Mississippi

US Air Force Personnel

Wayne Blythe, *Major, USAF—B-52 Pilot*

James Blackwood, *Captain, USAF—B-2 Pilot*

Jeff Hoffman, *Captain, USAF—C-130 Pilot*

Mark Foley, *Captain, USAF—F-15E WSO*

William Gerber, *Lt. Colonel, USAF—F-15C Pilot*

Dave Lowry, *Captain, USAF—F-16 Pilot*

David Miller, *Captain, USAF—F-15E Pilot*

Jerry Munford, *Captain, USAF—F-22 Pilot*

Vince Rawlings, *General, USAF—Air Force Pacific Commander (COMPACAF)*

Chris Tweedale, *Major, USAF—B-1B Pilot*

Steve Victors, *Captain, USAF—F-22 Pilot*

Tom Watkins, *Colonel, USAF—Schriever AFB Watch Commander*

Amy Weber, *Colonel, USAF—NORAD Watch Commander*

US Army Personnel

Sara Hayward, *Colonel, US Army—USAMRIID Commander*

Charles Warner, *General, US Army—Special Operations Command (SOCOM) Commander*

CIA Personnel

Tony Caputo—*CIA Operator*

Andreas Cruz—*CIA Operator*

Felipe Mendoza—*CIA Operator*

John Parks—*CIA Operator*

NSA Personnel

Allison Townsend—*NSA Analyst*

* * * * * *

Philippine Personnel

President Renaldo Aquino—*Philippine President (as of 17 May, 2021)*

General Ernesto Gonzalez—*Philippine Rebel General*

President Andres Ramos—*Philippine President*

* * * * * *

Chinese Personnel

Wei Chang, *Minister of State Security*

Sun Chen, *Admiral, PLAN—Captain of the aircraft carrier,* Shandong

Hao Chenxu, *President of People's Republic of China (PRC), Paramount Leader of China*

Tan Chun, *Commander, PLAN—Captain of the* ChangZhen 17

Lei Han, *Minister of Finance*

Hou Jianzhi, *Sergeant, PLA—Special Forces sergeant*

Cao Jinglong, *Captain, PLAN—Captain of* ChangZhen 16

Tien Pengfei, Captain, PLA—WZ-10 Pilot

General Quan, *General, PLAN—Fiery Cross Commander (as of 30 May, 2021)*

General Tao, *Fiery Cross Commander (prior to 30 May, 2021)*

Hu Tengyang, *Captain, PLAN—Captain of* ChangZhen 14

Huang Tengyi, *Captain, PLAN—Captain of* Kilo 12

Liu Xiang, *Minister of Foreign Affairs*

Zhou Yang, *Minister of National Defense*

Xie Yingjun, *Captain, PLAN—Captain of* ChangZhen 15

Zheng Yunru, *Major, PLAN—H6M Pilot*

Hu Yuran, *Captain, PLAN—Captain of* Kilo 6

Lin Zhang, *Admiral, PLAN—Southern Fleet Commander*

Xhao Zhen, *Captain, PLA— WZ-10 Pilot*

*   *   *   *   *   *

Taiwanese Personnel

Cheng-han, *Captain, ROCAF—F-35 Pilot*

Chia-ming, *Commander, ROCN—Captain of the ROCS Hai Lu*

Chia-wei, *Captain, ROCAF—F-CK-1 Pilot*

Chin-lung, *Major, ROCAF—F-16 Pilot*

Chun-cheih, *Vice Admiral, ROCN—Flotilla Commander*

Hsin-hung, Chief of General Staff

Kuan-yu, *Captain, ROCAF—F-35 Pilot*

Pai-han, *Commander, ROCN—Captain of the ROCS Hai Lung*

Shu-ching, *President of Taiwan*

Tsung-han, *ROCAF Commander*

Wei-ting, *ROCA Commander*

Wen-hsiung, *Penghu Defense Commander*

Yan-ting, *Minister of Defense*

Yu-hsuan, *ROCN Commander*

What Went On Before

China pushed to become the global economic power, engaging in a trade war with the United States. At the same time, they sought to expand their empire into the South China Sea by creating manmade islands and building military bases. The territorial waters China claimed were challenged in the World Court which ruled that they had no basis for making those claims. China ignored the ruling and continued to claim the waters surrounding the Spratly Islands. It was a claim that was continually challenged by warships of the United States, who conducted FONOPs (Freedom of Navigation Operations).

Along with their attempts to push into a world economy, China sought to establish the Yuan as world currency. Nations balked at using the Yuan as a trading currency, thus keeping China relegated as the world's second largest economy. Although many of the nations in Southeast Asia were swinging in China's direction, the Chinese government sought a quicker remedy to their sluggish economic gains. They devised a virus which would run rampant throughout the world and disrupt the various economies. China's goal was to emerge from the crisis as the number one economy. Markets fell as the highly contagious virus spread throughout the world. However, other events soon overtook China's attempts.

One general was fed up with the constant intrusion of the United States into what China viewed as territorial waters. One warship was targeted, but in a procedural lapse, the defensive systems were left in automatic mode and missiles launched. The USS *Preble* and the USS *Pinckney* fought valiantly but just didn't have enough time to fend off the sudden swarm of missiles. Hit several times, the USS *Preble* sank rapidly. Only twelve survived.

China rescued the twelve survivors and kept them hostage, claiming them as prisoners. The United States sortied their submarine fleet in case matters turned south. Angered with China's refusal to release the twelve sailors, United States SEALs conducted a rescue. This rescue was coordinated with a follow-on attack which leveled the island of Fiery Cross, the Chinese military installation from which the USS *Preble* was fired upon. In response, China devised a response along many fronts and sortied their own submarine fleet.

* * * * * *

In response to the American attack on the Chinese base on Fiery Cross Island, China fired submarine-launched cruise missiles at Anderson Air Force Base situated on Guam. Undersea battles ensued between LA-class fast-attack subs and the Chinese vessels who fired the cruise missiles and their accompanying escorts. Backed into a corner and not wanting to show signs of weakness, both nations reinforced their presences in the South China Sea.

After much deliberation, the United States launched attacks against the remaining Chinese military installations located in the contested Spratly Island chain. The destruction of those two bases prompted China to strike out against the two American aircraft carriers operating in the South China Sea, resulting in the sinking of one carrier and a cruiser. This ignited a regional war between the two superpowers, expanding into the East China and Philippine Seas. Most of the preliminary battles were conducted undersea between fast-attack submarines.

In the ensuing battles, the United States managed to sink one of China's aircraft carriers while damaging a second. China damaged a second American carrier as it was departing San Diego, thus limiting the firepower that the United States could bring to the Far East.

Nudged by China, North Korea mobilized its forces and began a march toward the demilitarized zone separating North and South Korea. China also showed signs of gathering an invasion fleet pointed toward Taiwan. Although the United States destroyed much of China's submarine fleet, they found themselves facing attacks on many fronts. They urgently needed to eliminate a second surge of Chinese submarines so that they could bring their carriers within striking distance.

Chapter One

Maryland City, Maryland
19 July, 2021

With a heavy sigh, Allison Townsend dropped her keys on the counter and deposited her armload of groceries. Exhausted from hours spent poring over satellite pictures of Chinese troop movements, she only wanted to collapse on her couch with a glass of wine, barely paying attention to the television playing in the background. Picking up the remote to the small television she kept in the kitchen, she turned up the volume.

As a newsman's low voice drifted through the room, she began lifting cans and boxes from the plastic bags. Times had become interesting and the hours long around the NSA ever since the US and China had begun exchanging shots. Placing several cans of vegetables in the pantry, Allison wondered when her schedule would return to normal. Pausing to stare at the shelves of food, she realized that she didn't have the energy to cook and thought about calling for a delivery from her favorite Chinese restaurant. With a sigh, she closed the pantry door and spun on the tiled floor, heading for the phone.

Glancing at the TV as she passed, she noticed a picture of a container ship behind the anchorman. Slightly intrigued, she grabbed the remote and again turned up the volume.

"…an unprecedented number of cargo ships lie anchored off California ports, waiting for their turn to berth at filled docks. The bottleneck stems from the low number of available truck drivers. We're going live to Los Angeles. Bill, what are you seeing there?"

The feed changed to show a man holding a microphone. In the background were a number of large cranes that served the port, silhouetted against the light of a dying day.

"Well, Tom, the docks here are filled with ships attempting to offload their cargo. As you mentioned, the problem comes from a nationwide shortage of truck drivers to carry away the cargo containers, and there's only so much room for storage here at the port. This is creating supply chain issues, and the entire nation is feeling the pinch with depleted shelves in many of the stores."

The screen again changed to show an aerial view of anchored ships by the dozens.

"As you can see here," the remote newscaster continued, "there are many ships arriving without places to offload their cargo. There doesn't seem to be an end in sight for the Western ports."

"Bill, have you heard anything about whether this is limited to the West Coast, or might this problem be cropping up elsewhere?"

"Tom, I haven't had the chance to speak with anyone in authority as yet, but we did receive this footage."

The video altered to another aerial view, this also showing ships anchored next to each other.

"This is from just outside one of China's ports and shows a similar scenario, ships anchored and waiting for their turn to enter ports in order to unload cargo. While the reasons for the delays there aren't known, I can only surmise that they are in a similar situation."

"Thank you, Bill."

Allison forgot all about calling to have her dinner delivered; forgot even about being hungry. Her mind drifted back to her day of poring over the Chinese port facilities, and she didn't recall seeing the docking berths filled as the newscast intimated. Other than military transport ships gathering, the activity surrounding the civilian port facilities had appeared normal. So, either she had been shown old pictures, which she highly doubted, or there was another reason why those ships were anchored.

There was the possibility that the news footage was taken some time ago, was stock footage, or a video of some other country altogether. Perhaps the news station had their facts wrong. Now that she thought deeper about it, one of those seemed the most likely scenario. However, as much as Allison tried to convince herself that the news footage was wrong, she was still stuck with the feeling that something wasn't quite right. Remembering that she had been about to order dinner, Allison alternated glances from the phone to the television, which had since moved on to another story.

Goddamn it! she thought, quickly pulling items from the grocery bag that required refrigeration.

Snagging her keys from the counter, Allison glanced longingly at her couch. Her evening of relaxing with a glass of wine was about to disappear, all because a misreported newscast had placed a bug in her head. Her mom's voice entered her thoughts, telling her that her focus toward work was why she couldn't maintain a relationship. With a sigh, Allison went out through her kitchen door and entered a humid Maryland night.

Minutes later, she found herself driving down the Baltimore-Washington Parkway on the way to Fort Meade and her offices at the National Security Agency. Showing her badge at the gate, she arrived at her parking lot, mildly pleased to be able to park closer to the building. As she strode the corridors to her office, she braced herself for the inevitable disappointment when she found that the news program had been wrong about ships anchored off China's ports. She was prepared to be very pissed at herself for going in to work, even though the drive was a short one, and having her night interrupted. Nights were her time away from the stress, and she hated to miss a single moment of solitude.

Entering her office, she threw on the lights, the overhead banks of florescent flickering to life. She gathered the day's photos and settled into her chair. With a sigh, she placed the magnifier on one picture and leaned over. Sure enough, the first port showed that there were both empty and filled berths — as normal. Verifying the dates and times, she saw that other Chinese ports were the same. The military transport ships were still anchored in the same positions, the staged troops and equipment remained in their bivouacs. Civilian activity levels appeared normal. It seemed that the news report had been wrong after all.

"Thought so," she muttered, selecting a different set of pictures.

The ships anchored off the ports showed up almost immediately. Just for grins, she pulled up pictures of the ports at Los Angeles and San Francisco. Those berths were full with cargo ships, along with a host of container ships anchored offshore. Allison returned to the ships riding off the Chinese ports and looked at them more closely. Puzzling...their decks weren't filled with containers. As a matter of fact, they weren't container ships at all. The little bug that had been buzzing in her head grew louder.

She had an idea of the type of ships she was looking at and had to verify them by pulling up images of them from the database.

"I'll be damned," she breathed, settling back in her chair.

Not realizing that a couple of hours had passed, Allison made copies of the satellite images she'd need come morning and fired off an email to her boss:

I think I know how China is going to solve their transport problem for the invasion of Taiwan. Let me know when we can talk.

* * * * * *

The next morning, Allison dragged herself back into an office that it felt like she had only just departed. Setting a stained mug of steaming coffee on her desk, she plopped down in her chair. In that instant, almost as if a button were placed on her seat, her phone rang. The display showed that it was her boss.

"Well, that was quick," she mumbled, knowing that her day was about to become even busier than it had of late.

"Allison," she said, picking up the handset.

"I just saw your email and attachments. My office, five minutes. And bring everything you'll need to convince a larger audience."

Allison didn't get a chance to respond before the line

went dead. It wasn't that her boss was an asshole, or really even a brusque man. But she knew he had a lot of balls to juggle and didn't waste much time on pleasantries. It had taken some getting used to, but she eventually came to realize that she couldn't take it personally. Allison spent a few minutes gathering the satellite footage she'd need, wondering what her boss meant by convincing a larger audience. The concept of speaking to groups didn't faze her. She had a bit of a reputation for confidently stating her analytical conclusions and it didn't really matter who she might be talking to.

Several minutes later, she walked into her boss's office. The first of the morning's rays filtered in through open blinds, the clear skies beyond the specially tinted windows promised another warm summer day.

Allison darted her eyes around the room, expecting to see others seated in the office. However, all she saw was a large-screen television and audio equipment on a rolling cart. On screen were the faces of General Dawson, Chairman of the Joint Chiefs of Staff, the Secretary of Defense, and several admirals that she didn't recognize.

The door opened behind her and in walked Bill Reiser, the NSA director. Greetings were quickly made as the director took a seat, leaving Allison to stand in the middle of the room, wondering where she was supposed to be. She now understood what her boss meant by a larger audience. It wasn't larger in the sense of numbers, but of rank in America's chain of command.

"Gentlemen, this is Allison Townsend," her boss said, waving her to one of the remaining seats in front of his desk. "She's the lead analyst who linked the ships anchored off the Chinese ports with the possible invasion of Taiwan. Allison, take us through what you found."

"Well, sir...sirs. I only brought physical satellite pictures and I'm not sure they'll suffice for a remote audience," Allison replied, her mind frantically combing through possible ways to present her findings.

"We should have the pictures you need online. You can use my computer," her boss replied, rising. "It's hooked in with the video conferencing software, so you should be able to broadcast what you need."

"Well, it...this will take me a couple of minutes to find what I need," Allison responded, remaining in her seat.

"Take your time," the NSA director said.

Seeing her boss standing behind his chair, Allison realized that he was serious in that she should occupy the seat and lead the meeting. Being familiar with the sequence of photos she required, it took less than the promised couple of minutes to be ready.

She selected an aerial view of the ships anchored off the California shoreline.

"This is a picture of the vessels waiting for their turn at the LA docks. The slips are completely filled with ships being slowly offloaded. Note the decks stacked with containers," Allison began.

The screen changed as she switched to a photo of the Los Angeles docks.

"So, with the docks filled and the slow process of ships being unloaded, it's easy to understand the reason why there are a large number of vessels anchored offshore."

The picture again changed to another dock area with about half of the slips filled with ships having their cargo transferred.

"This is one of China's busiest ports, and as you can see, they aren't full like those on our West Coast."

The scene altered as Allison selected another satellite image. This showed a number of ships anchored in a line.

"These ships, like those along the California docks, are anchored outside the same port I just showed. But, why are they there? They can't be waiting for dock space, as there is plenty of that. Even if there weren't enough dockworkers to offload cargo, no port authority would leave a ship anchored off the coast if there was room for them to dock."

The screen image blurred as it was magnified.

"This is another important distinction. These ships aren't cargo container ships but are, in fact, roll-on/roll-off ships, often called 'RoRo' ships. I believe that the People's Liberation Navy has modified the doors and ramps in order to carry armored vehicles and intend to use these civilian vessels for use as landing ships. We've observed them doing this a few times to test the feasibility. We were wondering how they were going to gather enough transports to make the invasion viable. Well, I think we now have our answer. This is how China is going to land the required number of troops and equipment."

The room was silent for a moment as the screen again changed to the high-ranking military leaders.

"Well, that fits with our suspicion that China was going to use civilian shipping to enhance their meager invasion capabilities. As you mentioned, Ms. Townsend, we have footage of them modifying RoRo ships and testing them with armored vehicles," one admiral stated. "We didn't know that they'd managed to modify so many."

"Ms. Townsend, are you sure that these ships are modified to carry military equipment?" another asked.

"Sir, I don't have solid proof yet, but I don't believe they'd have them anchored like this unless they were. If they were only ready to undergo modifications, we'd see that type of ship in drydocks. I've looked at the drydocks and they're empty. The positioning of these vessels, along with the staged men and equipment nearby, leads me to believe these ships are ready to receive heavy military equipment," Allison answered.

The admiral nodded. "That makes sense, thank you."

"So, gentlemen," Aaron MacCulloch, the secretary of defense spoke up. "Our reports indicated that China wasn't ready for an invasion of Taiwan for several reasons. One being that they didn't possess enough transport ships. It seems that this changes that equation."

* * * * * *

China's Invasion of Taiwan Will Require Civilian Assistance

There has been a lot of talk surrounding China's advances in anti-ship missiles, area deniability capabilities, and the development of their navy. But, for any invasion attempt against Taiwan to succeed, the endeavor will depend squarely on transport ships.

Although growing a formidable navy, Beijing lacks a crucial component to an amphibious assault: adequate troop transport and landing vessels. If China isn't able to put boots and armored vehicles on the ground, they stand little chance of establishing a foothold from which to advance to Taipei and capture the island.

That's where China's formidable civilian shipping industry comes into play, with their numerous roll-on/roll-off vessels and ferries. Since 2015, China has mandated that the Chinese shipbuilding industry comply with directives stipulating that bulk carriers, container vessels, roll-on/roll-off ships, and other capable vessels follow guidelines that allow them to be interoperable with the People's Liberation Army Navy.

While civilian shipping fleet

wouldn't be as battle-survivable as the dedicated transport vessels, they make up for this weakness by their sheer numbers. China's domestic shipbuilding industry is by far the largest in the world.

Any view of China's naval capabilities, especially when looking at their ability to invade Taiwan, must consider the navy's close relationship with civilian shipping.

* * * * * *

Philippine Sea
16 July, 2021

The USS *Springfield* had been patrolling the depths northeast of Palau Island when orders came down. They were to proceed with all speed to the passage where the Celebes Sea emptied into the Philippine Sea. They were to intercept another surge of Chinese submarines which were currently in the South China Sea and heading southeast.

Commander Cook understood that "with all haste" meant something different within the conflict zone. He would alter his heading and increase speed to twenty knots. That would allow for the LA-class fast attack sub to remain relatively quiet while attempting to head off any enemy boats trying to enter the vast expanse and depths that the Philippine Sea offered. The orders Cook received made it clear that the southern reaches of the sea were to be cleared of any Chinese underwater threats.

While proceeding to the new patrol area, Commander Cook was worried about the timing. He had a long distance to travel, and if he was to retain the advantage of remaining quiet, then it was conceivable that he and the lead Chinese boats would arrive at the narrow passage at nearly the same time.

Reports had come in of the successes of other boats that

had been directed to intercept the long train of Kilos streaming south. However, no one had any idea whether it had been the leading or trailing edges of the line which had been sunk, or the middle. Station-keeping subs had reported the Chinese diesel-electric boats departing at thirty-minute intervals, so it was very likely that any enemy submarine the *Springfield* encountered would have company in close proximity.

*   *   *   *   *   *

Philippine Sea
19 July, 2021

Sailing at twenty knots, it had taken the better part of three days to reach the outer limits of their new patrol zone. Commander Cook listened as it was reported that the depth under the *Springfield's* keel rose abruptly. They had just passed over the southern edges of the Philippine Trench. Not too far to the north was the Emden Deep, which descends to over thirty-four and a half thousand feet, rivalling the Challenger Deep located in the Mariana Trench. The edges of the seabed plateau that made up the Philippine Sea were essentially surrounded by these deep troughs.

"Make your speed ten knots and come to heading two seven zero," Commander Cook ordered.

"Aye, sir. Right standard rudder to heading two four zero, slow to ten knots," the XO repeated.

Commander Cook was guiding the *Springfield* through the passage separating the Celebes and Philippine Seas south of the Philippines. His goal was to cut through the northern section of the channel in order to catch any Chinese boats attempting to come through the deeper areas located to the south. If they reached the other side of the passage without finding any sign of enemy submarines, he planned to swing south toward Sangihe Island. There he would wait and listen for any Kilo attempting the passage.

"Sonar contact, bearing three four zero. Range sixteen thousand yards and closing. Aspect ratio moving right to left.

Screws indicate twenty knots. Labeling contact as Alpha One," sonar reported.

"Slow to five knots. Right standard rudder. Make your heading two one zero," Cook ordered.

"Aye, sir. Five knots. Right standard rudder to two one zero," LtC Malone mimicked.

"Sonar. Any idea what we have?" Cook inquired.

"It sounds like a Kilo barreling through the strait," sonar replied.

"Very well. We're treating Alpha One as a hostile. If we maintain our course and speed, how close will it pass by us?

"Sir, if we both maintain course and speed, Alpha One will pass within four thousand yards in about seven minutes."

"XO, make sure the fire control system is updated and ready forward tubes one and two. We're going to catch this bastard as he passes by. I want tubes three and four readied for any subsequent contact that crops up. We have to keep in mind that there's a good chance of others nearby," Cook said.

"Aye, sir. The FCS is updated. Tubes one and two showing green," Malone intoned.

"After we fire, we're going to head directly across the strait and wait for the next one to arrive. I want to take station five miles north of Karakelong Island."

"Aye, sir."

The foreign Kilo continued its eastward course, closing the distance to the *Springfield* at a rate of one mile every three minutes. Commander Cook listened to the sonar updates, ready for any indication that the Kilo had noted the presence of the LA-class fast attack boat lying in wait.

"Sonar, do we have any other traffic in the area?" Cook asked.

"Sir, we only have the fishing boats several miles to the north and that freighter we passed when we entered the strait."

Commander Cook wanted to sneak to the surface and have a look around. Or at least have a quick "listen" for enemy radars. Although the Kilos didn't have the modern capabilities of the Chinese nuclear fast attack boats, he didn't want to risk spoiling the setup. He had an enemy submarine about to land in his lap. Intel had the few Chinese airborne ASW assets operating further to the northwest, but that didn't necessarily mean there couldn't be any in the area. Seeing as the strait was out of range for land-based fighters from either side, it was possible.

"Alpha One five thousand yards, speed twenty knots. Course remains the same, zero niner zero. Aspect ratio changing right to left. Estimate the closest pass in thirty-five seconds."

"Copy, sonar."

The sonar gave a countdown to distance as the *Springfield* moved only fast enough to hold its position in the strong current flowing through the strait.

"Sir, ten seconds to closest pass," sonar called.

"Copy. XO, is the FCS updated with the targeting data?"

"Aye, sir."

"Fire one," Cook ordered.

"Torpedo away," Malone stated.

With a fixed gaze on the second hand, Cook waited for five of the ticks to click by.

"Fire two."

"Torpedo two away."

In the cold depths, two cylinders were forcefully ejected from within long steel tubes. Hitting the open water, they accelerated to sixty knots, one chasing the other like children playing follow the leader. Given clear instructions, the two Mark 48 torpedoes sped away from the loitering sub. A thousand yards away, the first made a turn to the south and began racing toward its target. The passive sensor within the heavyweight torpedo "heard" the Kilo submarine transiting less than a mile away.

Five seconds later, the second Mark 48 made its turn. Surrounded by dark waters, through which sunlight barely filtered down, the two deadly weapons began their final trek toward the unsuspecting Kilo.

"He's heard them. Alpha One accelerating, aspect ratio

changing. Looks like he's turning away," sonar reported.

"Very well. Make them active and cut the lines," Cook ordered.

"Aye, sir. Torpedo one active...torpedo two active. Time to target, one minute, forty seconds."

"Come right to heading zero three zero, make your speed twenty knots," Cook ordered.

The *Springfield's* momentum changed as the speed increased and heeled as it turned to the new heading. Cook wanted to get clear of the area, even though the two torpedoes were coming at the Kilo from different angles. If the Chinese vessel fired down the backtrack of the Mark 48s, Cook wanted to be far away from any searching sensors.

Two thousand yards from the Chinese submarine, the two Mark 48s turned on their active sensors. They followed the generated returns, easily keeping up with the Kilo as it turned south and accelerated. With the Chinese boat already sailing at near its top speed, there wasn't much it could do to elude the closing threats. With a forty-knot advantage, the two torpedoes rapidly closed the distance.

"Countermeasures deployed. He's turning again."

Picking up a new noise, the two Mark 48s altered direction slightly. Their onboard processors analyzed the bubbling mass of confusion. The lead torpedo correctly deduced that the noise wasn't from the target it was assigned and resumed its original course. The second torpedo wasn't so quick and continued toward the countermeasure. The second Mark 48 arrived at the bubbling canister and passed through, the sensors telling the fuse that it was as close as it was going to get. The thousand-pound warhead detonated, the explosion rocking the Kilo desperately trying to flee the threats chasing it.

The first torpedo closed in, and the proximity fuse ignited the warhead just forward of the engine room. The compressed water buckled the hull, sending powerful jets of water streaming into the interior. Those streams widened and several compartments gave way to the pressure. The hull collapsed and filled with seawater.

Unable to overcome the additional weight and with systems going offline, the Kilo was doomed. The captain fought to right the damaged boat and claw for the surface, but the weight of the incoming sea pulled the vessel deeper. The electric motors still drove the Chinese sub until the pressure became too much for the hull. Passing through the crush-depth, the hull gave way, silencing the terrified sailors huddled inside the last surviving compartments. With sparks barely illuminated in the dark waters, the sub went silent, the dark carcass settling slowly to the seabed.

"Sir, torpedo one has hit. I hear breakup noises."

"Copy. Register that one as a kill on a Kilo, possibly Chinese," Cook responded.

"Torpedo in the water, bearing one one zero, range one thousand two-hundred. It's gone active. Aspect ratio changing left to right, speed sixty knots. It looks like he fired down the backtrack of our own. I now hear two pinging behind us."

"Copy, maintain speed and heading. We need to get out of any search pattern range," Cook commanded.

The crew of the *Springfield* continued listening to the ranges increase and the bearings change as the two Chinese torpedoes entered circular search patterns. Tensions eased after several minutes once it became apparent that the two circling torpedoes weren't any longer a threat to the LA-class boat speeding away from the scene.

Cook held the sub on the same course and speed for another three minutes. Acutely aware that other Kilos might be heading toward the strait, the commander wanted to be in position to catch them if they tried to transit. Using the screeching of the dead Kilo's tortured hull for cover as it sank, Cook ordered a turn to the south toward Karakelong Island.

*   *   *   *   *   *

Philippine Sea
19 July, 2021

The sonar reports were very clear: a vessel was sunk some twenty miles north of their position. From the timing and location, either one of the Kilos that had sortied from their homeport had run into the Americans...or maybe it was an American boat that had been hit. His sonar operators thought they had briefly heard the surging screws of a Kilo, bringing Huang to the belief that the breakup sounds they heard had likely come from the demise of one of their fellow boats. The question that weighed on the captain's mind was whether the American attack was from an airborne source or from one of their attack submarines. Either was possible, considering the location.

Captain Huang had been ordered to hold a position near the straits leading from the Philippine Sea into the Celebes Sea. He had chosen to remain near a small island chain northeast of Karakelong Island, listening for any American warships attempting to transit on their way to the South China Sea. So far, all he and his crew had come across were freighters and fishing vessels plying the surface.

If the American attack had come from the air, Huang needed to get into deeper waters. Some of their aircraft had MAD gear and some didn't, but he didn't want to be caught in shallow waters where the chance of being discovered was greater. If the attacker was a sub, then the enemy captain would be looking to get out of the area. Huang knew from experience that American boats were quiet, but he also knew that his own diesel-electric sub was difficult to find when it was running slow on its electric motors. This might be Huang's chance to catch the American unawares.

"Steer heading three six zero. Increase speed to eight knots."

The Chinese Kilo started moving into the passageway separating the two seas, descending as the underwater terrain fell away from the dotting of islands. Far to the north, the groaning sounds of a sinking vessel could still be heard. With that background noise, finding an enemy sub attempting to flee might prove difficult.

Ten minutes later, Captain Huang's attention was captured by one of his sonar operators. The man visibly stiffened and then closed his eyes, pressing his hands against his headphones. He opened his eyes briefly to peer at the sonar scope before concentrating again on something he may have heard. Tension gripped Huang even more as he edged toward the man who was possibly deciding if he heard a whale or a submarine.

"Captain, sonar," the man finally said, "I think I hear a faint set of screws."

"Are you sure?"

"Sir, it's hard to tell with all the background noise, but...hang on, yes, there they are. Bearing three five five, range four thousand kilometers and closing, speed...speed twenty knots. Aspect ratio unchanging. I can't be positive, but it sounds like an LA-class submarine."

Huang was quick to react. Two and a half miles away was an American fast attack sub rapidly closing in on his position. If no change in course was made, the American would be on top of him in less than ten minutes. He had two choices. If he waited until the enemy vessel was closer, he could fire without giving the American captain much time to react. That would limit his opponent's ability to escape and to return fire. However, the closer the LA-class sub was able to get, the greater the chance of Huang and his boat being discovered.

The other choice was to fire now. With the American submarine being closer to the discordant sounds of the dying boat, there was the likelihood that the enemy captain wouldn't hear the approaching threat until it was too late. There were risks associated with either decision.

"Slow to four knots. Make sure the target information is put into the Fire Control System and ready forward torpedoes one and two."

"Sir, target data is validated and uploaded. Torpedoes one and two ready to fire."

* * * * * *

Captain Cook was eager to depart the scene of the attack. The twisting metal of the sinking remains was making it difficult for the sonar to hear anything else but he was reasonably sure that there was another Chinese Kilo within ten miles. He needed to get clear of the wreck and across the channel to be ready if another showed.

As the *Springfield* made its way south, Cook found himself second-guessing his decision to turn south so quickly. He should have worked farther east, away from the noisy interference, but the thought of catching a stream of enemy subs sailing into his sights was too great an opportunity to give up. Cook knew that he'd feel better once they gained some distance from the destroyed Kilo.

"Captain, sonar!" an excited voice called. "Active torpedo, bearing zero zero five, range one thousand yards, speed sixty knots. Aspect ratio unchanging."

"Hard to port, heading zero niner zero, full speed. Emergency dive, make your depth three hundred. Release countermeasures."

The executive officer repeated Cook's orders, but the commander only faintly heard them as his mind went over possible escape options. The proximity of the enemy torpedo narrowed his choices, and his chances. Even though the heading would enable the torpedo to cut a corner, Cook needed deeper waters if he was to evade the threat. To the east was a thermocline he could dip under, if he could only make it.

"A second torpedo has gone active. Range one thousand yards. Torpedo number one turning with us, range eight hundred."

Cook could hear the faint pinging of the active sonar locating his boat.

"Distance to the thermocline?"

The navigator looked to the XO and shook his head. "Sir, one thousand yards."

Traveling at double the speed of the Springfield, the

torpedoes following had a thirty-knot advantage. The report meant that the lead torpedo would catch up with Cook and his crew before they were able to reach the thermocline. They would come up short by two hundred yards.

"Release countermeasures," Cook ordered, willing the nearest Chinese Yu-6 torpedo to chase after the noisemakers and give them a few more seconds to reach a safer location.

*   *   *   *   *   *

Three days later, Tammy Cook was staring out the kitchen window while finishing up the kids' breakfast dishes. Across the road, another Navy wife was out tending to her small flower garden. Sunlight streamed down from the Hawaiian skies, filtering in through the lace curtains. Tammy pondered heading down to the park once the kids returned from school.

It had taken some time for her and Alan to get the on-base house, as they were a treasured commodity. They had been on the list for over a year, and she remembered the day they moved into the three-bedroom house; how warm and cozy the home made her feel, the contentment that she could become part of the housing community. Spending some time with the other wives might alleviate some of the anxiety and loneliness she felt when Alan was at sea.

Placing the last dish on the drain board, Tammy noticed that her neighbor across the street had paused in her gardening and was staring intently at something down the street. The other wife slowly stood, her garden tool dropping at her feet. Tammy tried peering to the side but was unable to see what her neighbor was looking at.

When the other wife put her hand to her mouth, Tammy had a sinking feeling. She knew what the other woman was looking at. Every spouse had seen that car pull down other streets and into other driveways, each wife feeling sick at the news someone else was about to receive. Terrified, Tammy followed as the neighbor turned her head, following the slow movement of the vehicle. The hood came into view, and then the rest of the car.

The vehicle slowed even more. Tammy lost all thought, the day dimming, as the car turned into her driveway. The outside world blurred as she collapsed in her kitchen and hot tears flooded down her cheeks.

"No…no…no…NOOO!!!"

* * * * * *

Philippine Sea
19 July, 2021

Lieutenant Carlos Lopez rubbed his eyes in an attempt to dispel the tiredness the last two days had brought. Ever since the orders had come down to locate and eliminate the Chinese submarines that had sortied on the 15th, his life had been relegated to fly, eat, sleep with the balance heavily leaning toward time spent in the cockpit. There were moments when all three were accomplished at nearly the same time. It wouldn't have been so bad, except that the standard flying hour limit had been waived.

Below the P-8, scattered cumulus clouds clawed for the heavens as if trying to escape their earthly bond, the tops becoming mere wisps before evaporating. Carlos thought they looked like gumdrops or wrapped kiss candies. He visualized dropping the Poseidon down and circling each cloud as if he was unpeeling the wrappers.

"Damn, I really need to get some sleep," he muttered over the intercom.

"You're right about that," the co-pilot returned. "Even that sludge they call coffee isn't doing the trick anymore."

Too tired to come up with a witty reply, Carlos merely grunted and returned his gaze to the skies below. Between the clouds, hurtled along by strong winds, the wrinkled texture of the Philippine Sea was a deep blue striated by white-topped waves. Somewhere under those waves lurked the silent hunters of China and the United States. The job of the three officers in the back was to pick out the quiet echoes left by the subs, determine if they were enemy vessels, pinpoint their location, and direct an attack by the highly modified 737.

Years of experience, first flying the P-3 Orion and then the P-8, had taught Carlos that it wasn't such an easy job to find the silent underwater predators. Even with the advanced gear they currently possessed, the steel killers were difficult to detect. The secret radar slung under the fuselage could pick out the tiniest of ripples on the surface and determine whether or not they were the result of a wake left by a submarine traveling under water. They could even sense temperature differentials in the water and analyze if the variances were caused by the cooling water of nuclear reactors. But still, even though the gear inside the Poseidon could see millions of square miles of ocean, it seemed finding an enemy sub was still a matter of luck, or perseverance…he wasn't entirely sure which it was sometimes.

Rumors had circulated from a P-8 squadron operating from the damaged airfield on Guam, that they had found and sunk two Chinese Kilo subs operating at the southern extremes of the Philippine Sea. While Carlos was part of a crew that had caused a submarine silhouette to be painted on one of the P-8s, they hadn't come across anything since. Intel had it that the Chinese had pulled their remaining nuclear submarines closer to their homeland and Taiwan. That same intelligence had a number of diesel-electric boats operating in the vast expanse that was the Philippine Sea, presumably placed there to keep the gathering U.S. carrier task forces from getting within striking distance of Taiwan.

The Chinese withdrawal of their surface forces, now supposedly concentrating near their naval ports and the upper reaches of the South China Sea, gave the American anti-submarine aircraft unrestricted access to the hunting grounds of the eastern Philippine Sea. To Carlos, China had made a mistake withdrawing. Even the threat of the long-range anti-aircraft missiles carried by the Chinese destroyers was enough to keep the slow, cumbersome ASW aircraft at least a hundred miles from any Chinese radar that was detected.

China allowing the P-8s, their associated drone companions, and the aging P-3s to roam at will was a sure way to have their fast-attack submarines located and sent to the bottom. It might take time, but the older subs that made up most of China's underwater fleet would eventually be found. And once they were, their odds of surviving were pretty darn low.

Carlos knew from talking to other pilots stationed at Kadena Air Force Base that the Air Force was sending F-22s aloft to cover the South and East China Seas. The reason for risking them so close to China was to prevent the few Chinese ASW aircraft from being able to have unrestricted access to those waters.

Bored with drilling holes in the sky, Carlos allowed his tired mind to wander. Growing up in San Diego, his two older brothers were both involved in gang activities. His dad had done his best to keep Carlos away from that lifestyle, but Carlos had been young and was determined to follow after his brothers, whom he worshipped. His two brothers did their best to shield Carlos, making sure he stayed in school, and that care had meant a few ass-beatings by one or both of his brothers whenever he missed a day.

The very next morning after graduating from high school, with the early morning sun streaming in through the threadbare curtain covering his bedroom window, he was roughly awakened by his brothers.

"Get up, you're coming with us," his eldest brother stated, grabbing the front of his stained T-shirt and pulling him to his feet.

Thinking he was about to be initiated in some way, Carlos remembered hurriedly dressing in his cleanest clothes and stumbling after his brothers. The fact that his dad met him at the front door and hugged him was confusing, but he put that out of mind as he raced after the backs of his retreating brothers and threw himself into the back of his oldest brother's convertible.

Carlos became even more confused when they pulled up

to a strip mall and his brother told him to get out. With a brother at either shoulder, they marched him toward one of the shops. When Carlos saw the United States Navy recruitment office, he slowed and then stopped.

He had tried to escape, but each of his brothers had a hand firmly placed on a shoulder. His next-oldest brother looked at him and shook his head. Hoping for some help, he looked up to his eldest brother, but that brother leaned down, getting into Carlos' face.

"Look here, you are going in there, you are going to sign your name, and you are going to become a Navy man. You probably think you should have a choice in the matter, but you don't. You are getting out of here and making a life for yourself that doesn't involve drugs, guns, and an early death. Do you understand that?"

There had been a look in his brother's eyes; Carlos knew he couldn't say no. He had never seen either brother exhibit looks of pleading, but it had been there that day. It was something he had never forgotten. That day in the parking lot had changed Carlos' life, possibly saving it. His brothers had sent him down a path to a completely different life.

Following basic training, Carlos had been selected to attend Officer's Training School, where he did well enough to be given a flight spot and was sent to pilot training. Throughout his training, his brothers were never far from his thoughts. He didn't make much money, but he sent most of it back home to his family. It was enough to allow them to move out of the impoverished neighborhood. The last he heard from home was that both of his brothers had completed their GEDs and were enrolled in community college.

"Pilot, CIC." The intercom call pulled Carlos back into the cockpit.

"Yes, sir, go ahead."

"We have a possible MAD contact from the Triton drone a hundred and eighty miles to the south of us. Come around to a heading of one seven five," Commander Martin said.

"Copy that, sir. Turning to one seven five," Carlos

replied.

The shimmer of the morning sun off the waters five miles below moved in the windscreen as Carlos banked the twin-engine P-8 to the south. Several straight white lines on the striated blue surface of the sea showed where a few vessels braved the war-ravaged waters, intent on delivering their cargo to foreign shores.

Twenty minutes later, the P-8 slid over the top of the MQ-4C Triton circling fifteen thousand feet below. Commander Martin, the combat information officer sitting in the fuselage, raised an eyebrow at the sensor operator. The drone was continuing to send information on the MAD contact it was still holding on to, but the crew hadn't been able to locate the object with their own equipment. It was frustrating; they could see that there was supposed to be something below the surface, but they were unable to establish contact.

"Pilot, CIC," Martin said.

"Aye, sir, pilot here," Carlos responded.

"Take us five miles south and then begin a descent to ten thousand."

"Copy. Heading five miles south and then down to ten," Carlos replied.

Commander Martin could easily set up an attack run based on the information the crew was receiving from the drone, but the detection system could only determine that something was there. It couldn't provide more in-depth information, such as type. Although there weren't supposed to be any friendly boats in the area, he wanted to make sure of what he was targeting.

Carlos again turned to a southerly heading and flew for half a minute before beginning a descent. Both pilots kept their eyes peeled for the drone miles below, even though they knew they were clear of its path. Slowly, the wispy tops of the clouds drew closer, the scattered puffs driven by moderate winds.

The Poseidon encountered light turbulence as the aircraft approached the cloud tops. The bumps served to remind Carlos that they were within an element of unseen forces, the P-8 flying through invisible waves. He knew the light chop the modified 737 was experiencing would be a completely different experience for someone flying something smaller. Someone flying a Cessna 172 through the same area where an airliner reported moderate turbulence would leave a white ring on the seat from the experience. That is, if they didn't outright suck up the cushion.

The wingtip flexed as the aircraft flew through the turbulence. In a bank, the left wingtip slipped through a cloud top, the mist swirling around the wing. The transient light in the cockpit dimmed as the aircraft was engulfed in a cloud, the brightness returning as it flew out the other side. Continuing its descent, the cockpit crew was subjected to alternating bursts of light, then shadow, as they flew in and out of clouds.

The Poseidon was thrown into clear air once again as it descended through the bottom of a cloud. Whereas the tops of the clouds were white and puffy, the bottoms were flat and gray, their shadows dimming the bright blue of the sea. As the altimeter wound down to ten thousand feet, Carlos eased out of the bank and pulled back on the control wheel.

"We're level at ten," Carlos called over the intercom.

"Copy that...thanks," Commander Martin replied.

The contact appeared to be heading eastward at about ten knots. Martin wondered if he was indeed tracking a Chinese submarine. So far, most of the ones found had been loitering near major passages. This one was operating near the middle of the sea. This increased the possibility that they had located a submarine belonging to a nation other than China or the United States. As foolish as that might be, the notion couldn't be wholly discounted, and thus the reason Martin wanted additional verification.

Based on readings coming from the Triton drone, Martin directed headings to place sonobuoys ahead of the slow-moving contact, alternating depths in order to optimize targeting data to be fed into the fire control system.

"Sir, I have a moderate contact on buoy Charlie Four with a faint reading on Charlie Five. Verifying this as contact

Alpha One," one operator intoned.

Commander Martin nodded. They had the bastard, and it was only a matter of time before they were able to positively identify what they had found.

"Alpha One heading one zero zero, speed eight knots. Classifying as a Kilo Class fast attack boat."

Although that identification more than likely made the contact a Chinese submarine, there were several other nations running the Kilo. However, the rules of engagement dictated that *any* Kilo in the South China, East China, or Philippine Seas was to be treated as hostile. If a nation was foolish enough to run the same class in the conflict area, it was their funeral.

"Okay folks, we're classifying this as a Chinese target. We'll lay another line ahead of the track and make a run," Martin stated.

That set the crews in the back and those flying the aircraft into motion as checklists were started, readying the aircraft for a live run. After dropping another line of sonobuoys, Carlos turned the aircraft away from the immediate area and made a wide circle. With the sub running easterly, they'd come at it from the south. Coming in from the beam would give the torpedo targeting systems the best chance of acquiring the Kilo and tracking it.

"Passive contact on Delta Five. Alpha One heading one zero zero, speed eight knots," an operator reported.

"Copy. Pilot, turn to heading zero one zero. Descend to five thousand and begin your attack run," Martin called.

"Aye, sir. Turning to zero one zero, down to five thousand. Beginning run," Carlos repeated.

The P-8 came out of its wide turn and flew northward. Shadows from the overhead clouds raced across a blue sea filled with white wave tops. Slung under each wing, Mark 54 torpedoes were attached to external hardpoints. Carlos selected two of the lightweight weapons and pulled the throttle back to adjust his speed. The fire control system would determine the drop points for each torpedo, the auto pilot also tuned to the FCS.

The aircraft bounced as it flew through the turbulent air closer to the surface of the sea. Carlos ensured that the Poseidon maintained the designated track, speed, and altitude. Glancing outside, all he saw were whitecaps that stretched to the horizon. Focusing ahead, he knew that there was an armed metal tube silently cutting through the depths. He was fascinated by the idea that they were striking at an unseen target, but he also felt a little sickened that the lives of nearly a hundred souls were about to be snuffed out. He had been in the business long enough to know that it was rare for anyone to survive a submarine sinking.

The aircraft shook differently as one torpedo fell free from its mount. The Mark 54 released and dropped toward the sea, a drogue chute coming out to slow the weapon and allow for an easier entry. Seconds later, the P-8 again trembled as a second torpedo separated, the aircraft wing bouncing. The Poseidon flew directly over the contact with two objects descending toward the choppy waters.

As the distant aircraft began to circle back around, and when each torpedo was just above the surface, sensors within each cut loose the drogue chutes. Fed with real time targeting information, the two lightweight torpedoes entered the waters. They were immediately inside the kill box and went active. The active pings located their target and they accelerated to forty knots, diving deeper below the waves.

"Torpedo One and Two have acquired Alpha One," an operator intoned. "Time to impact, twenty seconds."

A short time passed. "Alpha One is accelerating, now passing through ten knots."

Carlos's gaze centered on the drop area. Though his move had been made, he knew that a deadly game was now being played out, unseen by both attacker and prey. He imagined canisters tumbling from tubes as the sub captain released countermeasures; could see the noses of the torpedoes alter direction as they turned toward the sudden noise. Now it would be a matter of whether the targeting systems would hit their objective or be fooled into striking the countermeasures.

Meanwhile, he and the copilot were preparing for another run. If the first two torpedoes missed, then they would drop others in the hope of destroying the enemy vessel. However, they might first have to reacquire the target.

Underneath the waters, the submarine captain attempted to outrun the threat, releasing a multitude of countermeasures as he dove his boat deeper. He tried to buy time to reach the thermocline hundreds of feet below. The crew, filled with a surge of adrenaline from the sudden appearance of torpedoes, darted eyes toward the hull when the sound of pinging reached the interior. As the sound of the pings increased, so did the fear inside each sailor.

Carlos finished preparations and waited for instructions from the CIC. Suddenly, the water in the near distance buckled and an immense geyser shot skyward. Before the spray had completely settled, another fountain erupted. Seemingly in slow motion, the towering pillars of water fell back toward the sea. The wind-driven waves soon covered the evidence of destruction, leaving behind a rainbow sheen of fuel that slowly spread across the waves.

"I have breakup sounds," one voice stated over the intercom.

"That's a kill. Call it in," Commander Martin ordered.

*   *   *   *   *   *

Philippine Sea
20 July, 2021

Highlighted white with ash-colored valleys, puffy clouds drifted across skies partially covered by a thin overcast, thousands of feet above. The cockpit of the Poseidon was alternately flooded with bright sunlight and then subdued in gray as the sub hunter flew in and out of the scattered clouds. Below lay the deep blue of the sea, the color becoming leaden in the shadows of the clouds.

To the pilots of the P-8, it was just another unbroken patch of ocean. Time had become never-ending, one day blending into the next. It seemed to Carlos that no sooner had he felt the relief of the wheels settling onto the runway than he found himself again sitting at the hold line waiting for clearance to take off. The reports, the meals, the briefings, the times when his head hit the pillow, it all seemed a blur. Even the usual light-hearted banter was limited and felt forced.

The briefings included updates on the successes of the ASW assets, both above the water and below. Carlos had his doubts about the numbers of Chinese submarines listed as sunk. On the other hand, considering their own sinkings, perhaps they might not be so far off. The commander he'd flown with was leading the island in kills and had requested Carlos as his pilot for all of his flights.

"Carlos, you're my lucky charm," Commander Martin had joked during one briefing.

Carlos wasn't sure he wanted that moniker; to voice something like that was to jinx it. Not only that, but something like that could turn into a call sign. "Lucky" might be okay, but it wasn't often that fellow pilots pulled the positive thing out to determine call signs. He would probably get something like "Leprechaun" or worse, considering that the Lucky Charms guy says, "They're magically delicious." So far, he had escaped with being called "Lope" and he was fine with that.

With a sigh, Carlos shook his head to clear away the fog. The aircraft was on autopilot, following a programmed search pattern, but he couldn't afford to let his mind drift away. That was usually when the flashing lights and alarms appeared. It wasn't the diligence of the mechanics that kept the aircraft in the air, it was a direct result of his firm attention on the instruments and the surrounding skies, or so it seemed at times.

Seated in the fuselage, Commander Martin was also having difficulties remaining focused. As with everyone tasked with locating and eliminating China's submarine threat, the long, continuous days were taking their toll. Once this was over, Martin was going to put in for leave. He would hunt down some uninhabited corner of the world and do nothing but sleep. With the crew rest requirement waived, and the number of hours he'd been glued to his console far exceeding that, he had even contemplated calling his career done once his current enlistment was completed. He knew that was mainly the tired talking, but the thought kept surfacing.

"Sir, I have something on the sniffer," one operator reported. "Diesel fumes."

In Martin's mind, they had probably found some fishing or cargo vessel plying the waters of the Philippine Sea. But they were obligated to check it out. Even though the odds dictated that it wasn't likely a diesel-electric sub snorkeling to recharge its batteries, there was still a slim chance that it could be. Anyway, chasing down a trail might also make the time pass more quickly.

"Pilot, CIC. Turn to heading one seven five, descend to six thousand."

"Aye, sir. Coming around to one seven five and down to six," Carlos responded.

Taking the aircraft off autopilot, he banked it through a one-hundred and eighty-degree turn. He heard the exchange between operators in the back, and looked into the distance, searching for any visible wake showing on the watery carpet below.

With the easterly winds aloft, any "scent" they picked up would be coming out of the west. Coming down to a lower altitude would help narrow down the search. Carlos was familiar with the procedure. They would locate the scent again and determine a course to follow to remain in its path. Eventually, they would fly over the source, perhaps visually sighting it before they arrived. If it turned out to be a surface vessel, then they would climb and continue with the original search pattern. If there wasn't anything in sight, that meant the fumes came from something below the water. They would then begin a different kind of search, attempting to find a submarine situated close to the surface. More than likely, their radar would locate the waves generated by the submarine.

After several turns, the P-8 was able to follow the track of the faint fumes detected by the sensors. Carlos kept his view ahead, searching the vast expanse for any wake or vessel. This high up, the source could be to the left or right of their flight path, due to the different winds at lower altitudes. The friction of the earth caused winds to veer closer to the surface, curving right in the northern hemispheres and left in the southern regions.

Miles passed without any change in scenery. Nothing showed on the radar, and the farther the P-8 flew without a visual sighting, the more Carlos thought they might actually be on to something. They'd found foreign subs recharging before, but Carlos couldn't imagine why a captain would be doing so in open waters located in a war zone. Commander Martin had similar thoughts as they continued to track the scent. The radar was clear, yet the sniffer still showed diesel fumes, the concentration increasing as they drew nearer the source.

"I've lost the signal," one operator called.

Commander Martin directed Carlos to circle, picking up the trail on one segment of the three-hundred and sixty-degree turn and losing it on the opposite arc. Martin looked at the position of the MQ-4C drone, opting not to call it closer to establish a MAD reading. The radar showed the surface clear, and the pilots reported that they couldn't see anything. The winds were strong enough to cause several whitecaps, so identification of a snorkel was difficult from a mile up.

Martin ordered the Poseidon lower and laid a line of sonobuoys, each one floating down on a drogue chute before being released into the choppy waters. It wasn't long until the sensors found the noisy diesel engine.

"Sir, passive readings on Alpha Three and Four. faint signal on three, fading on four."

Martin noted the buoy locations showing on the scope.

"Signal fading on three, nothing on two or four."

The commander knew that meant the sub was heading away from the north-south line of sensors they had deployed. Directing the P-8 west, another north-south line was dropped. The operators listened for the slightest hint of a diesel engine, but all buoys remained silent. Being nearly over the contact, the radar would have a difficult time picking out the snorkel from the ground clutter. Martin thought about working further away from the contact in an attempt to get the snorkel on radar, but one of the operators interrupted that train of thought.

"Sir, I have a wave detection."

The radar slung under the aircraft had sensed a wave pattern coming from a submerged boat. Once detected, the pattern became obvious and showed up like an arrow pointing directly to the object. It revealed the stealthy hunter as if it were traveling on the surface. After confirming that there weren't any friendly submarines in the area, Martin issued an order. It was established that it was a diesel submarine they were tracking, so further verification of it being hostile wasn't necessary. The United States didn't have any in its inventory. Checklists were run and it wasn't long before the P-8 was set up on yet another attack run.

Flying low over the contact, the Mark 54 torpedoes didn't drift downward for long. Two of the potent weapons quickly ran up to their top speed of forty knots. The submarine captain didn't have a chance to issue orders before the 238-pound warheads detonated underneath the snorkeling Kilo. Water shot into the air. In the midst of the chaotic waterfalls, two larger parts of a dark tube rose above the surface. The broken submarine floated among the cascades of saltwater for a brief moment before the two sections sank back under the waves. It wasn't long before the sensors attached to the buoys recorded the groans of distressed metal. Commander Martin had added yet another marker to his reputation for locating and sinking China's silent killers.

"I tell ya, Carlos, you're my lucky charm."

"If you say so, sir."

* * * * * *

Taiwan Strait
20 July, 2021

Commander Brown studied the depth charts. He had the

USS *Connecticut* creeping along at four knots west of Kaohsiung City and southwest of Tainan City, both busy port cities on the western shores of Taiwan. His sub was positioned just where the shelf of the Taiwan strait began dropping off into the deeper waters of the South China Sea. The currents flowing through the narrow passage between Taiwan and China created sharp ravines on the sloping seabed, making it look similar to the hillsides of the American Southwest.

Brown was patrolling an area near the southern entrance to the Taiwan strait, listening for any indication that Chinese submarines might be loitering nearby. Intelligence reports indicated that China had pulled back their remaining nuclear fast attack boats, perhaps to use them as screens for the anticipated invasion fleet. The *Connecticut's* primary orders were to destroy any Chinese submarine it encountered, and secondarily to be ready to engage the invasion vessels if and when they sortied and departed Chinese territorial waters.

The commander knew that the second part of those orders would place the Seawolf-class boat at risk, as their position would be betrayed by the missile launches. Should that occur, Brown planned to fire his contingent of Tomahawks and immediately dart into the deeper waters, hiding near one of the trenches that ran through the area.

The first part of his orders was difficult enough to follow. The shipping traffic, although slowed tremendously by the regional conflict, was still busy enough to generate a background of noise. Although it hid the already quiet fast attack boat, it also hid his Chinese counterparts. Creating turbulence as it flowed over the rough terrain, the strong, northerly-flowing current that swung around the island nation and into the strait created its own noise. It was like being in a busy mall where a multitude of conversations blended into a solid wall of noise while trying to hear the faint whisper of one particular dialogue.

The *Connecticut* suddenly jolted, those on their feet stumbling. The sub wasn't going fast, so they weren't quite thrown from their feet. A loud screeching, a sound like metal grinding metal, penetrated the usual quiet of the control room. It was pretty easy to figure out that the submarine had collided with something.

Brown's first thought was that they weren't positioned where they'd thought and had run onto a shelf. The sound of the collision was his career being flushed. His next thought, all traveling through his mind at the speed of light, was that he was in a warzone and he was making an awful lot of noise.

"Full reverse, emergency ascent to one hundred feet," Brown ordered, the executive officer's replies barely heard over the noise.

The fast attack boat shuddered as forward momentum was lost, the screeching noise continuing. As the boat lifted, the sound diminished and then vanished altogether. Damage reports began coming in. The sub was taking on water. The pumps could handle the inflow of seawater, but Brown knew that too would make noise.

"Sir, sonar. I hear cavitation. It...holy shit. Sir, it's a Shang-class Chinese boat. I think we just hit one of their nuclear fast attack boats."

"Are you sure?" Brown inquired.

"I'd stake my life on it, sir," the sonarman answered.

"Goddammit!" Brown uttered through clenched teeth.

The damage reports continued filtering in. Some of the sensors on the bow were out of order, along with forward tubes five through eight.

"Ensure the target is put into the FCS. Ready tubes one and two. Remove the safeties," Brown ordered.

By removing the safety measures inherently built into the torpedoes, Brown allowed for the Mark 48s sitting in the tubes to be immediately armed rather than waiting for them to travel a certain distance. However, he was now facing an incredible dilemma. Normal procedure for an underwater collision was to stabilize the boat and surface to check the extent of the damage. However, surfacing in these waters wasn't entirely optimal. They were in international waters and in an area where China usually had one of their few airborne ASW hunters aloft. To surface now was more than likely a death sentence.

There was also an enemy sub who was only a few feet away, who now knew that the *Connecticut* was right on top of them...quite literally. Neither captain could fire upon the other, as that would mean taking their own boat out in the process.

As near as the commander could tell, the *Connecticut* was damaged but under control. It didn't appear as if it was going to immediately sink, and they had the potential to surface if absolutely necessary. However, traveling at any speed would result in them making a lot of noise. Brown decided they would deal with the nearby Chinese sub and make for Taiwan's nearest harbor. That might not be ideal, as their sub might be interned, but it was a far sight better than being sunk. The commander doubted he could make it to Japan, Guam, or Okinawa with the noise he'd be making during the transit...but first, he had to deal with the immediate threat. Then he could figure out a plan.

"Full ahead, come right to zero two zero," Brown commanded.

The submarine lurched ahead as the jet-pump propellors bit into the water, the deck canting as the turn was initiated.

"Contact Alpha One speed is increasing. He's cavitating badly. We might have bent a propeller. Aspect ratio changing. Range...two hundred yards and increasing."

Brown winced. The Chinese boat may be damaged, but it sounded like they'd hit the rear of the enemy vessel. That meant their torpedo tubes would be intact. The enemy captain was likely going through the same motions and ideations as Brown. That meant there could soon be the sound of active torpedoes heading their way. Shoot, with the noise they were making, the torpedoes could home in passively.

"Range four hundred yards and increasing. The best I can tell, sir, the target is doing ten knots. Bearing one eight zero."

"Fire one," Brown ordered.

The justification for firing with the other sub still so close was that Brown wanted to get off the first shot. Even though he might receive additional damage in the aftermath of the explosions, he was hoping he could destroy the Chinese attack boat before the opposing captain could fire his weapons.

"Torpedo one away and tracking."

Brown let out a small sigh. The danger of arming a torpedo so close and having it circle back around was that it might just start tracking its own boat.

"Fire two."

"Torpedo two away and tracking."

* * * * * *

A cargo ship sailing toward Kaohsiung City reported three, possibly four, distinct eruptions in the water forty miles west of the Taiwanese port city.

Chapter Two

Pentagon, Washington, D.C.
21 July, 2021

The creak of worn leather filled the plush room as Aaron MacCulloch leaned back in his chair. A large monitor dominated one side of his office. At the moment, the screen was blank but it would soon be filled with the stars and stripes of America's top brass in the Indo-Pacific theatre.

The staff that had set up the teleconference meeting had departed, allowing the secretary of defense a moment to himself. Leaning back with his hands interlocked behind his head, Aaron's mind meandered down several paths before centering on his career. He mentally sighed as he thought of his current position. It wasn't one he'd ever thought to be in, and he often wondered why he'd continued into politics following his retirement from the Navy.

The reason he often gave himself and others was that he wanted to continue serving his country, that it needed him. In the secret corners of his mind, he knew that was a lie. He loved this nation of his, but he had served his time and didn't enjoy the web of politics. Perhaps he had been afraid that he would become bored. Or maybe it was that he didn't know what else to do with himself. It's not that he had a storage closet full of hobbies…or any interests, to speak of. His focus had been on his career, and now he found himself at odds with any other kind of life.

Maybe he should take his wife up on her "subtle" suggestions that they purchase an RV and visit every national park. Her last subtle hint had literally been, "Aaron, we need to get an RV and drive to see every national park." Honestly, the thought of going to do anything other than what he was doing at the moment sounded appealing. But first, he had to see the United States out of the conflict with China. He would put his all into the next month or two and then seriously contemplate handing in his notice. Perhaps the entire cabinet should consider retirement, given how weary all of them were looking lately.

Almost to the second of the scheduled meeting time, faces began populating the monitor. The Secretary of the Navy, the Chairman of the Joint Chiefs, the Chief of Naval Operations, the Pacific Air Force Commander, the Commander of the Pacific Fleet, and the Commander of the Indo-Pacific Command all joined within thirty seconds of each other. The small talk was minimal as greetings were made.

"Thank you for attending, gentlemen," MacCulloch began. "We'll give the others a few before we begin."

As soon as he uttered that, the Commander of the Pacific Submarine Forces came into view, followed shortly afterward by the Third and Seventh Fleet commanders. Finally, the Commandant of the Marines came online. The requested attendees were all present.

"Okay, we have a lot to cover, so let's begin. Sooner started, sooner done. I know we've established contingency plans for the upcoming fight for Taiwan, but I have a meeting with the president following this, and I want to make sure that we're presenting the best solution. So, let's put aside the current plans and talk this through on a strategic level as if they don't exist. Let's start from the outset of a Chinese invasion," MacCulloch requested.

"Sir, the first indication that China is finalizing their preparations will be when they start loading up their ships. They'll load their equipment first while staging their soldiers closer to the ports. Thanks to the latest intel, they'll be using modified civilian roll-on/roll-off ships in addition to their military transports," General Dawson briefed. "They'll likely hold those vessels in port as they soften up the island's command and control facilities. We've observed a mass movement of their mobile cruise missile launchers toward coastal areas directly across from Taiwan. We don't know how long the initial bombardment will be, but we anticipate that a majority of the initial attacks will come from these mobile launchers, and from airborne bombers that won't need to leave

Chinese airspace."

"What are the probable results from these initial attacks?" MacCulloch inquired.

"Most of Taiwan's command bunkers are deeply buried, as are their communication cables. So, we don't expect Taiwan's communications to be severely impacted, at least not their hardline comms. It's the wireless and radio communications that may be disrupted. The antennas will be damaged, and I suspect that China will place jamming aircraft in the Taiwan Strait with escorts. They won't venture too close to the island, due to Taiwan's long-range air defenses, so their effectiveness will be limited.

"Aside from command and control facilities, China will probably focus their initial attacks against air defenses. Like our own doctrine, China will want to establish air supremacy over the island. With their homeland only a hundred miles away, they can be over the island in a matter of minutes, making it an easier feat. Now, considering that their airborne troops will probably figure prominently with any invasion attempt, air supremacy will be essential. That means they'll need the air defenses, both aircraft and anti-aircraft batteries to be neutralized. This is where we can expect their initial missile salvoes to be aimed."

"So, how are we going to counter this?"

"Taiwan has extensive surface-to-air defenses in place. We also have multiple Patriot missile batteries placed in deep bunkers positioned throughout the island. We had thought to use them to help defend against this initial onslaught. However, we're now thinking to hold these defenses back to use them as a trap against China's airborne forces when they arrive. Our goal here is to limit the number of forces China can put ashore while we whittle down their supply ships.

"Taiwan's Air Force will play their part in defending against the anticipated onslaught of missiles, but it should be noted here that Taiwan's Air Force is seriously outdated, and a large percentage won't survive the first day. Even if they aren't taken out in the air, their airfields will be destroyed. Either way, they'll be close to becoming ineffective within hours of the first missile being fired. So, I'd like to suggest that they be used before they're downed without firing a shot," General Dawson answered.

"Hang on a sec, Phil. Are you suggesting that we send them up against the missiles and possibly any Chinese aircraft that are away from their territorial boundaries?"

"No, sir. I'm saying that we utilize them to attack the Chinese homeland...specifically the mobile launch platforms. That may alleviate a lot of the pressure that China can initially bring to bear against Taiwan," General Dawson responded.

"Attack the Chinese homeland?" the Secretary of the Navy asked, incredulous. "Are you nuts? That will only serve to escalate this conflict."

"Well, sir, I'm merely suggesting that Taiwan *could* do that. After all, they're the ones under attack and are not constrained by the same rules of engagement that we are," Dawson replied.

"And that won't open the door for China to expand the war?" Secretary Chamberlain questioned.

"I think as far as the war between China and Taiwan goes, they won't be playing by the same rules. I believe that the Republic of China could directly attack the PRC without us facing any ramifications. After all, I seriously doubt that China wants an expansion of hostilities with us or we would already have seen that. I think we, meaning Taiwan, could get in one good shot against China's bevy of mobile launchers, and possibly their bombers, if they send them in the first wave."

"You're suggesting that we use Taiwan as our proxy to directly attack China," MacCulloch said.

"I am merely suggesting an alternative solution to Taiwan just sitting back and waiting to be attacked," Dawson replied.

The rest of the men on the screen were quiet as this suggestion was a new wrinkle. The previous discussions had centered on Taiwan using its outdated air force against the expected cruise missiles. That aircraft would be lost if the airfields were demolished and the pilots had to eject. Taiwan losing its air force within the first hours wasn't a new idea, but this new suggestion on how to use them before they were wasted was something to strongly contemplate. The risk was that China could take this as an expansion of the conflict with the United States, which was something to be avoided. It was a similar situation to China using North Korea to ease their own tensions.

To MacCulloch, the idea was appealing. It would be nice to get a lick in on the Chinese forces, which were hiding behind their territorial boundaries.

"Are you also talking about using the F-35Bs we gave them in this manner?" General Rawlings, the Pacific Air Force Commander asked.

"Of course. We have to keep in mind that they'll be the only effective aircraft on day two. They can be used to keep hitting the Chinese mainland, winnowing down the number of launchers. Or held back to fight against the invasion forces. The plan would be to operate the F-35Bs from roads and fields, and the Republic of China has already established protocols for operating them in such a manner. If we can maintain communications with the mobile airfields, we can hand down targeting data and hopefully reduce the amount of cruise missile platforms that China can launch from," Dawson replied. "Of course, defeating the launchers, or at least lowering their numbers, will also help us out when we opt to bring our carriers closer."

"I like this idea of hitting China at home. But this has the ring of being a suicide mission for the pilots. Has this topic been broached with Taiwanese officials?" MacCulloch inquired.

"We may have...well, sir, there may have been some open-ended discussions surrounding the matter," Dawson sheepishly answered.

"So yes is the answer."

"Yes, sir."

"And what did they have to say about this...suggestion?"

"Although the risks to the pilots are great, they were in agreement. Better to use what assets they have than just outright lose them. I think that's how they put it."

"So, just to get this right, your suggestion for inclusion into the contingency plan is to have the Republic of China launch their available aircraft when the first PRC missiles appear and hit the launchers?" MacCulloch asked.

"Yes, sir. That about sums it up."

"And the military leadership of Taiwan is okay with this?"

"Yes, sir. They were actually the first to bring this up when we were discussing strategy."

"Okay, what about their Navy? Can we achieve the same thing there? Deploying before hostilities begin and hitting the Chinese mainland?"

"That's a different animal. With the rare exception, their ships are mostly equipped with anti-ship missiles. Their plans are for their destroyers and frigates to leave port immediately. When the hostilities begin, they'll then focus on the invasion vessels, possibly even hitting them before they leave port," Admiral Crawford responded.

"Correct me if I'm wrong, but isn't their Navy comprised of hand-me-down ships? Will they even survive against the few remaining Chinese subs?" MacCulloch questioned.

"Their ASW gear is actually fairly decent. However, this scenario falls under the umbrella of using equipment while they can. Due to the pressure China has put on the rest of the world, the Republic of China has a very limited supply of missiles. They've been able to fully equip their ships, but that's about as far as it goes. The best use of their surface fleet will be to send the destroyers and frigates for a quick strike, then retreat out of range," Crawford answered. "The corvettes are mostly suited for anti-air missions, so they might be able to assist with the island's defense."

"So, the current belief is that Taiwan's air force, well, a greater percentage of it anyway, will be knocked out of any conflict within the first hours, and their Navy is only good for a single strike?"

"That's about the gist of it," General Dawson stated.

"So, if the island is to have any chance of surviving, this thing is going to land on our shoulders?"

The heads on the monitor all nodded their agreement with that statement.

"If I may interject a thought," Admiral Tillson, the Seventh Fleet Commander said. "This all sounds terribly one-sided, and to a certain extent, it is. But we have to be mindful that, even with the inclusion of civilian shipping, China's transport fleet is limited. Taiwan's fleet may be limited as well, but I think they'll still be able to put a pretty good dent in any invasion fleet China puts together. And if we can whittle down those launchers, then that will put us in a fairly decent position. After all, we've been able to knock their submarine forces down a considerable degree."

"I might include their front-line fighters in that synopsis as well, especially their J-20 fifth generation aircraft. They only had about fifty of them to begin with and we've destroyed nearly half of those," General Rawlings chimed in. "China may hold the advantage of proximity, but we have a big technological edge."

Jake Chamberlain, the Secretary of the Navy, cleared his throat. "I suppose that it's my duty here to remind everyone that we had our butts kicked a few times in wargames envisioning this very scenario. Our Achilles' heel in all this is our surveillance and communication systems sitting in low-earth orbits. China has demonstrated the effectiveness of their anti-satellite missiles. If they wanted to, they could threaten our ability to 'see' the battlefield. If they blind or deafen us, our battle management system becomes severely compromised."

"Well, we lost the HELIOS system installed on the *Preble* when it was sunk. But we've since worked to get the high-energy laser system integrated on the *Benfold, Kidd,* and *Fitzgerald.* All three of those destroyers are with carrier groups currently deployed in the Indo-Pacific region. The test results were encouraging, so perhaps they'll be able to help safeguard our satellites," Admiral Crawford replied.

"It's my understanding that we've moved several surveillance satellites to both Cape Canaveral and Vandenburg Air Force Base as a result of those wargames as a stop-gap solution to quickly fill any holes that might develop," MacCulloch stated. "We also have ballistic missile defenses which could be used. Other than that, we'll have to maintain our combat systems as best we can.

"Now, before we move on, I think that it's important to go back to the topic of any invasion fleet China puts together. We need to decide whether we prioritize transports or escorts."

Aaron remembered the heated discussions when this subject was raised previously, when they were originally developing contingency plans. Those present were divided on what they should concentrate on. The reasoning went that targeting the escorts would eliminate most of the short and medium range anti-air capabilities, thus removing the air defenses and rendering the rest of the fleet vulnerable to air and missile attacks. That would enable carrier and land-based aircraft to then get closer and take out the transports with greater ease. Dealing with the escorts first would remove one of the major threats that the carrier strike planes would face.

The counter argument was that the strait separating Taiwan and China was only a hundred miles wide. Any faster-moving transports could cover that distance in five hours. If American aircraft focused on the escorts, the invasion forces could conceivably land before the United States had a chance to effectively intervene. If the transport ships were the focus and sunk, then there wouldn't be an invasion to worry about.

Suggestions were floated regarding Taiwan mining the harbors, both at the entrances and along any route invasion fleets might take, but it was believed that blame would be set squarely on American shoulders, so the thought was shelved.

It was the same with any idea that Taiwan should strike at the Chinese ships riding in the harbors or anchored outside harbor entrances. The importance of maintaining China as the aggressor was paramount. Preemptive attacks would surely make it easier for China to justify an invasion of Taiwan, but most believed that this conflict would be resolved through a negotiated cease-fire. In that, as important as it was to approach any negotiation from a position of strength, world opinion also mattered. Thus, it was important that China be seen throughout as the disrupter of peace.

If Taiwan attacked China first, then China's invasion of Taiwan could be viewed as a valid course of action. While holding back might not help Taiwan in the short-term, no one wanted China to be able to cry "victim." The expressions on the screen told the story that no one wanted to have the targeting priority discussion again.

"Aaron, if it's all the same to you, let's not hash this one over again. I understand your desire to give this a fresh look, but do we really have to dive into this one?" Secretary Chamberlain said.

"Sir, I have to agree," the Chief of Naval Operations chimed in. "Our current plan is to focus our attacks on the Chinese escorts. I see no reason for that to change."

MacCulloch turned his gaze away from the monitor as he contemplated the request. He really wanted to make sure they had the best, most comprehensive solution for the likely invasion of Taiwan. After all, they only had one chance to get it right. To lose Taiwan to China would severely hamper keeping China from controlling the South China Sea. The best passage into those waters passed just to the south of the island, and they would essentially lose access to the Taiwan Strait. The American strategy of keeping China bottled up would take a critical hit. But, regarding target priority, they had talked at length and arrived at a plan. To open up that can of worms again might prove fruitless. Worse, it could serve to antagonize some of those present.

"I'm fine with that," MacCulloch finally said, returning his attention to the screen. "But before we leave this discussion behind, has anything new materialized that might change the plan as it currently sits?"

No one had any input. "Okay then," MacCulloch

continued. "What else do we need to discuss about Taiwan before we move on?"

"The plan calls for F-22s to be stationed out of range of China's long-range anti-air umbrella, sending them in when opportunities arise. I want to point out that we have two F-15EXs that we're testing. They each have the capability of carrying twenty-two of the long-range air-to-air AIM-120s. That's a lot of firepower that can help keep China from attaining complete air supremacy. Even though they're still undergoing testing, I'd like to put in a request to utilize them with the F-22s. Perhaps not to infiltrate too close, but to the edge of AMRAAM range," General Rawlings voiced.

"Vince, let me think on that. I'll have an answer to you within a couple of days," General Dawson responded.

Admiral Brickline, the Indo-Pacific Commander, spoke up. "I'm going to toss in my two cents. I'm fine with what we've discussed so far. It's imperative that we do not allow China to land their entire invasion forces, or ideally, to keep them off the island altogether.

"We have increased our presence on the island, placing a Marine brigade ashore. From the intel we've seen, China has eight Marine brigades ready. That doesn't include the six airborne troops they've staged. That's possibly fourteen brigades that we'll have to deal with. Taiwan has a number of soldiers under arms, but their equipment is archaic and won't stand up against what China possesses. So, unless we want to place more troops on the island, then we *cannot* allow China to land their entire invasion fleet."

"I'll tag onto what Shawn said. If China is able to land men and equipment, at a minimum, we've got to be able to interrupt their flow of supplies," Admiral Crawford stated.

"Okay, so I have to meet with the president in a couple of hours. What do we say about Taiwan aircraft attacking Chinese forces within their territorial limits? Not on a preemptive basis, but after China initiates hostilities?" MacCulloch asked.

Going from person to person, all were in agreement that, even though this sounded like suicide missions, they didn't have a problem with it as long as Taiwan concurred. The measure was penciled into the contingency plans.

"To summarize, Taiwan is to strike at Chinese mobile launchers and bombers the moment China's first strike is inbound. B-1 bombers out of Guam and B-52s from stateside bases will get airborne as soon as the invasion armada sails and hit the escorts once the ships leave the twelve-mile limit. Marine anti-ship missiles will also target the escorts, coordinating with Air Force units to achieve a time-on-target solution. The Taiwan Navy will depart immediately, moving into positions where they can hit China's invasion fleet, or fleets.

"F-22s, and possibly now the two test F-15EXs, will loiter out of range with tanker support and strike at targets of opportunity. With regards to the Korean Peninsula, aircraft will be assigned based on need. Do I have that correct?"

All those in the meeting nodded.

*   *   *   *   *   *

White House, Washington, D.C.
20 July, 2021

President Winslow wondered how this second term could be so vastly different from the first. He'd come to the office full of energy and armed with plans that were going to change the world. Sure, that energy had waned as the responsibilities had piled on, but he *had* changed the world — if the events over the past year and a half were a measure. The cakewalk of the first four years had evolved into a conflict with China, an unstable stock market, and rising inflation. That's not to mention a pandemic and a nation becoming divided along every conceivable line. Everything seemed to be changing too fast to keep up with. When he tried to write policies to keep inflation somewhat under control, that seemed to cause something else equally bad to pop up elsewhere. It was like playing whack-a-mole. He often wondered if he was going to end up in the hospital before the second term played itself out, and thanked God there wouldn't be a third.

"Okay…okay, thank you, Aaron," Winslow said, interrupting his Secretary of Defense's briefing on contingency plans surrounding China's likely invasion of Taiwan. "I'm quite confident you and your staff have the situation handled."

MacCulloch stopped mid-speech and looked up from the folder open on the table in front of him. Setting down the paper in his hand, he turned his gaze to the president sitting at the end of the table.

"Frank, that's what I'm trying to say. We don't have the situation *handled*. China is likely to throw their entire weight behind this invasion of theirs. For them, it's do or die. Although we've managed to sink nearly three-quarters of their submarine force, we still don't dare move the carriers closer. As we've seen in exercises, the firepower carried by even one of their subs is enough to take out an entire strike group. But that's not the half of it. We've still got to decrease their damned bombers, and the sheer number of cruise missiles currently deployed to China's coastline can overwhelm our defenses."

MacCulloch was determined to make the president understand the reality facing the country. He continued. "And then there's their invasion fleet, which we absolutely cannot allow to land. We've bolstered their defenses, but Taiwan will be vulnerable once they run out of missiles or the launchers are destroyed. If China manages to get enough troops ashore, we can consider Taiwan lost. We do have a considerable amount of firepower in the area, but firing cruise missiles will put our subs at a much greater risk. Unfortunately, that's nearly all we currently have to stop any invasion force. So, although we've managed some success, we're still at a disadvantage." He put his hands flat on the table. "Frank, that's just Taiwan. It doesn't even begin to address the Korean Peninsula."

"I understand the situation, Aaron. What exactly do you expect me to do about it? Is there something you need me to do?" Winslow said, frustrated.

The president rubbed his face with his hands. Just as with everything else, there didn't seem to be any easy options.

"There isn't anything I'm asking. I was just briefing you,"

MacCulloch replied, annoyance edging into his tone.

An awkward silence infused the room with the other attendees suddenly finding other very interesting things to look at.

"Look, I'm sorry. I've had a lot on my mind and sleep seems a distant memory. Thanks for the update, Aaron. I do have every confidence in the planning, and we can only do what we can do. We're nearly halfway through our sixty-day authorization window. So, my question is whether we'll have completed operations by the end of our allotted time?" Winslow inquired.

MacCulloch chuckled. "Well, I guess that depends on how successful we are at stopping the Chinese invasion. Because honestly, I think it may be a close-run thing."

"I'll give it another week or two before broaching the subject of an extension with congressional leadership. With the split in the Senate and the House, who knows if we'll get it, so we need to conduct ourselves as if we'll have to withdraw after our sixty days are up. With that said, have we seen any indications that China is moving toward their ships? And has North Korea moved beyond their staging areas?" Winslow questioned.

"Not as of this time. Both countries are still entrenched in their bivouacs."

"It seems they have everything in place, so why the delay? What is it they're waiting for? Hao must be aware of the timeline we're operating under. Is it possible that he's waiting for our authorization to expire before making his move?" Frank asked.

"I'm sure he's aware of our constraints, but with all due respect, sir, I doubt that's the reason behind the delay," General Dawson chimed in. "If China was waiting for us to pull back, then they wouldn't have moved their forces into the staging areas so soon. Being in temporary encampments for extended periods of time only serves to erode morale."

Tom Collier sat more upright in his chair. "If I may. It appears that China is waiting for North Korea to make their move. According to some of our analysts at any rate. That way, we'll have diverted some of our resources, and our attention, thereby upping the chances that they'll be successful. Along that same line of thinking, North Korea is most likely doing the same, waiting in order to better their chances of securing the Peninsula before we can do anything about it."

"So, Hao sets this thing up, and is now stalled because each side is waiting on the other to move? If this weren't so serious, it would be humorous," Winslow replied.

"Well, honestly, that's to our advantage in many ways. The longer we don't have to respond to an invasion in any theatre is more time we have to cut down on China's submarine forces," MacCulloch stated.

Inwardly, Aaron was relieved to see that the President was tracking the complexity they faced.

"True as that might be, we're also up against a timeline. Tom, how long do your analysts forecast this…standoff…to last?"

The CIA Director shrugged his response. "A day…three…a week."

"Okay then. So, is our plan to still bring in the carriers once we've eliminated their bombers?" Winslow inquired.

"That's correct, sir," General Dawson said. "However, we've modified our timeline. We're thinking that we should wait until China launches their attack. They'll use cruise missiles to soften up Taiwan, so if we wait, China will clearly place themselves as the aggressors, and we'll have fewer cruise missiles to deal with. The timing of luring their bombers out will be tricky."

"So, we're sitting back and waiting for events to transpire, then? Is folding back to become reactive a good idea? Plus, I'm again going to remind you that we may not have the time to do that indefinitely."

"China may not be able to hold off invading indefinitely either. It's our belief that they'll have to move soon, regardless of what North Korea does," Dawson replied. "With regards to being reactive, that's unfortunately where we sit on several fronts. I can assure you that we are being quite proactive in dealing with their undersea fleet."

"What about North Korea? Are we also waiting for them to move before we respond?"

"No sir. Even though it may stir up the nest, it's imperative that we strike first if we're to hold them off. In the opinion of the joint chiefs, and those of the staff in the Pacific, remaining on the defensive will be to our detriment. A preemptive strike into North Korea will help with our defensive withdrawals until Taiwan and the situation with China have been resolved. That's part of the operations plan we've drawn up regarding North Korea. We're asking a lot from the few troops stationed in South Korea, and allowing the North to strike at full strength will hurt our chances to stave off their attacks long enough."

"So, the suggestion is still to issue a warning to North Korea, giving them twenty-four hours to show signs of withdrawing, and then hit them if they don't comply?"

"Yes, sir."

"Very well. Fred, you'll see to it that North Korea receives our message, and General, you have my approval for the operation as laid out," Frank said.

The cabinet filed out, leaving the president alone with his thoughts. Frank gathered his papers, his mind focusing on the dangers and death his words would bring to thousands of soldiers, sailors, and airmen. This was not at all how he imagined his second term.

And so it begins. God help us all, Frank thought, picking up his stacked folders and exiting the room.

* * * * * *

Beijing, China
21 July, 2021

"Minister Liu, tell me why North Korea has not launched their invasion," Chairman Hao asked.

"Our inquiries into the matter have been met with

resistance. The only reply we receive is that they are dealing with logistical difficulties, which they say will take some time to be sorted out," the foreign affairs minister returned, his voice neutral in an attempt to cover his annoyance with the North Koreans.

"If you ask me, they are stalling until we launch our own invasion of Taiwan," Minister Zhou chimed in.

"Of course they are," the minister for state affairs responded, his tone sarcastic as if Zhou had told the meeting members the sum of two and two. "And you will find that their 'logistic' problems vanish the moment our ships set sail."

Hao paused to glance at the head of the intelligence apparatus, sometimes forgetting that the secretive man was even in the room. To forget that Wei Chang existed was a sure way to wake up to find one's career spiraling down in flames.

"I know that we were waiting for them to invade the South before we moved, but waiting only serves the Americans. We are quickly losing our submarine fleet and soon won't have anything to shield our invasion forces from the American subs. If we wait any longer, we are going to find that our invasion fleets are at the mercy of their missiles and torpedoes," Minister Liu emphatically stated.

"While we have sustained some losses, it is important to note that we have also inflicted considerable damage on the American submarines," Minister Zhou responded. "Are we forgetting that we have thousands of cruise missiles poised along our coastline?"

Zhou paused for a second, waiting for any rebuttal to his rhetorical question. When no one spoke up, he continued.

"Those missiles and the threat of our bombers will keep the American carriers away from the island. Our anti-submarine forces will hunt down any enemy submarine that fires on our fleets.

"We will push our forces across the narrow passage at top speed. Our ships will be able to cross the passage in a little over six hours, thus limiting their exposure. Once we land our Marines and their equipment, then any viable defensive measures Taiwan possesses will have to shift. With the American carriers held at a distance, that will allow us to resupply with decreased threats.

"The airborne brigades will occupy strategic junctions, forcing American Marines and Taiwanese troops to split their defenses. The Marines will push off the beaches and link up with our airborne forces, and strike for Taipei. We need to keep in mind just how weak Taiwan truly is. With the exception of the brigade of Marines the Americans landed, we will be facing antiquated equipment. Once ashore, we will overrun the island in time, especially with the air superiority we will have.

"I think there might be some here that forget the tremendous advantage that being only a hundred miles away holds. Our aircraft can cross the strait in minutes. With the threat of missiles holding the American carriers at bay, any counter air that the Americans can throw our way will be minimal, considering they will have to operate near or beyond the range of their aircraft. And any air support they do send to the island will bring the Americans within range of our long-range anti-aircraft missiles."

There was not a member sitting around the table that didn't suspect that the National Defense Minister's numbers regarding Chinese and American submarine losses were padded. Hao knew it for a fact, as he had eyes and ears within the ministry. China's submarine fleet had been devastated. There were currently very few subs still sailing, while the American sub losses were minimal by comparison. The true situation, in that regard, was much different from the one Zhou was attempting to portray.

Hao could see the writing on the wall. The defense minister was correct that they still held an advantage, but if they didn't launch their invasion soon, that would be lost. Their window was narrowing. There was also pressure from other nations to end the conflict.

Internally, the seams holding the financial market were close to coming apart. The drastic reduction of exports was limiting China's income. The downstream effect was that production had slowed to a near crawl, forcing many companies out of business. Foreign markets were clamoring for goods, but shipping was a bottleneck that held back the delivery of those. And to top that off, major corporations were beginning to pull out their manufacturing processes. China's financial market was on the brink of collapsing, and the unemployment rate was causing many to start complaining. At the moment, it was a mere whisper that Hao's government was attempting to suppress, but it could conceivably grow to a roar if the current situation went on much longer.

Hao knew that the conflict had to be wrapped up sooner rather than later if China was to survive afterward. If too much time passed, then someone else would fill the void of goods that China once supplied to the world. Already, pharmaceuticals were being moved to more American-friendly countries. But Hao was determined to pull every last bastion of rebellion under the People's Republic control. It was time to end the fight that began over seventy years ago.

"Minister Zhou is correct. We hold the advantage, and it is time to strike. While our original plan was to wait until North Korea struck South, as Minister Wei pointed out, if we continue with that strategy, then we will find ourselves sitting in our ports until the ships rust. So, gentlemen, we have a window of time in which to fulfill our unification goals and catapult China to become a global financial leader. Issue the instructions to proceed with invasion," Hao ordered.

All but one around the table smiled at the news. China would soon be whole, and the conflict ended. While their submarine fleet had been hit hard, they would emerge on the other side as the undisputed global leader. China would avert a financial disaster and continue their plans for expansion, which included upgrading their military capabilities.

Hao was the only one to notice Wei Chang's eyes narrow. The paramount leader wasn't sure if the countenance was because he didn't think the venture would be successful or if his expression was due to plans cycling through the state security minister's mind. The two men locked eyes. Minister Wei made a furtive motion, signaling that he would like to meet in private.

Folders were gathered and those around the ancient teak table departed in small groups. Hao noticed the smiles of the generals and admirals fade as they departed to face the coming battles. The minsters talked of events to transpire after Taiwan was brought under China's control as if the matter were already resolved. Hardly anyone noticed Hao and Wei remain in the room.

"The recording devices are off," Minister Wei said once the last person departed.

Hao nodded. He and Wei were the only ones who knew that the room was bugged. Hao had requested that move years ago so that his words couldn't be misquoted by those seeking to gain power. It was also so that he could use any words said behind the closed doors against others, should it become necessary.

"There is something we are missing here. I am not sure what it is, and that worries me," Wei stated.

"Zhou's reports are not telling the entire story of our losses," Hao offered.

"Everyone knows that. It is something else. We have every advantage in this upcoming conflict, and what our dear defense minister says is correct. Or, I should say, it *should* be correct. The Americans will not risk their precious carriers by bringing them in close enough to help Taiwan. Yet, they speak of aiding Taiwan. That should tell us that they are planning something that will allow them to."

"Surely you are not saying that they will strike at our mainland forces. No matter what else may be the case, I cannot believe that they will dare to widen the conflict," Hao responded.

"No, I do not believe they will do that, either. But we are missing something, and for the life of me, I cannot figure out what it is. Even with American aid, Taiwan is in no shape to defeat us. They might do a little harm, but that is all they are capable of. The submarines of the United States have the capability to sink a few of our invasion ships, but doing so will expose them to our anti-submarine assets. There are their bombers to worry about, but again, I believe they will be too few to sink all of our transport vessels," Wei replied, his eyes taking on a faraway look. "So, what are they up to?"

Hao knew better than to state the obvious with the wizened old man. America wouldn't widen the war by attacking China's mainland. That would make them more vulnerable, opening themselves up for China to attack American bases on Okinawa, Guam, and possibly even Japan. They also wouldn't risk their precious carriers. But the state security minister was right. The United States was not just going to sit back and let China invade Taiwan. They had missiles and aircraft, but not enough to completely stop China.

"Perhaps they plan on taking out our satellites?" Hao mused.

Wei thought for a moment longer. "We have plans for removing some of theirs, yes?"

Hao nodded.

"And we have others ready to launch to replace any lost. Our sources indicate the Americans have a similar plan as well."

"It could be that the United States is planning to focus on the North Korea invasion and willing to sacrifice Taiwan. Perhaps they think they will still have us hemmed in and can reclaim Taiwan through diplomatic channels and worldwide pressure?"

Wei stopped in his tracks and turned to face Hao.

"Hao, you are smarter than that. America will not let Taiwan go after announcing their recognition. We would then be able to take control of the South China Sea, and they are not about to let that happen."

Hao nodded his acceptance of that fact. There would certainly be a battle with China and the United States over Taiwan. Wei folded back into silence, lost in his own thoughts.

Hao took the moment to hash through his own knowledge. Taiwan's military capability would soon be reduced. As had been discussed, most of their equipment was obsolete. The initial cruise missile bombardments China was planning would reduce Taiwan's air force and navy to the point of being worthless. Any navy vessel which escaped their ports would have to deal with what was left of China's submarine fleet and escort vessels.

That left the small force of Marines the United States had on the ground and Taiwan's troops, bereft of armored vehicles. Any real defense of the island therefore fell to America, and with their carriers away from the action, they would have to rely on their long-range bombers and aircraft flying out of Okinawa. If the Chinese mainland remained a safe haven for China's mobile launchers and aircraft supporting the invasion, then Hao didn't see how the United States could grab the upper hand. Wei's doubts made Hao second-guess everything, but he was at a loss as to why.

Wei sighed, his focus returning to Hao. "I do not see what it could be, but yes. We are missing something, Hao. And we need to identify it soon."

"Are you suggesting that we stall the invasion?" Hao inquired, a dangerous glint forming in his eyes.

"No, Hao, I am not," Wei said, shaking his head, his gray wisps of hair waving with the motion. "We should not have waited this long. We need to move while we still retain this window of opportunity. I will think more on this and let you know if I come up with something."

Minister Wei rose from his seat and walked toward the exit, his stride strong despite his age. He patted Hao on the shoulder, leaning in to whisper, "Let us hope Zhou's...enthusiasm...doesn't ruin this opportunity."

The old man continued toward the door. The secretive minister had said many things in that one sentence. Hao remained behind a moment longer, thankful that the powerful minister of state security was in his corner. Or at least he hoped that to be the case.

* * * * * *

United Nations, New York, New York
22 July, 2021

Small groups gathered within the foyer, their conversations blending to create a continuous background of noise. The echoes rose and fell with crescendos of laughter punctuating the open space. Mixing in were heeled shoes clacking on the tiled floor as other delegates made their way toward the chamber.

Standing off to one side, as if attempting to hide in the shadows, Elizabeth Hague tried focusing on her notes, her eyes narrowing in annoyance at the reverberating clamor. She wasn't going to say anything she hadn't already iterated, but she needed to strongly assert that the United States wasn't messing around with the warnings it had delivered.

Even though they'd been warned how any mass staging of men and equipment close to the DMZ would be viewed, North Korea had ignored every missive. Now Elizabeth was to put a firm timeline on the North returning from their aggressive stance. The United States Ambassador to the UN knew North Korea wasn't engaging in its usual saber-rattling; they intended to strike south.

The briefing she received was that they were waiting for China to begin their invasion of Taiwan before attempting their reunification. Even though China had shown signs of assembling an invasion force before, it had come as no surprise that China had accelerated their plans following the official recognition of Taiwan. Elizabeth would have put every cent of her savings on China invading, following that bombshell, whether they had originally planned to or not.

Going through her notes again, she wondered why she even bothered issuing these warnings. Everyone in the foyer, those already in the chamber and those yet to arrive, all knew what was coming. Yet, there was protocol, a decorum that had to be observed in the diplomatic circles she ran in. Even with a conflict raging throughout the Far East, there was still a game that had to be played on many levels.

Those men and women fighting there sure don't view this as a game, she thought, feeling a little ashamed at thinking of the power struggle between China and the United States as some kind of game.

The noise in the foyer began to fade, conversations ending with nods or claps on the shoulder. One by one, the small groups disbanded as the time drew near for the scheduled meeting. Elizabeth put away her notes and smoothed over her suit jacket, checking her pants for any visible lint. In this arena particularly, appearances mattered almost as much as the conveyed points. Or rather, they helped carry the message.

Ambassador Hague pushed through the doors, pausing just on the other side of the entrance. The din of conversation was replaced with the sound of voices conducting translation checks and the creak of chairs as delegates took their seats. Taking a moment, Elizabeth surveyed the room. As she was usually busy thinking about the upcoming business, it was seldom that she took in where she was. If any of her friends in college had told her that she would one day fill her current position, she probably would have laughed and asked to have some of what they were on. She was such a different person now than that carefree young woman she had been in those days.

Losing a family will do that, she thought.

The memory of losing her husband and six-year-old daughter in a car accident years ago nearly caused Elizabeth to lose her cool demeanor. It had taken her a long time to come out of her depression and have the courage to again face the world. And to keep that at bay, she thew herself into her work and sealed that part of her life behind thick doors with sturdy locks. Once in a while, those doors flew open. When that happened, the flashflood of emotions would have Elizabeth sobbing uncontrollably, curled into a ball on the floor of her loft.

Brushing away a small tear that had formed, Elizabeth cleared her throat, sighed deeply, and recalled her steady mien. With confident strides, she made her way down the carpeted path. She knew eyes followed her progress; she was the United States representation of what was transpiring in the Far East.

Some of those gazes were filled with anxiety, others with curiosity, a few with animosity. Elizabeth acknowledged the greetings of allies and friends, ignoring those who were definitely neither. Taking her seat, she opened her briefcase and extracted a series of folders.

The Secretary General opened the meeting, and several issues were discussed before Elizabeth was given her chance to speak.

"The Chair recognizes the United States."

"Thank you, Your Excellency," Elizabeth said, nodding as she rose.

Keeping her gaze focused forward, she began. "The United States has a message to convey to North Korea. The mobilization of reserve forces and the staging of first and second tier units near the Demilitarized Zone destabilizes the region and constitutes a direct threat to South Korea."

Elizabeth turned her gaze to the North Korean delegate. "You have been warned that this action would be viewed as hostile and would be responded to as such. To date, not only have you ignored the pleas to pull back and promote regional stability, but you have actually increased the number of military units massing near the border. This threat of hostilities leaves us no choice. You have forty-eight hours to begin withdrawals with a completion timeline of seventy-two hours for all units to be back in their bases. That timeline starts at midnight tonight, Coordinated Universal Time. Non-compliance will result in the United States and South Korea acknowledging this massing of forces as an act of aggression, and we will take the steps we deem necessary to ensure the safety of its citizens."

"We will not be threatened by you, nor by anyone else. The peace-loving nation of the Democratic People's Republic of Korea is engaging in peaceful maneuvers on its sovereign territory. We will not be subject to the threats initiated by the United States. We will withdraw when we have completed our military exercises and not one hour before," the North Korean ambassador countered.

"While we recognize your right to conduct military

exercises, massing your troops on the border presents a direct threat, and, as I previously stated, it will be treated as a hostile action," Elizabeth said.

"And as I said, the Democratic People's Republic of Korea is conducting military exercises within our borders."

"Mr. Ambassador, we both know that isn't true. Everyone in this room, including yourself, knows that you aren't merely conducting an exercise, but instead are staging troops as a prelude to resuming hostilities. Not a single military formation has departed its staging area, which only serves to prove that this 'military exercise,' as you call it, is a sham. It is a threat to peace in the region, a peace that has lasted for nearly sixty-eight years."

"Your words are the real threat, as are your troops stat—" the North Korean ambassador started.

Elizabeth interrupted, "My second message is directed toward the People's Republic of China."

"Do not talk over me," the North Korean ambassador complained.

"I have the floor, sir, so it is you who is talking over me. I have delivered our message to you. I am not looking for a discussion. I am now moving on to another matter. If you feel you would like to voice something additional, or to begin a discussion centered around your withdrawal, please await your turn.

"Now, as I was saying, my second message is for the People's Republic of China," she continued, turning back to the assembly as a whole. "The United States had accepted Sweden's offer of negotiating a cease-fire, which, as you know, was spurned by the People's Republic of China. Now we have indications that China is gathering an invasion fleet, with the purpose of invading the sovereign nation of Taiwan."

"Ms. Hague, I am not sure where you are getting your information," the PRC ambassador interrupted, "but it is incorrect. There are plans to conduct military exercises in the near future that have nothing to do with the current situation between our nations."

Elizabeth focused her gaze on the Chinese ambassador, holding it for a long moment. "By 'situation,' are you referring to the regional war, the one that you started and then refused to negotiate an end to? Is that what you mean, Mr. Ambassador?"

Without waiting for an answer, as the question was meant to be rhetorical, Ambassador Hague continued. "Do you honestly expect me to believe that you are planning to conduct a military exercise in the middle of a conflict? Please do not insult my intelligence, or that of everyone in attendance. You are preparing for the invasion of Taiwan. So, let me warn you that the United States will view any fleet heading toward Taiwan as a direct threat, exercise or not, which will be answered accordingly."

"Ms. Hague, am I to take that to mean the United States will fire on Chinese vessels operating in sovereign waters? Does the United States plan to escalate the crisis, as you did when your country attacked the peaceful habitations in the Spratly Islands?"

"I will not discuss matters of escalation with you. Everyone here knows the truth of your destabilizing actions in the region and your wanton destruction of an American vessel operating in international waters. The United States will gladly discuss a cease-fire and bring an end to hostilities between our countries. Would you be willing to talk about a cease-fire, Mr. Ambassador?"

"I, of course, cannot answer that question, as I do not have the power to conduct policy decisions. I will happily pass along your request."

"We will eagerly await Beijing's response. Please be sure to also pass along our warning. Your excellency, the United States cedes the floor."

* * * * * *

Zhanjiang, China
23 July, 2021

The silence of pre-dawn draped across the encampment

as tendrils of fog snaked their way among the tents and equipment. As the sky lightened, the mist that had been hovering near the ground rose to blanket the expanse of sleeping soldiers. Beads of moisture gathered on the chilled metal and windows of parked vehicles, trickling like sweat down the sides of armored machines designed to deliver death.

In the east, the sun rose, a ball of orange shining through the thin layer of mist. Like a lethargic beast rising from the deep, the light signaled for the camp to slowly come alive. The fog swirled around moving bodies, rejoining in silent collisions. Voices drifted through the soup, rising to a crescendo of shouts that caused the land to forget the peace of the previous silence.

In the distance came the sound of diesel engines, their exhausts shooting plumes of warmer air into the chilly morning. On one side of the sprawling camp, treads squealed as armored vehicles maneuvered over churned soil. With the clanking of metal pervading the area-adjacent railroad tracks, tanks and armored personnel carriers climbed awkwardly onto railcars where they were lashed in place.

The mist thinned under the warmth of the sun, light and color starting to replace the gray mist. Whistles rang out in a dozen places. Soldiers responded to shouted commands and the ground vibrated as the boots of running troops slammed onto it. Formed into regimented columns and rows, expressionless faces stared straight ahead, ignoring the passage of sergeants searching for the slightest deviations in dress and countenance. Equipment was carefully inspected.

When all was in order, commands were relayed via radio. The sound of diesel engines grew in volume and soon the soldiers could see the dim silhouettes of transport trucks driving through the camp. Emerging out of the mist, throaty engines drove past, the trucks slowing as they approached their pre-determined parking places. With squealing brakes and the hiss of compressed air, the trucks came to a halt.

Barked orders erupted from those leading the formations, and troops headed for the vehicles. The smell of unburnt fuel was pervasive as soldiers threw their gear into the back of the idling trucks, clambered aboard, and sat on worn, wooden bench seats. Conversations were sporadic as the convoys started out for their long trip to the harbor. They were one of many groups heading for the port facilities. Most of the Chinese Marines were glad to be moving instead of spending another monotonous day in their staging area.

* * * * * *

Zhanjiang, China
23 July, 2021

Low clouds hung just above tall buildings rising a short distance from the gray-green waters of the Zhanjiang harbor channel. White wakes trailed all manner of craft plying the waterway; ferries carrying Friday morning commuters, junks motoring on some errand, and ships slowly working their way toward their assigned docks. In amongst the busy waterway, large hovercraft left the confines of Amphibious Transport Docks to practice maneuvers on the choppy waters as other crews readied their vessels for the upcoming invasion.

Just inside the harbor channel entrance, roll-on/roll-off ships were nestled against concrete docks jutting into the wide river. The rumble of engines reverberated down city streets as heavy trucks crawled along, waiting their turns to offload heavy armored vehicles chained to trailer beds. At the docks, armored personnel carriers and tanks rolled up modified ramps to park in the civilian ships. As the day progressed, full vessels were replaced by empty ones and the process started again. It would take several days for the eight brigades of Marines and their equipment to load onto both civilian and military transport vehicles.

Out in the bay, anchored destroyers and frigates pulled tight on their chains against a rising tide. The full roll-on/roll-off ships joined the growing armada, waiting for the signal to sail.

* * * * * *

NSA Headquarters, Fort Meade, Maryland
23 July, 2021

Mike Collins sifted through a multitude of intelligence reports that had been dumped on his desk. As a deputy chief for the NSA Operations Directorate, Mike had the responsibility to put together reports for the director based on intel received from the other directorates. In one folder, signals intelligence had noted increased radio traffic between China's regional headquarters and those units staged in temporary locations.

Satellite photos matched with the increase in signals traffic. Several pictures showed long progressions of troop transport trucks while others showed train cars loaded with all types of armored vehicles. Near the port facilities hosting China's collection of landing ships, lines of tanks and armored transports were being loaded onto civilian and military shipping vessels. Mike ignored the numerous sheets that detailed specific units, equipment types and numbers, along with troop figures. In all, the numbers showed that eight Chinese Marine brigades were on the move.

Mike opened another folder, this one detailing the mobile missile platforms China had moved to the eastern coastlines. There had been very little movement of units in the past forty-eight hours. On the photos, each mobile launcher system and the attached radar vehicles had been circled in red with small notations marking whether it had moved, its attached unit, and what type of launcher it was.

The deputy chief leafed through the stacks of photos. As he passed over one, something different caught his attention. Going back to it, he saw that two mobile platforms had been heavily circled with large, drawn arrows pointing at them. Someone wanted these two launchers to be noticed. Glancing at the annotations on the side, he read that these were Dongfeng-17. That rang a bell. Turning to the back, he noted the analyst who'd previewed the photo. Looking through the directory, he found the number and dialed.

"Allison Townsend," a woman said upon answering.

"Allison, Mike Collins here."

Mike could sense the hesitation on the other end.

"Yes, sir. What can I do for you?"

"I'm looking at one of the pictures you annotated. It's the one of a pair of mobile launchers you've circled and annotated as Dongfeng-17s. Remind me what their importance is," Mike said.

"Oh yes, those. I'm glad you found them. I mean, I'm glad someone spotted them. I mean, I usually hand-carry items of interest like that, but I was busy at the time. I was meaning to follow up this afternoon."

"Yes, yes...you did fine. What about these mobile platforms? What's so special about them?" Mike interrupted.

"Well, sir, those are medium-range ballistic missiles that specifically mount China's DF-ZF hypersonic glide vehicle," Allison stated.

Mike's heart missed a beat as a small amount of adrenaline was released. The United States had little answer to China's hypersonic missile, which was labeled as a "Ship Killer." Traveling at speeds up to Mach 10, those missiles supposedly had the capability of sinking a Nimitz-class aircraft carrier by kinetic energy alone, or so some theorized. And they were capable of evasive maneuvering, making them even more difficult to target with conventional means.

"I take it by their positioning near the eastern coast and the fact that you marked them so a blind person could see them, that China may be getting ready to use them."

"Yes, sir. It's my belief that they're going after one or more of the carrier groups currently in the Western Pacific. Or at least presenting the threat. There's no other reason for moving them to their current location," Allison answered.

"I concur. There's another picture here which you appear to have *annotated* in a similar manner. This one has Dongfeng-21 in the side notes."

"Now that one is theorized to deploy a maneuverable reentry vehicle in the future, but I don't think the ones shown are there for that role. Their range in the anti-ship role is limited. There are other versions that can either support nuclear or conventional warheads. They may be there to use against Taiwan, but there's one additional use. China also uses those missiles in an anti-satellite capacity. It's what they shot down their malfunctioning satellite with. It only makes sense that China would want to remove our low-orbit surveillance satellites prior to their invasion," Allison explained.

"So, it looks like they're going all-in on Taiwan. Thank you, Allison…well done," Mike said, setting the receiver back in its cradle.

Mike again reviewed the synopsis sheets attached to each stack of pictures. China was definitely on the move. The synopsis sheets of the signals intelligence and the satellite photos, when combined, spoke a single message: China was about to invade Taiwan.

Chapter Three

Word quickly spread as the intelligence resources attached to the Pacific Fleet headquarters drew the same conclusions as the national security analysts. Not only was China about to launch two invasion fleets aimed at Taiwan, but it appeared that they were about to test their new hypersonic weapon. The United States could ill afford having another of its carriers sunk, especially by a missile launched at them from China's mainland, over a thousand miles away. If that occurred, it might very well signal the end of American naval dominance. However, global opinion might assume the same thing should the United States move away from the upcoming conflict zones in order to be out of range.

* * * * * *

White House, Washington, D.C.
23 July, 2021

Shadows stretched long across the green expanse of lawn as the sun arced down toward the horizon. Those residing in the capital city hoped the night would bring relief from the hot, humid day. Men in suits with coiled wires protruding from their jacket collars wandered the grounds, ever vigilant for an intruder. Deep inside the white building, those who formed much of America's policy sat in an air-conditioned room to discuss the ramifications of recently discovered intelligence.

President Winslow eased into a chair that he was becoming all too familiar with. Even though many others prior to him had sat in the very same chair, Frank was willing to bet he was close to setting a record for the number of hours of butt-to-seat contact in this room. It felt as if the chair was permanently conforming to his contours. Soon, he might stand up and the chair rise with him.

Glancing at his watch, Frank knew that it was still light outside but that it would be long dark before they emerged from within the confines of the Situation Room. The table was nearly full with members of his cabinet, their ties loosened as they also realized they were in for a long session. Even though the HVAC system recycled the air numerous times per minute, there was still a faint odor of varying colognes vying with melting deodorants, and both were slowly losing to the growing hint of a locker room.

Three still-photos occupied the large screen mounted against the far wall. The left half of the monitor showed an aerial picture of a section of China's coastline with several areas circled in bright red and white. The right side of the screen was divided in half again with the upper quadrant depicting a closer picture of a mobile launcher. The bottom half showed a collection of others that were similar but with different missile container shapes.

Frank had read the intel synopsis of what the pictures were and what that meant, immediately realizing that things were about to significantly change.

"We're all here, so let's get started. Aaron, will you tell us what we're looking at?" President Winslow asked, pointing at the screen.

"If it's all the same to you, I think General Dawson is better suited to explain," the Secretary of Defense stated. "General, if you will?"

"Of course, sir."

General Dawson opened one of the folders stacked on the polished table to his front. Clearing his throat, he reached for a laser pointer and stood.

"As you can see here on the left," the general began, the laser dot circling the marked positions, "the red circles indicate where China has moved up DF-17 mobile launchers. Those are medium-range ballistic missiles designed to carry their hypersonic glide vehicles. Our analysis concludes that China has done this to either conduct a launch against our carriers operating in the western Pacific, or placed there as a deterrent against us moving said carriers closer to support Taiwan.

"Even though we have HELIOS systems aboard several destroyers in the task forces, those systems are still in the testing process. This means we can't positively rely on them to counter the hypersonic weapons. Furthermore, we don't have an effective defense against them. Their speed and ability to maneuver plays havoc with our tracking capabilities, along with our anti-air missile's ability to intercept these high-speed vehicles.

"The only good news is that these hypersonic missiles of theirs are also in the testing process, even though China signaled that they were operational several years ago. Their last test conducted less than a year ago missed the target by twenty-four miles. If I would hazard a guess, I would say that the mobile launch platforms were placed there so we would think twice about committing our carriers close to Taiwan."

"What is it that makes you think they're only threatening, General?" Frank asked.

"Because China wouldn't want to be embarrassed by launching weapons at us and having them miss by that much," General Dawson explained.

"Makes sense," Winslow responded.

The other cabinet members all nodded in agreement.

"Now, these others are the more worrisome of the two. These launchers house the Dongfeng-21s. I know that in itself doesn't mean a lot, but they're medium-range missiles with a range of nearly two-thousand miles. That weapon has three possible configurations. One is an anti-ship version that can be mounted with a maneuverable reentry vehicle, clearly a problem, but those we see in the photos don't have those attached, so we can discount them being used in an anti-ship role, like the DF-17.

"That leaves either conventional or nuclear warhead configurations. Obviously, the greatest concern is if they're carrying nukes. They can deliver a 500kt nuclear payload to anywhere in Japan, Okinawa, or Guam. They might even consider nuking our task forces. Of course, they can also hit the same targets with conventional payloads, the most likely scenario."

"Could it be that China is truly going all-in in their

conquest of Taiwan? I mean, how far do you think they'll go?" Winslow asked.

"We're not sure," Tom Collier answered. "China has long sought to bring Taiwan under their control. It's an obsession of theirs that has ebbed and flowed depending upon who was in charge. But it's never been far from mind. President Hao is practically salivating over it. It's well within the realm of possibility that China will escalate matters in order to conquer the island."

"Including a nuclear exchange?" Winslow inquired.

Tom shrugged. "In my thinking, anything is on the table for them."

General Dawson stared at the CIA Director for a moment, and then nodded his agreement.

The room grew quiet with the proclamation. Until voiced, the thought of the two superpowers' conflict escalating into a nuclear confrontation had remained in the deep background. Before that utterance, Frank had still thought they could control the situation. Now they were approaching the brink of that worst case scenario. Most in the room just stared at the circled image of the launchers, the proof their fears might become reality.

Along with the others, Frank stared at the still-images of the mobile missiles. He felt as if he were aboard a speeding train, and there was nothing he could do to stop it. The thought that China might launch a nuclear weapon in order to achieve their goals suddenly seemed to be a real possibility. Surely no one would escalate to that level in an offensive manner. Nuclear weapons were defensive deterrents to ensure other nations didn't use them. Threat of nuclear strikes belonged in the realm of rogue nations such as North Korea or Iran, not First World nations actively engaged in commerce and tourism. Still, the pictures warned of a different reality.

"In light of this, I'm bringing our Pacific forces to DEFCON 2," Defense Secretary MacCulloch recommended.

At the start of hostilities, the third and seventh fleets, along with other units stationed in the Far East, were brought to

DEFCON 3. This step up would order all armed forces in the Pacific to be ready to engage in six hours. Of course, readiness levels had already increased to frontline units in Korea, Japan, Guam, and Okinawa with the massing of North Korean troops and the conflict with China.

"I agree," Winslow stated.

"Other than preparing to attack our forces, there are two other likelihoods. One is that they're presenting them as a deterrent to us getting involved in the defense of Taiwan. Secondly, China also uses those platforms as anti-satellite weapons," General Dawson briefed.

The screen changed to show a larger view of the launchers circled in white. This photo included an overlay of a yellow line.

"This line," Dawson said, the laser tracking the length of the yellow stripe, "is one of the orbital paths of two of our Keyhole satellites. You can see that those launchers sit adjacent to the path. So, it's extremely likely that China is planning to use those platforms to take out our low-earth surveillance satellites passing over the region."

The abyss Frank felt he was standing next to faded somewhat. The surge of adrenaline that had pumped into his system receded and he felt the thudding of his heart slow. What the general said made the most sense. China was likely not contemplating engaging in a nuclear conflict over Taiwan; in every scenario, the destruction of US satellites would be their priority. Winslow mentally sighed.

"Now, they've demonstrated the ability to knock out low-earth satellites recently. As previously briefed, there have been recent wargames played out along this specific scenario. Our ability to bring our firepower to bear depends on our communication and data-sharing infrastructure. It's paramount to the success of implementing our strategies. It's also our weak-link and easily exploited.

"China has the capability to threaten all of our low-earth orbiting satellites, and as we've recently observed, our higher-orbiting communication systems as well. We're in the midst of developing a mesh system which will provide redundancy and make our systems more survivable. But we're not there yet. So, if China is indeed readying itself to use its anti-satellite weapons against us, we need to deploy more Keyhole satellites to Cape Canaveral and Vandenburg, and ready Delta rockets to carry the payloads. Considering what's coming, it's imperative that we be able to speedily replace any gaps."

"I thought we were already doing that," MacCulloch stated.

"We are, sir, but we need to increase the measures already in place. It's much easier to shoot down a satellite than to launch a replacement. While they aren't numerous, China has enough operational anti-satellite weapons to give us a headache, if not completely disrupt our operations, and therefore our strategy. We need to be able to match any losses with ready replacements...and quickly," Dawson replied.

"Okay, I'll see what can be done," MacCulloch responded.

"Speaking of time, when do we anticipate China and North Korea will launch their offenses?" Winslow inquired.

"With what we've seen recently occurring in China, the estimation is that China's ships will be ready to sail in ninety-six hours. North Korea will then likely start their invasion within the following days. They're ready, so it really depends on how engaged they want our forces before launching their own," Dawson answered.

"So, with what we've talked about before, that means China will likely start firing their cruise missiles in a day or so," Frank said.

"Yes, sir. We can anticipate the first launches occurring in the next twenty-four hours," Dawson stated.

"Frank, that means Taiwan needs to get moving. Their naval vessels are ready to deploy and their air force has been placed on alert. Their ships will move out of their harbors within..." MacCulloch glanced at the clocks set to the different time zones, "well, it should start happening within the hour. The two submarines they operate have already departed. Once the first Chinese missile is fired, their air force will take to the air."

"I'd like to circle back to the satellite question," Frank began. "We've already been attacked by China, resulting in the loss of one of our surveillance satellites. If China is indeed looking to escalate the conflict in that regard, are we situated to counter them?"

"We have some defensive measures in place, and there are offensive operations ready," MacCulloch responded. "As General Dawson mentioned, we may encounter disruptions, but so will China. However, we're trying to reserve that operation for phase two of our planned campaign...the drawing out and annihilation of their bomber force."

Frank nodded. The discussion surrounding Taiwan seemed to have come to an end.

"As a side note," the Secretary of State chimed in, "we're only a little over twenty-four hours away from the end of the ultimatum we presented to North Korea."

"Any sign that they plan on pulling back?" Frank inquired.

Still standing, General Dawson shook his head.

Frank sighed. "Okay, once the deadline has passed, you're free to launch a preemptive strike as outlined in OPLAN 5015."

With those words, Frank knew the real battle with China over regional control was about to commence. He felt the tension knotting his gut. In the back of his mind was still the lingering possibility of China firing nuclear weapons at American bases or carriers. Would Hao risk world condemnation in order to secure Taiwan? There was no doubt that the fallout wouldn't only affect the thousands in the blast zones, but China's financial future. If they did fire a nuclear weapon, countries would most definitely shun China, thus erasing their years of effort to become a world economic power. Would Hao risk all of that? How far would he go? Frank's deepest worry was that he didn't have answers to those questions.

In addition to his fear about China's intentions, were the possible plans of an unstable government also known to possess WMDs. The fact that North Korea had nuclear capabilities changed the nature of what the United States could do. Unlike China, there was no doubt in anyone's mind that North Korea would use their nuclear arsenal, should America be about to overrun their country.

The warm yellow of interior lights glowed from within homes and apartments as night descended on the city and its surrounding environs. Gathered around dining tables, meals were enjoyed as families told their stories of the day. In other abodes, blue glows shaded faces as people congregated in front of televisions to watch their favorite series. Unknown to all, except for a very few, there were policymakers assembled in a deep underground room discussing the very real possibility of a nuclear exchange between superpowers.

* * * * * *

Zuoying Port, Kaohsiung City, Taiwan
23 July, 2021

Lights glowed against the grey clouds hanging low over the southernmost major Taiwanese city. Most of the city's workforce were contemplating their beds, their thoughts not far from the ever-present threat that lay only a hundred miles across the strait. The conflict between the United States and China rang all around the island nation. The build-up of transport ships created even more than the usual tension in the populace.

Up and down the island, the Taiwanese navy made ready to sortie from their naval ports. Word had come down that the Chinese invasion of Taiwan was imminent, and it was imperative that the naval vessels put to sea. Tugs were in continuous motion in the black waters of naval ports, moving with a sense of urgency to assist destroyers, frigates, corvettes, patrol boats, and fast attack missile boats away from their berths.

In the Zuoying District north of the city, xenon lights shone brightly across the naval dockyards. With sea bags draped over their shoulders, sailors strode briskly toward waiting ships. Matching stride, their multiple shadows from the many lights stretching across concrete piers followed in varying shades of darkness. In the middle of the harbor, several warships motored slowly toward the narrow entrance, waiting for the arrival of the few remaining still glued to the docks. One by one, the Tsoying Naval Base docks were being emptied of warships.

Shouts drifted through the night, ropes were hoisted from stanchions and tossed into the water with heavy splashes. Wake boiled around a tugboat from its prop biting into the water as it guided the ROCS *Fong Yang* away from its concrete pier. The distance between ship and dock increased as the ex-Knox-class frigate eased away from the shore.

Aboard the vessel, the CIC was busy as offensive and defensive systems were brought online and checked. The ship carried four Hsiung-Feng 3 supersonic and four Hsiung-Feng 2 subsonic anti-ship missiles capable of striking at long range. In addition, it housed four lightweight torpedo launchers as well as an anti-submarine rocket launcher. It was one of twenty-two such active frigates with a similar configuration.

Water churned behind the vessel as the warship started forward, a light wake arcing out from the bow unseen in the darkness. The officers and sailors in the bridge guided the *Fong Yang* through the busy harbor, easing toward a large group of waiting warships.

In the lead of the frigates, corvettes, and missile boats, two Kee Lung-class destroyers started for the open waters of the Taiwan strait. The old warships were once the cream of the crop, Spruance-class destroyers purchased by Taiwan and upgraded. Aside from the anti-submarine gear, the ships each contained eight Hsiung-Feng 3 anti-ship missiles capable of reaching out to two hundred and fifty miles.

Actively pinging, the two destroyers, the ROCS *Tso Ying* and the ROCS *Ma Kong* made for the choppy open waters. In the darkness beyond the breakwaters was a battleground for which the older vessels were mostly outclassed. China's pressure against nations willing to sell arms to the Taiwan had proved effective. However, the island nation had been able to upgrade the older systems, bringing its aging fleet up to something that could prove deadly.

Ranging further out in the night were ASW helicopters searching for signs of China's submarines, which surely had to be lurking near naval port entrances. All across the island, from the major naval ports to the northeast and east, other ships set out from their harbors. Three separate armadas, comprising a majority of the Taiwanese fleet, hit the open waters ahead of the commencement of China's attempt to invade.

*   *   *   *   *   *

The Shang-class nuclear fast attack sub slowly patrolled to the southwest of Kaohsiung City, Taiwan. The Chinese captain, Xie Yingjun, knew that there was an American submarine somewhere near the southern end of the Taiwan strait, but he hadn't been able to firm up the enemy sub's location well enough to take a shot. All his crew had been able to find were hints. One time, they had found a temperature differential in the water which may have been from the passage of a nuclear boat, but they were never able to zero in on the American's position. Another time, sonar thought they'd heard a faint noise, but lost it against the background of a cargo ship transiting the area.

Xie had received orders to patrol near the Tsoying Naval Base. He and his crew knew that the long-expected invasion of Taiwan was coming, and they were to be on the leading edge of it. The rules had changed. Although they were to hold off striking land targets for now, any warship emerging from the harbor was now fair game. To Xie, that could only mean that the launching of the cruise missile attacks that were to proceed the actual invasion was only hours away.

Changzhen-15 might be a part of that equation at some

point, but Captain Xie hadn't received any targeting orders other than Taiwan's fleet should it put to sea. Xie's theory was that China didn't want to reveal their hand too soon, but Beijing also didn't want Taiwan's fleet deployed. The danger Xie worried about wasn't so much the warships docked in the harbor, but rather the silent American boat he knew in his gut was also loitering nearby.

On the positive side, his boat hadn't been attacked, so if there was an American boat nearby, they didn't know the *Changzhen-15* was here. That might give Xie a slight edge, but it certainly didn't feel like much. It wasn't but a few days ago that they had picked up a horrible screeching that sounded like someone had run aground. But the explosions and subsequent breakup sounds that followed indicated that two vessels had sunk. Although he couldn't be positive about what had transpired, it demonstrated that the waters around Taiwan were getting awfully crowded.

The *Changzhen-15* captain felt that the war with America was mostly an unseen one, waged underwater between opposing fast attack vessels. Although not very detailed, the reports he received from Yulin Naval Base made it seem that China was holding its own against the Americans. That wasn't much of a surprise to Xie. Their nuclear boats were on par with the LA-class the Americans operated and, their diesel-electric subs, although old, were also difficult to detect. He'd been briefed about the new American airborne ASW capabilities, but they didn't seem to be making much of a difference, if the reports were to be believed. Xie had no reason not to trust his superiors.

He knew that the American carriers had been forced away, and the only fleet that was any threat to the invasion was the one Taiwan possessed. And if they stuck their nose out, Xie was there to make sure to bloody it. He would feel much better if he knew he was the only one in the vicinity. Then it would be easy: strike quickly and move until he was again able to hit the ships. Perhaps Taiwan would wait until China fired their land-based cruise missiles, in which case, the ships would certainly be part of the initial target list. If that was the case, then Xie wouldn't have to put his crew and boat at risk.

"Captain, we have multiple vessels coming out of Tsoying," sonar reported.

That call removed any hope Xie had of remaining just another patch of water. He moved closer to the sonar station.

"I have two destroyers, Kee Lung-class. Bearing zero three zero, range fourteen thousand yards, moving right to left. Speed ten knots and increasing. They are actively pinging. Labeling as Alpha One and Two."

Xie acknowledged the report. If the enemy fleet were sortieing, Xie knew there would be ASW helicopters screening the vessels. He hoped the noisy waters of the strong current would hide them from the dipping sonars.

"Slow to maintain position," Xie ordered.

The slow speed would make minimal noise.

"Ready tubes one through four."

Changzhen-15 had six forward tubes. The first two were loaded with YJ-18B supersonic anti-ship missiles. The remainder housed China's newer Yu-9 heavyweight torpedo. His initial plan was to use the two missiles against the destroyers then launch two torpedoes against any other ships which emerged. He would save two for the American sub, should it make its appearance.

Following his initial attack, he planned to escape to reload, and then move back to strike again. Where he retreated depended on where the enemy ships headed.

"Alpha One and Two aspect ratio changing. Targets turning north and accelerating through twenty knots. New targets coming out of port. Three Cheng Kung-class frigates. They are also accelerating. It appears they are following the two Alpha targets. Labeling the new targets as Bravo One, Two, and Three."

The ships were turning north and speeding up. Xie knew the ships were capable of thirty knots, which meant that it wouldn't be much longer until distance became a factor. His Yu-9 torpedoes cruised at forty-five knots, only accelerating to sixty knots in the final stage of the attack. The ships were nearly three miles away with the distance increasing. With only a fifteen-knot speed advantage, it would take nearly twenty minutes until his torpedoes hit, the weapons covering twelve miles. Every minute he waited would only make the situation worse, especially considering that the maximum range of the weapons was only twenty-eight miles. Any delay and the enemy fleet might outdistance the Yu-9s.

"Target Alpha One and Two with one YJ-18B each. Target Bravo One and Two with one Yu-9 apiece," Xie ordered.

"Sir, fire control system is updated. Tubes one through four are ready."

"Fire One."

*   *   *   *   *   *

"Passive contact, bearing two zero zero, range two thousand yards, unknown speed and type."

The report came from the *Fong Yang's* helicopter operating three miles to the southwest of the lead ships exiting the harbor. The CIC officer peered at the situation board. The lead destroyers had turned north, planning to meet up with the flotilla departing the harbors of Keelung in the northeast and Hualien City in the east. The ASW chopper reported that it was moving farther to the west in order to triangulate what it found and perhaps better determine what it was. Another helicopter from the *Tso Ying* reported that it was on its way to assist.

As the dipping sonar was being reeled in, the pilot was peering through the night toward the contact's position. Somewhere out there was a Chinese submarine. He felt it in his gut. After all, it would be negligent of the PRC to not be monitoring Taiwan's major naval port. The problem was that there was the possibility that the contact might also be an American submarine. They knew one was supposed to be patrolling the southern end of the strait, but not its precise location.

Across the darkened waters, several position lights shone

from ships braving the conflict zone. Movement a half mile away caught his attention. Something disturbed the choppy sea. Suddenly, a bright flash broke the uninterrupted dark. The burst of light resolved itself to become a tongue of flame that accelerated as it climbed above the sea. The arcing trajectory flattened.

The pilot stared unmoving for a couple of seconds as the streaking trail of flame, which seemed ready to pass overhead, descended and was now headed directly for him. Once he realized the threat, there wasn't enough time to evade. The YJ-18B anti-ship missile was in the process of accelerating to its terminal speed of Mach 3 when it slammed into the side of the S-70C(M)-2 Thunderhawk. With a brilliant flash of fire, the chopper exploded, raining pieces of hot metal into the sea. Spinning wildly, the large rotor slammed into the water, kicking up a fountain of spray. A hundred yards away, another tall column of water rose into the night from the supersonic missile crashing into the strait.

While the *Fong Yang's* CIC crew were processing the sudden radar blip and subsequent loss of their helicopter, the bridge watched as a second long trail of fire streaked into the sky. It flew over small flames that were licking upward from fuel burning on the surface and raced toward one of the lead destroyers.

The fire control systems aboard the ships identified the sudden target as hostile. Phalanx Close-In Weapon Systems rotated toward the target, which was now accelerating past Mach 2. Barrels began to spin, spitting out 20mm tungsten rounds at 4,500 rounds per minute. The onboard computers tracked the target and the outgoing rounds, making adjustments as the bullets were walked to the target.

The speed of the YJ-18B made the task of adjusting difficult, especially considering it was still accelerating. Pillars of water shot into the night as the heavy rounds impacted the sea, the columns forming a line as they marched toward the speeding projectile. Jamming systems attempted to interfere with the supersonic weapon, if it was homing via radar. Flares shot into the night, their bright incandescence shimmering off the sides of ships and the dark waters.

If there had been time, the night would have also been filled with the fiery streaks of anti-air missiles, but the Chinese missile traveling at one thousand, eight-hundred miles per hour didn't leave enough time for the defensive weapons to engage. At that speed, it took a mere six seconds to cross the three miles. Although the Phalanx system was designed to put the first bullet on target, that was against slower moving, constant speed targets.

The YJ-18B, now speeding through the night at Mach 3, plowed into the side of the ROCS *Ma Tong*. Once inside the ship, the 660-pound warhead shredded the interior, knocking out many systems and starting fires on multiple decks. The destroyer slowed dramatically and began to settle as it took on water. Flares continuously illuminated the skies until the last one fell into the strait with a hiss.

A flash of light again lit the nighttime skies, a following roar reverberated off the waters. First one, and then a second missile left the ASROC launcher aboard the *Fong Yang*. The anti-submarine rockets flew out over the sea on a backtrack course from the anti-ship missiles that had emerged. The fact that Taiwanese ships had been attacked left no doubt as to the nationality of the contact.

The flame propelling the rockets lasted only moments as Mark-54 lightweight torpedoes were dropped on the spot where the missiles had risen from the strait. Dropping below the choppy waters, the torpedoes entered a circular search pattern, each one turning in opposite directions. Additional rockets left the decks of two other frigates.

*   *   *   *   *   *

Captain Xie ordered *Changzhen-15* to turn west and increase speed following the launches.

"Descend to three hundred feet," Xie added.

He regretted that his vessel wasn't one of the versions

that was upgraded with a vertical launch system. If he had had that capability, he could have launched an attack that targeted a dozen or more ships at once. As it stood, he was now on the defensive while the forward crew reloaded the four torpedo tubes that were now empty. He opted to reload them with the Yu-9 torpedoes, as he would remain quieter when he turned to reengage. He would also be able to remain at depth when conducting attacks, making it less likely to be found via a MAD contact.

Captain Xie knew that he would only be able to keep up torpedo attacks for a limited time. The enemy warships were now heading north at thirty knots, his maximum speed. At best, he would only be able to keep up. But with having to maneuver between attacks, he would slowly lose ground until he was too far away for his torpedoes to be effective. At that point, he would ascend and fire the YJ-18Bs until he ran out. If he was patient, he knew he could conceivably destroy the armada sailing north, thus depriving Taiwan of a large portion of its navy.

"One missile hit," sonar reported.

Xie glanced at the time. Less than half a minute had passed since his first order to fire. The two torpedoes now accelerating to their maximum speed of sixty knots, would still take nearly seven minutes to catch the fleeing targets.

"Two torpedoes in the water, range three thousand yards, aspect ratio continuously changing. Sir, it seems like they've entered a search pattern and are actively hunting."

The fact that the deadly threats were searching meant that they hadn't yet picked up his boat. The weapons were dropped where the YJ-18B missiles emerged and not where his sub had fired. The missiles, along with the torpedoes, had been given differing tracks so the enemy couldn't easily just fire down the reverse track and locate the *Changzhen-15*.

"Increase speed to twenty-five knots," Xie ordered.

It was imperative that he quickly depart the area, as there were bound to be more torpedoes fired his way. He had just hit one of their lead destroyers, and those sailing with it weren't going to be happy. If anything, there would be choppers overhead within minutes and he wanted to be far away. The turn west was both to remain in range of the Taiwanese ships and because south would be the most likely direction an attacking sub would take to get away. He would only keep up the speed long enough to clear the immediate area. While he formulated plans for a continued attack, Xie still worried that there was a lurking American threat.

*   *   *   *   *   *

The *Fong Yang* sailed past the stricken destroyer, which had taken on a list. Thick smoke billowed upward from the warship that was lying dead in the water, waves lapping over its fantail. A missile boat had pulled alongside and was lending whatever aid it could. Calls had gone out to the base and two ocean-going tugs were on their way. From the shape of the *Ma Tong*, those in the bridge of the frigate doubted the tugs would make it in time.

The CIC officer listened to the incoming reports regarding the torpedoes that were searching for the Chinese sub, the threat still out there somewhere in the dark. The helicopter that was on its way to aid the *Fong Yang's* chopper arrived on the scene of the downed bird. Bright spotlights stabbed into the night, illuminating the dark waters. The beams revealed flotsam drifting on top of the choppy waves, but no bodies. With the menace still out there, the spotlights blinked out after a thorough search, and the ASW helicopter sped south in an attempt to locate the submarine responsible for the attack.

Minutes later, the seas around one of the *Fong Yang's* sister ships began to boil. Steam rose up along the sides of the vessel thick enough to completely obscure the aft end of the warship. Like the *Ma Tong* before it, the ship suddenly slowed, its momentum carrying it past the dissipating steam cloud. It took only seconds for the frigate's stern to vanish under the sea, the waves turning the ship parallel to the swells. Waves began splashing against the superstructure as the ship sank lower. The surrounding waters were soon inundated with sailors exiting the interior of the ship, searching for anything to help keep them afloat.

The Yu-9 fuse had triggered underneath the vessel, just forward of the engine room. The two-thousand-degree chemical reaction had melted a third of the underside of the ship, allowing the sea to pour into previously watertight compartments. With sailors still plunging into the waves, the frigate's bow rose into the sky and the ship's stern vanished. The warship's progress into the deeps slowed and then halted as the watertight forward compartments held.

As the bow bobbed above the waves, another frigate was engulfed in steam as a second torpedo was ignited directly under its keel. With the entire center of the ship melted under the tremendous heat, the warship sank almost immediately, taking eighty percent of its crew with it.

The first ship continued bobbing on the waves for a full minute until the weight of the stern dragged the vessel under.

* * * * * *

The time to target for both torpedoes had expired. One of the unfortunate aspects of the Yu-9 was that it didn't create an explosion by which one could directly ascertain a hit. The torpedoes were fairly reliable, but unless the weapon sank a vessel, it was difficult to determine whether the attack had been successful.

"Break up noises. Sounds like a single vessel," sonar called.

Xie acknowledged while continuing to listen to reports on the searching enemy torpedoes. *Changzhen-15* was gradually closing the distance on Taiwan's navy and Xie was reasonably certain they were drawing out of the detection range of the circling torps.

A minute later, sonar reported the sounds of a second ship's metal being twisted from the pressures exerted on it. Two ships sunk for four attacks. Captain Xie was a little disappointed with the results from the YJ-18 anti-ship missiles. As far as he could determine, one of the missiles had hit without sending the targeted destroyer to the bottom. However, it was surely out of action. He was stymied as to what had happened to the first missile, but was glad he'd reloaded his tubes with torpedoes. There would come a time when he would be forced to use the missiles, but for now, he was going to rely on the proven effectiveness of the Yu-9s.

"Tubes loaded, sir."

Xie nodded to his second in command. "Turn to heading three five zero. Ready tubes one through four."

Xie knew it wouldn't be long until he had to ascend to begin using the YJ-18 anti-ship missiles. The data from four new targets were uploaded into the fire control system and two minutes later, another four torpedoes were speeding toward the remaining ships.

* * * * * *

Twenty-five miles west-southwest of Tainan City and south of the Penghu Island chain, the USS *Mississippi* glided through the Taiwan Strait.

"Here comes the navy," the sonarman joked. "It sounds like a herd of stampeding buffalo."

Commander Joe Wright knew his sonarman was referring to the Taiwan ships that were departing the Tsoying Naval Base. Heading up the western seaboard as they journeyed north at high speed, the sound of their thrashing propellers grew louder as they drew nearer to the patrolling Virginia-class submarine.

"Transient, bearing one three zero, range, uh…damn, I lost it. Sir, it appears as if it was beyond the first convergence zone, perhaps even the second one."

Commander Wright thought for a moment. With the noisy waters, the sonar could have picked up anything. However, with the emergence of Taiwan's western fleet, the coincidence was hard to dismiss.

"That was definitely an explosion. Bearing one one zero, range fifty-one thousand yards."

"Isn't that the position of the Taiwan naval vessels?" Wright inquired.

"Aye, sir."

"Just the one explosion?"

"Aye, sir. At least as far as I can tell."

"Anything further from the transient?"

"Negative, sir."

Commander Wright visualized the scene in his head. Numerous ships were steaming north off Taiwan's western shores. Behind them, his sonar had caught a transient sound with an ensuing explosion. There was no doubt in Joe's mind that the convoy was being attacked. If it weren't for the transient sound, he might have thought it could have come from China's mainland. Somewhere south or southwest of the fleet, a Chinese boat was lurking.

If he was right about the situation, then the other ramification was that China and Taiwan were now at war.

"Make your heading one one zero. Increase speed to fifteen knots. Maintain depth," Wright ordered.

"Aye, aye, sir. Heading one one zero, speed fifteen knots, maintaining three hundred feet," the XO repeated.

Minutes later, sonar reported the breakup sounds of two ships. The lack of explosions erased all doubts that the attacks were coming from a Chinese submarine, probably one of their Shang-class boats; those were the ones most likely to be firing the Yu-9 torpedo. That weapon didn't explode like the majority of those in use, but rather used a chemical reaction to melt the area around the target.

The enemy captain had likely fired a combination of those torpedoes and anti-ship missiles. It appeared that at least one missile and one torpedo had struck their targets. In view of the successful attack, the Chinese captain would likely chase after the fleeing ships and attack as long as he could. That meant the Chinese nuclear fast attack sub would pass close to the *Mississippi*.

"Sir, the signal is coming and going, but I'm pretty sure I'm picking up active pings. The bearing is zero one zero. If it's outside of the first convergence zone, then the range is fifty-four thousand yards."

"Standard rudder left to heading zero niner zero, slow to ten knots," Wright ordered.

The executive officer repeated the instructions.

"Steady on zero niner zero, speed ten knots," the helmsman reported moments later.

The change in course and speed was to avoid what was surely a counterattack from Taiwan. The last thing he wanted was to enter the kill box of a searching torpedo. Instead of seeking out the enemy submarine, he'd let it come to him. That might allow for additional attacks, but it might also keep him away from any itchy trigger fingers. The one advantage he held was that any submarine hoping to sustain its attacks on the surface ships would have to match their speed, or at least come close to it.

At the moment, the naval ships were steaming north at thirty knots. That was also the maximum speed of China's nuclear fast attack boats. The faster speed, though, if the enemy captain was indeed following, would make them easier to detect.

*   *   *   *   *   *

Water arced away from the bow as the *Fong Yang* dove into yet another cresting swell, the bow wave settling back to the sea with a hiss. Turbulent water streamed down the sides of the frigate as it raced northward with the other warships. The crew hoped they were only dealing with one submarine and weren't speeding into the waiting sights of another. The one was proving difficult to locate, and there was the worry that continued attacks could effectively eliminate this contingent of Taiwan's navy before it had a chance to strike back.

Fong Yang's helicopter had been unsuccessful in finding the Chinese sub to the south. The only conclusion the captain could reach was that the enemy boat had either moved to the west, or maybe it had been there all along. With other choppers screening the convoy to the north and west, the assisting Thunderhawk was free to maneuver as needed to locate and eliminate the threat. As the *Fong Yang* was directing activities against this particular enemy submarine, the captain ordered the ASW helicopter to proceed northwest and begin searching southwest of the fleet.

Three seconds after the order was transmitted, another frigate was nearly engulfed in boiling seas. The warship was momentarily hidden behind a cloud of steam, coming out the other side with its nose diving into the unsettled waters as it slowed. The aft portion of the underside had melted away from the torpedo, the two boilers and turbine shaft dropping out of the bottom. In moments, the bow of the ship rose as the sea started washing over the sinking rear end. Only a handful of crew in the superstructure managed to escape before the ship vanished under the waves.

Just a few miles to the east glowed the lights of the cities that covered Taiwan's west coast. Hidden within the night lights was the populace the naval ships were supposed to protect, but were instead being systematically eliminated by a single submarine. The people, tossing in restless sleeps, were unaware of the violence occurring just a few miles from their front doors.

Over the next fifteen seconds, three other ships fell victim to the enemy submarine attacking from somewhere out in the darkness.

*   *   *   *   *   *

"Sir, that's four more breakup sounds," sonar reported.

Commander Wright shook his head. "Well, there's not much we can do about that right now."

Joe hated not being able to march southeast and intercept the Chinese sub earlier. There were lives being lost. But he hadn't wanted to be caught rushing to the scene or be mistaken for a Chinese boat by a searching weapon. An active torpedo, once in its kill box and released from being wire-guided, didn't know friend from foe. It identified a target and homed in on it. Wright didn't want to be chased by torpedoes meant for another. Instead, he'd stick with his original plan and wait for the Chinese captain to sail into his sights, so to speak.

The *Mississippi* patrolled silently, slowly drawing closer to Taiwan's western coastline. Over the next twenty minutes, sonar reported four additional losses. The distance between them was increasing, and Wright was beginning to worry that he had missed either the Chinese sub or the enemy captain's intentions.

The one good thing with the increasing distance of the surface vessels was that the waters were becoming clearer, sound-wise. The bad thing, that also meant it was easier to hear the *Mississippi*, even though they were currently the quietest boat.

"Sonar contact, bearing zero three zero, range twenty-five thousand yards, moving right to left. It's definitely a Shang-class sub, sir. Moving at twenty-five knots. Labeling as Alpha One."

Another few seconds passed before sonar again intoned, "I have Alpha One's course at zero one zero."

Wright examined the chart. With the intersecting lines, the Chinese submarine would pass within twelve thousand yards. The closer the distance between the two underwater hunters, the easier it would become to detect the *Mississippi*.

"Maintain heading and depth. Slow to five knots," Wright ordered.

The slower speed would make it more difficult to detect, as there was little to no chance of cavitation. The Chinese captain was taking quite the chance, racing after the Taiwanese fleet. But Wright knew he would probably take the same risk, had he a large percentage of the Chinese fleet in his sights.

"Ready tubes one and two," Wright ordered.

"Aye, sir. Both tubes showing green."

Wright would wait a little longer to attack, letting the

Shang-class nuclear boat get closer. With the noise the Chinese sub was making, he'd let the torpedoes passively track the vessel. If needed, the tracking mode could be changed up until the wires were cut.

*   *   *   *   *   *

Downwash whipped the surface into a frenzy as the Thunderhawk hovered several feet above the waves. The cable attached to the dipping sonar quivered, the device had just entered the water and was lowering. Having given up on locating the enemy sub to the south and guided by the *Fong Yang's* CIC, the chopper flew to a position southwest of the fleet. Here the hunt would begin anew for a threat that was methodically eliminating the ships. It was imperative that they locate the Chinese boat.

The sonar operator, intently listening for any hint that the Chinese vessel was in the area, suddenly yelled and frantically clawed at his headphones, throwing them away from his ears. The pilot looked down at the cable trailing into the depths, searching for a threat that could cause such a reaction.

The cable had angled off to one side. The surface of the water suddenly bulged upward, and the cable slackened. The pilot was moving the chopper back when an eruption of water geysered upward. Water splashed heavily across the windshield, and the Thunderhawk was tossed up and away. Nearly snatched from his hands, the pilot wrestled with the controls as he attempted to restore the situation.

Unseen beyond the fountain of water that nearly engulfed the helicopter, the dipping sonar was tossed into the air by the eruption. The attached cable rose with it, sailing through the rapidly spinning rotors. Cut loose, the sonar was flung away, falling back to the sea a quarter mile away.

As the pilots were fighting the chopper, a second eruption of water blossomed upward. Being farther away, the fountain, mixed with oil and debris, splashed down on top of the rotors. The helicopter was driven toward the surface of the sea.

With new forces shoving at the chopper, the pilots found themselves again battling against a loss of attitude. Red and yellow caution lights flared in the cockpit, along with warning buzzers. The large volume of water flooded the intake of one engine, shutting it down. Most of the water, thankfully, was thrown off to the sides by the rotors. Seawater rained down, the blades acting like an umbrella.

In moments, the second blast of water fell back into the strait. The pilots just managed to wrangle control. Below the chopper, a sheared cable swung over a forming slick of oils and debris that popped to the surface. Before long, the swells smoothed over the violent upheavals. Underneath the waves, the remains of a Chinese Shang-class fast attack submarine sank toward the shallow bottom, taking with it one hundred souls.

The pilots of the Thunderhawk were able to restart their engine and flew back to their ship. It didn't take long to figure out that the Chinese submarine, which had eluded contact for so long, had been sunk. Although the kill wasn't confirmed, the cessation of attacks on the fleet led to that conclusion.

*   *   *   *   *   *

With the loss of the *Changzhen-15*, there wasn't any communication to China's armed forces regarding the successful attacks. Chinese naval intelligence noted the Taiwan navy setting out from their ports, and even noticed a subsequent absence of several ships sailing up Taiwan's western seaboard. But there was no immediate connection that the missing ships had been sunk by a Chinese submarine. That link wouldn't be established until much later. Even though orders had been issued for submarines to attack Taiwan's warships if they emerged from their ports, those orders only pertained to the underwater fleet. China wasn't yet aware that they were now at war with Taiwan.

As the Thunderhawk pilots were wrestling their chopper for control, a Chinese Y-8Q anti-submarine warfare aircraft entered the area. They were unaware of the attacks against the Taiwanese navy vessels and thus weren't concerned about flying close to the Penghu Islands and the bristling defenses that were scattered throughout the chain of islands.

Flying over the strait south of the islands, the crew searched for any indication of American submarines. Tired from nearly continuous missions over the Taiwan Strait and the northern sections of the South China Sea, the crew inside the fuselage struggled to maintain focus on their screens.

Radar showed the naval vessels sallying forth from ports in Taiwan. Soon, they would be wary of such a force, but for now, they were only on the hunt for American submarines that had to be patrolling the strait between Taiwan and China. The important thing was that the radar also showed that the skies around the four-engine turboprop were clear of American aircraft. Having lost one of their number to the appearance of enemy fighters over the East China Sea, the pilots were wary. The American warships were far to the east, so they didn't pose much of a threat. It was those flying out of Okinawa, Japan, or even from Taiwan. However, for the moment, the crew was free to conduct their business without interference.

Their orders were clear: Find and eliminate any American submarines in and around the Taiwan Strait. Those lanes needed to be cleared before the arrival of China's invasion fleets that were to set sail in a few days.

Sensors aboard the aircraft registered a disturbance in the water and altered course. Moments later, the MAD sensor from the thirty-foot boom jutting from the rear picked up something metallic. Reversing course, the sensor was again able to pick up a presence. The surface radar was clear of ships at the location, so the contact was presumed to be a submarine. However, with Chinese subs known to be patrolling near Taiwanese ports, the nationality of the underwater contact wasn't assured.

*   *   *   *   *   *

"That's a kill, sir," sonar stated.

"Very well. Right standard rudder, set your course to one niner zero. Increase speed to fifteen knots," Commander Wright ordered.

"Aye, sir. Right standard to one niner zero, speed to fifteen knots."

"Prepare a flash message to COMSUBPAC. Inform them of the Chinese attack against the Taiwanese naval fleet by a Shang-class sub and its subsequent sinking. Send along our data," Wright added.

"Aye, sir."

Minutes later, a transmitter surfaced and sent the flash message. The device sent its compressed message in less than a second and then vanished back below the waves. Commander Wright ordered the *Mississippi* to clear the area, even though it was a long-range attack against the Chinese boat. Sonar had the area free of enemy surface vessels, but operating so close to China, there was always the risk of ASW aircraft. In the shallower waters, the risk of MAD detection was all too real.

* * * * * *

Subsequent passes by the Y-8Q over the area revealed that the contact was on a southerly heading and traveling at approximately fifteen knots. That information fit in with the profile of a submarine underway. After affirming the target course and speed, the crew directed the Y-8Q to a perpendicular course. From four dispensing holes, sonobuoys were dropped into the night.

"Faint contact on buoy Alpha Three. Target speed fifteen knots, contact fading," an operator intoned.

The lumbering aircraft made a wide turn and came around on a reciprocal heading, dropping additional buoys further ahead of the contact.

"Faint contact on Bravo Three. Contact course is one niner zero, speed fifteen knots. Contact signal increasing."

A moment later, the operator confirmed that they were hearing an American Virginia-class sub that was passing close to one of the sonobuoys. That information was enough for the officer in charge. The sound of checklists being run thought filled the intercom following his order to engage the contact.

The Y-8Q made another wide turn and descended. The rays of a near full moon caught the tops and leading edges of the wings as the aircraft went into a shallow bank. Below the turboprop, a layer of clouds hung motionless, looking like a white mattress that stretched for as far as the eye could see. Moonbeams highlighted the tops, shading the valleys a light gray.

Rolling out of its bank, doors opened from the belly of the Chinese aircraft. Maintaining a steady course and speed, the aircraft droned toward a computer-configured drop zone. A minute later, two objects fell from within the aircraft. Glowing under the light of the moon, the cylinders drifted below drogue chutes meant to slow their fall and ease their entry into the unseen waters.

Moments later, the two Yu-7 lightweight torpedoes entered the cotton ball cloud layer and vanished from view. Dropping from the bottom of the low-hanging ceiling, the weapons entered the strait and began their search. With information received from the buoy just prior to submerging, the two Yu-7s quickly found their target and sped up. Ten seconds after sinking below the waves, the torpedoes went active.

Upon hearing the active torpedoes, the American submarine increased speed and dove. Countermeasures were released, but to no avail. The Yu-7s plowed through the noisemakers and detonated alongside the fleeing sub. For the second time in a short period, the surface of the Taiwan Strait became littered with the debris of a submarine settling to the bottom.

* * * * * *

Word of the attacks against their naval vessels was quickly received by Taiwan's command centers. Units were placed on high alert, but that was the limit of the initial communications. Being late at night, it took some time to contact Taiwan's leadership. They then had to compile information from the sometimes conflicting intelligence, so the first moments were spent determining exactly what had happened and compiling damage assessments. After the assessments had been completed, it became clear that Taiwan naval forces had been directly attacked by China and the two nations were now at war.

The plan for the surface fleet had been for the three separate flotillas to join up and wait for the Chinese invasion fleet to appear. The Chinese attack altered that strategy. As a matter of fact, it changed a lot of plans. The armadas were ordered to still meet, but instead of waiting, they were to immediately speed north toward the Chinese port of Zhoushan. Taiwan's navy would go on the offensive. Their primary target was one of the fleets gathering for the invasion, and they would strike it with their long-range anti-ship missiles.

The moment that it became clear that Taiwan naval forces had been attacked by a Chinese submarine, orders were sent to the armed forces, including those stationed in the Penghu Islands. All services were free to engage any Chinese military asset. That communique set into motion the anti-air units buried in tunnels carved throughout the island chain.

Chinese aircraft had continually pressed into Taiwan's airspace. The incursions were meant to intimidate the island nation and to measure its responses. With that constant threat, the anti-aircraft batteries were already prepared for orders to engage.

The radar facilities had been tracking a Chinese aircraft that was flying over the Taiwan Strait. When orders came down freeing the weapons, it didn't take long for the Tien Kung III missile batteries to target the enemy plane.

Roars woke the island residents as flames shot from hidden mobile launchers. Rocketing through the flames, anti-aircraft missiles flew from their containers. Those who happened to be looking outside observed fire trails arcing into the night sky where they quickly entered the low cloud layer. Accelerating to Mach 7, the missiles could be briefly followed from the ground due to fiery glows within the clouds. After the short interruption, the night again settled back into quiet, leaving a nervous population to wonder exactly what had occurred.

* * * * * *

The celebration aboard the Yu-8Q was short-lived as sensors alerted a now startled crew that they were being targeted by anti-air radar systems. The pilot started a sharp turn to the west. Behind the aircraft, flares were ejected into the slipstream. In the bright light of the moon, orange flares arced out and then slowly floated downward.

The copilot had his head craned out of his side window, peering back toward the Taiwan-controlled islands. Beyond the descending flares, he saw another set of glows coming from within the cloud layer. The glimmerings quickly brightened and then became more distinct as the Sky Bow III missiles sped from the top of the clouds.

More flares were ejected as the numerous missiles arced toward the turning aircraft. The deadly projectiles ignored the countermeasures, and instead continued tracking the lumbering aircraft. With wide eyes, the copilot watched the missiles, traveling at over four thousand miles per hour, converge on him.

The first missile detonated adjacent the outer right-side engine. Shrapnel penetrated the cowling, severing fuel and oil lines, and punched into the rapidly-spinning turbine blades. Trailing a sheet of flame, the engine came apart. The drag and thrust differential pulled the aircraft into a steeper bank to the right.

The Yu-8Q bucked as a second missile exploded next to the fuselage, perforating the thin skin. Pieces of metal flew inside the aircraft, slicing through flesh and bone. Screams of pain punctuated the interior, which had been filled with cheers only moments ago.

With warning bells and lights filling the cockpit, the pilot fought to keep the aircraft from rolling inverted. At the same time, he reached over to shut down the stricken engine in order to put out the fire and to reduce the drag imposed on the aircraft. His copilot was glued to his window and the pilot had to yell to get his partner's attention back inside the aircraft to assist.

The night lit up again when a third missile exploded just outside of the cockpit on the right. Fragments of metal shredded the window and cockpit on that side. The sharp whistle of wind screamed into the cockpit as pressurization, which had been bleeding from the holes in the fuselage, was lost in an instant. What remained of the windscreen became covered in blood as pieces of metal tore into the copilot. His severed head was sucked out of the large hole in the side of the aircraft, his limp body slumping against the constraints.

The pilot's arm, reaching for the emergency cutoff for the number four engine, went numb as shrapnel shattered it. Lightheaded from the sudden lack of oxygen, he did his best to keep the plane upright. In confusion from blood loss and lack of air, the pilot reached for his emergency oxygen, forgetting that his right arm didn't work.

The aircraft shuddered as another missile slammed into the number three engine. The pilot stared at his arm, confused as to why it wasn't working. The answer seemed close, but hovered just out of reach. The information coming from the flashing lights and instruments were also confusing. Looking out through his portion of the still intact windscreen, he wondered why the clouds were at right angles to the aircraft. Nothing made any sense.

What is that noise? the pilot thought just before he slumped forward.

With the right wing engulfed in flame, the Yu-8Q rolled inverted and began a dive. Weakened and under tremendous pressure, the right wing separated. Spinning violently and trailing fire, the plane plummeted. At first it was just a glow inside the clouds, but then the aircraft was spit from the bottom of the thick cloudbank and slammed into the sea. China was now down to six functioning Y-8Q ASW aircraft. The opening shots between China and Taiwan had been exchanged.

Chapter Four

East China Sea, north of Taiwan
24 July, 2021

The clocks ticked past the midnight hour, signaling that another day had technically started. Those caught up in the quickly escalating events in the seas surrounding Taiwan were mostly unaware of the new calendar date. That was especially true of those sailing in one of the three fleets that had set out from Taiwan's naval ports. They were far too busy trying to stay alive and keep their units somewhat intact. News filtered in to the other two fleets of the sinkings on the western seaboard. Everyone manning their stations knew that the night wasn't over, and that the conflict with China would last until Beijing gave up, or the island was overrun and the cities left in smoking ruins. It wasn't only life and death for those on the frontline, but the possible end of a nation and its way of life.

* * * * * *

Sailing northeast out of Keelung Harbor, Taiwan's two other destroyers led an armada of frigates, fast attack missile boats, patrol boats, and a corvette. The makeup of the flotilla looked very similar to the one that had set forth from Tsoying Naval Base. Being the most northerly ships, they had deployed later than the others that had left the east and west coasts. The plan had been to sail slowly to the northeast and let the other two task forces join them. However, in light of the attack, the Keelung task force would now sail at top speed to the northeast, where they would then proceed on a zig-zagging course to allow the others to meet up.

The lead vessels were aware that there was a good chance that a Chinese submarine was sitting out in the dark, ready to ambush the task force. ASW helicopters ranged out ahead of the warships, passing Heping Island Park on their way into open waters.

The bright beam of the Keelung Islet Lighthouse stabbed

out into the night, briefly illuminating the ships as the lamp circled. To the west, another beam of light from the Yehliu Lighthouse penetrated the darkness. The stream of warships sailed between the two beacons, spreading out into protective formations once they hit the open waters.

* * * * * *

"Multiple contacts, bearing zero three zero, range forty thousand yards, passing slightly right to left. Lead vessels speed fifteen knots and increasing."

Captain Cao Jinglong nodded to the sonarman. The report was expected, although it came sooner than he thought. The naval ships from the Chilung naval base were putting to sea. Cao hadn't expected them for another day or so. It appeared Taiwan was being cautious and deploying before China began their attack. Captain Cao appreciated that China's leadership had foreseen that this might occur and sent orders that any Taiwan ships moving out of their harbors were to be attacked. It's best to take care of matters while the warships were boxed in rather than deal with the headache they could cause later.

Cao weighed the options of waiting for the ships to pass closer versus attacking at a longer range. If he waited, then there was the chance that the fleet steaming out of the harbor would alter their course, taking them further from *Changzhen-16's* position. Currently, Cao and his crew were slowly patrolling north of Taiwan between Mianhua Islet and Huaping Isle. There would undoubtedly be ASW air assets searching the area around the flotilla with their dipping sonar. Although the waters were noisy, there was certainly a chance of being found in the shallow waters.

However, if Cao chose to attack now, then that might decrease the number of attacks he could make if the fleet turned away. The range to the nearest ships was already near the limit of his torpedo's reach. Any further away and he'd have to rely solely on his anti-ship missiles. Unlike torpedoes, the launching of missiles would be heard and seen, and merit prompt retaliation. That would draw attention toward his position and force him on the defensive as he withdrew from the area. It would be some time before he could attack again, especially seeing how the surface ships could travel at the same speed as the Shang-class boat.

It took only a few moments of thought before Cao arrived at his choice. He would attack with what he had in the tubes, two YJ-18 anti-ship missiles and four Yu-9 torpedoes. The missiles would force him to move to another position before attacking again, but better to get in one attack now rather than waiting and possibly being found. The distance from the warships would also give him time to exit before any ASW assets arrived. Surely there wouldn't be any helicopters operating this far from the ships.

*   *   *   *   *   *

"Transients, bearing two eight zero, range three thousand yards," sonar called with a tone of excitement.

Commander Patrick Sims turned his head sharply. They were operating just a couple of miles west of Mianhua's rocky shores and a contact so close was a surprise. His immediate concern was that the transients that sonar had picked up could be a Chinese boat firing on them. How they would have heard the loitering LA-class sub was a mystery, but that wasn't Patrick's worry at the moment.

"Make sure the location is in the FCS and prepare tubes one and two," Sims ordered.

His stomach knotted as he waited for anything further from sonar. If an enemy torpedo went active, then he'd deploy countermeasures and fire his torpedoes.

"Make your heading zero eight zero, maintain speed at five knots," Patrick added.

If the USS *Columbus* had been fired on, given the distance between his boat and the transient sound, he wouldn't have much time to evade. His only hope would be to use the shallows and the uneven, rocky bottom that surrounded the nearby islet. Sims longed to issue the order to deploy countermeasures and speed around the island, but if his boat hadn't been located, that action would certainly make it so.

"Those transients are definitely missiles firing," sonar reported.

Sims mentally sighed as some of the tension left his shoulders. If those were indeed missiles, then his boat hadn't been located. Sea-launched missiles were for either surface or ground targets. If the *Columbus* had been targeted, in this environment, he probably wouldn't have heard the torpedoes until they had gone active.

"Sir, sonar contact. Bearing is zero eight zero, range two thousand, five hundred, aspect ratio moving to the right, speed increasing through seven knots. I make it to be a Shang-class boat. It sounds like he just commenced an attack on the Taiwan ships sailing out of Keelung harbor."

"Very well. Update the FCS," Sims commanded.

"Fire control system updated with the contact," the XO relayed.

"Fire one."

A Mark 48 torpedo was ejected from its tube. It increased speed to sixty knots, racing through the nighttime waters. Wire unspooled from behind the weapon so that it could receive additional updates and instructions. Time to target was one minute, forty seconds.

*   *   *   *   *   *

The S-70 Thunderhawk flew a hundred feet over the top of the swells, the sea tinted green as the pilot looked out through his NVGs. The chopper was one of many that screened the ships deploying from the naval base. With the attack against the ships sailing from Tsoying Naval Base, more helicopters were sent out in an attempt prevent more losses. As small as the Taiwan navy was, it could ill afford the loss of any ship if it was going to inflict any significant damage to the invasion fleets.

In the distance to the east and southwest, faint lines of white marked where the rolling swells of the East China Sea crashed against the rocky shores of two islands. The crew's current mission was to ensure the waters between the two upthrusts of land were clear of Chinese subs. There was intelligence that the Americans were also operating in the area, so it was imperative that a positive identification was made.

A mile and a half away from the Thunderhawk, the night was interrupted by a blaze of light coming from the surface of the sea. At first, the pilot thought it might be a flare, but quickly discarded that thought as the ball of fire rose, arcing over the water. The trail of flame winked out just as another one broke the surface. The two pilots knew instantly that submarine-launched missiles had been fired, the two weapons now headed toward the ships steaming to the northeast.

The pilot altered course as he radioed back the inbound threat. The radar plot showed two objects speeding past his location to the east, heading toward the ships fanning out a little over twenty miles behind. It took over a minute to reach the location where the missiles had emerged from the sea. Knowing that the enemy captain would fire the missiles so as to disguise his position, the pilot flew a little past and brought the chopper into a hover.

The dipping sonar had barely lowered when the operator said he had a passive signal. The contact was most surely a Chinese Shang-class sub that was moving along at ten knots to the north of the chopper. Reeling in the sonar, the pilot prepared two Mark 54 torpedoes and sped toward the location where sonar had indicated the presence of a Chinese submarine. Not wanting to give the enemy time to evade, the pilot dropped two torpedoes upon arriving near the contact's last known location.

The two lightweight torpedoes released their drogue chutes and had just entered the sea when a large mound of water formed nearby, bursting into a fountain shooting into the sky. Another followed on the heels of the first. The pilot knew that something had struck their target, and his eyes immediately spun around to the operator in the back. The operator stared back with wide eyes and shook his head. There was nothing they could do to stop the weapons they had just dropped. They could only hope that the American sub was outside of the Mark 54's search patterns.

*   *   *   *   *   *

"Number one torpedo hit," sonar stated.

Five seconds passed when the sonarman informed Commander Sims that the second one had struck the Chinese Shang-class sub. Moments later, he said he heard breakup sounds, confirming the kill. Sims knew that the Chinese captain had conducted an attack against the Taiwan navy. Attention was likely to be drawn to the area and Taiwan's nervous ASW forces might be a little trigger happy. It was time to leave.

"Left standard rudder to three five zero, increase speed to ten knots," Sims ordered.

"Torpedoes in the water, two actively pinging. Range fifteen hundred yards and closing, aspect ratio unchanging. They have us, sir," sonar reported.

"Belay that last order. Maintain zero eight zero, increase to flank speed," Sims commanded.

The sub surged ahead.

"Deploy countermeasures."

Two canisters shot out from the back to the boat, tumbling in the waters as they sought to draw the two deadly weapons away from the steel tube containing one hundred and twenty-nine souls. The lead Mark 54 turned away from pursuing the speeding sub. Its processors analyzed the new contact and determined that it wasn't the correct target. It then reacquired the *Columbus* and resumed cutting through the dark waters.

As the weapon drew closer, the crew could hear the faint acquisition pinging and mentally willed their captain to pull them out of the fire. More countermeasures were ejected as the sub sped toward the perceived safety of the underwater outcroppings extending from the nearby islet. The Mark 54s drew closer, their searching ping intervals coming faster as they approached.

Shortly after dropping their torpedoes, the pilots of the Thunderhawk watched another blossom of water rocket into the nighttime skies. Their hearts sank as they knew they had sent a friendly American submarine to the deeps. Although it had been a matter of horrible timing, the crew of the S-70 would feel that remorse for the remainder of their lives.

*   *   *   *   *   *

The two cruise missiles' rocket motors cut out and the YJ-18Bs transitioned to their turbojet motors. Being within their sprint range, they soon achieved their terminal velocity of Mach 3. Each of the supersonic anti-ship missiles had one of the Taiwanese destroyers targeted as they raced seven feet above the crests. They would complete their journey in approximately forty seconds.

Fire controls systems aboard the vessels immediately analyzed the incoming contacts and determined them to be hostile targets. With the warning from one of the ASW helicopters who had witnessed the launches, officers commanding the combat information centers authorized weapon releases.

The residents of Keelung working late shifts were treated to a light show in the waters beyond the lighthouse. From the decks of the two destroyers, along with numerous frigates and missile boats, Sky Bow system anti-aircraft missiles sped from their launchers and raced into the night. Flames abruptly flared in the dark, streaking away from the warships. Arcing tails of fire trailed away, glowing as they entered the low clouds before vanishing altogether.

The defensive weapons tracked their two speeding targets, arcing down toward the sea. The distance difference from the attack on the ships traveling up the western coast and the one on the ships sailing out of Keelung allowed for a better defensive reaction. The missiles designed to take down fast attack aircraft maneuvered to intercept the threat, but the high velocity of the attacking missiles still made intercepts difficult.

Many of the missiles raced out of the low clouds only to impact the surface of the sea at high speed, sending up spouts of seawater as the projectiles missed their targets. However, several of the missiles passed close enough that their proximity fuses caused the warheads to detonate alongside the YJ-18Bs.

The second Chinese anti-ship missile came apart and splashed into the sea. The first made it closer, crashing into the waves only three miles from its target. While the battle above the surface was being fought, four undetected Yu-9 torpedoes continued toward their targets under the waves.

There wasn't any thunderous explosion to mark a torpedo's hit. There was only an engulfing steam cloud that signaled the end. Taiwan lost another frigate and three more fast attack missile boats.

In the two attacks against their fleet, Taiwan had lost eleven of the seventy-one ships that had sortied. But because *Changzhen-16* was sunk before having the chance to communicate, China was still unaware that two of its submarines were responsible for initiating hostilities against Taiwan.

*   *   *   *   *   *

Beijing, China
24 July, 2021

The incessant ringing finally penetrated through the thick layers of sleep, the sound turning from some vague unknown that invaded dreams to something more recognizable. With a groan of discontent, not wanting to be pulled from deep slumber, Hao rolled over and opened his eyes. A nightlamp flared to life at the touch of a finger. With bleary eyes blinking under the sudden light, the Chinese leader picked up the phone.

"Yes," Hao answered.

"Sorry to bother you, sir, but this is urgent," a voice said on the other end of the line.

"Fine, fine…what is it?"

"Sir, Taiwan has attacked several of our units."

With those words, the mist of sleep vanished. Hao rolled off his bed and stood, his eyes roving through the dimly lit room for his clothes. Still listening to the update, Hao found the clothes from the previous day draped over a chair. Hurriedly, he slipped off his pajamas and dressed. The ministers and general staff were in the process of being notified and were on their way. Hao hung up and ran a comb through his hair before heading to the situation room.

It took a while for the others to arrive, each one looking as weary as Hao felt. The initial rush of adrenaline had worn off and now he wanted to crawl back under the warm covers. President Hao had learned that the damage caused by Taiwan's attacks wasn't as serious as he'd first imagined upon hearing the news. The initial picture that had formed was of fields of burning equipment positioned near the coastal areas and invasion ships full of equipment resting on the bottom of the seas.

"Minister Zhou, fill us in on the events of the evening," Hao requested once everyone had gathered.

The National Defense Minister nodded toward Admiral Lin, the southern fleet commander.

Clearing his throat, Admiral Lin began, "Sir, at approximately 21:00 local time, part of the fleet stationed in the Taiwan Tsoying Naval Base put to sea. There are two possible reasons for this mass departure. One, they planned to attack one or more of our invasion fleets. Two, they sought to pull back out of range prior to our attack in order to preserve their ships.

"We had one of our nuclear fast attack submarines stationed off the harbor to alert us if and when Taiwan's warships left port. We lost contact with *Changzhen-15*. They have not responded to any of our attempts to communicate and are presumed lost. It is not verified that Taiwan is responsible, but satellite footage revealed that one of their anti-submarine helicopters was in the area at the same time we lost contact.

"At approximately 22:30 local time, following a report of one of our anti-submarine aircraft sinking an American submarine, an anti-aircraft battery positioned in the Penghu Islands targeted and shot down that aircraft in international airspace. At 23:00 local time, another flotilla of ships departed Chilung Naval Base in Keelung. We lost contact with another nuclear submarine we had stationed off the harbor for reporting purposes. Again, a Taiwanese ASW helicopter was observed in the area. As of this time, we also cannot establish contact with *Changzhen-16*.

"A third set of ships also departed the eastern side of the island. All of these units are currently heading north north-east at top speed. Our intelligence thinks that they are attempting to reach positions where they can engage our invasion fleet gathering at Zhoushan. At their current speed, they will be in range of their long-range anti-ship missiles in four hours. In seven hours, they will be able to fire their medium-range missiles.

"Currently, they have sixty-one ships, giving them the capability of launching nearly four hundred anti-ship missiles at targets of their choice. The escorts we currently have near the anchored ships cannot possibly handle that many missiles if they arrive at the same time. For the invasion of Taiwan to be successful, it is imperative that the Taiwanese naval vessels are eliminated. Or, at the very minimum, the number needs to be drastically reduced."

"Admiral Lin," Hao said, "I want to go back to the sinkings and attack on our aircraft. Were our monitoring submarines in international waters?"

"To the best of my knowledge," Admiral Lin nodded.

"Admiral, is there a chance that our submarines attacked and that we are now looking at a form of retaliation?"

The admiral shook his head. "We have not received any communications indicating that our submarines conducted an attack."

"So, and this is critical, what you are telling me for sure is that Taiwan attacked one of our aircraft without provocation, and possibly sank two of our submarines? And that now they are steaming to attack one of the ports where one of our invasion fleets sits?"

"That about sums it up, sir."

"Minister Zhou, do you concur with this assessment?" Hao asked.

The defense minister nodded. Hao knew that he wasn't being told the entire truth, but he opted to hold that knowledge close to his chest for the moment. He was building a file in case events didn't go as planned. However, Hao also knew that the defense minister would gain power should they be able to conquer the breakaway nation. That was something he'd have to deal with at some point, but for now, he opted to ride the wave to achieving one of his, and China's, major goals.

"And you are recommending that we engage the Taiwan ships?"

Minister Zhou and the general staff nodded, the other ministers holding back their thoughts on the matter.

"Very well. We were going to be in a conflict with them inside of twenty-four hours anyway. Approved," Hao stated.

Admiral Lin had said it would be four hours before Taiwan was in a position to attack. He would like to grab another few hours of sleep, as that was likely to become a rare commodity in the coming days.

He had been woken with the urgent assumption that recent events comprised an emergency. Although they were significant, one airplane shot down and two submarines sunk hardly constituted a crisis. What was significant was the fact that Hao, and China, now had a valid reason to conduct an attack against Taiwan without having to shoulder the negative worldwide opinion that would have followed.

The meeting ended and everyone shuffled tiredly out of the exit. Hao followed the others into the hall, thinking about how to best take advantage of what had transpired. Hao thought about how to turn the world's perception of China as the aggressor into that of the victim. Hao refocused when he noticed Minister Wei drop back.

"A moment of your time, perhaps?" the minister for state security asked.

Hao nodded and Wei handed over a folder. "A little light reading."

Hao opened the folder and found a copied set of communications regarding orders sent to the submarine fleet to attack Taiwanese warships.

"Were you aware of this?" Wei softly inquired after Hao closed the folder.

"Zhou proposed something similar earlier," Hao whispered.

"And you ordered this?"

Hao shook his head.

"I thought not. It seems our dear minister of defense might be issuing policy," Wei stated.

"It will be dealt with, but later. It is not the time for internal changes. Let him charge ahead. Once we have taken Taiwan, then the issue will be addressed."

"I hope you are correct in taking this strategy, Hao. Let us hope that everything works out," Wei said.

Hao gave the minister for state security a look out of the side of his eyes. He didn't appreciate the thinly veiled threat.

Ignoring the look, Wei made an offhanded comment. "Were you aware that our submarine fleet has been virtually wiped out?"

Hao stopped in his tracks. He'd seen the damage reports. They depicted that China had lost some of its submarines while inflicting a number of losses on the American side. Nothing in them came close to mentioning that the submarine losses were that drastic. He assumed it was the combined threat of the subs and numerous anti-ship missiles in China's possession that kept the American carriers at bay. Hao suddenly had a vision of being surrounded by American attack submarines and the damage they could inflict on the invasion fleets.

If what Wei said was true, and the Americans knew, then the Americans could very well bring their carrier groups into play in the defense of Taiwan. What had seemed like an inevitable victory only moments ago started turning sour in Hao's mouth. Surrounded by his generals and admirals, Hao watched the retreating back of his defense minister with increased anger. If the planned invasion failed because of Zhou's incompetence, Hao planned to see his head hanging in Tiananmen Square. Of course, that could only happen if he managed to keep his own head attached.

Hao continued walking, unsure if the building anger was because of his defense minister or because he hadn't been supplied with the information firsthand. There had been a time when he had eyes and ears everywhere. His pipeline into the defense ministry had dried up of late, no doubt thanks to Zhou. Wei would of course have his fingers everywhere, so it was not a surprise he had the information. Hao worried about the things Wei wasn't sharing. The old man truly understood the power of information, and that probably contributed to his longevity. What Hao would give for an hour inside the man's head. One thing was for sure, he was going to get the right numbers before the day was out.

Forgoing his planned nap, Hao veered toward his office. While the rest of the nation slept, a weary Hao plopped into his chair. Centered on his desk was a sealed folder. Opening it, Hao stared at the contents. Contained within was the information he had planned on spending much of the day acquiring. It was the true number of submarine losses. Hao placed the papers on his desk after reading through them. He leaned back, his fingers rubbing his eyes.

If the numbers were accurate, they portrayed a picture that was worse than even he had imagined. China had nine submarines remaining…a grand total of nine operational subs. The papers, which had to have come from Minister Wei, didn't show the positions of those remaining, but they didn't need to. The Americans had effectively managed to eliminate most of China's underwater force.

Considering the information and Minister Zhou's insistence that the conflict continue, Hao wondered if the defense minister's actions were a result of incompetence or whether he was purposely sabotaging the war effort. It could be a power play against Hao to show the Central Political Bureau that he wasn't capable of leading the nation. It could also be that Zhou was embarrassed by the losses and chose to present a rosier picture of the conflict. Any of those three could be true. The one truth was that China was now vulnerable to American submarine attacks.

Hao wondered if he should call off the planned invasion and seek out Sweden's proposal of a cease-fire with the Americans. After all, they still held the advantage of forcing the American carriers away. China would still control the South China Sea by proximity. Things could return to the way they were before, and China could rebuild, coming to a parity with the Americans before trying again.

However, Hao knew that he wouldn't be in power when that opportunity again arose. He would be viewed as the man who had failed to unify Taiwan. No, he couldn't allow that to happen. He knew he had gone all-in when this started, and he had to remain true to his chosen course. China still had thousands of anti-ship missiles with which to keep the Americans at bay. Taiwan was no match for the might China still retained and would be squashed like a bug, even if the Americans intervened with their subs. China had hundreds of ships they could utilize for the invasion, so it would be over quickly. Besides, once China sailed, North Korea would come storming down and the Americans would have their hands full.

Hao placed the papers back into the folder, unlocked a drawer, and slid the contents into his desk. There they joined others he had collected. The invasion would work…it had to.

* * * * * *

The top echelon in Beijing went their separate directions, the news received deemed insufficient for any further discussions. Those would come later when China unleashed a full-scale conflict against the island's armed forces. Although China was now aware that hostilities between the two nations had been initiated, they believed them to have been started by Taiwan. They weren't yet aware that the actions of the night were far from over.

*   *   *   *   *   *

Zhoushan, China
24 July, 2021

When word came of the Chinese attack, orders went out to two diesel-electric submarines owned by Taiwan. They were to proceed with all caution and attack the Chinese invasion ships both berthed and anchored in the ports around Zhoushan. It was part of Taiwan's plan to attack the ships, but the original one had called for the subs to wait for the ships to sail and attack them in conjunction with the surface vessels. The Chinese attack altered the strategy, allowing Taiwan to go temporarily on the offensive.

The ROCS *Hai Lung* slid quietly out of the East China Sea and neared the Pushen Channel. Even in the middle of the night, the harbor areas around Ningbo and Zhoushan Island were busy with traffic. Above the muddied waters, lights shone from the city, and a dozen other towns dotting the coastlines of the mainland and nearby islands. Bright lights illuminated the abundant ports with the constant sound of equipment drifting across the waters. Although not nearly as busy as the pre-SARCov-19 days, and the days before the conflict with the United States, ships still navigated their way to and from the numerous berths.

Since receiving his orders, Commander Pai-Han had eased his aging submarine closer to the Chinese major harbor and naval base. His boat held very few advantages over the modern sensors the Chinese warships possessed. The only true edge was the quiet nature of the slow-moving submarines operating on electric engines, so Pai-Han was taking it slow and easy. He and his crew were vulnerable, being this close and in such shallow waters. China was sure to have placed underwater sensors, but Pai-Han was counting on the hectic activity of the harbors to hide him.

"Sonar contact, bearing three five zero, range eleven thousand yards, moving right to left, speed four knots. Classifying contact Golf One as a Jiangkai-class frigate. He's actively pinging."

"Acknowledged," Commander Pai-Han responded.

Sonar constantly updated Commander Pai-Han on the positions of the frigate that was actively patrolling the channel. So far, it was the only warship identified as guarding this particular entrance. The captain of the *Hai Lung* itched to ease the periscope above the waters and confirm what sonar was telling him. There was always the possibility that another ASW ship was holding steady in a different location. However, if the frigate was pinging, they'd certainly have their radars active, would pick up the periscope, and in these relatively calm waters, it would all be over.

Lying close to the bottom just outside of the channel, Pai-Han was waiting for his chance. He longed to retaliate against the nation that had constantly harassed, threatened, and now attacked his country. He could back off and just unleash a volley of Tomahawk cruise missiles, but there was a good chance that the defenses would shoot down most of what he fired. If he could sneak into their harbor, he could do a lot more damage and perhaps even escape undetected. So, remaining patient was critical, as it was in any submarine operation.

"Sonar contact, bearing two zero zero, range eight thousand yards and decreasing. Aspect ratio unchanging, speed six knots. Based on screw sounds, I make contact Hotel One out to be a large merchant vessel."

That was the report that Pai-Han was waiting for. Even though the vessel was still an hour way, Pai-Han had the crew make ready to follow the ship in. The news heightened the tension within the control room. Waiting off the coast of a major enemy harbor provided its own pressure. But now that the crew knew they were about to head into action, engaging the enemy inside their own harbor, the stress level substantially increased.

The frigate continued patrolling back and forth as the

cargo ship drew closer. Pai-Han was pleased that the aspect ratio of the freighter remained unchanged. That meant that the ship was going to pass close to the *Hai Lung* and it wouldn't require much movement on their part to achieve the first part of the plan. Too much maneuvering might alert the frigate to their presence.

It seemed as if an eternity passed before the crew could hear the faint churning of the large propeller driving the cargo ship. When the sound began to fade, Pai-Han issued his orders.

"Turn to heading two one zero, make your speed four knots."

The ship had slowed upon reaching the outer islands. As long as the ship didn't anchor, it would gently navigate through the channel's turns, proceed under the Zhujiajian Strait Bridge, and enter the expanse of the inner harbor and all its adjacent channels. There the crew of the *Hai Lung* would go to work. As the Chien Lung-class attack boat eased behind the cargo ship, there were many in the crew that didn't expect to live through the night.

Being so close to the large ship effectively rendered the passive sonar useless beyond a short distance. The vessel was nearly empty and thus part of the propeller was above the surface. The noise of the propeller churning the water drowned out any other sounds circulating through the depths. Pai-Han watched the sub's position as it was updated via the inertial navigation system, allowing the navigator to anticipate the cargo ship's turns. The moment sonar reported an aspect ratio change, Pai-Han ordered a turn to the expected headings, making minor adjustments until they were again right behind the merchant vessel.

When the ship turned south and slowed even more, the commander knew that they had passed the frigate and were beyond the first layer of Chinese defenses. That didn't mean they weren't detected, or couldn't be, only that they were further than many had expected to make it. The sighs of relief were almost tangible within the tension-filled atmosphere. Pai-Han was thankful for the near creeping speed the ship was making. Even though it was nighttime, and the *Hai Lung* was in the ship's wake, if they were going much faster, the sub's wake might be visible on the surface of the channel.

Based on continuous updates from sonar, Commander Pai-Han kept his aging diesel-electric sub trailing the cargo ship as best as he could. He tried to keep a level tone even though his stomach was tied in knots. It was an odd feeling because he didn't expect to live long enough to attempt an exit and had come to terms with that. The anxiety didn't come from the fact that he was trying to infiltrate a major Chinese naval base. His desire was to inflict damage on those who were threatening his country and he was worried that he'd be located and sunk before being able to fire a single torpedo.

"Increased screw sounds from Hotel One. Captain, I think he is reversing," sonar reported.

"All stop. Hard left turn to heading one eight zero," Pai-Han ordered.

What little vibration that ran through the sub halted as the electric motors ceased driving the propellor shaft. The deck tilted as the boat came around to the new heading. The surface vessel's abrupt reverse could only mean that the ship was coming to a halt. That meant one of two things: tugs were either about to push the ship into a berth or it was about to drop anchor. Pai-Han didn't want to drift under the ship and have that heavy hunk of iron dropping on top of his boat. If that happened, he wouldn't have to wait for a Chinese frigate to end him, as he would already be dead from embarrassment.

"Splashing sounds. He's dropped anchor."

That could only mean that the *Hai Lung* had successfully penetrated the harbor. The INS navigation system showed that the boat was in the middle of the Qitou Ocean. He knew that there were several Chinese naval ships berthed on the southern part of Changshi Island with the majority of the fleet docked in and around Dinghai Port. The latter was difficult to get to and the islands surrounding the port negated any torpedo attack. He'd have to go after the ones at Changshi

However, he couldn't just launch from his current

position as there were dozens of anchored ships around him that weren't part of the invasion force. Any sinking of a civilian ship would quickly turn world opinion against Taiwan, and that was something they didn't need at this critical juncture. The government was having a difficult enough time formulating friendly relations with any nation because of the pressure China placed on those countries.

Possessing older satellite photos from the Americans, Pai-han had a reasonable idea of where the anchored ships were. He was in the middle of them, but he had to be wary. Some of the ships were bound to be in different locations, and he didn't want to move arbitrarily lest he run against an anchor chain and start pulling a surface vessel. Aside from the possible damage to his own boat, that action would surely draw undesired attention.

If he was in the midst of a group of anchored ships, then he might be able to briefly raise his periscope to get a better picture of his situation. He could use his radar to truly get an enhanced idea of what he was dealing with, but a foreign search radar in the middle of the ocean feeding the numerous harbors would raise a few eyebrows.

"Up scope," he commanded.

The periscope slid silently upward in its tube. Pai-han had his eyes on the lens before the scope cleared the surface. Water ran down the lens as it emerged into the clear. Bright lights from the shorelines danced across the muddy waters, silhouetting the dark outlines of ships tugging at their anchor chains. The sheer number of vessels hid the shoreline in all directions. Pai-han panned around quickly, keeping the periscope above the surface for only a couple of seconds and hoping that the anchored ships blocked the radar signature.

"Down scope."

The commander reviewed the recorded video, searching for a northwest route to the outer edge of the ships. He scanned the video multiple times before hitting pause. Searching the overlapping hulls, Pai-han, his executive officer, and the navigator discussed the best way through. They selected a route where they'd pass under one ship after another. With the tidal currents pulling at the anchors, the best bet was to go straight under the ships as the chains would stretch ahead of the vessels.

"Right standard rudder to heading three one zero, make your speed three knots," Pai-han ordered.

It was still a dangerous move negotiating his way through. A slight change in the current could push his boat off course and he'd only know when the screech of an anchor chain dragged against the *Hai Lung*.

Slowly, the sub eased beneath the massive steel hulls, passing one after another. The inertial navigation system finally showed the submarine to be in a position where Pai-han thought they were past the final layer of shipping. The commander risked another peek of the periscope to verify that the water between his boat and the docked invasion ships was clear.

As the lens cleared the muddy ocean, he had a clear view of the distant island. Through a highly magnified view, bright lights cast several invasion ships in stark detail. Armored vehicles were slowly rumbling up modified ramps where they'd vanish inside. Helicopters hovered over open decks, their spotlights detailing crated supplies carried in nets slung underneath. Pai-han marked the array of ships secured to concrete piers, the fire control system accepting each input of course and distance.

To the right of the activity was another island. The captain of the *Hai Lung* knew that dozens and dozens of ships laden with equipment lay on the other side, anchored in the narrow passage between Xiaoqian Island and the major city of Zhoushan. He itched to attack those ships that were crammed together, but they were protected by the island. Maneuvering to get into a position to fire torpedoes would be too risky. Perhaps he would target them with his Harpoon missiles once he completed his torpedo attacks.

The modest naval base was comprised of one large concrete pier and three smaller ones. Each of the three smaller ones held a single ship with the large one having room for three moored vessels. However, at one end of the large dock, three ships were tied side by side, making five ships berthed there. Pai-han allocated one torpedo for each of the visible ships.

"Ready tubes one through six," the commander ordered.

"All tubes showing green, the XO replied.

"FCS updated?"

"Yes, sir."

The torpedoes were given a course that would take them parallel to the targets. At a set distance, they would then turn and home in on the docked ships. That was a protective measure so the *Hai Lung* couldn't be pinpointed by the backtrack of the torpedoes. Pai-han felt the internal knot he'd been carrying release. He had attained his goal of arriving at an optimal firing position. The anxiety hadn't completely gone away, as he knew he had a fight coming. He'd do his best, but the Qitou Ocean would likely become his grave, along with the sixty-six others of his crew.

"Fire One."

Over the next eighteen seconds, six Mark 48 torpedoes were ejected from their tubes. Each sped to sixty knots, silently racing through the murky waters. One followed the other as they reached a programmed distance, turning to a heading that would take them toward the unsuspecting ships taking on cargoes of armored vehicles.

Once the weapons were away, Pai-han ordered a turn that would take them back inside the boundary of anchored merchant ships. As the sub passed the first ship, the forward crew loaded additional Mark 48s into their tubes.

Assured that they were surrounded by surface vessels, Pai-han ordered, "All stop."

Also on his command, the *Hai Lung* slowly descended until it settled on the silty bottom. Pai Han and the rest of the crew would sit there, quietly attempting to ride out the storm that was sure to come.

*   *   *   *   *   *

Dark wavelets lapped against the steel hulls of the three ships berthed against the brilliantly lit dockside. The floods of light turned night into day, rendering the riding lights of distant ships and the glows from nearby cities to mere pinpoints within inky voids. The heavy clanking of treads, the rumbles and whining of engines, and the shouts of workers directing the movement of armored vehicles rode the night air, the noises as intense as the blares of light.

Tanks and armored personnel carriers waited in long lines for their turn to roll up ramps and vanish into the interiors of waiting ships. Heavy-lift helicopters added their beat of rotors to the turmoil of sound as they came roaring in, hovering momentarily to lower their loads.

With so much noise permeating the area, dockworkers and soldiers alike stared with astonishment as a huge mountain of water abruptly rose, completely engulfing one of the ships. Most gazed with interest, wondering what might have fallen overboard that could cause such a huge splash. Others wondered if one of the helicopters had crashed. The curious expressions quickly turned to confusion as the vessel was itself lifted in the massive column of water. Those who were nearest the ship heard a deep, rumbling roar accompanying the commotion.

Large waves rolled away from the scene, vanishing into the surrounding darkness. Cascades of water washed onto the dock and onto the ship's decks as the vessel settled back into the water. The confusion of the onlookers was short-lived as the roll-on/roll-off ship continued settling and took on a significant lean. Moments later, the huge vessel rolled over, snapping the heavy lines that had been holding it secure to shore. A jagged tear spanning the width of the hull revealed that the ship had almost been torn in half.

Another geyser rocketed into the night air, lifting a smaller ship that was second in line. The vessel, nearly full of equipment, broke in half, crashing back down in two distinct parts. Equipment standing free on the decks slid, crashing into the dark waters as both the bow and stern angled more and more to the heavens. Without much fanfare, the civilian ship slipped below the surface with only the superstructure remaining above the waves.

Most workers had only run a step or two before the third ship rose up on its own fountain of muddy water. Tanks rolling up the rear ramp were tossed into the night. Some of the armored vehicles hit the water with splashes of their own while others fell heavily among workers, soldiers, and rows of parked armored personnel carriers. One tank was flung high, tumbling as if in slow motion before crashing, turret down, onto a group that was just beginning to flee.

Onrushing water created pressures that blew open hatches and doors. The third ship joined the others as it took its load of equipment to the bottom of the harbor, along with the lives of crew and loaders alike. Seconds apart, more explosions rocked the other docks as additional Mark 48 torpedoes tore into the stationary ships. Three additional ships rested their torn hulls on the muddy bottom.

The process of moving armor and supplies onto ships came to an abrupt halt. Considering that the sunken ships effectively choked access to the docks of Changshi Island, that was a status that was likely to hold for the foreseeable future.

*   *   *   *   *   *

Sonar reported the hits of the six Mark 48s that were fired. What they couldn't tell was how effective the attacks were. The only way to tell if a ship was sinking was to listen for the groans of metal warping under high pressures, but the shallow waters near the docks didn't allow for the kind of water pressure that could bend metal. For all Pai-han and the crew knew, they could have hit the shoreline. However, sonar soon told of increased activity as frigates and destroyers churned the waters in search of the enemy sub they now knew to be in the area. Sonars actively probed the ocean and Commander Pai-han hoped that the anchored ships surrounding his boat would provide a shield and keep him from being located. The silt bottom was relatively flat, so it wouldn't be difficult for the searchers to "see" the shape of the *Hai Lung* protruding above the seabed should they begin probing among the anchored vessels.

* * * * * *

Hangzhou Bay, China
24 July, 2021

As the *Hai Lung* crept its way through the Chinese outer defenses, its sister ship was attempting the same, forty miles to the northwest. Riding the wake of a slow-moving cargo vessel, Commander Chia-Ming crawled past the island chain that stretched from Ningbo to Shanghai. It took much longer for the *Hai Hu* to work its way through, but eventually the Chien Lung-class submarine managed to get inside the vast expanse of Hangzhou Bay.

Chia-Ming's original plan was to target the berthed ships taking on military cargoes at the Dinghai Port and other docks along the southwestern peninsula of Zhoushan Island. However much the commander tried to squeeze through to get a decent shot, he was thwarted by numerous frigates actively patrolling the entrances. Unknown to the crew of the *Hai Hu*, Commander Pai-han's successful attacks had placed the Chinese ASW forces on high alert. Frustrated, Chia-Ming withdrew into middle of the Hangzhou Bay to weigh his options.

Anchored in the middle of the bay's channel were nearly a hundred ships that intel had identified as vessels that were highly likely to participate in the upcoming invasion of Taiwan. The problem facing the commander was that he had no way of knowing if the ships were loaded with military hardware or not. Sinking an unloaded ship would put a dent China's efforts, but sending a loaded vessel to the deep would truly hurt them.

If the two boats sent to attack the shipping, along with the warships currently steaming north, were to take out loaded ships, then it could sorely hamper China's invasion attempt. Maybe even enough that China would substantially delay their plans or even bring them to a screeching halt.

Another alternative to targeting the docked ships was to reload the torpedo tubes with Harpoon missiles and either fire from his current position, or back off to a more secure location within deeper waters. However, that would limit the number of weapons he could launch and thus reduce the amount of damage he could inflict. Whenever he opted to fire his missiles, either as a first strike or as a later attack, his position would be revealed, or at least his location narrowed down. So, the choices were down to firing at ships without knowing their status or heading back out to launch missiles.

It would have been nice to impede dock operations by sinking berthed ships, but with his inability to sneak into the harbor, that was no longer an option for his torpedoes.

"Make your depth sixty feet," Chia-Ming commanded.

The older diesel-electric sub slowly slid through the dark waters of the bay, leveling scant feet below the surface.

"Level at sixty feet."

"Up scope."

The periscope slid up, the lens breaking the surface. Chia-Ming saw the darkened silhouettes of hundreds of ships tethered at the end of their anchor chains. The commander marked the mass of vessels.

"Down scope."

With so many ships overlapping each other, he could just do a spread fire pattern based on the center of the flotilla he had marked. It was a simplistic approach but could be effective, much like it was during World War II. With the number of ships riding at anchor, it would be difficult to miss.

Chia-Ming motored his boat several miles away from the ships in order to give himself some breathing room and make his exit easier. The complication to the entire operation was that the entire bay was less than fifty feet deep, with the exception of channels dredged for shipping purposes. The shallow waters limited the ability to maneuver and increased the exposure risk. From a distance of six miles, six Mark 48 torpedoes were forced from their tubes and were soon speeding toward targets.

Knowing that the incoming tidal bore that swept through the bay at nearly forty knots would soon be upon him, Chia-Ming urged his crew to set records with reloading the six torpedo tubes. It was imperative for him and his crew to be out of the bay when the tide turned lest they be swept along with the current.

*   *   *   *   *   *

The pilot of the Y-8Q ASW aircraft rubbed his eyes, attempting to alleviate the tiredness. The loss of two other aircraft meant that the workload had to be picked up by the remaining six. The war with the United States had stretched the scarce ASW airborne resources thin, which meant that the crews barely had time to rest between sorties, but it was vital that a shield be kept to ward off American submarines.

That was the very reason they had been awakened. Apparently, there was a chance that an American sub had penetrated the defenses around the busy port of Zhoushan and attacked the shipping there. Their orders were to ferret out the enemy boat and sink them before they could do more damage.

That was easier said than done. Normally, the shallow waters would allow the Y-8Q to detect the sub with their MAD gear. However, the sheer number of ships anchored in the middle of the Qitou Ocean made that a near impossible task. The pilot looked down at the cloud bank hanging low over the water, obscuring the harbor areas. The rays of the near full moon reflected brightly off the top of the blanketing layer with the light from the cities glowing faintly through the clouds. The lack of visible contact with the surface didn't make it easier.

The autopilot turned the four-engine turboprop to a new heading as it followed a preset search pattern. The lack of anything to do other than monitor the instruments added to the weariness the cockpit crew felt. Although unvoiced, both pilots thought their presence in the search to be near useless, but orders were orders. Going a step further, the pilot seriously doubted that it was an American submarine they were after. He knew about the unwarranted attack on their fellow aircraft by Taiwan and concluded that it was one of their submarines they were searching for.

"Pilot, command center," a voice said over the intercom

"Pilot, go ahead."

"One of the frigates operating in the Hangzhou Bay had a momentary radar contact and wants us to check it out. Turn to heading three four zero, descend to ten thousand."

"Copy. Coming left to three four zero, descending to ten."

The pilot reached up and flipped off the autopilot, thankful to be doing something. He banked the aircraft around, noticing that the cloudbank ended near the edges of the island, presenting a clear picture of the darkened waters of the bay. To the left were numerous red, green, and white riding lights of anchored ships.

As the pilot rolled out on the new heading, he glanced again toward the ships. Moonlight caught a fountain of water shooting into the air around one of the ships, the droplets at the edges looking like glittering diamonds in the moonlight. As the water was settling back to the surface, another towering column of water lifted one of the smaller ships clear of the bay. For the next twenty seconds, the cockpit crew watched as four more geysers engulfed ships slated for the invasion of Taiwan.

The aircraft leveled off past the cloud layer, the combat information center chief directing the aircraft to the position where the frigate had the momentary radar contact. With the explosions that encompassed the ships, there was no doubt in anyone's mind that the contact came from a periscope that had been raised. With the nearest anchored ships miles away, the search would be infinitely easier than it had been over the Qitou Ocean.

The copilot put the search parameters in the computer and the pilot again selected the autopilot. The bay was extremely shallow, so if there was an operating submarine, the thirty-foot MAD boom would find it. It took several turns along the grid pattern before the crew in back had a contact. Marking the spot, the Y-8Q descended to five thousand and began deploying sonobuoys.

Mountains of muddied water again began rising among the ships, each one denoting where another torpedo struck. The stricken ships settled to the bottom, several with their top decks awash while others showed only their superstructures. Whether they sank fifty feet or a thousand, any cargo they carried in their holds was lost.

The initial buoys dropped into the shallow depths came up empty, but each pass over the contact revealed that something was definitely there and moving.

"Faint signal on buoy Hotel Five, growing louder...now a faint signal on Hotel Four. Strength on Hotel Five is increasing. We are definitely looking at a Chien Lung-class diesel-electric sub. Speed increasing through seven knots."

A minute later, with two of their Yu-7 lightweight torpedoes hanging on pylons armed, the Y-8Q swung around on an attack heading. Staring ahead into the night, the pilot could almost visualize the submarine sliding along beneath the surface. The aircraft shuddered as the two weapons were released, dropping through the night. Once they hit the muddy waters of the bay, it didn't take long for the torpedoes to acquire their target, producing two more towering columns of muddy water. Debris and a fuel slick confirmed the kill.

In the eyes of the ASW vessels patrolling the waterways, the submarine responsible for sinking eighteen ships had been silenced. The commanders breathed a little easier as they resumed their patrols.

* * * * * *

Tainan Air Force Base, Tainan, Taiwan
24 July 2021

After the meeting with Taiwan's civilian and military leadership, it was decided that Taiwan would go on the offensive against China. Strictly maintaining a defensive stance would allow those across the strait to achieve and maintain the upper hand. As much of Taiwan's weaponry was older, it could be easily destroyed before having an opportunity to be utilized. Many of their aircraft and other weapons were kept in underground bunkers, keeping them safer from attack. Regardless, it wouldn't be long until China established air supremacy.

The decision to take the fight to the Chinese mainland was made to reduce the number of weapons China could bring to bear against Taiwan. Each mobile launcher that was taken out meant that there were two to four fewer weapons that could hit the island. If enough were destroyed, the rain of firepower that was expected to fall might be slowed to a trickle, allowing the full might of the Taiwanese armed forces to operate against the anticipated invasion.

One by one, F-CK-1 Hsiang Shengs rolled out of their fortified bunkers. With the tapered ends of missiles protruding from underwing hardpoints, staggered formations of the attack fighters taxied to the runway. Upon reaching the end of the hold line, there wasn't any hesitation on the part of the pilots as they immediately rolled onto the active runway. Long tongues of flame shot out from the rear of the aircraft, the darkened silhouettes rapidly picking up speed. The heavily laden fighters bounded into the air, the streaks of fire vanishing as the throttles were taken out of afterburner.

Captain Chih-wei advanced his twin throttles as the roar of the preceding aircraft rolled across the airfield. Turning to align with his half of the runway, Chih-wei didn't hesitate to push the throttles forward. The F-CK-1 instantly responded, accelerating down the runway. Reaching takeoff speed, Chih-wei eased back on the stick mounted on the right quadrant. The lights of the city ahead vanished as the nose lifted. The main gear left the paved surface, and the aircraft became lighter as it entered the realm it was designed for.

Pulling the throttles out of afterburner, Chih-wei grasped the gear handle and jerked it upward before going for the flap lever to clean up the attack fighter. The Hsiang Sheng was almost immediately wrapped in a cottony environment, the lights of the surrounding city becoming a soft glow as if a distant memory. Almost as quickly, the twin-engine fighter blasted through the low cloud layer and entered a much different world. A nearly full moon hung silently in the heavens, its silver rays shimmering down to grace the cloud tops. Stars glittered on the periphery of the bright light, their cold sparkles twinkling as if alive.

Behind Chih-wei, three other aircraft zoomed into the night skies and joined on his wings. Across Taiwan's air bases, other laden attack fighters roared down runways and surged into the night.

"Sugar One, Candy flight, flight of four, airborne passing angels minus fifteen," Chih-wei radioed.

"Copy Candy flight, radar contact. Turn right heading zero niner zero, climb and maintain angels minus five."

"Copy, Candy out of angels minus thirteen for angels minus five, turning right to zero niner zero," Chih-wei responded.

Sugar One was an E-2 flying to the east of the island. The crew of this particular Hawkeye was in charge of assembling the aircraft into attack formations. A second E-2, designated as Sugar Two, would be directing the actual aerial attacks against the Chinese. Circling over the Taiwan Strait to the west were two F-35Bs. Their mission was to passively listen for electronic signals emanating from Chinese radars, passing the information on to Sugar Two. The focus of the early missions was to locate and destroy Chinese radars associated with anti-aircraft defenses, in particular the long-range HQ-9 missile platforms situated within range of Taiwan's airspace.

Chih-wei and the rest of his flight circled to the east, ensuring they were outside the range of China's air defense network. There were others flying in different holding patterns and at staggered altitudes. In all, one hundred and twenty F-CK-1s and one hundred-eighty F-16s took to the skies.

"Candy flight, contact Sugar Two on button two."

"Candy switching to button two. Candy flight, button two, go."

After receiving confirmation from the rest of this flight, Chih-wei turned his radio to channel two. He checked in on the new frequency with the others of his flight before calling the second E-2.

"Sugar Two, Candy flight on freq, level at angels minus five."

"Candy flight, loud and clear. Execute Hotel," Sugar two called.

"Copy. Candy flight executing Hotel."

To his wingmen, Chih-wei called, "Candy flight, execute Hotel."

Three separate double clicks over the radio indicated that the other three in his flight heard and acknowledged his order.

The attack plan called for five different ingress routes toward the Chinese coastline. Alpha through Foxtrot was the most southerly route, swinging very wide to the south of Taiwan and angling to the northwest at a predetermined point. Golf through Lima's route encompassed swinging just south of the island and then heading west. Mike through Papa took the aircraft directly over the island. Quebec through Tango circled north of Taiwan, and the remainder swung far north. All the attack runs were to be flown at three hundred feet or less. Targeting data would be relayed from the F-35Bs to the E-2 and then to the attacking aircraft. When they were within range, the fighters would climb and fire their AGM-88E anti-radiation missiles.

Flights of F-16s armed with AIM-120s also circled to the east, ready to engage any Chinese fighters that attempted to interfere with operations.

To the west, a gleaming line marked the cities that ran in a near continuous line up Taiwan's western seaboard. Sending his flight into tactical, Chih-wei brought his throttles back and lowered the nose. The Hsiang Sheng fighter nosed down toward the cloud deck nearly twenty thousand feet below. Moonlight glimmered off the top of his wings as his aircraft dropped through the night. Heading southwest, Chih-wei aimed his flight toward the southern end of the island.

Nearing the top of the cloud layer, the captain eased back on the stick to decrease his sink rate. Wisps floated over the top of his wings, the bed of cotton turning to violent spins of horizontal tornadoes behind the aircraft as wingtip vortices took the clouds in their grips. The LANTIRN (Low Altitude Navigation and Targeting Infrared for Night) system presented a clear picture of the sea below. Also keeping an eye on his radar altimeter, Chih-wei eased down through the layer. The system obtained from the Americans didn't contain automatic terrain following, so he had to rely on his own skills to keep from crashing into the water racing past only a few hundred feet below.

Levelling off at three hundred feet, the bottoms of the clouds fled past the canopy. Chih-wei felt like he could reach up and run his fingers through the overcast. Looking to his left, he was rewarded with the faint glow of formation lights coming from the other element. A glance to his right showed his wingman in position, glued to his wing. Clear of the clouds, Chih-wei signaled his wingman back into a chase position.

Rounding the southern tip of Taiwan, Chih-wei turned to the westerly heading as noted in the briefing. With alternating glances between dials, the outside, and the checklist strapped to his leg, he began the process of arming the missiles slung under his wings.

* * * * * *

The four-engine jet aircraft slowly picked up speed, seeming to take an eternity to become airborne. Eventually, the KJ-2000, with its rotating disc atop its airframe, lumbered into the night. With the Taiwanese attacks on one of China's aircraft and presumably against shipping targets within Chinese harbors, it was vital to get an airborne command post aloft as soon as possible. It was slowly dawning on China's military leadership that Taiwan was attacking preemptively, and not just going after the stray aircraft or two, which meant that the territorial boundaries no longer provided safe havens.

Anti-aircraft defenses were alerted, and more were beginning to come online. With less than twenty-four hours until the onset of attacks against Taiwan, it was critical to protect the mobile cruise missile sites that were vital to the upcoming invasion.

It didn't take long for China's early warning and command aircraft to identify numerous aircraft loitering east of Taiwan. The radar operators followed the aircraft as they left various holding patterns and descended. Some of the radar tracks were lost due to the low levels that Taiwan's aircraft were flying, but the Chinese crews managed to stay in contact with several flights as they flew toward China's shorelines.

*   *   *   *   *   *

Xiamen countryside, China
24 July, 2021

Hydraulics whined as the four-tube launcher angled upward from the bed of the eight-wheeled truck. The airborne command center had notified the battery of eight transporter erector launchers (TELs) that enemy aircraft were on attack profiles for China's mainland. With a clunk, the TEL locked into its vertical firing position.

The KJ-2000 flying miles inland forwarded targeting data to the HT-233 long range search and targeting radar, which in turn passed the information to the eight launchers under its control. Operators verified the data and assigned two targets to each of the individual units. Upon receiving the order releasing the weapons, the command to fire was given.

Long tongues of flame flared in the dark as rocket motors ignited. Missiles rose out of their cylinders, each trailing their own wake of fire. Gaining speed, they accelerated into the night skies. Streaks of fire filled the countryside as long-range anti-aircraft missiles arced over a nation still asleep, the citizens unaware that they were now at war with their neighbors across the strait.

* * * * * *

The Chinese KJ-2000 Mainring AWACs operators saw the number of aircraft filling the skies east of Taiwan and knew they wouldn't be able to single-handedly manage the battlefield. The officer in charge sent a call requesting a second command aircraft. Once it arrived on station, the two would divide the combat zone. One Mainring aircraft would manage the aerial combat while the second would take over intercepting the inbound Taiwanese attack aircraft.

The commander's next call went out to airbases hosting China's frontline fighter aircraft. With the invasion underway, many of the squadrons maintained a number of readied aircraft. When the alert came in, pilots scrambled to grab their gear and raced to waiting vehicles. In the late hours of the night, boots pounded across tarmacs, the sound echoing across sleepy bases.

Crew chiefs readied the sleek attack fighters, opening canopies and lifting stairs to the sides of cockpits. Placing helmets on canopy rails, pilots eased themselves into the tight confines and strapped themselves in. Each sorted through a myriad of thoughts: flight leaders ran tactics through their minds, contemplating who was assigned as wingmen and what degree of trust they had in the skills of their fellow pilots. Element leaders wondered if they'd be able to maintain flight integrity through skies filled with planes. New pilots nervously hoping they wouldn't make fools of themselves — or find themselves being shot down.

Helmets were at last donned, and soon the bases reverberated with the roar of jet engines coming to life. Pins and chocks were pulled. Under the direction of ground personnel holding lit wands, the powerful jets taxied out from their revetments. Taking the runway, afterburners flared behind rapidly accelerating J-20, J-16, and J-10 fighters as they took to the skies. The last of the aircraft rocketed into the night, the roar of engines fading. The first wave of the Chinese response was on its way to a battlefield only a few miles distant.

When flights checked in with the command aircraft, the

first were directed toward the low-level enemy aircraft flying attack profiles. One flight of J-20 Mighty Dragon aircraft was sent high above the Taiwan Strait to provide air cover. At the moment, there were twenty Taiwan aircraft that were all angling toward China's mainland. Five flights of four were scattered around the island: two to the north, two to the south, and one directly west. Their low altitudes made it difficult to keep them on the radar screen, but the radar operator aboard the KJ-2000 had a pretty good picture, even if he lost one or two of the flights for moments at a time. Behind the first wave, other aircraft were forming up on similar attack routes. Targeting the first wave, the operator sent the information to the ground missile defenses and to the attack fighters that were coming online, assigning targets to both missile battery and aircraft alike. The operators had to juggle defenses so that missiles and fighters didn't occupy the same airspace at the same time.

At the fighter bases, telephones rang as recall rosters were run through. Soon, streets were filled with additional pilots rushing to their bases.

*   *   *   *   *   *

Chih-wei flew through the initial point on his attack run. Making a slight turn, he advanced the throttles, accelerating to five hundred forty knots. He knew that a search radar had painted him, and he nervously scanned the time remaining until launch. There would only be approximately eighty miles between him and the belt of Chinese air defenses when he launched his volley of anti-radiation missiles, putting him well within the parameters of the numerous anti-aircraft missile batteries.

"All units, threat condition Mike One. Repeat, threat condition Mike One."

Shit! Chih-wei thought. "Mike One" meant that ground-to-air anti-aircraft missiles had been fired.

As if in response, Chih-wei's threat receiver went off. A fire control radar had targeted him. The captain punched off the warning light and tone, ignoring it for the moment. Instead, he focused his attention on keeping his F-CK-1 out of the water and on the upcoming launch point. Flying at nine miles per minute, the countdown went quickly. A last glance at the weapons control panel informed him that the missiles were armed and properly selected.

Chih-wei pulled up, climbing toward the brightly lit moon. He squeezed the button on the control stick. One TC-IIA anti-radiation missile flew off its rail and streaked into the dark. Chih-wei was momentarily blinded by a sudden flash of light as the missile flew past the canopy, the trail of fire arcing toward the heavens. For a brief moment, it appeared as if the Taiwanese captain was attacking the moon. Three other anti-radiation missiles (ARMs) rippled off the other rails.

A glance to the side revealed other trails of fire streaking away from his wingmen. Together, his flight had just fired sixteen missiles toward mobile radar targets inside China. Each missile received its targeting data from Sugar Two, who would issue mid-course changes in the event they became necessary. All across the strait, twenty aircraft delivered a first-round volley of eighty missiles which arced over the narrow waterway. The sensors aboard the missiles would passively home in on the radar signals emitted by the anti-aircraft batteries. If the radars turned off to move or to avoid being targeted, a secondary sensor aboard the missiles would hunt down the vehicle via infrared guidance. Once launched, there was a high probability that the target would become a kill. The best defense was to shoot down the ARM, set up decoys (such as popping chaff and aiming a radar signal into its midst), or hit it with low-intensity lasers that interfered with its targeting sensors.

Chih-wei rolled his aircraft one hundred and thirty-five degrees and pulled. It was time to start worrying about the missiles that were racing toward him at over Mach 4. Somewhere in the skies over the strait, the first stages of the Chinese long-range anti-aircraft missiles were falling toward the seas as the second stage motors ignited.

Descending back toward the seas, showing green in his monitor, Chih-wei thumbed his countermeasures. Canisters shot away from the Hsiang Sheng attack fighter, releasing clouds of chaff. Hopefully, his return to the low-level environment, coupled with a confusing radar picture, would divert the missile or missiles sent his way.

As if laughing at his hopeful thoughts, the threat receiver again sent a shrill tone. He'd been targeted by an HQ-9 missile that had gone into its active homing cycle. The Chinese weapon received guidance from distant radars until it neared its target; it would then rely on its own radar to strike home. That way, the missile battery radar could shut down, keeping its presence off the air as much as possible.

With the ocean swells rolling just scant feet under his aircraft, Chih-wei banked hard to the right and punched out more chaff. He glanced back over his shoulder to see if he could determine where the missile was and maneuver accordingly. The sight of multiple fiery streaks descending out of the heavens caused an additional jolt of adrenaline to flood his system. Each of the tails of fire seemed to close in on his flight in slow motion.

Chih-wei had a difficult time turning away from the volley of anti-aircraft missiles, but he knew that if he didn't, there would be a good chance that the ocean waters would take care of what the enemy missiles were sent to do. Turning back to the front, Chih-wei unloaded his aircraft by pushing forward on the stick, thus reducing the Gs. He then rapidly rolled to the left and pulled. The G meter flipped up to over 8 Gs as the captain again punched out countermeasures.

A flash in the distance caught his attention. A ball of flame flared in the night, quickly fading. One of the HQ-9 missiles had caught his number four wingman as he was attempting to maneuver.

The proximity fuse of the weapon detonated the 280-kg warhead near the wing root. White-hot shrapnel tore through the fuel system, igniting the volatile fuel. In a tight turn, the explosion forced the jet too far over. Before the pilot could register what was happening, the attack fighter slammed into the strait at over five hundred knots. The aircraft disintegrated.

Unseen by Chih-wei, other HQ-9s followed his number two wingman. Ignoring the radar picture that the chaff presented, a missile cut the corner of the maneuvering aircraft. The first missile passed behind the aircraft and crashed into the sea before exploding. However, a second missile also cut a corner and angled directly toward the fighter. Flying at two thousand five hundred miles per hour, the projectile flew directly over the top of the canopy and detonated. Shrapnel punched through the glass and tore into flesh and bone. The pilot was already dead when his plane plowed into the surface, sending a bright plume of water into the moonlight.

Chih-wei let his aircraft descend to a hundred feet over the top of the waves, and then down to fifty feet. Maneuvering at high Gs at that altitude and at night, while flying at over five hundred knots, he had to put his entire concentration into staying aloft. Sweat ran down his face from the exertion, his body weighing almost seven times its normal weight. He squeezed his leg muscles and abdomen to keep blood in his head, breathing in quick gasps. Rolling in the other direction, with the waves seeming to brush his cheeks, Chih-wei let loose yet another bundle of chaff.

While straining, Chih-wei waited for the explosion that would set off a myriad of warning lights. Focusing on keeping the high-speed fighter out of the drink, he didn't dare risk a peek to determine what was happening around him, but the suspense of not knowing was overwhelming. He almost wished something would happen, so he'd know for sure.

As with his wingman, the first missile targeting him flew past and crashed violently into the sea. The second turned to keep on track of the racing aircraft, but a timely turn of the F-CK-1 forced the weapon to the outside, and it was unable to correct itself before smashing into the waves.

Rolling into another turn, Chih-wei noticed that his threat receiver was clear. Somehow or another, the missiles had lost track. Breathing hard, the captain rolled out of his turns and reoriented himself. Finding himself off his egress route, he turned to an intercept heading and glanced to the side. He couldn't find any sign of his number four wingman, but he did spy the formation lights of his number three. As his radar was off, he wasn't able to see whether number four was just out of position or was actually gone.

"All units, threat level is Alpha One. Repeat, threat level is Alpha One."

Chih-wei shook his head. That call meant that enemy fighters were now airborne. Intercepting his egress corridor, he turned toward the Tainan air base.

"Candy flight, contact Tainan Approach."

"Copy, Candy switching to Tainan Approach. Candy flight, go button four."

There was a pause that seemed to drag on forever. Normally, his number two would respond immediately. The silence meant that his wingman was either off frequency, couldn't hear his order, or he wasn't there anymore. After a moment, his number three answered. That was it. Only one aircraft responded. Somewhere over the strait, he had lost half of his flight.

His number three wingman joined up on his wingtip and the two were vectored down through the weather. Landing in formation, the two Hsiang Sheng attack fighters taxied in to refuel and rearm. Sweating, Chih-wei climbed down from the aircraft, the night air feeling chilled against his flight suit. He headed to a waiting van to be taken to his debriefing, knowing the night was far from over.

* * * * * *

In the middle of the Taiwan Strait, the Tien Chien IIA anti-radiation missiles heading for their targets passed underneath the HQ-9s tearing after the aircraft that launched them. The Taiwanese ARMs were given mid-course guidance from the second E-2 orbiting east of the island. The missiles homed in on the radar signals emitted from the search and fire control radar systems controlling China's long-range anti-aircraft batteries.

The passive sensors followed the radar signals as they hopped through various frequencies, keeping track of their targets by the position logged internally. Even if the radars went off the air, the TC-IIAs kept on track with the last known position and would home in on infrared once they drew closer.

Around the scattered vehicles that made up the longer-range anti-aircraft batteries, short range anti-air missiles came to life. They leapt from their launchers to streak after the Mach 6 ARMs that were coming within range. Most civilians missed the hypersonic weapons that tore through the nighttime skies and descended onto unsuspecting mobile radar platforms. Lines of fire arced out of the night, ending with sharp echoing booms which rolled through the countryside. Fragmentation warheads punched shrapnel through antenna and dishes, perforating the thin-skinned vehicles. Of the eighty TC-IIAs originally fired, sixty-one reached their targets. One by one, the radars controlling China's air defenses began to go dark.

* * * * * *

The initial Chinese alert aircraft checked in with the command aircraft. They were given intercept headings and altitudes. Even though they would be in the Taiwan Strait in a matter of minutes, they would be too late to stop the first wave of Taiwan's attacking aircraft. Thus, a majority of the J-16 and J-10s were assigned targets that were part of the second wave of enemy warplanes. With the short distances between adversaries, afterburners lit up the nighttime skies as pilots raced to intercept their targets.

On the opposite side, the E-2 responsible for targeting noted the appearance of Chinese fighter aircraft and issued a threat warning. Noting the enemy surge toward Taiwan aircraft conducting a second wave of strikes, the CIC commander gave the order for the orbiting F-16s to be sent into the attack. The hundred miles of water separating the two nations was about to become a whole lot busier.

*   *   *   *   *   *

Sugar Two's CIC commander looked at the radar screen and was worried. Although the jamming emanating from the Chinese mainland was only marginally effective at the range the E-2 was, the major knew that there had to be some of China's 5th generation attack fighters that lay hidden. If they were closer, the radar might be able to pick up the aircraft, but that would place the vulnerable airborne command post within range of the numerous long range anti-aircraft weapons that China possessed.

He had several flights of F-35Bs positioned near the western coast of Taiwan that the two Chinese Mainring command aircraft hadn't picked up yet. To his thinking, that was almost a verification that there were Chinese J-20s that *he* couldn't see. Even though American intel had shown that China's J-20 numbers had been significantly reduced, it wouldn't take many to completely disrupt operations.

The major also understood that he was only looking at the leading edge of the fighters that China would throw their way. It was therefore important that they overwhelm this initial pack of fighters and deal all the damage they could. Taiwan was currently on the offensive, but everyone with any sense knew that wouldn't last the night. Before long, China's superiority in both numbers and equipment would begin to force Taiwan into a more defensive mode.

There wasn't anyone in the chain of command who didn't understand that Taiwan's survival depended on the United States. The island nation had the capability to inflict considerable damage, but it couldn't win a protracted battle against China. It was therefore vital that the Americans be allowed to move their carrier strike groups within range. To make that possible, there were several specific targets that the Americans had requested be taken out. If the Taiwan Air Force managed to live through the next few minutes and the second wave of anti-radiation missiles managed to hit their targets, then that would, hopefully, open up the possibility of striking China's mobile cruise missile platforms.

*   *   *   *   *   *

"Panda flight, turn left heading two seven zero, descend to angels plus five."

Orbiting to the east of Taiwan, Major Chin-lung had been expecting the call. After all, China wasn't going to take attacks on their homeland lightly. Being assigned to the air superiority role, the major knew the radio call meant that Chinese aircraft were in the air and heading toward Taiwan's attack aircraft streaming to the west.

"Panda left to two seven zero and down to angels plus five."

Chin-lung brought his agile fighter around to the new westbound heading. The airspeed indicator edged upward as the major eased the nose down and headed for flight level three zero zero (30,000 feet). Three additional F-16s followed his maneuver. Chin-lung listened as more fighting falcons were vectored into the upcoming fight. The jet jumped as external fuel tanks were jettisoned, the steel tanks tumbling down through the night. With a quick nudge of his wings, he sent his second element out to tactical before sending his wingman into a chase position. Lighter and more maneuverable, and carrying six AIM-120 air-to-air missiles, Panda flight was ready to duke it out with China's frontline fighters.

Six miles above the earth, Chin-lung stared into the moonlit skies. Nothing was visible, but the major knew that the skies ahead were filled with aggression. He felt the sweat form inside his flight gloves, and his stomach was gripped with nervous tension. The event he'd been training for, and worried about for even longer, was upon him. Here he was racing toward what looked to be a huge, messy fight. With the ejection seat reclining back at thirty degrees, Chin-lung sometimes felt like he should be watching a football match instead of being strapped to an agile rocket.

* * * * * *

With a second KJ-2000 command aircraft joining, the battlefield, from the Chinese point of view, was split nearly the same as their counterparts'. One AWACs managed the air-to-air intercepts while the other controlled those against the Taiwanese aircraft over the strait conducting attacks against the homeland.

With more aircraft taking off from airbases to join the defending forces, the operators aboard the Mainring aircraft were better able to put together packages to send against the attackers. Armed with long-range PL-15 active radar guided missiles and PL-10 short-range infrared-homing air-to-air missiles, flights of J-16s and J-10s were sent east. Targeting data was replicated from the KJ-2000s to the fighters in order to reduce their electronic signatures. Once in range and specific targets selected, PL-15s ignited and sped away from their rails. Given the shorter distances, the trails of fire arced downward, giving the appearance of a fireworks show being conducted in reverse.

The operators aboard the E-2 controlling Taiwan's attacks against anti-aircraft emplacements noted the reduced number of ground-to-air missiles that rose against the second wave of attacking aircraft. However, threat receivers in the F-CK-1s still activated as Chinese fighters made their appearance known. In addition, mobile launchers that survived the first wave of attacks fired.

Hsiang Shen attack fighters shed chaff bundle after bundle in attempts to lure the radar guided missiles astray. Several of the weapons saw the larger targets appear and diverted from their trajectories. F-CK-1s pulled up at their launch points at about the same time as the Chinese air-to-air missiles began arriving. Another eighty anti-radiation weapons roared into the night.

With aircraft banking wildly to return to the low-level

environment and to avoid the incoming threats, explosions dotted the darkness like dancing fireflies. Some of the PL-15s blew up in the midst of chaff clouds. However, there were many that found more significant targets. Shrapnel flew into airframes, smashing through engine components and severing fuel and hydraulic lines. Long tails of fire blazed for short periods of time before burning aircraft crashed into the Taiwan Strait.

As attack fighters were violently splashing into the waves, a second wave of Tien Chien IIA fired by the aircraft maneuvering at high Gs began to drop out of the heavens. Salvoes of short-range anti-air missiles rose up to meet the ARMs, some finding their mark. Bright flashes of light appeared in the nighttime skies, followed by meteor-like trails of fire from burning debris. Others that made it through the defenses fell among radar trucks, shredding the vehicles and those manning the systems.

Although not all the mobile platforms had been destroyed, a large gap in China's air defenses had been created. That had come at great cost. Of the twenty Hsuing Yings attacking in the second wave, fewer than half survived. Those fortunate few who made it through the barrage of missiles returned to their bases to take on fuel and armaments, readying themselves to engage once more.

* * * * * *

Miles below, Major Chin-lung saw faint flickers of light flashing in and out of existence. Although he was on a different frequency, he could imagine the discordant radio calls as the low-flying aircraft attacking China's ground-based air defenses attempted to avoid the Chinese missiles chasing after them.

The major was being vectored toward China's airborne fighters to alleviate the pressure being applied against the strike fighters. The four AMRAAMs tucked on the wing pylons were all armed and the two AIM-9X on his wingtips stood ready in case the distances between the two adversaries closed to within range of the sidewinders.

Chin-lung kept the information being replicated to his screen in his crosscheck, watching as the distances to the nearest Chinese aircraft decreased. The nervousness the major felt seemed to intensify and then fade as his F-16 sliced through the cold air. His eyes searched through the night, but he knew that it was unlikely he'd see other moon-lit aircraft. If he'd been equipped with LANTIRN gear, he might, but those had been reserved for those skimming the wave tops.

"Panda flight, turn left heading two four zero. Bandits will be on your nose, eighty miles. Cleared to fire," Sugar Two radioed.

Chin-lung clicked twice on the transmit button and banked his agile fighter around to the new heading. He knew that his second element would automatically turn, but he looked over out of habit. He saw the formation lights a mile off his wingtip and swept his gaze back to the radar screen. Two targets had been selected for his radar-guided missiles. He pressed the trigger and an AIM-120 ignited and roared off the rail. Trailing a stream of fire, the missile sped away, the glow quickly fading as the weapon accelerated to Mach 4. Subsequent presses and three additional long-range air-to-air missiles departed into the dark.

As the last AMRAAM streaked past the cockpit, four bogeys suddenly appeared on his screen. The airborne threats were only sixty miles away. Chin-lung's threat receiver immediately went off, and the major knew that he'd just been fired on by China's J-20 stealth fighters. They became visible on radar only after the doors on their weapon compartments opened.

Out of long-range missiles, there wasn't anything Chin-lung could do to defeat the newcomers. The major banked the F-16 hard, letting the nose fall into a descent, and shoved the throttle into afterburner. Having expended all of his long-range weapons, it was time to head back to base to rearm. But first, he had to shake the incoming Mach 4 threats.

* * * * * *

A majority of China's aircraft that roared aloft to meet the Taiwanese assault were directed against the low-level threats. Being alert aircraft, the mostly J-16 and J-10 attack fighters had been armed with PL-15 long-range radar guided and PL-10 short-range infrared missiles. The few J-20 remaining in China's active inventory were assigned an air superiority role. Their mission was to counter any aircraft that Taiwan sent against the J-16s and J-10s.

It wasn't long before the operators aboard the Mainrings identified Taiwan fighters racing to the west at altitude, presumably to protect their low-level assets. Mighty Dragons were sent east to intercept, making themselves known only when they were ready to fire. The air-to-air missiles from both sides streaked toward each other, passing beneath a cold moon.

* * * * * *

Taiwanese captain Kuan-yu rolled his neck and shoulders, trying to relax the tension the he felt building. He and his flight were being vectored in an arc to the north of Taiwan in order to take some of the Chinese aircraft by surprise. While looking toward the moon, he noticed an object quickly streak past the lit surface only a few thousand feet above his altitude. He was attempting to locate the fast-moving eastbound object when a second one also crossed in front of the celestial object. Although only briefly silhouetted, the captain was fairly sure he'd seen the clear outline of a Chinese J-20.

Kuan-yu thought briefly about the risks of breaking radio silence, but the information was too important. This was especially true as the aircraft weren't showing up on the replicated data painting his screen.

"Sugar Two, Mango flight. Two J-20s just flew past, eastbound at angels plus ten. Am pursuing."

"Copy Mango. Upload data when acquired," the E-2 responded.

The airwaves came briefly alive as the Hawkeye

commander made adjustments to his plans.

Hoping that his second element observed his maneuver, Kuna-yu shoved his throttle forward and pulled back on the stick. The F-35B arced upward at nearly its 7g limit with the captain straining against the inflated G-suit. The nose of his aircraft rolled past the white orb hanging passively in the sky. Kuan-yu held the stick as the plane nosed its way past the vertical and headed back toward the horizon. Inverted and level, the captain rolled upright and allowed the Lightning II to accelerate.

Selecting the sidewinders, Kuan-yu scanned the skies ahead, hoping to locate a hint of the enemy aircraft he had observed. As his eyes roved the night, a tone briefly sounded in his helmet, indicating that the missiles had found a hotspot to lock onto. Kuan-yu double checked his radar to ensure that there weren't any friendlies in the specific direction. Mostly assured that the tone was coming from one of the Chinese aircraft, he looked at the spot again and was rewarded with a signal that the weapon could "see" its target. On one screen, Kuan-yu saw the infrared-composed image of the rear of a Chinese Mighty Dragon in straight and level flight, the exhaust flaring more heat than the rest of the aircraft.

With a quick lock-on to the heat source, the doors of the weapon bay opened and one of the AIM-9Xs fell away, followed quickly by a second one. Off to the side, Kuan-yu saw his wingman's missiles speed ahead, tracking a second target. A mile to the side, faint trails of fire arced through the night air as his other element located and fired on other enemy fighters that Kuan-yu hadn't seen. The data was uploaded to the E-2 so they could incorporate the new threats into their planning.

As the missiles passively tracked the heat sources, the Chinese pilots were unaware that their presence had become known. Kuan-yu's first missile literally flew up the tail pipe of the Chinese stealth fighter, detonating inside. Shrapnel sliced through several of the turbine blades. The imbalance imposed immense centrifugal forces on the rest, and the fans shredded themselves, throwing additional metal fragments through engine components. The high-speed splinters cut through the protective wall surrounding and tore into engine number two. Flames from the jet engines coming apart under their own momentum reached far behind the damaged J-20, providing more than adequate heat sources for the second missiles closing in at over Mach 2.

The second sidewinder exploded aft of the flaming stealth fighter, causing additional damage to the rear end. Shedding pieces of metal in its wake, the aircraft's nose abruptly pitched up. At the same time, the canopy of the aircraft flew into the slipstream, followed shortly afterward by a rocket motor carrying the pilot's seat away from the stricken warplane. Racked by stresses beyond its capability to absorb, the fifth-generation fighter came apart in mid-air.

Seconds later, another J-20 flamed as a heat-seeker exploded directly underneath the exhausts. As with the leader, a long tongue of flame trailed behind the fighter. The wingman pulled on the handles and was thrown into the brutally cold atmosphere. Trailing fire, the aircraft nosed down and began a long, spiraling journey toward the waters below.

Flashes marked where a third J-20 was hit, a fiery path tolling the Mighty Dragon's demise. The number four wingman, alerted by the explosions of the others in his flight, thumbed the countermeasures button. The sky behind the fighter lit up with a dozen flares arcing away. More were ejected as the pilot pointed the nose down and rolled, pulling 9Gs. The two AIM-9Xs targeting the last aircraft were drawn toward the hot flares, both detonating in their midst.

The element leader noted the misses, but opted to turn on his radar to get a lock onto the fleeing fighter. Quickly targeting, he fired two AIM-120s. The pair of radar-guided missiles followed the J-20's maneuvers and exploded, tearing into the wing root. Under high-G and weakened by fragmentation warheads, the right wing tore away from the aircraft. The Chinese pilot never managed to complete his Split-S maneuver. Pieces of the aircraft were flung outward as the fighter spiraled violently down for seven miles.

In a chance meeting in the middle of the night, with neither side able to see the other, China lost a fifth of their remaining stealth fighters in one battle. However, the threat sensors in the F-35Bs came alive as they themselves became known to China's air superiority forces.

Being within range of both Chinese long-range ground-to-air and air-to-air missiles, Kuan-yu and the rest of his flight soon found themselves on the receiving end of China's attention. Limited to 7Gs, the pilots weren't able to maneuver as tightly as they would have liked. The Taiwanese pilots made sure their radars were off and applied their afterburners in attempts to outrun the threats launched against them. However, unknown to them, a second flight of J-20s had been accompanying the first. They were too late to do anything to assist their fellow pilots, but they were able to locate the fleeing F-35Bs and fire PL-10 heatseeking missiles.

The appearance of the J-20s just a few scant miles away as the weapons bay doors opened startled Kuan-yu. Flares and chaff filled the surrounding skies. He and his wingmen tried to elude the threats, but it was all too little and too late. Chinese infrared tracking missiles came in too fast and detonated near the Lightnings IIs. Soon, four more parachutes floated down from the frigid heights.

*   *   *   *   *   *

As with the Chinese land-based anti-aircraft systems, when the fights came within range, Taiwan's Sky Bow II and Sky Bow III long-range ground-to-air systems came to life. Even though the battlefield was "managed" by command aircraft on both sides, the skies over the Taiwan Strait became a chaotic back-alley melee. Taiwan's low-level attackers were fired on from the air and ground. In turn, Taiwan's air and ground defenses attacked Chinese aircraft. The air became thick with weapons and airborne platforms, especially as each nation fed more and more aircraft into the fight.

Rockets rose from Taiwan's outer Penghu Islands and

from batteries along the western shores of the main island. So much chaff was dispensed into the prevailing easterly winds that radar pictures became fuzzy in some areas. As the bundles of foil spread out, tiny regions became almost like Faraday cages slowly working their way to the east, confusing radar returns.

Aircraft on both sides were destroyed or had to limp back to their bases with parts missing. Taiwan had nearly three hundred F-CK-1 and F-16 operational attack fighters at its disposal, not including the squadron of F-35Bs that had been delivered. While China had more in its inventory (over six hundred J-20, J-16, and J-10 aircraft), a third of them were scattered between the northern, western and southern sectors.

With the planned invasion, China had moved several wings within range of Taiwan, but the actual number of aircraft available to the fight was nearly even. The initial difference was that all of China's frontline fighters were thrown into the fray to combat Taiwan's aircraft, while a percentage of Taiwan's fighters were assigned to conduct attacks against China's mobile missile platforms. That meant that Taiwan was outnumbered in the air superiority role, and the losses were showing that mismatch.

However, China was cautious about venturing too far into the strait lest the full weight of Taiwan's land-based air defenses come into play. Observing the successes of their long-range attacks, the Chinese commanders aboard the KJ-2000s were content to continue with that stratagem.

Taiwan's commanders were also watching their losses and becoming concerned. It was expected that they would sustain more than their counterparts, due to having to allot many of their assets to the ground attack role, but the numbers of aircraft available were dwindling. The silver lining was that the number of Chinese ground-to-air missiles had slacked off substantially. The Taiwanese commanders presumed that Phase One had been successful in that they had knocked out a vast swath of the mobile launchers. Now, they were ready to move into the next stage of their operations.

* * * * * *

Across the breadth of the island, many woke to the sound of diesel engines rumbling past as transport vehicles, mounting boxed launch chambers, rolled out of hardened shelters. Motoring along dark roads, hundreds of vehicles drove to pre-determined sites and began the process of setting up their launchers.

Shouts accompanied the idling engines at each transport erector vehicle location, the crews working to bring their battery into an operational status. With the sites already surveyed, it was really only a matter of connecting with the command vehicles and putting the erectors into launch position. After verifying their precise GPS location, one by one the crews checked in and notified the command centers that they were online.

With the help of American satellites, a target list was updated with the latest coordinates. Those were then fed to the various batteries, and the individual missiles were given their objectives. The authorization for weapon's release came down. With a ripple effect, volleys of missiles flew out of their chambers, quickly vanishing into the low overhanging cloud base.

To the pilots fighting in the skies over the island and the strait, the sight was almost mesmerizing. Hundreds of fiery streaks tore from the silver-topped clouds, looking like a flock of blazing crows being chased out of a forest. Just as suddenly as they appeared, the tails of flame winked out as the Hsiung Feng IIE cruise missiles transitioned from their solid fuel rocket boosters to the turbofan engines that would carry them to their targets.

The missiles continuously updated their positioning with a host of GPS satellites. Once over land, that was backed up with Terrain Contour Matching software that compared the surroundings with pre-recorded maps.

The Chinese KJ-2000 airborne command posts saw the massive launch coming out of Taiwan. Each of the aircraft had the ability to track a hundred targets, but the number coming from their cross-strait neighbor overwhelmed the screens. Operators had to filter out most of the radar returns, and the commanders were faced with difficult choices. They wouldn't be able to manage the sheer number of targets, both missile and aircraft.

The choice was to either disregard the inbound storm of missiles and focus on Taiwan's aircraft already aloft, or they could break up the missiles into hundred-unit batches and direct airborne and ground defenses there. If they were to focus on the aircraft, they would release the remaining ground-to-air assets to defend against the cruise missile targets that flew within their sectors. That would effectively reduce the forces they could bring to bear to achieve air superiority.

Alternatively, directing their attention toward the cruise missiles could leave their air superiority assets to function on their own. That meant the aircraft would have to rely on their own radars, thus making them more susceptible to the opposing forces. It was either lose valuable aircraft or lose whatever ground targets Taiwan was after. Neither option sounded favorable. In the end, a hybrid solution was adopted. One of the Mainring command posts would continue with the air war, while the second one would divert its J-16 and J-10 aircraft from attacking Taiwan aircraft to targeting the cruise missiles. The ground-to-air defenses were optioned off to select their own targets with the emphasis on the enemy weapons currently crossing the middle of the strait.

*   *   *   *   *   *

Chih-wei lifted off from Tainan airbase, this time with two Wan Chien air-to-ground cruise missiles strapped under his wings. Between debriefing his last flight and briefing the next attack, there hadn't been time to share stories or rumors with any of the other pilots. However, it wasn't difficult to read the tales written in the eyes of those who made it back. It had been a harrowing experience for everyone, and soon they were to go back out and do it again.

The captain was actually happier with his current assignment for two reasons. First, he felt the low-level environment was more survivable than what the F-16 and F-35 pilots had to face. Having drawn the air supremacy role, those pilots would be up there with their asses hanging out in the wind. At least the F-35 boys had the advantage of stealth, but the F-16s would be spotted from the moment they retracted their gear. Chih-wei only hoped that their mission against China's air defenses had been helpful, even if that wasn't the primary reason for the strikes.

But the main reason was because of what he was about to deliver. They were now going after the Chinese cruise missiles TELs (Transporter Erector Launcher) in the hopes that the expected bombardments would be less severe and give Taiwan a fighting chance to defeat China's invasion forces. Still, if it also gave the fighters miles overhead a better chance of surviving the night, then Chih-wei was satisfied.

Chih-wei climbed through the low cloud cover and emerged into an isolated, moonlit world. Banking east, he contacted Sugar One and headed toward his assigned orbit. As he flew low over the mountainous backbone of the island, Chih-wei thought about the two flight members he had lost over the strait.

Taiwan's search and rescue units had deployed into the straits and the scant few snippets he'd heard was that they had been able to extract pilots out of the drink. Remembering the previous flight, he seriously doubted that anyone who'd flown with him would be located, either alive or dead. He thought about racing over the tops of the waves and knew that if he had been hit, he would have become just a dark smear on the water.

His flight of four had been rounded out by the surviving members of other flights. Thankfully, this mission wouldn't be as difficult as the one before, as the cruise missiles had a much longer range. They'd be close to the outer limits of China's remaining ground-to-air missiles and from Chinese airborne PL-15s, unless things had drastically changed since he'd landed.

As Chih-wei envisioned it, this would be as close to a cakewalk as any combat mission could be.

As soon as he reached his assigned orbit, Sugar One switched his flight over to Sugar Two's frequency.

"Candy flight on button two," Chih-wei radioed after checking in with his flight.

"Copy Candy. Climb and maintain angels minus fifteen."

"Copy. Candy flight out of ten for angels minus fifteen."

Throttling up, Chih-wei started a gradual climb up to the new assigned altitude. As soon as he leveled off, Sugar Two called.

"Candy flight, turn left heading two six zero. Execute Whiskey Charlie."

"Candy to two six zero, executing Whiskey Charlie."

The code wasn't truly some vastly secret one. It merely meant that he was cleared to fire upon rolling out on the new heading. Coordinates of the targets had been uploaded to the two cruise missiles and updated by the E-2. Somewhere to the west, at the precise locations fed into the weapons, were two mobile launch platforms. Chih-wei had no idea of what the exact targets were, only that China's mobile cruise missile vehicles were being targeted.

As he turned to the west, Chih-wei was a little surprised that he hadn't yet been targeted, even though he was further east than the last attack run. He could see in the replicated data that there were Chinese aircraft in range, yet his threat receiver remained silent. Thankful for the breathing room, Chih-wei reached his release point with relative ease and pressed the trigger. The F-CK-1 bucked upward as the heavy weapons were dropped, their turbofan motors igniting. Unseen in the darkness, the cruise missiles slowly dropped away. Flying low over the water, they joined their ground-launched relatives in crossing the width of the Taiwan Strait and heading into China's interior.

The missiles fired from the ground and airborne platforms rolled through Chinese defenses. Attack fighters sent air-to-air missiles against the horde of weapons reaching their shores, while the few remaining long-range ground-to-air batteries released the last of their projectiles. With each minute that passed, the number of Taiwanese cruise missiles decreased. But those surviving the desperate push by China rolled across rocky shores and beaches. They dropped to anywhere from fifty to a hundred feet above the terrain and proceeded to race inland at nearly ten miles per minute.

Chih-wei turned back toward the airfield, thankful that this mission hadn't been as harrowing as the last. He knew that cushion couldn't possibly last and wondered how his wife was doing. Was she safe? Did she make it to a fallout shelter? Those were questions he desperately wanted answers to, but there was no possible way to know at the moment. He'd have to survive the night in order to find out.

China had deployed many of their mobile cruise missile vehicles close to their eastern shorelines. Those batteries were a mix of ground attack, for the planned invasion of Taiwan, and anti-ship weapons, to provide a deterrent against American warships seeking to enter the South China Sea. The prepositioning of those systems decreased the time Taiwan's cruise missiles would require in order to reach their individual targets.

From launch, it took most of the missiles fifteen minutes to reach their targets. Even though many were brought down, many more made it through, thanks in part to the sacrifices Taiwan's pilots made in reducing the number of anti-aircraft batteries that could be brought to bear.

Reaching their final approach, the HF-2A and Wan Chien cruise missiles climbed to avoid any obstacles. This allowed their imaging infrared terminal guidance sensor (IIR) to home in on a specific target. The IIR seeker was part of a digital target recognition system that compared an infrared image against digitalized files stored within the guidance computer. Once the target was verified, the cruise missile made the necessary adjustments to hit the optimal aimpoint. The entire attack run minimized any electronic emissions, thus making it more difficult to spot and defend against.

Those manning the batteries that were spread across the landscape became anxious when the short-range air defenses came to life, sending streaks of flame rocketing into the heavens. Amid the roar and swoosh of missiles firing, anyone outside could hear a high-pitched whine coming from the surrounding darkness. That sound was the last many heard as fourteen-hundred- pound warheads detonated overhead, obliterating mobile launchers.

Although China had thousands of cruise missiles scattered throughout the country, Taiwan's attack put a sizable dent in their inventory. In particular, eight of their deployed DF-17 sites had been completely destroyed. The United States had requested that these hypersonic anti-ship glide vehicular "ship-killers" specifically be taken out.

* * * * * *

Given the successes of the cruise missile attacks, regional command officers were taken to task by their superiors in Beijing. That rolled downhill until it hit the combat information center commanders flying in the two KJ-2000 airborne command posts.

They observed Taiwan's aircraft that had fired ALCMs (Air-Launched Cruise Missiles) as they began landing at airfields. Their presumption was that the attacks weren't over, and that the planes were rearming for additional sorties. There was also the possibility that Taiwan had more ground-launched missiles at their disposal. With pressure coming from above, something had to be done to prevent additional damage to China's arsenal of ground-launched missile forces.

Without any attack fighters armed with something other than air-to-air weapons, the officer in charge of the Chinese air operations knew there wasn't much he could do about Taiwan's GLCMs. He would refocus most of the air assets toward enemy aircraft flying at the lower altitudes, with the few remaining J-20s still fulfilling the air superiority role. However, his eye kept wandering to the two aircraft loitering to the east of Taiwan.

With the distance and the constant orbital patterns, he ascertained that they were Taiwan's command and control E-2s. He'd originally thought they might be tankers, but there hadn't been any signs of Taiwan's attack fighters pulling up to take on fuel. Besides, just like their own forces, there wasn't a need for them, with the bases being so close.

If he could manage to eliminate those two air assets, then the structured attacks against the homeland would become virtually leaderless, at least for a while. Perhaps there was even a possibility of sneaking a flight of J-20s through Taiwan's defenses. With the battlefield centered around the island, the officer's eyes ventured further south. He wanted to stay away from the northern routes, which would take them too close to the American forces stationed in Japan and Okinawa. It was worth the risk to divert a flight from their escort duties. Contacting a four-ship of J-20s, he sent them on a circuitous route around the fight. His only concern was for the two bogeys that were orbiting hundreds of miles away farther to the east, radar blips that the operators hadn't been able to determine the purpose of.

At nearly the same time, Taiwan's combat information officers pondered their losses to the opposing fighters. The attack fighters had been shot down at an alarming rate, making it difficult to keep up the tempo of operations. Taiwan's plan had been to hit China with everything they had and to keep up the pressure for as long as possible. Keeping their adversary off balance was the best way to inflict damage and to send a shock wave of doubt into the minds of China's generals. It was felt that if they were to let up, even for a short period of time, that would allow China an opportunity to recover and go on the offensive. If that happened, it would effectively end Taiwan's freedom of the skies and remove their ability to freely fire long-range ground-launched missiles.

So, too, did Taiwan's CIC officer's eyes turn to the two Mainring aircraft orbiting a good distance behind the frontlines. If he could take away the airborne command posts, then China's fighters would be forced to switch on their own radar systems in order to continue with their defense. That would highlight their positions and make it easier for Taiwan's commanders to coordinate the intercepts, especially against the J-20s, which were quickly becoming a thorn in his side.

Even though they had already lost four of their highly valued F-35Bs, the officer in charge directed a flight of the fifth-generation fighters on a northerly route to shoot down the two KJ-2000s directing China's fight. That path would mostly keep the attack fighters away from having to fly over the Chinese mainland, thus coming under fire from the still-functioning ground-based radar sites.

If successful, the officer was fairly certain he could extend Taiwan's momentum for a while longer.

* * * * * *

While the air battles raged in the night skies over the Taiwan Strait, there was a different one being waged in the East China Sea north of Taiwan. Following the attacks against the naval vessels sailing from the western and northern ports, the remaining ships steamed to the northeast at high speed. As the northern port ships led the massed departure of Taiwan's navy, the western and eastern port ships came together and sailed in their wake.

The radar operators aboard the ships nervously eyed the numerous Chinese aircraft miles to the southwest. However, they all seemed preoccupied with Taiwan's attacking air forces, so none of them turned their attention toward the ships. Carefully staying out of range of China's shore-based short- and medium-range missiles, the flotillas paralleled China's shoreline as they sped to get within missile range of China's eastern fleet port of Zhoushan.

Orders finally filtered down from Beijing to anti-ship missile batteries stationed near the coastal region, and to H-6K bombers located in the eastern regions. In the middle of the night, bomber crews were awakened, driving bleary-eyed down empty streets to arrive at the main gates to their bases. The echo of car doors slamming rang across parking lots, followed by the thud of boots along well-lit corridors as aircrews rushed to briefing rooms. Outside, ground crews worked feverishly to load long-range YJ-100 anti-ship missiles onto the six, wing-mounted pylons. Given the shortage of CJ-100 Long Sword hypersonic missiles, and the priority of those given to the ground rocket forces, the bomber units had to be satisfied with the slower version that was also able to reach out to the distances required.

At the request of the United States, several CJ-100 vehicles had been targeted by Taiwan's cruise missile attacks. But Taiwan's focus had been on the ground attack cruise missile sites, so many of those launchers had survived the initial attacks. Upon receiving orders to fire on Taiwan's naval ships, CJ-100 command vehicles received data from passing satellites and assigned targets to each of the launchers. Brilliant flames lit up the countryside as rockets roared from their launch tubes. The arcing trails of fire were soon extinguished as turbofans kicked in to carry the warheads on their two-hundred-mile journeys.

With so many Chinese missile launches at once, operators aboard Taiwan's destroyers, frigates, and missile boats had to filter out many of the enemy aircraft from their radar screens in order to better provide a coordinated defense. Understanding that there were only two Chinese anti-ship missiles capable of reaching the ships, the CIC officers knew that it was imperative that the weapons, capable of hypersonic flight in their terminal phase, be eliminated as far out as possible.

As the vast carpet of anti-ship missiles closed to within a hundred miles, the decks of many ships flared brightly as medium and long-range anti-air missiles ignited. SM-2s and SM-1s flew off their rails, their vaporous trails arced through the night, fiery tails that quickly turned to pinpoints of light as they sped away. Rails spun to the vertical position and additional weapons slid up from below deck to attach. The launcher then rotated, and the decks were again covered in fire and smoke as more weapons raced away toward targets beyond visual range.

Many of the newer SM-2 missiles were able to hunt down their targets. Fragmentation warheads exploded near anti-ship projectiles flying at or near wave-top levels. Shrapnel hit control surfaces and seared through the thin skins to cut into guidance systems. Out of control, the Chinese weapons slammed into the sea. However, many of the older SM-1 missiles, attempting to intercept their low-level targets, either lost contact or just outright missed.

When the incoming projectiles flew within sixty miles, more ships joined the defensive action. TC-2N medium-range weapons joined the fray of anti-air missiles racing into the night. Datalinks provided mid-course guidance to lower electronic emissions, thus reducing interference to the missiles themselves. Ships, spread across miles of ocean, became awash in fire and smoke as the sixty-one remaining ships fired at the inbound threats.

The number of CJ-100 anti-ship missiles fired was intended to overwhelm the layered defenses of Taiwan's naval ships. But the concept of overwhelming a strike group was intended to succeed against five or six escorts, not over sixty. Even though Taiwan had a mix of modern and antiquated weaponry, sixty warships could put up one hell of a blanket defense. The daunting number of threats headed against the armada were beginning to whittle down.

From the first long-range missile that was fired against the Chinese swarm, it was four minutes until the CJ-100s broached twenty miles. Short-range TC-1 missiles that were part of the Sea Oryx system sped away from their twenty-four- and twelve-capacity launchers. The combat management systems aboard the ships provided targeting data, with some of the systems hosting autonomous versions that allowed each missile to locate and track their own targets.

These infrared homing missiles were better suited to hit the approaching threats, as they could "see" the hot exhaust coming from the CJ-100 turbofan engines. Just over the horizon from the ships speeding through the sea at thirty knots, flashes of light marked where the TC-1 missiles intercepted their slower-moving targets.

However, several of the hypersonic missiles were able to penetrate the barrage of missiles sent up in defense. Entering into their terminal phase, the Long Sword 100 anti-ship missiles accelerated to Mach 5. The infrared-seeking counterthreats had a difficult time adjusting their trajectories, and most splashed into the waves.

After hearing the continuous roars and swooshes of departing anti-air missiles, the Taiwanese crew's eyes grew large when the buzzsaw of the Phalanx close-in weapons system begin spitting out 20mm rounds. When one heard that sound, they knew that the inbound threats were dangerously close.

A loud metallic *whang* reverberated across the waters as the first CJ-100 tore into the side of the ROCS *Si Ning*, a Kang Ding-class frigate sold to Taiwan by France. The monstrous warhead obliterated the interior of the warship, knocking out the ship's power and control systems. With its bow diving into the East China Sea, the vessel slowed instantly. The sea turned the stricken ship until the waves were abeam. Smoke roiled out from the gash in the ship's hull, red fires occasionally glimmering through the dark smoke. Listing to portside, the *Si Ning* began taking on water and settled lower.

Surviving crews fought to put out the fires and get the ship back under command, but the damage to the fire control and power systems proved too great. Ten minutes after the missile struck, the order was given to abandon ship. Given the nature of the mission and the distance back to Taiwan, the *Si Ning* was subsequently sunk by a torpedo from the ROCS *Wu Chang*, which had pulled alongside to rescue survivors.

The scene became a familiar one as six additional hypersonic missiles came barreling in. Within minutes, Taiwan's navy had lost one frigate and six more fast attack missile boats. Sixty-one warships had been culled down to fifty-four, and they were still two hours away from coming within range of the Hsiung Feng III missiles. The officers and crew knew that they were in for a very long night.

*   *   *   *   *   *

Anti-ship missiles continued chasing after the Taiwanese warships. At sea, the men and women on the vessels fought for their lives, sending volley after volley of short, medium, and long-range anti-aircraft missiles skyward. Although China sent fewer weapons on the second volley, it was still enough that several of the missiles broke through the defenses. Slowly, the ships sailing north were being eliminated.

On the Chinese mainland, crews departed their briefing rooms and made for their loaded H-6K twin-engine jet bombers. Many had been startled by the announcement that Taiwan had initiated attacks against China, a war which was currently being conducted in the nighttime skies.

Although many of the pilots were aware that hostilities against the island nation were supposed to have begun within the next twenty-four hours, the news of the attacks angered them. They didn't know whether they were upset at having been attacked or because Taiwan had beat them to the punch. Maybe it was a mixture of both, but indignant tones filtered through the chilled air as individual crews were dropped at the bombers sitting in revetments and hardened shelters. Wanting revenge, they climbed aboard and strapped in, running through pre-start checklists.

As if echoing the feelings of the men and women, the deep roar of engines broke the stillness of the night, the noise increasing when pilots advanced the throttles to get the large airframes rolling. The six long-range anti-ship missiles slung under each of the wings made the bombers look heavy, like they should be sinking into the asphalt instead of rolling along it. Looking at them as they trundled down lit taxiways, it seemed impossible that just two jet engines would be able to provide enough thrust to lift the birds into the air.

Like a busy airport during the holidays, bombers were stacked along taxiways as they waited for their turn to take off.

Exhaust fumes blurred taxi and runway lights. Bright landing lights constantly lit the runway as each aircraft nosed around to align with the center stripes. This was followed by the roar of jet engines screaming to push the weighted aircraft down the long expanse of pavement.

To those waiting in line, each H-6K appeared to be moving in slow motion, the planes not seeming to pick up speed. That also seemed true to the pilots as the bombers rumbled down the runway, the airspeed indicator moving like a sloth manning a DMV desk. After nearly a mile and a half, each bomber reluctantly raised its nose gear. It seemed that would be the extent of effort the aircraft could muster, perhaps preferring to return to the warmth of its shelter. Finally, the main gear separated from the runway, the behemoth scratching for every foot it could gain. One by one, the flights and squadrons departed their bases and turned north.

The formations of H-6Ks climbed, the air traffic control stations ensuring that they stayed away from the battles waged between opposing fighters. The flight plan called for the bomber streams to fly north and then to the east to circumvent the fights and also keep them away from Taiwan's long-range air-to-air and ground-to-air missiles. Although China could draw from bombers stationed in the north, south, and west, they were still smarting from the number of planes shot down by the United States.

Their route took the bombers west of Shanghai before they turned to the east. The course took extra time, but it was necessary if China was to preserve their deterrence. It didn't take much effort to send GLCMs toward the naval vessels, but to get the bombers aloft and into attack positions was a complicated affair. First, the crews had to be called up in the middle of the night and make it to their bases. Then there was the process of organizing attack routes and weapons selections. Finally, there were extensive briefs to ensure everyone was on the same page. Unlike the nearly automated processes surrounding mobile launches, getting a bomber into the air and on target was a very human-involved process, and that took time.

Although that investment of time brought a tremendous amount of firepower to bear, it also allowed Taiwan the time it needed to come within range of their anti-ship missiles.

*   *   *   *   *   *

Sitting on the horizon, moonlight shimmered across the East China Sea, the rippling shapes always changing in the nearly calm waters. The glow was enough to highlight superstructures and create dark voids in the recesses, making ever changing geometrical shapes of light and shadow. Inside the confines of the steel containers, rooms reeked of emotion. It had been a harrowing four hours for the men and women since departing Taiwan's major ports, but fifty ships had survived the journey so far.

Combat information centers had been busy fending off the near continuous anti-ship missiles sent from the Chinese mainland, but now the mood in the ships changed. Being within range of the Hsiung Feng III Brave Wind supersonic missiles, it was time to go on the offensive, even if only momentarily.

The target list was divided among the surviving ships that carried the medium-range weapons, the data subsequently passed down to each missile. The ROCS *Fong Yang* sliced through the water at high speed. The hiss of bow waves falling back into the sea was overridden by the abrupt blare of an alarm that echoed across the water. From the rear deck of the warship, a long sheet of flame roared, shrouding the stern in a cloud of smoke. A cylindrical object emerged from within a mounted container and shot into the air. The main motor, and two strapped-on solid-fuel rockets, accelerated the weapon as it was propelled aloft.

Gaining speed, the HF-3 tore through the night; the tail of fire streaming behind looked much like a Saturn launch of old. Three additional warnings blared from the ship, followed by an equal number of missiles leaving the deck of the frigate. Along the rows and columns of ships, one-hundred-and-forty rockets were fired into the dark, their flames disappearing once they accelerated to Mach 2-plus. Randomly weaving and employing electronic countermeasures to evade China's defenses, the missiles would complete their two-hundred-and-fifty-mile journey in ten minutes.

In the war at sea, the tables had been momentarily turned, and China would soon be facing another volley of cruise missiles heading toward their territory. As the HF-3s came within range of China's air defense systems in and around the Zhoushan archipelago and Ningbo, short-range missiles soared skyward. The Brave Wind IIIs, with their sudden sharp turns, were difficult to track. The electronic countermeasures they emitted fooled some of the Chinese anti-air missiles, but were worthless against those employing infrared seekers.

Small explosions dotted the general northwesterly route of the striking cruise missiles, each marking the end of a Taiwanese threat. The remaining HF-3s streaked past the outlying islands and raced across the Qitou Ocean, passing almost directly over the *Hai Lung* resting quietly on the bottom of the busy harbor. Several of the Mach 2 projectiles turned for the island of Aoshan. On the terminal portion of their runs, the active radar guidance systems identified the nearly two hundred giant oil storage tanks that covered the entire island. One by one, the HF-3s exploded over China's largest oil storage facility. The tanks burst, emptying their contents into spill containment areas surrounding each section.

Subsequent missiles set the oil alight, sending flames licking skyward. It didn't take long before the entire island was on fire. The facilities became a conflagration that sent reddish-orange flames towering into the night skies. Spilling over the containment pits, burning oil ran down the island and spread out into the water, engulfing the numerous oilers docked there offloading their tanks. Workers in the process of loading and offloading barely had time to react before they were engulfed in flames, their screams lost within the catastrophe.

The oil ships exploded from the heat. Visible rings of condensed moisture rolled away from gigantic blasts. The explosive booms were heard as far away as Shanghai. Flaming pieces of tumbling debris soared high, arcing back down to the waterways where they landed with heavy splashes. The seas became dotted with fire until the fuel was exhausted.

The sheets of flame were rocked by internal explosions, sending more fiery gouts of material up and out. The heat burned off the low cloud cover that had been hovering over the ports. Dark smoke roiled from the fires, hiding stars and the setting moon. Ash drifted like black snow across Zhoushan, covering avenues that ran between towering skyscrapers. The island looked like it was an erupting volcano.

More missiles transited Hangzhou Bay and slammed into the massive refinery complex along the shore south of Shanghai. As impressive as the Aoshan fires were with their columns of flame that extended thousands of feet into the air, the refineries inside the massive complex were inundated by sharp explosions that tore the mechanisms apart. Liquid gas and refined fuels went up with explosions that filled the night with flashes of blue and white and momentarily turned night into day.

Miles of pipelines and storage tanks erupted, sending flaming shrapnel hurtling across the complex. The surrounding towns were startled awake. People flung back curtains to see the night skies filled with flashes, like massed artillery bringing the end-times to their shores.

The rest of the HF-3s plowed into the shipping anchored in the bay. Armor-piercing warheads easily penetrated the hulls of civilian and military transports alike. Self-forging fragments shot downward from their shaped charges, punching through engine compartments and ship bottoms. Jagged tears along the keels allowed seawater to pour in faster than bilge pumps could counter. More ships were added to those already resting on the bottom from previous submarine attacks.

Vice Admiral Chun-chieh stood in the CIC of the ROCS *Kee Lung*, the Taiwanese destroyer serving as flagship to the naval ships pushing northward. Facing a difficult decision, he stood before the situation board with his hands folded behind his back.

China's attacks had been relentless and the fleet had lost twenty-one ships in the mere four hours it took to reach their current firing positions. While they had fought their way to a position where they could fire their longer-range HF-3s, they still had a hundred miles to go before they drew within range of the over one hundred and forty Hsiung Feng II missiles still at his disposal. To close that distance would require another three hours of sailing time. If China kept up the rate of fire of their anti-ship missiles, pushing on could very well risk the entire fleet.

Only the eighteen frigates and eighteen fast attack boats remaining carried the shorter-ranged and slower HF-2. One of the options the admiral was weighing was to split those ships off on their own attack run. Considering what China had thrown at them, he seriously doubted that the thirty-six ships would make it to the launch point on their own. If they were to pull within range, they would need the defensive firepower of the entire flotilla. Chun-chieh ruled out that scenario.

Another option was for the entire armada to abandon the idea of a second attack and head east for the open waters. If they did that, they would come under the protective umbrella of American air cover in short order, eventually making it to their carrier strike groups operating in the western Pacific.

And then there was the third solution, which was to continue pushing ahead with the entire armada, defending the ships still carrying anti-ship weapons. The dilemma for the admiral wasn't an easy one to realize, but that's why Taiwan's high command had put him in this position. If Chun-chieh elected to turn away now, he would be leaving behind Taiwan's best chance to curtail China's ability to successfully invade his nation. However, if he ordered his ships forward into another attack, there was no guarantee that they would even make it into a position to launch their remaining missiles. It came down to numbers. Each frigate and missile boat that was sunk meant another four HF-2s that couldn't be fired, along with their defensive firepower. If enough were sunk, then the effort wouldn't have been worth it.

One of the problems facing the fleet was that they were running out of anti-aircraft missiles. Taiwan only had enough to field a full complement for each ship, which should have been enough for a single battle. However, China seemed determined to eliminate Taiwan as a naval force and had sent endless waves of anti-ship weapons their way. Even now, the combat information center was filled with orders arranging defensive fire and the faint whoosh of anti-aircraft missiles could be heard streaking from their rails.

Chun-chieh felt with near certainty that there might not ever come another favorable opportunity to strike this hard at China. A piece of his heart sank along with each of the ships lost. His precious navy, one he was so proud of, was being cut apart, demolished one ship at a time. But this was also the situation they had prepared for. Everyone in command and every woman and man under their command understood that a Chinese invasion had never been an "if," but a "when." If he were to turn tail now, then he would have to run the gauntlet a second time in order to again get this close. He never wanted to go through this situation again. Thus, he reached a decision. The remaining warships would continue, pushing to come within the hundred and fifty-mile range of the HF-2s.

* * * * * *

Streams of H-6K bombers flew north of Shanghai, circling around the major port city. Unknown to the crews, supersonic missiles fired from the ships they were targeting were already speeding across the East China Sea, en route to the ports surrounding the Qitou Ocean.

Once the heavy aircraft crossed the shoreline, they turned to southeasterly headings. That allowed them to stay within the twelve-mile territorial limit, and thus remain within their safe haven from American fighters that were prowling in the East China and Yellow Seas.

The airframes shook as YJ-100 anti-ship missiles were released from the wing pylons, the aircraft wanting to lift higher with each release of weight. Slowly pulling away from the aircraft, the weapons dropped through the night. Completing the circle around Shanghai, the bombers turned south and proceeded back to their individual bases.

The last formations to release their weapons saw pinprick flashes of light through the overcast layer covering the distant harbors of Zhoushan. A vast orange glow began forming and the clouds melted away, replaced by a wide expanse of flames licking upward. Pilots watched as the columns of fire grew into a raging inferno. Dense smoke, darker than the night, billowed into the sky, rising as high as the bomber force that flew six miles above.

Flying at subsonic speeds, the YJ-100s took considerably longer to cover the same distance that the HF-3s flew in ten minutes. For the warships striving to close within firing range of Chinese shores, the incoming swarm was a replay of the action they had been seeing since steaming out of their ports. Trailing fire, long-range defensive weapons soared away from ships on intercept courses. That was followed by medium, and then short-range missiles. Flying slower than their CJ-100 cousins, the intercepting defensive weapons had an easier time hitting their targets. Twenty-five minutes after dropping from their pylons, the YJ-100 anti-ship missiles that managed to make it through the fading Taiwanese defense screen began arriving. Chun-chieh's nightmare had arrived.

*   *   *   *   *   *

"Aster flight, turn left heading two niner zero. Execute Kilo Juliett."

Two clicks on the transmitter button signaled his acknowledgement. Unaware of the naval vessels fighting for their lives a hundred plus miles to the east, Captain Cheng-han brought his throttle back to idle. Rolling left, he let the nose of the F-35B fall through the horizon as he began a steep descent toward the East China Sea.

He and his wingman had taken off from Chiashan Air

Base for their third sortie of the night. Although feeling stretched from a long night of beyond visual range engagements with Chinese fighters, the adrenaline-fueled night kept Cheng-han alert. This new mission was one to cause little white rings to develop on the seat cushion.

Upon tucking the gear in their wells and contacting Sugar One, the captain and his wingman were told of their new assignment. At first, Cheng-han was excited to be going directly after a high-value target deep inside China. But then reality caused his excitement to tone down a notch or two...or five. To reach his objective, he would have to fly inland and thus would be exposed to China's radar defenses. While his aircraft's stealth capabilities kept him out of sight at distances, his route would likely take him inside the range where China's search radars could see him. Rolling out on his assigned heading, the two F-35Bs of Aster flight dove for the deck.

Cheng-han's aircraft plunged into one of the scattered fog banks lying off the coast, his LANTIRN system providing a clear view regardless of the weather. Advancing his throttle as he pulled back on the stick, the captain brought his single-engine fighter to level flight. At a hundred feet, swells raced past his nose. Five hundred feet behind, his wingman flew across the sea, so low it appeared as if the F-35B was a stone skipping across the water.

Small islands whisked past, their silhouettes only slightly darker than the surrounding seas. Expecting to hear his threat warning go off at any moment, Cheng-han streaked into Sanmen Bay. With a quick glance, the captain ensured that the AIM-120s tucked into the weapons bay were selected and armed. Once he arrived at his final approach point, he would definitely become exposed the moment he opened the weapons bay doors, and would therefore have to fire quickly. His one hope of survival was that the missiles fired by his fellow countrymen and women were effective in taking out China's anti-air defenses.

Flying alongside Tianwan Island, Cheng-han banked hard left. Vortices swirled the muddy waters as his wingtip sliced through the air scant feet above the bay. Rolling out into a new waterway that opened up, the pilot saw a couple of headlights beaming from a long bridge that spanned the Shepan Channel. With a quick correction, the F-35B rose up and zipped over the structure. Surprised motorists heard the jets rocket past. Looking out of their windows, they searched the skies but were unable to find the jets that had again been swallowed by the night.

Easing the fifth-generation fighter to the right, Cheng-han flew up the narrowing channel of Qimen harbor. Village lights, appearing on either side, followed the aircraft as it slid over the top of another, partially completed bridge. The captain yanked the Lightning II hard around a sharp bend, feeling pressure build against his legs and abdomen from his inflating G-suit.

A string of lights glowed from larger villages and neighborhoods that sprang up next to the tapering waterway. Cheng-han watched as bridge after bridge whisked under his nose, the channel becoming a river as he proceeded further inland.

The terrain rose, the flatlands near the coast transitioned to become rugged and mountainous. The bridges became a series of dams meant to tame the river steaming out of the highlands. As soon as Cheng-han rolled out of one turn, he was forced into another by the winding nature of the waterway. On both sides, steep hills rose higher and higher.

Passing a dense series of villages, the F-35B shot out of a valley and flew into a series of ravines which threaded their way through rugged terrain. And still the threat sensors remained silent. Cheng-han didn't need his G-suit to put tension in his gut as it was already there. Still maintaining a westerly heading, the captain felt like he had been flying for an hour but noted that he was only thirty miles inland as the crow flies. At nine miles per minute, he had only been winding his way through enemy territory for a little over four minutes. He still had nearly a hundred miles to go. Ten minutes was a long time when things could go horribly wrong at any moment.

Tall ridges rose above, silhouetted against the glow of Tiantai sitting in the next valley. Cheng-han imagined batteries of short-range IR missiles and 20mm cannons sitting atop the sharp crests, their rails and barrels tracking his F-35B as it raced through the ravine. His mind envisioned the flare of a rocket motor sending a fast, agile missile tearing off its rail and sprinting toward his streaking jet. His plane would come apart in the air and he'd slam into the ground knowing only that something wasn't right. It was a relief to see the glow of the cities fade behind without him becoming just another piece of scattered wreckage.

Working through the mountains, the two F-35s crossed low over saddlebacks, rolling inverted at the ridgetops to slice into adjacent valleys. On one such crossing, Cheng-han flew up one tree-covered slope, the individual trees a green blur in his display. Cresting the ridge, just as he began rolling inverted, wind shooting up the opposite slope caught his fighter and lifted it higher than he intended. His breath caught as the threat warning flashed. He was suddenly exposed to a nearby radar actively searching the skies.

Willing the signal to vanish, he pulled back on the stick to keep his aircraft from climbing higher. The nose reluctantly crossed back through the horizon line and the altimeter started decreasing. The sensor went quiet and stayed dark as the F-35B powered down the reverse slope. Cheng-han hoped that the operator at the radar station was either dozing and didn't notice or thought the momentary blip that appeared on his screen had been an anomaly.

With each glance, Cheng-han noticed the decreasing distance to his launch point. The two targets replicated on his screen continued their individual orbits. If their positions altered and they started heading away, then he'd know that he and his wingman had been discovered. Flying next to the steep, forested hillside, Cheng-han felt as if he'd been at the controls a year for every minute that passed since he'd crossed inland.

Minutes later, as the captain was weaving through a narrow valley, he noted a particularly tall ridge blocking the far end. Cheng-han took a deep breath. They'd made it. Rocketing up the slope, instead of rolling down the opposite side, he kept the F-35B climbing. Cheng-han angled for one of the KJ-2000s hidden in the darkness, flying some six miles above the undulating terrain.

The weapons bay doors flung open and Cheng-han pressed the trigger three times. Almost immediately, his threat warning told him that a search radar had found him, followed by a fire control radar. Three AMRAAMs streaked away into the night. The E-2 flying hundreds of miles away saw the weapons leave and issued targeting instructions. The AIM-120s instantly veered and accelerated toward the large AWAC aircraft. Flying in a chase position, his wingman fired three additional long-range air-to-air missiles, the Hawkeye sending the target information for the second Chinese airborne command post.

With adrenaline coursing through his system, Cheng-han rolled upside down and pulled back for the protection that the mountain passes afforded. Unseen in the distance, ground-to-air missiles flew off their rails and raced into the sky toward him. Punching out flare and chaff countermeasures, the F-35B streaked for the ground. The captain knew he was in a race for his life, though, even if he made it into one of the narrow valleys, he wasn't guaranteed an escape. China now knew for sure that he and his wingman were there and would hunt them relentlessly. He had arrived at the point he'd hoped to be but had chosen not to think about. The egress would be considerably harder than his flight into the interior.

*   *   *   *   *   *

While directing the fight against Taiwan and monitoring the progress of the J-20s he sent against their command posts, the Chinese CIC officer was startled to see two bandits appear on his screen. His amazement didn't last long as he recognized the appearance for what it was. The enemy commander had conducted the same kind of operation as he had, and considering where his aircraft were, he must have done it at about the same time. Directing the pilots to conduct evasive maneuvers, and knowing in his heart that they would prove fruitless, the commanding officer issued instructions to the J-20s.

The drone of the four-turboprop engines changed as the pilot throttled back, the deck angle changing as he rolled and began a steep descent. Outside, three projectiles trailing fire changed direction to keep angling toward the large aircraft. Their guidance systems noted that they had entered their terminal phase and the onboard sensors started actively homing. It didn't take long for the Mach 4 AIM-120s to reach their objective.

The first exploded between the two engines on the left wing. Fragments sliced through the wing and both engines. The outboard engine's prop began spinning faster as the control box was destroyed, the prop running away. That created additional drag on that side. The pilot fought the aircraft's sudden tendency to roll into a hard left turn. Warning lights flashed amber and red in the cockpit as the inboard engine came apart in a ball of flame.

The next detonated close to the fuselage near the right wing's trailing edge. Screams punctuated the interior as white-hot shrapnel tore into several of the operators, blood splashing across control panels. Wind whistled as pressurized air rushed out of the holes, loose paper flying across the cabin to be sucked out of the aircraft. The interior air fogged from the instant chill and decompression, and the crew who were still able to scrambled to don their emergency oxygen masks.

A flash blinded both pilots as the third AMRAAM arrived, obliterating the windscreen and ending their valiant fight to save the damaged aircraft. Spiraling down, the KJ-2000 took several minutes to fall out of the sky. A towering explosion marked where it crashed into the wilderness.

It was much the same story with the second Chinese airborne command post. The efforts to evade the radar-guided missiles went for naught. One missile strayed away, drawn toward the deployed clouds of chaff. However, two were more than enough to down the large turboprop. It too crashed, scattering wreckage over a mile of forested hillside. China was now down to their last two airborne command posts.

* * * * * *

The Chinese KJ-2000s were fleeing for their lives, and instructions relayed to China's stealth fighters were received. No matter what happened to the command aircraft, the flight leader knew that they wouldn't have the replicated data for very much longer. Even though they were further away than the hasty plan had called for, it was either fire now or wait. Waiting would mean having to turn on their own radars and thus make them more visible to the Taiwanese forces. In their current position over the Philippine Sea to the southeast of Taiwan, highlighting themselves like that could lead to a very short existence.

The two Hawkeyes were well within range of the Mighty Dragons' PL-15 missiles. The radar operator aboard the maneuvering Chinese AWACs still had the E-2s targeted, the long-range air-to-air missiles accepting the data. In the light of a moon fading below the horizon, missiles dropped from open weapons bays and ignited. They shot forward, quickly vanishing in the night.

As with Taiwan's F-35Bs attacking the KJ-2000s, threat sensors came alive once the weapons bay doors opened and the aircraft lit up on search radars. The crews of both E-2s recognized the danger from multiple bandits that abruptly appeared on their scopes. Sending out alerts to the aircraft under each command aircraft's control, the two turboprops turned away from the threats and began a rapid descent. Flares and chaff flooded the slipstreams behind each of the command centers.

Halfway to their targets, the PL-15s suddenly lost their mid-course guidance from the KJ2000 directing them. Without the bursts of data, the missiles lost their targets. The guidance systems switched to their internal radar homing. Five of the eight immediately reacquired their targets. The three malfunctioning missiles flew onward for several minutes before they safed themselves and crashed into the sea after running out of fuel. The other five continued forward, arcing down toward their descending targets.

One of the PL-15s chased after a dense cloud of chaff, but the other four ignored the countermeasures and leapt after the slow, plodding command centers. Three exploded in rapid succession, tearing one of the E-2s apart. The aircraft tumbled and disintegrated, scattering airplane pieces across a vast expanse of the Philippine Sea.

The last PL-15 detonated underneath the number two engine. Shrapnel tore through the cowling and sliced into the rapidly spinning turbine blades. The jet engine came apart as pieces of the turbine were flung outward at high speed. A ball of flame coughed to the rear. This ignited free-flowing fuel and the descending aircraft streamed fire from the stricken engine.

Pieces of the disintegrating engine shattered the control box governing the propeller. This caused the prop to run away and speed out of control, tearing away from the engine. Still spinning, it was flung back, tearing through the upper wing. It knocked into the rotating radar disc mounted atop the fuselage, taking out a slice before ripping through the horizontal stabilizer and taking the outer tail with it as it trailed aft of the Hawkeye.

The aircraft attempted to roll over to the right due to the asymmetric thrust and missing part of the tail structure. Straining to hold the control wheel to the left and keep the E-2 upright, the pilot reached over and pulled the fire T-handle. The fire light extinguished as the flames were snuffed out, and the fuel on the right side shut off. Having descended far enough, the shrapnel cutting into the fuselage didn't create the same explosive decompression as it had aboard the KJ-2000.

In the command center, two operators administered first aid as best as they could to another crew member whose upper arm was only attached by a couple of tendons and a narrow strip of skin. The pilots were able to maintain a semblance of control through the use of trim. In the dark, at low level, the E-2 limped west toward Chiashan air base. It was out of the fight.

Within moments of each other, both sides lost their battlefield management platforms. The tempo of the night operations over the Taiwan Strait was intense. However, the mostly orchestrated battlefield turned from being semi-controlled to one that was more chaotic. Aircraft relying on the command centers found their information had suddenly vanished and had to turn on their own radars to compensate. Air-to-air combat narrowed the battle from strategic fights spread over a wide area to tactical ones encompassing only a few square miles.

Led by squadron and flight commanders, flights moved to engage their opposite number. Taiwanese attack fighters rose from airfields to deploy air-launched cruise missiles at remaining Chinese mobile sites. Rockets soared from the island to streak across the strait. Instead of relying on the E-2s for targeting data, these weapons received their information from orbiting American satellites.

* * * * * *

As the damaged E-2 limped toward base on one engine, the crews of two other Hawkeyes scrambled across the tarmac to get their aircraft airborne. Taiwan's doctrine relied on having the command posts online, especially seeing they were outnumbered and outgunned in most regards. China's J-20s were wreaking havoc. Taiwan could have brought their F-35Bs in to do the same, but they needed them over the strait, passively monitoring electronic signals. This was necessary to pass on the data for the cruise missiles to home in on.

Even though the F-16s were getting in their licks, they were under pressure from the moment they departed their airfields. Both countries' long-range anti-aircraft missiles were also taking their toll. The skies were being cleared of aircraft by the minute.

Miles to the east of the fight, two American KC-135R tanker aircraft flew racetrack patterns as they orbited over the Philippine Sea. Following along at scattered altitudes was a squadron of F-22s that were pulling up to one of the refueling booms whenever they needed topping off. Accompanying this armada, staging out of Kadena Air Force Base, was an E-3 Sentry AWAC that was following the battle between Taiwan and China.

When the command-and-control aircraft noted the Chinese bombers showing up as they lifted off from their bases, the F-22s topped off and made ready for an intercept. Taiwan had accepted some of the ground targets the United States had requested, but had turned down the appeal to go after the heavies. If America wanted to diminish China's bomber fleet, they'd have to do it themselves.

The American radar operators aboard the converted 707 followed the bomber streams as they joined up and flew to the northeast. The entire American fleet of aircraft shifted positions to shadow the Chinese bombers, remaining just out of range of China's fighters prowling the skies around Taiwan. When the bombers looped north of Shanghai and dipped into the East China Sea, pilots and operators stood ready to surge the sixteen Raptors forward.

The radar operators keenly observed the flight paths of the H-6Ks. When the bombers started hugging China's coastline, it became apparent that they weren't going to venture past the territorial boundaries. Still, those participating on the mission, and those observing from afar, hoped that China would send their heavy aircraft farther out. When radar screens lit up with additional bogeys coming from the bombers, everyone involved knew that the likelihood of catching the enemy fleet was dashed. China had launched without exiting their territorial boundaries.

Word came down from Pacific Air Force Command that the F-22s were free to engage any Chinese aircraft outside of the twelve-mile limit. With a spray of jet fuel flowing past the stealth aircraft, the last of the Raptors disengaged from the boom. Fading out of sight, the Raptor joined with the others in the inky darkness.

*   *   *   *   *   *

Coordinating with the Taiwanese E-2s, sixteen F-22s rushed forward under the guidance of the E-3 AWACs. The sudden appearance of four bogeys on the radar to the northeast of the island and subsequent attack on the Hawkeyes brought a slight change to the American plans. The Sentry spent the next moments directing frequency changes for the F-22 squadron and analyzing the battlefield.

The loss of the E-2s created instant chaos among Taiwan's attack fighters moving to launch points and the aircraft maneuvering to protect them. Operations turned into a confusing tangle of radio calls infusing the airwaves. The CIC officer aboard the E-3 noticed that the Chinese were experiencing similar confusion with the loss of their airborne command centers.

A free-for-all erupted between the two sides with individual flights engaging each other. One result was that Taiwan's aircraft carrying ALCMs and slated for attack runs were no longer being properly sequenced. Some of the orbiting aircraft departed their holding patterns to start their run-ins. However, with the loss of Sugar One and Two, most remained in their holding patterns like fighters in their corners, waiting for the bell to ring. They held there, straining at the bit, waiting for additional E-2s to arrive and resume control.

The choreographed strategy of the aerial battlefield was broken by what was essentially a technical failure. The airborne command centers, with their advanced equipment capable of handling a hundred different engagements, enabled the smooth application of firepower. They were the primary reason for the success of beyond visual range fights, as they allowed the fighters to remain dark with regards to operating their individual radar systems. Effective use of weapons systems was rendered almost impotent by these failures of command.

It took several minutes for the operators working in the E-3s fuselage to come to grips with the mayhem and to organize the frequencies for the F-22s streaking west. Once they had a handle on the attack sequencing for the Taiwan aircraft still running around their oval racetracks, the aircraft control crew began contacting individual Taiwanese pilots to reestablish order. With restored confidence, F-CK-1s started departing their altitudes to again begin flying their assigned attack routes.

One operator handled the sequencing and attack runs while another managed the F-22s. Another of the fifteen crew members crammed at their consoles started to direct the Taiwanese F-16s running intercepts against Chinese J-10, J-16, and J-20 fighters. Nearly half of the Falcons providing air cover were out of the fight, either in the process of returning to base after having spent their missiles or were already on the ground rearming. With a plethora of Chinese targets across the strait, the F-16s weren't long in the air after takeoff before they had fired their long-range air-to-air AIM120s and had to return for more. It amounted to little more than flying a traffic pattern.

This was the case on both sides. Ground crews worked as fast as they could to get aircraft back into the air, but the process was almost as lengthy as the time it took to take off, acquire targets, and return. Many of the aircraft had to queue up in order to receive arms. Consequently, some aircraft lifted off only half loaded.

All the while, the American E-3 flew west to get closer to the battle in order for the radar to see further into China. The main concern for the CIC officer in charge (and for the operator directing intercepts for the squadron of Raptors) were the Chinese J-20s. One of the first actions, upon seeing the four blips suddenly appear, was to direct a flight of F-22s toward the Chinese stealth fighters.

* * * * * *

The cold, silvery rays of light faded as the moon dipped below the horizon. From the air, it left behind a dazzling heavenly display, as if the sky had exploded and sprayed a million glittering dust particles across a background of black. Arching across the night skies glowed the endless spread of the Milky Way, both hiding and revealing its majesty of power and mysteries.

A shiver raced up his spine. For just a brief moment, Captain Steve Victors felt a deep chill, as if he had become a part of the freezing expanse of the heavens above. He sometimes felt the beauty of the universe deeply when flying, especially on clear nights like this one. Steve pulled his attention away from the heavens tonight, as he couldn't afford to lose himself in the moment. There was danger lurking in the dark skies ahead.

The radar blips toward which he and his flight had been vectored had vanished. The four Chinese J-20s that had attacked the Taiwanese E-2s had again become invisible once they had fired their missiles and closed their doors. Steve knew finding the fifth-generation assets would be a matter of luck. The advantage was that the Chinese pilots didn't know they were there, either.

Racing through the skies nine miles above the black void that was the Philippine Sea, Steve listened to the busy airwaves as the E-3 sought to establish control over Taiwan's aircraft. Taiwanese E-2 Hawkeyes were in the process of getting airborne, but until they arrived on station, the Sentry would attempt to manage the battlefield.

Captain Victors eased the throttles back a touch as his F-22 crested Mach 1.5. They were approaching the airspace where the Chinese fighters had briefly materialized. Odds were that the J-20s had turned tail once they fired and were making for the Chinese border. Long range thermal sensors weren't picking up much, so it was doubtful that the pilots were using afterburner to fly away.

Latest intel had it that the J-20 might not be capable of super-cruise (the ability to maintain Mach speeds without the use of afterburner), so the flight of Raptors should soon be catching up to the fleeing Chinese aircraft.

"Cobra flight, turn left heading two eight zero. Target will be at your twelve-o'clock, forty-three miles, angels plus ten, speed five-fifty," the E-3 operator intoned.

Steve clicked twice on his transmit button and eased his aircraft twenty degrees to the left. The replicated data suddenly showed four bandits nearly forty miles away. The abrupt appearance of the enemy aircraft must mean that China's forces were experiencing chaos from their own command center losses. Otherwise, the opposing aircraft wouldn't have turned on their own radars and thus become visible to the passive sensors aboard the E-3.

Steve's first thought was to creep closer to the fleeing aircraft and engage them with the AIM-9X sidewinders tucked into the side weapon compartments. Although they were gaining on the four J-20s at nearly five miles a minute, it wouldn't be much longer before the Mighty Dragons entered China's territorial limits. There was also the fact that Steve wanted to remain clear of China's considerable long-range ground-to-air arsenal. Although the F-22s radar signature was minuscule, that changed when the weapons bay doors opened in order to fire.

Captain Victors switched over to the AIM-120Ds sitting in the main weapons bay. The missiles received targeting data from the E-3, which would also provide mid-course guidance until the AMRAAM entered its terminal phase. Steve saw that he had a lock. Traveling at one and a half times the speed of sound, the doors opened and two AIM-120Ds were ejected from the racks. Free-falling for a second, the rocket motors ignited and the air-to-air missiles sped ahead of the fighter.

Noting their danger, the four J-20s turned off their radars and went dark. Losing their mid-course guidance, the lethal projectiles activated their radars. Traveling at four times the speed of sound and having a closure rate on the targets at thirty miles per minute, the guidance system was within range to acquire the Chinese fighters.

In the dark, the Mighty Dragons punched out flares and chaff while starting to maneuver at high-Gs in an attempt to evade the incoming threats. Two of the eight missiles fired veered toward the deployed countermeasures, but the other six soon entered their no-escape envelope. In a series of flashes seven miles above the earth, two J-20s came apart. With their fighters disintegrating under them, the pilots ejected into the frigid slipstream.

A third was hit, but the pilot managed to get his ailing aircraft back under control. With one engine out and tears in the airframe, he started a shallow descent toward home, all the while wrestling to keep his J-20 upright. With pieces flapping in the airstream, the usually narrow radar picture was enlarged. Four minutes after first being hit, two more AIM-120s came streaking out of the night sky. Two explosions in quick succession threw the stick from the pilot's grasp and the J-20 slewed sideways. In a long streamer of flame, the aircraft shed pieces as it plunged toward the East China Sea.

On his return flight, Captain Victors looked again at the stars, thankful to be alive. The American incursion into the fight was short-lived. Having fired their contingency of AMRAAMs, the American F-22s turned back toward their tankers before returning to Okinawa. The E-3 maintained control of Taiwan's side of the battle until Taiwanese E-2s arrived. It then flew back to its original orbit to monitor the situation, returning to Kadena Air Force Base long after the sun again rose.

* * * * * *

It was a ragtag group of ships that arrived within range of the HF-2 anti-ship missiles. For seven hours, Taiwan's naval fleet had come under sustained fire from China's ground and air-launched weapons. Out of the seventy-one ships that originally set out from their harbors, only twenty-two made it to the launch point. Each loss had decreased available defensive firepower, which meant that an increased number of Chinese anti-ship weapons made it past the defenses. The last hundred miles was littered with floating wrecks and fuel slicks. The back of Taiwan's navy had been broken.

The battle for the skies had been waged during the same

hours that the navy had fought for its very existence, neither truly knowing of each other's desperate battles. To the forces on both sides, whether on sea or in air, the night seemed like it would never end. The world appeared stuck in an eternal darkness. But, as the ships approached their goal, the skies to the east lightened as if a curtain on the night's destruction was slowly being raised.

The anti-ship missiles directed toward the naval vessels and their exhausted crews were fewer as China had expended much of their inventory in the attempt to destroy Taiwan's capability to wage naval warfare. To those manning their stations, the reprieve was like a draft of cold air rushing through the heated interior of a forge.

Against a horizon turning blue, fifty-six Hai Feng II missiles roared into the fading night skies. With the mission accomplished, Admiral Chun-chieh departed the combat information center and made his way to the bridge. Upon firing the last of their weapons, the flotilla turned east with the hope of making it to the umbrella of protection Japan and the United States afforded. The admiral reached the bridge in time to see the skies flare purple, red, and orange, the fanfare announcing the sun's arrival.

Chun-chieh stared at the beauty of the upcoming dawn, the peaceful times of his years at sea crowding his mind. There was nothing like the wide expanse of blue stretching endlessly in all directions, the feel of a ship riding the gentle swells, the salty breeze against his cheeks on the open decks.

Blares suddenly rang from the ship's speakers, screaming of another volley arriving from China. Many of the vessels' magazines were empty of defensive missiles. On some ships, only the Phalanx guns were available to defend what remained of the Taiwanese navy. When the buzzsaw sound of the chain guns entered the bridge, the admiral closed his eyes, holding fast to the distant memories echoing inside.

*   *   *   *   *   *

A fiery sun crested the horizon, spreading its light across the ports in and around Zhoushan. Thick black smoke boiled into the morning from towering orange flames still covering the entirety of Aoshan Island. Across Hangzhou Bay, dirty smoke drifted from a fire-ravaged refinery. Across the waterway from the burning island, the rumble of diesel engines and clank of treads vanished as men and equipment were diverted away from the unusable docks. Workers puzzled over how they were going to clear the concrete berths of sunken ships.

In the surrounding cities, the eyes of the residents were drawn from the massive oil fires when ground-to-air missiles again streaked into the morning skies. The final delivery of cruise missiles from Taiwan's navy had started to arrive. Several of the subsonic weapons were brought down, but many found their targets crowded into the narrow waterway of Shenjiamen Harbor.

The armor-piercing weapons punched through the hulls of waiting ships. More sharp explosions reverberated down Zhoushan's avenues, the island's ports absorbing the brunt of Taiwan's anger. A concussive blast of heat rolled over ships berthed at the many docks and through waterfront neighborhoods as an ammunition ship was hit. A second ship carrying fuel evaporated as an anti-ship missile plowed into its side and detonated.

The two explosions shattered windows for miles around; glass rained onto the streets beneath high-rises. The concussive waves struck nearby anchored ships, forcing them to capsize and begin taking on water. Two berthed ships were lifted clear of the water, their bows deposited on the docks. The explosions also caused three incoming HF-2s to fly out of control and splash into the harbor.

The attack only lasted a moment, but the destruction left behind was as if a typhoon had whipped through the area. Spirals of smoke from stricken vessels joined the massive conflagration erupting from Aoshan Island.

Across the breadth of China's mainland, the smoldering wrecks of missile transport erector launchers and radar vehicles sent columns of smoke rising into the early morning skies. Other thin wisps marked the graves of aircraft. In the bays, fuel slicks, surrounded by floating debris, shimmered under the morning sun.

* * * * * *

Commander Pai-han had listened as sonar reported the explosions that had rocked the port several hours ago. Thinking that the *Hai Lung's* sister ship had started creating havoc, the sub captain had opted to sit tight. If the *Hai Lu* was active, then surely China's ASW forces would be alert, even though sonar hadn't heard any of their ships nearby.

That changed with the recent sounds of explosions being heard. The other sub could have sat it out in a similar manner to the *Hai Lung*, but Pai-han was doubtful. From the sheer number of hits, it sounded more like cruise missiles were arriving. The commander thought perhaps this presented his chance.

"Make your depth sixty feet. Once we're clear of the bottom, come right to zero two zero, speed five knots," Pai-han ordered.

The *Hai Lung* eased off the silty bottom. Working slowly through the anchored ships, the Taiwanese diesel-electric boat crept toward the channel through which it had entered. The sound of explosions had ended before the sub had fully left the bottom, but the commander hoped the inevitable chaos following the attack would continue long enough to cover his escape.

As the boat progressed across the Qitou Ocean, Pai-han conducted an internal debate. He still carried more than twenty weapons onboard. If he managed to escape, then he could use those against whatever invasion fleet China sent against his homeland. But, he was also inside one of their major ports, with those same ships lying at anchor. If he waited, then he could be fairly assured that any ships he hit would be fully loaded. The problem was that they would also be more heavily protected by ASW forces.

Pai-han was still debating on the best use of his remaining weapons when he turned the *Hai Lung* north to pass through the narrow passage under the Zhujianhaixia Bridge and entered the Pushen Channel.

"Sonar contact, bearing zero zero five, range two thousand yards. Aspect ratio unchanging, speed ten knots. Classify as Renhai-class destroyer coming through the channel."

Pai-han's internal debate cleared immediately. Coming right at them through the narrow waterway was one of China's newest guided missile destroyers. It carried the most advanced Chinese ASW sensors, including a larger bow sonar. The decision where and how to use the next round of weaponry had been answered for him. If he didn't fire, and do so immediately, the destroyer would certainly find him, if the ship hadn't already. With the aspect ratio unchanging, it seemed likely that the vessel already knew the *Hai Lung* was there.

"Update the FCS and fire tubes one through three," Pai-han commanded.

"Torpedo one away," the XO stated. "Time to target, sixty seconds."

With the destroyer in the narrow channel, Pai-han knew that there was little the Chinese captain could do to evade the Mark 48 torpedoes.

"Torpedo two away."

The commander expected to hear sonar report the sound of splashes from enemy ASROC torpedoes hitting the water.

"Torpedo three away."

The *Hai Lung* was in shallow water. If the destroyer continued on its present course, it could ram the sub. The disadvantage of the enemy warship in an enclosed space also worked against the sub; it too couldn't maneuver out of the way.

"Time to target, thirty seconds."

Commander Pai-han felt tension clench his gut. He had believed that he and his crew wouldn't live through their attack on the Chinese ports and was at peace about it. However, now that the slim chance of an exit had presented itself, the commander wanted to live to hit the Chinese invasion fleet again. That was looking less possible by the second.

"Aspect ratio changing. Moving slightly from left to right. Target is accelerating through fifteen knots."

Pai-han now knew that he hadn't been previously spotted, but the Renhai-class destroyer had become aware of the threat. The narrow channel didn't allow the warship to maneuver and by the time it discovered the Mark 48 bearing down on it, it would be too late to even fire one of its Yu-7 torpedoes down the backtrack.

The Mark 48 heavyweight torpedo passed under the bow of the destroyer, tripping the proximity fuse. A thousand pounds of explosive lifted the front of the ship clear of the water, sending a tall gout of water skyward. The early morning sun caught the outer droplets, creating jewels of fire from the refracted rays.

With a massive gash tearing away the bow of the Renhai-class destroyer, the ship slammed back into the water just as the second torpedo detonated under the keel. Another fountain of water blossomed around the vessel, this one breaking the back of the warship. Seconds later, a third explosion tore the ship in half, the aft end rolling upside down. Forward momentum was halted, and the bow half of the ship settled lower in the muddy waters.

The crew didn't need sonar to tell them that all three of the heavyweight weapons had hit the Chinese ship. Pai-han immediately ordered a reversal of course. His original exit plan had shattered like the destroyer. He would have to find another way out with China's ASW now alerted to his presence.

*   *   *   *   *   *

Twenty-four hours later, Pai-han guided the *Hai Lung* into the more open waters of the East China Sea. Once there, he sent a message and headed east. A return message provided coordinates for the sub to rendezvous with the USS *Frank Cable*, a submarine tender. That was a meeting the *Hai Lung* never made. Later, along with intel and contact reports, it was surmised that the Chien Lung-class submarine ran afoul of a Chinese Kilo-class sub in the Philippine Sea. Searches throughout the years never found any sign of the wreckage, but the victories scored by the *Hai Lung* and *Hai Lu* were recorded in legacy.

*   *   *   *   *   *

Major Chin-lung eased off the brakes and cleared the active runway. A breeze flowed inside as the F-16's canopy lifted off the rails and eased skyward. Clicking one side of his mask from his helmet, the major took in a deep breath of the cool air. Under the rays of the morning sun, his body felt like it was made of rubber from the long night. Chin-lung noted the lack of other aircraft as the sleek fighter rolled along the paved taxiway. He knew that the toll had been heavy, but not the true extent.

The night had been full of engaging targets and maneuvering to evade enemy missiles intent on knocking him out of the sky. He lost count of the number of landings to refuel and rearm he'd made, but he relaxed knowing that this was to be his last for the time being. Almost as if they were vampires, the coming of the sun had chased China's aircraft back to their bases. Of course, that was likely due to the fact that Taiwan had run out of air-launched cruise missiles and had therefore called off its attacks. But Chin-lung preferred the analogy of the Chinese pilots being monsters of the night.

Reclined back in his seat with his flight suit soaked with sweat, Major Chin-lung didn't care the reason why the fight was over. He was also too tired to think about the friends he'd lost, the pilots who were forever grounded, their voices silenced. With the sun shining into his cockpit, he could almost imagine himself lounging on the beach with only the sound of the incoming waves for company.

A bounce startled the major awake. He'd been drifting off, but was now again fully conscious. That would only last until the next relaxing thoughts of sunlight and gentle surf came and he found himself thinking of lying on the warm sand…a bounce startled the major awake.

Ground crews directed him into one of the shelters carved into the hills extending from the highlands to the west. Inside the large cavern, fuel trucks motored across the concrete, along with other vehicles pulling trailers full of missiles. Chin-lung followed the yellow lines, easing into a parking place. With a signal from the crew chief, the major pulled the throttle back, pulling it over the detents. The engine wound down, coming to a stop.

Finishing his shutdown checklist, Chin-lung eased off his helmet and stared at the other parked F-16s and F-CK-1s. All of Taiwan's remaining attack fighters had been directed to Chiashan Air Base where they were tucked into mountain hangars. Taiwan had been on the offensive for most of the night, and had done everything it could to whittle down China's capabilities. The major knew that Taiwan would be on the defensive from here on out. Whether they had done enough remained to be seen.

*   *   *   *   *   *

Fishermen and sailors navigating the straits that night returned to ports with stories they'd tell endlessly around hearths and dinner tables. Their tales spoke of lights materializing inside the low overcast skies, becoming fiery trails that rained down through the night. Those fires, like meteorites splashing down to the liquid earth, hissing as the seas extinguished the burning demons.

Those who watched through patches of clear sky described the hundreds of meteors that streaked through the heavens, at times appearing to be a solid wall of flaming arrows.

The night proved costly to both China and Taiwan. The escalation from the single submarine attack evolved to become one of the world's top ten air battles of all time. Taiwan had sent over a hundred and thirty Hsiang Sheng aircraft and a hundred-forty F-16s aloft against China's one hundred and fifty J-16s, twenty J-20s, and nearly two hundred and fifty J-10 attack fighters.

The cruise missile attacks against China's shipping had successfully sunk nearly two regiments worth of equipment and supplies, a force that China wouldn't be able to readily replace, forcing changes in their planned invasion timetables. China's attack fighter strength had been hit hard, along with a severe reduction in their rocket forces inventory. Taiwan's attacks against China's mobile missile launchers and China's relentless attacks against Taiwan's navy had depleted a huge chunk of their available missiles. China would now have a more difficult time invading Taiwan.

However, those Taiwanese successes had come at a cost. Taiwan's navy was now almost non-existent, and a large percentage of their air force had been shot down or damaged to such a degree that they could only be used as spare parts. Only thirty-one F-CK-1s and fifty-seven F-16s survived intact to see the dawn, though, thankfully, most of the pilots were rescued. China, however, was down to thirteen of their vaunted J-20 fighters. They had lost just over half of their J-16s and over a hundred J-10s through the night.

A number of Taiwan's GLCMs had been expended, along with a vast majority of their ALCMs. They still retained a large number of ground-launched anti-ship missiles hidden away in underground bunkers and twenty F-35Bs to supplement their remaining aircraft. Their ground forces were largely intact and would now have to shoulder the burden against China's invading forces.

The opening tempo of the war for Taiwan had left both sides breathless. Although sorely depleted of several components of their vast military machine, China had withstood what Taiwan had thrown at it. Now it was their turn.

Zhoushan Harbor Attack

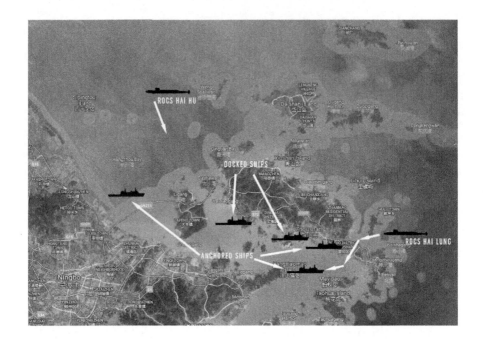

ROCS Hai Lung Attack

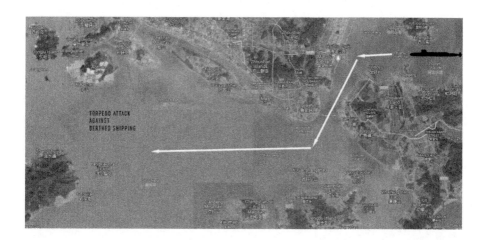

ROCS Hai Hu Attack

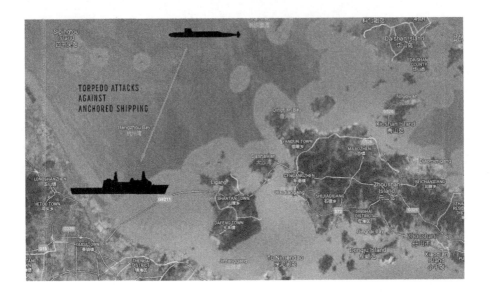

Chapter Five

Warm weather spread across the United States. The Saturday was like any other. Smoke wafted from backyards with steaks, hamburgers, and hotdogs tossed on heated grills. Bursts of laughter rang amid the gentler background of conversation. The sounds of kids at play echoed throughout neighborhoods, competing with the chug of mowers and the smell of cut lawns.

As the day wore on and the afternoon sun smiled down on picnics and barbeques, the news coming out of the Far East started making its way through media outlets and social media. Although the war with China was never far from anyone's thoughts, eruptions of laughter slowly turned to more serious discussions. China had attacked Taiwan and a full-on fight was going on.

Standing in the warmth of the sun, with the smell of steaks in the air, many found it difficult to imagine the air and naval battles that were being reported…a war underway a half world away. Slowly, people became glued more and more to their phones, some retiring indoors to see the latest news. Families who had loved ones serving overseas knew that the danger had increased and sent prayers of protection. Mothers, fathers, and spouses suddenly found it more difficult to breathe.

*   *   *   *   *   *

White House, Washington, D.C.
24 July, 2021

The sun that had risen over the Far East had yet to set on the East Coast. The warm, humid day was winding down. Families had finished with their dinners and were settling in their comfortable seats to watch movies or their favorite series. Some were starting to venture out for a night on the town or take in a show.

President Winslow knew that there would be no such relaxation for him tonight. Watching satellite footage show the dawning of a new day over the Taiwan Strait, Frank wondered what exactly had driven him to want to become President of the United States. It had been a dream of his for many years. But now, he was striving to remember the reasons he'd wanted it so badly. The rationale behind the drive was lost to him now. He supposed many dreams were like that. They took so much energy to accomplish that there was little left to enjoy once they became reality.

Sitting and watching Taiwan and China battle thousands of miles away for most of the day took something out of him. The fight with China was about to enter another dimension. And that was aside from the fact that North Korea was also about to erupt. He knew that the weariness he felt was nothing compared to the exhaustion it was about to become. Part of him longed to let China have Taiwan and the South China Sea just so he could get some rest. But he knew that couldn't happen. He would somehow have to drum up the energy to see this through.

He glanced at the clock…7pm. It was eight in the morning over the strait. Not much had occurred on either side for the past couple of hours. For all appearances, it seemed that the battles that had raged for most of the day here were over for the time being. Even though fires smoldered throughout China, and black smoke roiled above one of their oil storage farms, it was difficult to determine exactly how hard they had been hit, but the news coming out of Taiwan, made it pretty easy to see how they had fared.

Winslow was only partially listening to General Dawson recap the sequence of events. The president knew what had happened. After all, he had cancelled all of his appointments for the day in order to sit and watch the events as they unfolded. He recalled how quickly matters escalated and felt overwhelmed by the sheer number of aircraft battling one another. It had been so surreal, an odd sensation that was still present. Events long dreaded had happened.

"Although we won't know for sure until we study the intel more deeply, it would appear that the Taiwan navy is lost as an effective force. They still have some of their attack fighters, but there aren't enough to provide an effective counter to what China can bring to the table. Taiwan may be able to engage in small regional fights, providing they can get their aircraft airborne, but that's about it," General Dawson briefed.

"General," President Winslow interrupted, his mind too tired to take in all that the general was saying, "what do you mean 'providing they can get their aircraft airborne?' Why wouldn't they be able to?"

"Well, sir. The presumption is that China will take out the runways and will seek to keep them out of commission. Doing so will prevent a majority of Taiwan's attack fighters from taking off. The only aircraft they have that don't require runways is the squadron of F-35Bs that we sold them. I believe they still have most of those, but that's a small fighting force."

"Thank you, General. So, it's been quiet for a little while. Can we expect that to continue, or will events pick up again?" Winslow inquired. "I guess I'm asking what we can foresee happening in the next twenty-four hours?"

"That's tough to say, sir. The preliminary data makes it appear that Taiwan hurt China with their attacks, but I can't say just how bad at the moment. It may have forced China to reset their timetable while they divert the equipment stranded at the docks. A couple of days at least," General Dawson answered.

"I'd like to note that our initial intelligence reports estimate that China could have lost the equivalence of two Marine regiments. The Taiwan navy hit their ships pretty hard," Secretary of Defense MacCulloch interjected.

"Agreed, sir," Dawson stated. "Several ships that we believe were allocated for the invasion were sunk. While the navy focused on shipping, Taiwan's air force concentrated their attacks against China's long-range anti-aircraft batteries and their mobile cruise missile launchers.

"But, as to what the next twenty-four hours holds, that is anyone's guess. Taiwan appears to have spent themselves on offensive operations. I expect that they'll fall back into a defensive mode, using primarily ground-to-air missiles for defense. If China does decide to open air operations against the island, then Taiwan will likely expend their remaining fighters to counter that.

"Furthermore, if our initial estimates are close, then China has lost quite a few of their aircraft. I personally doubt that they'll risk what they have left in retaliatory strikes. More than likely, China will utilize their cruise missile inventory to pound the island, perhaps starting within the next few hours. That aerial bombardment may last for several days prior to the invasion force setting out from their harbors. Once Taiwan's defenses have been whittled down, then China will send in their aircraft."

"I know you mentioned a more in-depth study of the intel is required, but what do we estimate the losses on both sides at?" Frank asked.

General Dawson opened a folder and flipped through several papers before withdrawing a couple of them.

"As I mentioned previously, sir, Taiwan's navy is pretty much done for as an effective fighting force. Out of the seventy-one ships of varying types that set sail, only fourteen remain afloat. Those are currently heading east with plans to link up with task force 70 east of Japan. We'll rearm them and they'll assist the two destroyer squadrons providing escort duties.

"We're still processing data from the airborne battles, but our initial estimate is that Taiwan has lost two-thirds of their frontline attack fighter strength. At the moment, all of their remaining aircraft are stationed at Chiashan Air Base on the eastern coast. The airfield there has hangars built into the hills and should be able to withstand any anticipated missile attacks.

"It's difficult to guess how many aircraft China has lost. A rough estimate places their losses almost equal to Taiwan's. They may have had upwards of two hundred fighters shot down."

"I say it's a damn shame that we couldn't get their bombers. That would have alleviated some of our problems," MacCulloch stated. "But we do have victories of a different sort. One, it looks like Taiwan was able to put a serious dent in

China's rocket forces. That should make it easier to defend against an invasion.

"Two, amidst all the chaos, Taiwan's military leadership accepted some of our requested target lists. Specifically, they were successful in taking out several of China's DF-17 launchers. If you'll remember, those are the ones that are used to hoist their hypersonic anti-ship missiles into a low orbit. It should be noted that those rockets can also fire their anti-satellite missiles.

"And three, China expended a lot of their long-range anti-ship missiles against Taiwan's fleet. My guess is that they didn't expect Taiwan's navy to put up the kind of fight that it did. Like General Dawson said, we'll need a more comprehensive study of the intel, but I would say that they fired off a majority of their supersonic anti-ship missiles.

"That's the real victory for us. I can't imagine Beijing being too happy about that. I'd hate to be the one that gave the order to expend their missiles. But I'm glad for it; it removes one of the larger threats to our carriers, once we begin operations near Taiwan. Their bombers provide the only true long-range threat to our task forces for the interim. Again, it's too fucking bad we weren't able to hit those."

"Correct me if I'm wrong, but isn't that supposed to be the next phase of our operations against China?" Winslow questioned.

"It is," MacCulloch replied.

"And when will we be ready to commence that next phase?"

"Confirming the latest Chinese submarine losses, I can confidently state that we've eliminated a majority of their subs from the Philippine, South China, and East China seas," MacCulloch said. "Now, having said that, the Chinese boats that are still out there are still a threat. I'd like to have our P-8s continue to scour the area for another week.

"Admiral Crawford tells me that their diesel-electric submarines will also be close to having to recharge their batteries around that time. I can't believe they'll do that at sea after what happened to them the last time. That means most of their underwater fleet will have to retire to territorial waters. We'll be able to pick them up then and track them. Once those are out of the way, I can say that phase one will be complete. After that, we'll need to shift some assets around, and then we can move forward."

"Aaron, need I remind you of the time limit we're up against?" Frank said impatiently. "Thirty days have passed since I enacted the War Powers Resolution, which only gives us thirty more days until I have to ask Congress for an extension. I don't see a problem with that, but you never know. Inflation and this continued pandemic are stretching things pretty tight.

"The grumbles of dissatisfaction are already rolling through the corridors. I'd rather this was settled before I have to go crawling in on hands and knees. I mean, can you imagine if the opposition party decides to make a statement and we have to pack things up in the middle of this fight? We stand to lose more than the South China Sea."

"Do you think they'd actually do that?"

Frank's chuckle was not one of amusement. "Oh, I've seen stupider things happen. I wouldn't put it beyond some people to make waves just for their fifteen minutes in the spotlight. You have your week, Aaron, but that really starts putting us up against a wall. If it goes beyond that, then we're going to have to reanalyze what we're doing."

"I hope Taiwan can hold out that long," Secretary of State Stevenson added.

"That is the hope of us all," Frank replied. "I'm sure I don't have to remind anyone here what the consequences of losing Taiwan are."

* * * * * *

The loss of the *Mississippi* created a hole in plans to have the quiet hunters positioned to both intercept China's invasion fleets and to track any remaining diesel-electric subs once they neared the surface to recharge. The USS *Seawolf* and the USS

Jimmy Carter were positioned off Hainan Island and off the port of Zhanjiang, monitoring the southern Chinese invasion fleet. The only other nearby submarines were the USS *Texas,* patrolling in the southern reaches of the South China Sea, and the USS *Missouri* positioned off Guam.

Orders went out to the two Virginia-class submarines to work their way toward the Luzon Strait. The passage separated Taiwan from the Philippines and was the largest entrance into and out of the South China Sea. Filling one gap created two others. The southern waters of both the Philippine and South China Seas were now without benefit of coverage. It wouldn't be long until the United States would need to force passage into the Philippine Sea from the south.

Thousands of miles to the east, a gangplank was pulled to shore. Splashes marked where heavy mooring lines were cast into the water. Without fanfare, a tugboat eased the dark cylindrical object from the pier. None of the sailors aboard were happy with the recall, but all understood the purpose. There was a war to the west, and they were needed. Navigating the channel out of Pearl Harbor, the USS *Hawaii* slowly motored under the summer sun. Once clear of the entrance, the Virginia-class boat slid under the water. It followed the same path of the USS *North Carolina* by three days. With very few exceptions, and the three reserve boats currently being outfitted, the United States now had put its entire Pacific submarine fleet out to sea. It was now all-in to finish the undersea battle with China.

*   *   *   *   *   *

Beijing. China
25 July, 2021

The numbers floated off the page like a cartoon, seeming to detach themselves and grow larger. Hao and the rest of the military leadership were discovering one of the axioms of warfare that was true regardless of generation. It was impossible to accurately predetermine the ammunition required for any battle. Conservatively estimate, add in percentages for variables, and then double it. It was an old adage, and that still didn't seem enough.

One of those numbers chilled Hao more than the others...the CJ-100 supersonic anti-ship missiles. The expenditures that China's rocket forces had directed toward removing the Taiwanese navy as an effective fighting force had accomplished its goal, but it had come at the cost of draining most of China's supersonic anti-ship weapons. That was a loss that even China's vast manufacturing economy wouldn't be able to shortly remedy.

Hao understood that China's aim of invading Taiwan was now at risk. Without the threat of those weapons, the United States would be able to intervene with their carrier task forces. China was vulnerable. Hao felt a growing tightness in his chest as he thought about the upcoming invasion plans. Throughout his years climbing China's political ladder, he'd learned to listen to feelings of trepidation like those he was currently experiencing. Every fiber of his being was telling him to cancel the invasion of Taiwan, or to delay it at the very least.

They were losing the undersea submarine war. Even now, some of their deployed subs were having to leave their patrols in order to travel inside territorial boundaries. They had lost one of their carriers, and the other was still too damaged for use. It didn't take a genius to figure out that China was on the verge of losing the initiative.

Even though indications were that they had destroyed a greater percentage of Taiwan's air force, the two countries had broken even with regards to total losses. The advantage of proximity was still heavily in China's favor, thus their ability to attain and keep air supremacy over Taiwan. That and their bomber force were the only advantages that China still enjoyed.

Taiwan had hit a number of ships, but those could be more easily replaced by China's shipping industry. It wasn't Taiwan that had Hao so worried and on the verge of canceling the entire operation. It was the distant swell of American forces which were converging around Taiwan. Due to China's history, there was a cultural fear of being invaded. And the vulnerability that stemmed from the expenditure of missiles fed directly into that anxiety.

With Indonesia, Malaysia, and the Philippines pushing back against China's claims, coupled with American bases in Japan and South Korea, China felt the pressure of being closely surrounded. That claustrophobic paranoia was the predominant reason for China's regional aggression and had been throughout their long history. This situation was a chance for China to break out from the stranglehold around it and to propel itself from an impoverished nation into the world's number one economy.

Hao stared at the reports, wondering if they shouldn't have waited. There had been unfortunate circumstances which had brought on the current state, but he could have done more to reduce the tension and stave off the conflict with the United States. There was never any doubt that China was going to invade Taiwan. But they would have been in a better position to do so in six years. Now, Hao worried that events had been triggered too early. There was a way to make it look like China was a peaceful nation and seek out the offered cease-fire.

The problem was that he experienced that same tightness in his chest when he thought of halting the invasion plans. He remembered something his father said years ago. When facing self-doubt, return to a place where you were sure of your decision. Stick with the path you were sure of at that moment in time.

Taking a deep breath, Hao felt the worry ebb. China had destroyed Taiwan's naval and air forces, bringing China a step closer to unifying the breakaway republic. The American carriers were still at risk if they came within range of China's long-range rocket forces. And, the United States' battle doctrine relied heavily on its network of satellites, which were extremely vulnerable. No, this was still the right time to launch China into becoming a world power. Hao straightened the reports and placed them back into a folder.

Morning light streamed in through the tall windows, the partially open heavy drapes seeming more of a shield separating Hao from the masses than the thick walls. It had been a long night of watching events unfold. The ebb and flow of emotions had worn down almost everyone as the night progressed. The rising of the sun had served as a signal ending the bout. Taiwan had gone to their corner and had been unable to answer the bell. The momentum had changed; it was China that was now in the driver's seat. It was time to determine what changes Taiwan's attack had forced on their plans.

Pushing his internal debates aside, Hao focused on the briefing. Even though they had covered the same issues throughout the night, Minister Zhou felt it important to summarize the current situation.

"Our pilots withstood the brunt of the attack, knocking down most of Taiwan's air force in the process. After firing a few missiles, their navy has turned tail and is heading east at top speed. We managed to sink or severely damage fifty-seven of their warships. While this preemptive attack came as a surprise, it actually benefits us. In the past twelve hours, we have eliminated their navy and hit their air force so hard that they will be ineffective when we take the initiative. The lack of naval vessels and aircraft will make it easier for our marine and airborne combat units to conduct their landings."

Hao nodded, agreeing with the minister of defense. "Are we absolutely certain that this was a preemptive strike by Taiwan?"

Minister Zhou returned Hao's gaze as if the Paramount Leader had asked if he was sure that two and two was four.

"As certain as we can be. We were all there when Taiwan downed our aircraft operating in the Taiwan Strait," Zhou answered.

Hao again nodded. "I am aware. I believe Minister Liu was going to have our UN ambassador make some statements, and I want to be sure of their accuracy. If we are all sure of Taiwan's culpability, then we can move on. What is our current situation? What changes to our plan are necessary?"

"We lost several aircraft defending ourselves. Their attacks against our missile sites were focused and hit us pretty hard. But we will have enough remaining to see us through the conquest of the island. It is the same with the ships that were sunk. We have enough men and equipment to complete our unification effort," Zhou stated.

"And the Americans? There is not a doubt that the United States will come to Taiwan's aid. That means they will send their carriers. With our ammunition expenditures, especially in the realm of anti-ship missiles, will we be able to threaten their involvement?" Minister Wei inquired.

"Yes, defeating Taiwan's navy required the use of many rockets. We have begun constructing fake sites in addition to pulling reserves from our inventory. They cannot know our situation, so the deterrence is still a factor.

"Our bombers also provide long-range threats to their strike groups. With the demise of Taiwan's air force, we will be able to push our bombers out to even greater ranges. If their carriers approach, we will be able to launch anti-ship missiles from outside the limits of their combat ranges, thus keeping our bomber forces intact. I might also add that we have several of our hypersonic anti-ship ballistic missiles ready to launch. If we use those to take out two more American carriers, then the war with them will be all but over. That will leave the Americans with just two carriers in the Pacific, and they will not risk those defending Taiwan."

The room fell silent. Although the hypersonic missiles were a tremendous threat and extremely difficult to counter, those around the table questioned their true operational status. There was some discussion centering around the weapons' accuracy, and the operational nature was designed more as a deterrent to American carriers. More testing was necessary to pinpoint the accuracy issues, but no one wanted to mention the problems China was having with one of its important weapons systems.

"So, we still possess the capability of keeping the Americans away and defeating Taiwan. My question now pertains more to the issue of any scheduling delays," Hao said.

"Our timetable has been pushed back four days so that

we can divert equipment that was slated to be loaded at the Aoshan harbor."

"So, you are saying that we will be ready to begin phase one of operations in four days?"

Minister Zhou nodded. "Phase one of our attack is slated to begin on the evening of the 29th."

"Very well. Before we adjourn, let us briefly discuss the issues we are having in India and Hong Kong," Hao directed.

The minister of foreign affairs cleared his throat. "Much like the last uprising, we are in the process of clamping down on dissidents. New laws and curfews are being implemented in order to curb the violence. Furthermore —"

"Intel off the street says that our enforcement officials are killing minor dissident leaders from the previous uprising," the minister for state security interrupted.

"Is that true?" Hao asked.

It wasn't that he disagreed with the tactics. Harsh measures were sometimes necessary to instill certain lessons. The people of Hong Kong had been entitled for far too long, and now they were having to learn a painful lesson. The sooner they accepted that they were part of China and not some Western World democracy that promoted corruption, the better off they would be. Hao asked his question out of simple interest.

"No. What we have discovered so far seems to be a false flag operation. It is most likely propagated by the Americans, either directly or via a proxy. I think it is an operation designed to divert our attention," Minister Wei answered.

"Well, shut it down before the flames of rebellion spread too far. I do not care how. I am tired of hearing about these movements. I want results. What is the situation regarding India?"

"Cross-border shootings that have escalated. India fired on our border troops and we responded. In order to establish a safe zone, we have made several deeper incursions and are holding onto the territory. India has moved two new regiments opposite our forays. So far, they appear content to watch and wait, perhaps there to counter any additional attacks," Zhou briefed.

"Hold what we have taken, but do not go any further. We will revisit the situation once we have conquered Taiwan."

Hao didn't need to add that taking Taiwan would cause India to think twice about participating in a border dispute with China. As a matter of fact, many nations would stand up and take notice, allowing China a greater freedom to expand.

Hao remained as the others filed out of the room. The farmer in the picture on the wall seemed to mock him, the peaceful scene a tantalizing glimpse of the life Hao could have enjoyed. If he had just made a couple of different choices, he wouldn't be sitting in this ancient room, mired in difficult choices.

The conflict with the United States was actually going better than he had anticipated, but Hao knew that China was at risk of losing its momentum, of having the initiative ripped out from underneath them. He had hoped that North Korea would have made their opening moves by now, but the madman leading the secretive country was playing China. They weren't going to move anywhere until China showed their hand. Hao had sought to use the tiny nation to divide America's resources, but that was also what North Korea was doing, letting China draw off American troops so they would have a better chance at their own unification.

Hao knew that America was under a time constraint and had contemplated waiting them out. Their congress might just pull the plug with the rampant inflation they were experiencing. The problem was that China was dealing with the same issues. Although it was being kept from the world as much as possible, China's inflation was undeniably worse.

Everything was being done to keep the economy afloat, even sacrificing some of its future growth potential. However, that could only be kept up for a limited time and China was quickly approaching the moment when that wouldn't be possible any longer. China's imports, and more importantly, their exports, had been dramatically reduced due to the hostilities in the South and East China Seas.

Even though civilian shipping hadn't been targeted, very few foreign vessels were willing to negotiate the war-torn passageways. That only exacerbated the problem facing China, and brought the focus to just how much reliance there was on commerce transiting the South China Sea. It would be too easy for the United States to blockade China and bring their trade to a halt.

China was cornered, but came under fire whenever Hao sought to expand to give them some breathing room. Hao understood that his motives weren't entirely altruistic. Although he sought to expand China's influence to improve his impoverished nation, to improve their way of life, he also wanted to make a name for himself in the process. After all, everyone wanted to leave a legacy behind. And his was to bring Taiwan under China's control. That would be the start to pushing his enemies back from China's frontier.

* * * * * *

The world watched and waited following the initial battles between China and Taiwan. Those expecting events to quickly spiral were disappointed, yet relieved, when nothing more happened. As the hours of the next day passed, and then another day, anxiety eased. However, no one was under the illusion that the battles in the Far East were really over. Everyone knew that a Chinese armada would soon be heading toward Taiwan, and for that reason, the tension never truly dissipated. The media outlets didn't allow it. There was an endless string of broadcasters that brought in an equally endless string of pseudo-experts that seemed to materialize out of the woodwork.

* * * * * *

United Nations, New York, New York
27July, 2021

It took every bit of control for Elizabeth not to interrupt the Chinese ambassador currently spewing complaints about

Taiwan's unprovoked attacks against China. He provided footage of missiles leaving the Penghu Islands and striking something in the night skies. Elizabeth would certainly love to know where he'd gotten those videos being shown. The ambassador stated that the falling aircraft trailing flames was a Chinese plane patrolling in international airspace.

"This was no accident, but a deliberate attack by Taiwan against a Chinese military asset. The breakaway island has shown itself to be a consistent, destabilizing force in the region. Due to this unprovoked attack, China is officially declaring war on Taiwan. Too long have we stood patiently by, letting Taipei provoke and disrupt the peace. The time has come to remedy the situation."

Elizabeth couldn't stand it any longer, not that she was planning on it anyway.

"Mr. Ambassador, you are incorrect with your assertion that this was an unprovoked attack by Taiwan. You, sir, are the ones that initiated acts of violence against Taiwan," Elizabeth remarked, turning her gaze from the Chinese ambassador to encompass the entire chamber, "making China, once again, the aggressor in the actions between the two countries. As I have said time and time again, China is the instigator! They have attacked the world with the release of SARCov-19; they have deliberately introduced chaos and have destabilized our market economies, and furthermore, they continue their pattern of unchecked military aggression against the sovereign nations around them.

"I am going to play the actual, unedited radio communications between a Taiwanese helicopter and its ship, conducting anti-submarine operations against a Chinese nuclear fast attack boat *inside* of Taiwan's territorial waters. Included in the recording are the cockpit communications between the helicopter crewmembers."

Elizabeth then nodded for the recording to be played. The voices on the tape spoke Mandarin but were translated for those in attendance. While many had difficulties following the military idioms, they were able to get the gist of what was being said. All of a sudden, there was a subdued explosion, followed by warning bells and curses from the pilots. At that moment, Elizabeth cut off the replay.

"That explosion you heard was a Chinese submarine being sunk. Before that were discussions of attacks against Taiwanese naval vessels traveling in their territorial waters. Those were tracked back to the Chinese fast attack sub that was found and fired upon, again *inside* of Taiwan's territorial boundaries. That happened not once, but on two separate occasions."

"Those could have been manufactured or been taken from any time and place," the Chinese ambassador countered. "Ladies and gentlemen, as is usual, the United States is seeking to confuse matters by making up facts. China did not, nor have they been, conducting operations within any country's territorial limits."

"No, sir. We both know that isn't true." A display went up on a large screen. The image showed a thermal picture of the helicopter in question. Coordinates were dominantly displayed, along with a red line around Taiwan depicting the twelve-mile limit.

"This is the helicopter in question during the time of the radio transmissions. As you can see, they are well inside Taiwan's territory," Elizabeth continued.

"Again, those are lies propagated by the United States and are meant to undermine China. I will say it again, China has not, nor will we operate submarines inside foreign territories."

"Hmmm...have you recently heard from your Shang-class submarine positioned outside of Tsoying Naval Base?" Elizabeth asked.

"I am not privy to such information," the Chinese ambassador replied. "Even if I were, I would not answer a question such as that. As you seem to have difficulty hearing my words, I will say it a third time. We did not have any vessels operating outside of international waters, nor did we strike at any Taiwanese assets until after we ourselves were attacked.

Our response to Taiwan's aggression was made in defense."

"I hear your words just fine, Mr. Ambassador. It's that I'm denying them any credibility, given the counter-evidence I'm providing. If you like, I have video evidence of the attacks in question."

"This evidence you claim to have can easily be manufactured and the bottom line is that America simply cannot be trusted. I have also given evidence of an attack against a Chinese military aircraft, yet you want to dismiss that."

"I am not denying the attack against one of your aircraft. I am stating that it was after your attack on Taiwan's ships. You directly attacked a sovereign nation, and you seem surprised that they retaliated. You were the first to strike, and are thus, by the very definition, the aggressor."

Turning to again address the entire chamber, Elizabeth continued, "I have come before this assemblage many times regarding China's unchecked aggression. Each time we have stood back and done nothing. China attacked the United States in international waters. They have previously attacked fishing boats from other countries to bully them from fishing grounds. And now, they have attacked yet another nation in their drive to make the claim that the South China Sea is theirs.

"How long are we going to sit back and do nothing about this? How long are we going to allow China to ignore World Court rulings? Is it going to be after they swallow up one nation? Or will that number rise to two before we decide to do something about it? Perhaps three is the magic number. Maybe there isn't a number; maybe we'll just leave China to do as they will. Ladies and gentlemen, that is what Beijing is counting on…that this legislative body will be too scared to act.

"I make the motion to bring about sanctions for a third time, hoping that those in this chamber will recognize China's aggression for what it is. The civil rights violations being conducted in Hong Kong right now should demonstrate that China does not care about peace or the well-being of others. Stop this in its tracks…please."

Elizabeth sat. As expected, the resolution she had brought up for the third time didn't pass. However, it did bring several NATO nations to recognize Taiwan's sovereignty. While the European nations weren't ready to join an alliance to sanction China, it was a step. How it would help Taiwan in the upcoming war remained to be seen.

*   *   *   *   *   *

Even though the United States had warned North Korea about massing military men and equipment near the DMZ, the decision was made to delay any attacks. If the North wanted to wait on China before they attacked, then the United States was only too happy to let them. It allowed for additional stockpiles to be amassed and for defensive lines to be better prepared. A resupply line was created between Japan and Pusan, South Korea. An LA-class fast attack submarine was stationed near the narrow strait separating the two nations to prevent China from slipping in one of its subs to disrupt operations.

On China's end, they repositioned their three remaining nuclear fast attack boats into positions around Taiwan to protect their invasion fleet's route. All the diesel-electric boats, four Kilo-class and two Yuan-class, had been issued orders to return to coastal waters in order to recharge. The plan detailed the quieter nuclear subs to screen the invasion vessels, to interdict any American subs which would surely be positioned to attack the initial invasion fleet.

The feeling within China's inner politburo was that they just had to last long enough to get troops ashore in Taiwan. From there, resupply missions should provide enough soldiers to drive quickly to Taipei. Once they occupied the island, they would turn Taiwan into a bristling fortress and there would be little anyone could do to remove them. China would then bide its time and rebuild its forces, coming out on the other end stronger than ever. And once the hostilities came to an end, which they surely would, then commerce would flood into China. The economy would again prosper, and they would become the global economic power they were always meant to be. All that had to be done was to keep the American military at bay for the next two weeks.

*   *   *   *   *   *

East China
29 July, 2021

A three-quarter waning moon hung in the sky, the bright surface and darker craters so clear it seemed as if one could reach out and touch the surface. Silver rays caressed upper limbs like a light snow on Christmas day. Moonbeams shimmered across the undulating surface of the Taiwan Strait, thousands of sparkling diamonds changing shape and shadow with each rise and fall of the swells.

On both sides of the glistening waters, nervous men and women hunched over radar scopes, the soft glow highlighting their facial features. Systems stood poised and ready, like a spring trap quivering in anticipation, waiting for the delicate shift that would set swift violence into motion. The battles that had been waged over the narrow passageway had faded with the morning sun; the day carried anxiety and taut nerves, but was also filled with expectations.

In mobile control rooms spread up and down the eastern coast of China, many pairs of eyes watched the slow progression of seconds marching on digital readouts. Across darkened landscapes, China's remaining mobile missile batteries had their launchers pointed to the heavens. Green lights steadily shone on control boards, each representing a giant cylindrical weapon poised and ready. All waited on the steady countdown of time.

One second turned to the next, and the next, and the next. Switches were moved from standby to ready, more lights illuminating as missiles became armed. The digits on control vehicle clocks showed 58...59...00. At 23:00 Beijing time, lights flared across the eastern Chinese countryside. Solid-fuel rocket motors ignited, sending long gouts of flame roaring from containers. Long-range cruise missiles rose from their tubes. Fireballs arced across the night sky, joining with hundreds of others to create a show worthy of the best Perseid had to offer.

On the other side of the strait, Taiwanese search radars saw the threats rising from China's shores. As the information was being passed to fire control radar systems, the screens fluctuated, sometimes showing fewer targets, sometimes many times the initial number. Chinese airborne jammers were active on the west side of the passage. Taiwanese systems started frequency hopping as they attempted to elude the Chinese jamming.

Both sides knew that wouldn't last long because China would have to let up on their efforts lest the jamming interfere with the cruise missiles tracking. They only wanted to let the weapons get closer to Taiwan to reduce the effectiveness of defensive fire.

The systems on the outlying Penghu Islands were the first to be able to break through the jamming and identify the low-flying threats. Sky Bow surface-to-air missiles sailed from their housings, arcing over darkened homes filled with sleeping families. In addition, Patriot anti-aircraft batteries provided another layer of defense.

The Patriot radar gathered the data on the numerous tracks, examining each to analyze the potential target's size, speed, altitude, and heading. The system then decided whether the tracks were legitimate ones or only clutter created by radio frequency interference. Once the system classified the tracks as aircraft or missile threats, the tracks appeared on the radar screen. The radar operators examined the data as one of the subsystems sent out pings to determine if the tracks were friendly.

Based on these factors, the tactical control officer sent the information to the tactical director who then ensured again that the incoming tracks weren't friendly aircraft, certifying that the targets were hostile. The engagement was then delegated back to the Patriot battalion, where the tactical director selected a battery and ordered them to engage. The data was uploaded into the missiles. Once the tactical control assistant pressed the "engage" switch, the system selected missiles to fire. In a seeming continuous roar, Patriot missiles left their individual containers to soar aloft.

The decks of the warships that remained behind became awash in smoke as they added their own arsenal of anti-aircraft missiles. Streamers of fire tore out of harbors, quickly becoming glowing dots in the night sky before fading altogether.

The two forces met in the middle of the strait. On one side, dark objects, their tops bathed in reflected light, streamed a few feet above the rolling crests. On the other, streaks of fire fell from the heavens on intercepting courses. Dots of fire flashed one after the other as proximity fuses set off two-hundred-pound warheads. Shrapnel ripped through the fortified skins of the cruise missiles, shredding the internal components. Towering splashes erupted in the night as damaged missiles smacked into the waves at high speeds.

On the eastern side of the island, with the first radar warnings, pilots raced from alert rooms. Lights mounted high on the hangars carved into the foothills illuminated rows of sleek attack fighters. Boots thudded on concrete, adding to the noise of aircrews readying aircraft. Pilots raced up ladders and eased into the tight confines of cockpits. One by one, jet engines started, their roars echoing through the vast chambers, drowning out all other sounds.

With the smell of jet exhaust permeating everything, F-16s, F-CK-1s, and F-35Bs taxied from their parking spots. Giant doors rolled back, and fighters emerged from their underground shelters, their hardpoints bristling with air-to-air missiles as they rolled quickly down taxiways. Without pause, aircraft took the active runway and accelerated. With afterburners trailing long streamers of fire, what was left of Taiwan's fighters leapt into darkened skies.

The only interruption of the continuous fiery exhausts was a lone E-2. Once airborne, the Hawkeye turned east over the Philippine Sea, climbing so that it could see over a wider area. Once established in an oval holding pattern, the airborne command post began to establish control over the battlefield. The crew was aware of what had happened to the previous command posts and understood the risks. With the increase in the air-to-air missile ranges, even circling a hundred miles behind the front lines didn't provide the measure of comfort that it used to.

The attack fighters climbed quickly to ten thousand feet, high enough that they cleared the ridges and peaks that ran the length of the island. Leveling off, the pilots of the various aircraft fired mixed loads of AIM-120s and Sky Sword II missiles. The E-2 operators picked up the launches and assigned targets to each of the medium and long-range weapons, controlling the missiles until they entered their terminal phases.

Once the Taiwanese fighters released weapons slung underneath wings, fuselages, and weapons bays, the pilots would turn east and descend. The mountain ranges provided cover against Chinese search radars operating near the strait. Flying in a box pattern, the attack fighters came around for landings to rearm before again taking to the skies to fly the same routes.

The attacks a few days prior by Taiwan had put a huge dent in the number of mobile platforms China possessed, but not enough to completely eliminate the long-range threats. China had used the days in between to resupply, pulling many from their storage facilities. The fact that China was having to empty their reserves for this contest meant that their once seeming endless supply of missiles was becoming limited. China's cruise missile batteries were reaching a critical point.

Chinese radars picked up the Taiwanese aircraft as they crested the mountains. With targets showing up barely a hundred miles away, surface-to-air missiles began responding. When the aircraft dipped below the mountain crests, the fire control radars lost their lock on specific targets. Some of the HQ-9 anti-aircraft missiles crashed into Taiwan's thickly wooded slopes. Others flipped to their passive IR sensors and found a bevy of heat signatures. Some of the missiles followed the Taiwanese aircraft through their maneuvers. Those that cleared the mountain ranges found a dazzling array of flares slowly descending through the night and turned to intercept the heat sources.

Chinese HQ-9 anti-aircraft missiles came streaking over the mountain ridges at over Mach 4. Explosions dotted the night sky as the weapons plowed into the midst of flares. In other instances, at varying points in the moonlit sky, fiery tails would erupt and stream behind stricken aircraft. Those tails of fire would slow and drop from the heavens, beginning their short journey into the sea.

Inside China, an array of attack fighters stood ready to deploy. Pilots waited in ready rooms, poised to take to the air to defend their homeland. They wouldn't go on the offensive just yet. That was going to lie on the shoulders of the rocket forces for the interim. If Taiwan again initiated attack runs toward China, then the massed fighters would leap into the night and take the fight to the island nation. But, as long as enemy planes remained engaged in defensive fire, China's military leadership was content to let the long-range surface-to-air missiles carry the load.

It wasn't long before the Hawkeye radioed warnings. There were many Chinese cruise missiles that had survived the defensive gauntlet that Taiwan had sent skyward, and they were entering their final phases to targets spread throughout the island. Aircraft were directed back to the runway at Chiashan so they could land and be hangered before the ground attack missiles hit. It would be a close-run thing, the pilots rapidly landing one after another without the peacetime spacing. Aircraft rolled briskly along taxiways, scooting into the underground hangars. The huge hangar doors began closing as the last F-16 rolled inside.

Due to the threats coming from a major power only a hundred miles away, Taiwan had built an extensive network of underground bunkers. Inside these redoubts lay defensive missile systems that could be rolled out to fire on opposing forces. Many of these tunnels were also home to Taiwan's long-range anti-ship weapons systems. The radar systems for both ground-to-air and surface-to-surface were mobile and could be driven out of the caves, activated, the weapons fired, and everything then returned to the underground cover. The idea was to launch and retire before counter fire could arrive. It was from these defensive bunkers that Taiwan hoped to defend against a Chinese invasion.

With the warning coming from the E-2, the mobile defensive vehicles drove back into redoubts. Thick steel doors then closed, sealing the soldiers and equipment inside. Much of the army had been removed from their bases and driven into caves dug into the mountains. Knowing that China would likely use long-range artillery and missiles to destroy Taiwan's military, the underground shelters were Taiwan's attempt to protect its armed forces.

Knowing that the runway was apt to be taken out, the Hawkeye turned to the east. The crew would fly to Okinawa and initiate operations from there going forward. Previously, other E-2s had departed for the American air base. If the runways were effectively kept out of operation, then Taiwan's air defenses would center around the F-35B squadron. It wasn't much, but it was better than nothing.

Following positioning derived from China's BeiDou Navigation Satellite System, the courses the cruise missiles flew began to diverge as they sought out their targets. Those with targets positioned on the Penghu arrived first. Climbing to better identify their targets, the GLCMs compared the terrain with internally stored maps.

Short-range anti-air weapons shot up from around the island chain, one of the last layers of defense for targets of military importance. Radar-guided 20mm and 40mm barrels swiveled as they tracked their targets, spitting rounds into the darkness. Some intersected the five-hundred-mile-an-hour projectiles, plowing furrows as they crashed and tumbled.

Three missiles dove into the single runway on the main island. Their delayed charges allowed the weapons to bury themselves deeply before the warheads detonated. Gouts of dirt, rocks, and pavement flew outward, leaving behind three large craters along the length of the runway.

Additional bunker busters arrived, slamming into hardened shelters on the northern end of the airport. Chunks of dirt and foliage flew from the tops of the buildings, the structures camouflaged to blend in with the surroundings. Blocks of concrete fell into the hangars, shattering as they smacked onto the painted floor. Massive booms echoed throughout the empty hangars. Though the structures were weakened by the onslaught, they held up to the initial hits.

Other missiles flew directly over some targets, dropping shaped charges comprising a mix of anti-personnel and anti-armor munitions. Flashes and small detonations spread over areas like electrified hail. Equipment left out of the underground bunkers was shredded, exploding as fuel tanks were punctured. Blossoms of fire from secondary explosions ripped through the night.

The interiors of the bunkers reverberated as additional penetrator missiles attempted to punch through. Floors and equipment vibrated with each explosion. On the outside, warheads crashed through tree limbs to bury themselves deeply, the delayed explosions uprooting trees. Parts of the wooded landscapes soon began to resemble the dead moon floating overhead.

As if a tidal wave moved across the island, explosions then rocked Taiwan's west coast. The warheads targeted anti-aircraft launchers, spreading cluster bomblets over wide areas. More missiles crashed into known command and control centers, buildings collapsing under the concussive blasts. Explosions rocked the capital city. One cruise missile struck the central tower of the Presidential Office Building, a second one sailed through the main entrance before exploding inside. Brick, mortar, marble, glass, and concrete were blasted onto the ten-lane avenue in front. The tower collapsed like a felled oak, crashing onto the thoroughfare.

More hit the Ministry of National Defense, spraying chunks of concrete across the wide square. Targeting Taiwan's leadership, missiles flew over the walls of the presidential residence to shatter the main buildings. The houses of the general staff were also hit, though none were injured, as they were already ensconced within command bunkers. The casualties from the assassination attempts were mostly staff and soldiers of the Sixth Special Corps standing guard, although in a few homes, the bodies of family members lay in smoking ruins.

The rumbling blasts echoing through the city were hardly felt in the deep Heng Shan Military Command Center complex. The center lay hidden under a hollowed mountain that resembled the United States Cheyenne Mountain Complex. Tunnels connected to other military bases and resources and were impervious to 20 kilo-ton nuclear yields.

The focus of China's initial attack centered around anti-air defenses and the command-and-control structure. Antenna farms adjacent to communication centers were annihilated, along with central telephone exchanges. Cell phone centers were also on the initial target lists. Had China been able to hit every target, Taiwan's ability to regroup and organize would have been sorely hurt. But the defenses downed a number of the first cruise missiles, thus preserving much of their infrastructure.

All of the airports were rendered inoperative with their runways cratered. As soon as the attack was over, bulldozers and personnel moved out of bunkers and began the restoration process. Within two hours, the runways were all marginally back in operation. It didn't take much to destroy the paved strips, but it also didn't take much to restore their functionality.

Even though all of Taiwan's fighter inventory was on the east coast air base of Chiashan, crews worked to restore all of the runways and repair what they could of the environment. If China wanted to waste weapons with taking out bases that Taiwan wasn't using, then that was fine; it might possibly save the destruction of more important assets. Repairing the damage made it appear that Taiwan was using the bases, thus inviting them to be on future target lists, forcing China to waste more of their rocket forces.

Passing over the strait in a low earth orbit, a Chinese

Yaogan-series reconnaissance satellite scanned Taiwan and its outlying island chain. Analysts pored over the high-resolution pictures to determine the extent of damage delivered by the opening cruise missiles' attack. Damage assessments were disseminated to the military commands and target lists were updated.

Although the attacks hit some of their targets, the only truly effective strikes were those against surface structures. Blast debris fanned out from the government buildings in Taipei and photos depicting the airfields presented cratered runways. Craters also marred the tops of the fortified hangars, but without any sign of penetration. Uprooted trees lay around blast sites like pick-up-sticks, but that was the extent of the damage coming from China's attempt to destroy the underground refuges for Taiwan's defensive systems. Some remarked that the only truly significant outcome of the initial attack was that it reduced the number of Taiwan's anti-aircraft missiles, which were already limited.

Heat signatures from smoldering fires marked the ruins of stationary assets such as the close-in surface-to-air defensive emplacements, many of them surrounding the military bases that were struck. Several of the larger bases had coils of smoke spiraling skyward from missile impacts. Many command and communications buildings were piles of rubble, rebar-studded chunks of concrete protruding from collapsed slabs and freshly turned over dirt mounds.

On the ground, coming from deep within several crumpled structures, the faint cries of those trapped and injured could be heard. Streams of water from broken pipes ran down through cracks and crevices, the dripping trickles intermingling with the moans of the injured and the occasional shouts for help. Crews emerged from their shelters into a changed environment, with ruins all around. Instead of the warm glows of electricity that were indications of life, they were greeted by stark moonlight. A mix of silver highlights and alternating shadows deeper than black made for eerie scenes in the broken landscape. Some crews were sent to restoring base functionalities while others began the hard work of trying to save those trapped under tons of rubble.

After China's target lists were updated, orders were disseminated to rocket battalions and hence to batteries scattered across the countryside. Hydraulic motors hummed as transporter erector vehicles angled their loads toward the stars. Data was transmitted to individual missiles which sent corroborating information in return. Countdown times began, the times for each battery different in order to attain specific time on targets and to mass the weapons to overwhelm Taiwan's defenses.

With some of Taiwan's communication centers offline due to antenna farms being destroyed, it was hoped that the coordination of defensive fire would be decreased. The deterioration of the command-and-control structure was China's primary goal. But they also wanted to diminish the anti-air defenses so that China could claim complete air supremacy over the island.

Starting with the western-most batteries, cruise missiles began launching from their mobile vehicles. Similar to a wave at a ballpark, missiles launched from tubes in a ripple effect that slowly spread to the east. For the second time that night, a bevy of ground attack cruise missiles raced into dark to speed toward the Taiwan Strait like a migrating flock.

Crossing over beaches and rocky cliffs, the flock flew over waves undulating in the moonlight. They sought the lands which lay beyond the horizon. Hallway through their journey, they were again met by a horde coming out to answer them. The two sides met in a mighty collision. The suicidal projectiles coming from the island sought to destroy themselves against the sides of the invaders, defending their homeland from invasion.

Fisherman rising over crests and lowering into troughs witnessed flashes of light in all directions. Those were followed seconds later by sharp explosions that reverberated over the waters. Some of those plying their trade witnessed towering columns of water rise above the strait as high-speed projectiles plowed into the swells. The weapons sent out in defense were all wiped out within a minute, leaving many of their targets settling toward Neptune's locker. However, like before, missiles made it through the defenses to strike at the island again.

High-speed weapons slammed into the thin hulls of warships still anchored in harbors or attached to piers. The smaller vessels quickly succumbed to the warheads detonating deep within. Large gashes ripped down the hulls, the dark waters of the harbor spilling inside. The inrushing water gathered momentum as the ships listed. Mooring lines snapped, the thick ropes whipping violently through the dark as the mighty warships slowly rolled over.

The runways up and down Taiwan's west side were hit again, undoing the progress of the work crews. Craters rimmed with hunks of pavement and the twisted metal of repair efforts again made the surfaces unable to be used. On the eastern side of the island, Taiwan's remaining attack fighters stayed in their underground shelters. Following the night air battles days ago and fending off China's initial wave of cruise missiles, long-range air-to-air missiles had become scarce.

Citizens of the major cities lining the western coast woke to explosions rocking the cities, most of them concentrated on the nearby airfields. Forested ridge lines overlooking the metropolis areas also received their share of attention as the Chinese weapons sought out overlooking defensive positions. As fright seized hold of the denizens, hallways and streets became crowded with people seeking shelter. Above the general commotion, many heard the high-pitched whines of jet engines as they crossed overhead, much like Londoners heard the sound of the V-1 rockets in World War II. The passing sound of the cruise missiles was followed by echoing explosions rolling over homes and businesses.

Balls of fire soared skyward as the missiles detonated, sometimes followed by powerful secondary blasts. Tracers from weapons systems arced into the sky, the gunners seeking to get a lucky hit. Several systems tracked the incoming missiles, the tracers following a more defined path as the guns adjusted.

Fiery streaks raced aloft as short-range surface-to-air missiles locked onto the low-flying targets. Several fireballs erupted above populated areas, the defensive fire downing Chinese weapons. Hot shrapnel rained down on people fleeing to underground shelters.

Numerous missiles again hammered at the Heng Shan underground complex, attempting to knock out the central command center. Lights dimmed for brief moments in some sections from the continuous hammering topside. Generators were brought online to ensure a constant flow of power.

Several taller hills around the cities were hit, the cruise missiles blasting known cell phone tower locations. Suddenly, as if a tap were shut off, the tracers and trails of flame ceased. No longer heard were the sounds of missiles passing low overhead. Small fires burned in the wooded hills, spirals of smoke drifting upward in the moonlight. In the cities, sirens howled and the acrid odor of burning buildings wafted down the streets. It took some time for the all-clear signal to reach those huddled in shelters. Many were hesitant to return to their homes following the second missile attack from China, unsure if there was going to be a third.

* * * * * *

"Bandit One Zero, turn right heading two seven zero, descend and maintain three hundred. Contact Sugar One on three three five point four."

"Copy. Right to two seven zero. Departing one eight zero for three hundred. Switching to three three five point four."

Captain Jeff Hoffman turned the control wheel. The C-130 begrudgingly rolled to the right, the near full moon drifting across the windshield. In the turn, Jeff pulled back on the throttles, the drone that had been infusing the aircraft for the past hour and a half changing pitch as the power was reduced. Strung out in a line behind Hoffman, seven other 130s followed suit.

As the lead pilot, Jeff sent the others to the new

frequency given by the E-3 circling a couple hundred miles to the east. They were about to check-in with the Taiwanese E-2 coordinating the island defenses. Flying out from Kadena Air Force Base, the eight C-130s had been placed in a holding pattern while China's missile attack on Taiwan was underway. Once the missiles tracks vanished, and without additional launches being observed, the 130s were released to begin a low-level ingress to the island.

Moonlight highlighted the constant-speed propellers as they rotated, the upper wings and fuselage bathed in the reflected glow. Dropping out of the heights toward the dark void of the Philippine Sea, Jeff pondered what the next hour would bring. He was currently two hundred miles from Taiwan's eastern shores, hoping to be able to sneak under the radar to deliver the hardware strapped in the cargo compartment.

The mountains running the length of Taiwan should provide some cover from Chinese search radars as the stream of 130s drew near. Jeff's concern was any airborne AWACs aircraft China might have aloft. If they saw the inbound Hercules, they would undoubtedly direct fighters to intercept. There was also the possibility that China had some of their stealth attack fighters patrolling the Taiwan Strait or even over the island itself, although Taiwan's ground-based radars should be able to pick those up. Generally, any nation's fifth generation aircraft operating in stealth mode were difficult to see outside of twenty miles.

After checking in with the formation to ensure they were all on the correct frequency, Jeff contacted the Taiwanese Hawkeye.

"Sugar One, Bandit, flight of eight, on freq passing through fourteen thousand."

"Copy, Bandit. Radar contact. You are cleared to proceed," Sugar One responded.

If China chose to launch another attack while the 130s were inbound, then the ingress would be aborted and the 130s would return to their initial holding pattern. The world became green-tinged as the captain pulled down his night vision goggles. The co-pilot was responsible to call off instrument readings when necessary, backing up what Jeff was seeing on the outside.

With radar altimeter calls from the co-pilot, Jeff pulled back on the control wheel while advancing the throttles. The propellors changed their pitch angle and began to again pull the aircraft through the air. The Philippine Sea swells seemed as if they would sweep up and slap the underside of the 130, the large cargo aircraft seeming to skip across the surface.

With each passing mile, Jeff expected to feel the aircraft shake and hear the sharp clap of a missile exploding nearby. He was constantly leaning forward, scanning the skies for a fiery trail that would betray an inbound missile, but he was relieved to only see the shimmer of the moon hanging overhead.

Jeff was finally able to pick out the dark outline of land rising from the flatter expanse of the sea. Taiwan lay ahead. Radar showed the other cargo aircraft strung out behind, each one maintaining a mile separation. Bringing the 130 in a southerly arc, Jeff still scanned the heavens. If they were going to be hit, it would likely come while they were lining up for their supply drop.

A tall line of ridges rose to the west and still the threat sensors remained silent. Crossing over a rocky shoreline, Jeff brought the 130 to a northerly heading. The onboard computer tracked the drop point and gave a heading based on weather conditions. The land below was dark, either due to China's attacks taking out the power grid or from a mandated "light's out" policy. Either way, Hoffman saw a darkened landscape below his aircraft.

At the initial point, he moved the four throttles forward and started a climb. The aircraft had already been depressurized, so there wasn't any delay with lowering the rear ramp. In the back, the roar of the engines magnified as the top door raised inside and the rear ramp lowered into position. The crew chief unsecured the load and double-checked the parachute attachments.

Holding the aircraft steady, Jeff maintained the airspeed, altitude, and heading as precise as he could. Wind coming over the mountains caused a little turbulence as the 130 droned along the eastern coastline. In the view of the NVGs, he saw the runway environment that was to be the target drop. Machinery was pouring out from underground shelters, looking much like ants storming from a kicked nest. The runway, taxiways, and ramp areas were all heavily cratered, and crews were racing to repair the damage before the next missile attack.

The computer judged the timing right for the conditions and the green light lit. A drogue chute was dispatched into the slipstream. Inflating, it pulled a larger chute from its pack. It, in turn, pulled the entire palleted loads from the interior. Jeff held the 130 as steady as possible as the load shifted, altering the center of gravity. The aircraft wanted to climb as the cargo shifted aft on its way out the rear door. From the rear of the Hercules, supplies exited the aircraft and swung under huge parachutes as they drifted toward the ground.

Follow-on C-130s droned over the Chiashan airfield, dropping load after load of AIM-120 air-to-air missiles. The supply drops might not reverse Taiwan's shortage of the long-range weapons, but those that arrived were greatly welcomed. On the airfield, crews raced out of shelters to break down the loads and return them to the hangars before the next wave of attacks. Inside, personnel immediately began the process of arming the remainder of Taiwan's air defense aircraft.

*   *   *   *   *   *

Over a long and sleepless night for Taiwan, China sent one additional swarm of cruise missiles. It was with a sense of relief that the island nation emerged from shelters into the dawn of a new day. For whatever reason, daylight reduced the terror that night attacks brought, as if the sun's rays could somehow lessen the explosive power of the weapons.

So, it was with a collective release of pent-up breath that people watched the sun crest the mountains in a display of hopeful color. Ridges were darkly silhouetted against a painted sky. The eastern half of the island appeared to be on fire, but one they welcomed. The sun climbed, spreading light and warmth across the nation. Varying in density and volume, pillars of smoke scattered across the Taiwanese wilderness rose to taint the morning sky. Denser columns from burning buildings and smoldering ruins climbed above populated areas, spreading out to eventually bathe the island in an orange-brown hue.

A stunned nation wandered down rubble-strewn streets, wondering what they should do. Was it their duty to go to work as if it were a normal day? Should they head to government offices to help with the clean-up or volunteer in some other capacity? Fire departments were busy attempting to put out the fires, doing their best to prevent them from spreading. Search and rescue personnel were responding to downed structures to see if they could save anyone pinned in the debris. Other emergency services were deployed to restore order and to begin cleaning up the streets, as if these ordinary actions could somehow right the overwhelming destruction.

All the while, eyes kept straying to the smoke-filled skies, wary for a return of the missiles. Some startled at any sudden sound, their fight or flight response taut with apprehension. Those manning the underground command and control bunkers noted that port facilities and airfield infrastructures, with the exception of the runway environment, were free of damage. It's not like that was news, as Taiwan's military leadership knew that China would need both facilities intact in order to conduct a successful invasion. Without working ports and airfields, China would find it difficult to maintain a flow of necessary supplies. Although the port facilities were rigged with explosives, Taiwan couldn't afford to blow them just yet, as they needed their own inflow, even though very few ships would now risk docking in their ports.

Chapter Six

Andersen Air Force Base, Guam
30 July, 2021

Moonlight stretched across the runway environment, frosting the tips of the grass growing between the runways. With the colored lights outlining the runway and taxiways, the airfield almost seemed like it could be part of a festive scene. Most of the damage from China's attack had been cleared. There was evidence that repairs were being made to the fuel farm and construction had begun on the ruined hangars.

Vans raced across tarmacs, pausing for clearance to cross the active runway. Each slowed and came to a halt in front of the B-1B and B-52H bombers parked between the two runways. With bags in hand, the crews crawled under the aircraft and disappeared into the bellies of the massive war machines.

The B-1Bs were sleek with their wings folded back, looking eager to leap into the air and slice effortlessly through the thin, high-altitude atmosphere. The B-52Hs had a charm of their own, but appeared more as workhorses with twelve AGM-158B cruise missiles hanging from wing hardpoints. The historic bomber looked like it punched its way through the air rather than conforming to the physics of flight. The BUFF (Big Ugly Fat Fellow, as it was endearingly called), had eight additional Joint Air to Surface Standoff Missiles (JASSM) stowed internally. Unseen, the B-1B Lancers each had twenty-four of the cruise missiles tucked into its three internal weapons bays.

As each crew member settled into their positions, checklists were started. Soon, the quiet of the night was broken by the roar of jet engines coming to life. Lights blurred from exhaust plumes, the ramps smelling of burned jet fuel. As Taiwan's defenses were attempting to deal with yet another Chinese missile attack, bombers stationed on Guam started taxiing out of their parking places.

In the night, B-52s lined up and began a mass exodus from the island base. Thunderous roars marked the departure of each heavy bomber, their eight engines forcing the heavily laden bomber into the air. Dark silhouettes faded and then merged with the night.

Once the Stratofortresses lunged skyward, the B-1Bs began their takeoffs in more glamorous fashion. Afterburners lit up the darkness, the flames marking the progress of the Lancers as they accelerated down the runway. The airfield was a continuous flow of departing aircraft, reminiscent of the nuclear alerts during the cold war.

As the last B-1B thundered into the air, the fiery trail of the afterburners cutting off and the sound of the aircraft receding, quiet returned to the base. Operations Plan 5015 was an inclusive one that incorporated several contingencies, one of them involving a preemptive strike against any North Korean invasion threat. The bombers, carrying more firepower than some nations possessed, were the first aircraft to get airborne as the operations plan commenced.

*   *   *   *   *   *

Osan Air Force Base, South Korea
30 July, 2021

As the citizens of Taiwan were emerging from their shelters, nearly a thousand miles to the north, a gray-painted, four-engine jet rolled down a parallel taxiway. The near windowless aircraft marched past hardened shelters housing F-16s under their protective covering. Inside the hangars, personnel clambered over, around, and under the attack fighters, readying them for their next flights. Missiles hung on every pylon and wingtip, the agile jets looking both deadly and overloaded. Pilots climbed attached ladders, snugging themselves into confined cockpits.

The large enhanced 707 taxied past the activity in the hangars, past a widened area designed as a staging area. One each side, four F-16s were lined up and waiting. Helmeted pilots reclined in their seats and watched as the large E-8C JSTARS rolled past.

The E-8C's nose compressed as the pilot braked at the hold line to runway 09R. Exhaust trailed behind the four idling turbofans, faint shadows from the moving fumes forming irregular patterns on the concrete.

"Osan Ground, Ronin One Zero ready for takeoff, runway zero niner right."

"Roger, Ronin One Zero. Hold short and contact Osan tower on three zero eight point eight," Osan ground control radioed.

"Three zero eight point eight."

After switching, the pilot contacted the tower. "Osan tower, Ronin One Zero holding short, runway zero niner right."

"Copy, Ronin One Zero. You are cleared for takeoff, runway zero niner right."

The pilot moved the four throttles, the aircraft grudgingly rolling forward. As the aircraft turned to align with the centerline, the pilots squinted into the early morning sun sitting low in the sky. Moving the throttles to full power, the E-8C picked up speed as it rolled down the runway, the center lines passing under the nose faster and faster. The nose wheels lifted then finally the mains. The ground battle management aircraft climbed into the clear morning skies, ready to direct offensive operations against North Korea.

* * * * * *

The JSTARS aircraft took station to the south southeast of Seoul. The operators within the fuselage plotted vehicle movements on the other side of the DMZ, marking ground targets in among the massive North Korean staging areas.

Once the command post had the information the officers felt was needed, word went out to initiate phase one of the operational plan. Drones that had been circling were directed north along predetermined routes, focusing primarily on the western sectors of the Korean Peninsula. Their job was to present a force of aircraft on attack runs, forcing North Korean search and attack radars to become active.

As the drones neared the DMZ, North Korean operators became nervous as the screens depicted a multitude of aircraft streaking north. Having observed plenty of American and South Korean simulated attack runs in the past, officers in command posts calmed their air defense operators to "wait and see" readiness.

The radar blips approached the border and then crossed into the forbidden airspace. With the hostile aircraft crossing the frontier, commanders alerted outposts and additional radars came online. "Wait and see" was over. With the invasion of North Korean airspace, orders were handed down to the air defense units, freeing them to engage the incoming threats.

From mobile trucks, missiles were fired. Trails of smoke erupted across the entire frontier as North Korea launched their long-range KN-06 missiles. Shorter range ground-to-air missiles soon flew off their rails, adding their firepower to the layered defenses the north had along their border.

With the first weapons racing skyward, the drones turned back south. South of the DMZ, F-16s out of Osan and Kunsan Air Force Bases streaked along on low-level routes, scooting toward the DMZ. Miles south of the demarcation line, the Falcons zoomed skyward. With the data replicated from the E-8C, the AGM-88E advanced antiradiation guided missiles received targeting information.

As the North Korean surface-to-air missiles were homing in on the retreating drones, antiradiation missiles flew off the Falcon rails. The passive sensors found the specific radar signals precipitated from radar vehicles and installations and homed in. The F-16s, upon completing their attack runs, spit out countermeasures as they conducted high-G maneuvers to reverse their courses and dive back toward the low-level environment.

Black puffs marked where the air defenses of North Korea were successful, the Mach 4-plus weapons destroying the swarm of drones sent over the DMZ. The AGM-88Es sped over the distance, arcing down out of the morning skies. Following the signals to their origin, laser proximity fuses detonated the fragmentation warheads. Shrapnel ripped through radar dishes and the vehicles they were attached to. Blood splattered over screens as heated metal tore into flesh and bone.

Seeing the strategy, North Korean commanders ordered many of the mobile radar stations to go offline in order to preserve them for the coming offensive. The AARGMs that suddenly lost their target switched to their active mode, scanning the area with infrared sensors and locating their previous targets. When the radars were turned off, the antiradiation missiles were able to continue homing in on the radar sites. Balls of fire and smoke denoted successful attacks, the mobile units being hammered under the onslaught from dozens of missiles.

*   *   *   *   *   *

The bomber formations temporarily assigned to Andersen Air Force Base flew north, following the general path of the outer island chains that separated the Philippine Sea from the Pacific Ocean. The goal was to remain out of range of China's long-range threats and to avoid radar detection from any AWACs aircraft they might have airborne.

Major Wayne Blythe leaned back in his seat, attempting to stretch his back. Looking through the cockpit window to his left, he saw the last of the moon's rays as they fanned out over an endless sea of black. The yellow-hued moon was split by the curvature of the horizon and was in the process of being swallowed.

Off of the nose, a sparse string of lights marched north, coming from the island communities on the east side of the Philippine Sea. Wayne watched as the moon slid further below the horizon, and then unceremoniously dipped from sight. The lack of moonlight opened a greater vista, the heavenly stars taking their turn onstage.

On long flights, conversation within the B-52 ebbed and flowed. During the quiet moments, there was just the vibration of the airframe leaving each crew member alone with their musings. Wayne thought about the preemptive strikes that were about to be conducted against North Korea. The previous war on the peninsula didn't really receive much in the way of notoriety, crammed as it was between World War II and the Vietnam War.

Not privy to all the information, Wayne only knew that the north had massed troops near the DMZ. That might just be their usual posturing, but considering the current conflict with China, he didn't think this was the North just saber-rattling. It would make sense that North Korea would take the opportunity to launch an invasion while the United States was otherwise occupied. Whatever their intent, it was enough of a threat that America was launching a preemptive strike.

With the sky brightening to the east, Wayne thought about all the other aircraft flying in formations behind him. His thoughts then wandered to the troops on the ground, thankful for his position nine miles above the earth. This strike against the North might just be enough to cause them to leave their bivouacs and start their invasion. That meant an ugly ground war that the soldiers were to endure. As far as Wayne understood things, the ground troops had to hold out for two to three months before help arrived. That sounded an awful lot like the soldiers were being used as cannon fodder.

The light blue of the eastern sky slowly turned to a mass of color as the sun neared the horizon. The colors swirled and changed like a kaleidoscope, nature continually painting its marvels on an ever-changing canvass. A flare of yellow shot into the cockpit as the tip of the sun peeked above the corner of the earth. Several minutes later, the rays colored the rest of the world, turning a land of shadows into one of substance.

Ahead, the spread of the sun's glow brought the east coast of Japan into sharper focus. Wayne readjusted himself, tightening his harness. The DME on the nav instruments counted down as the B-52 neared a waypoint. Passing over the lat/long coordinate, the Stratofortress began a gradual turn to the left, the rising sun passing to the rear of the aircraft. Crossing over the narrow width of Japan and entering the Sea of

Japan, the intercom again came alive, this time with the crew members reciting checklist items.

High over the Sea of Japan, the B-52 shook as the first AGM-158 Joint Air-to-Surface Standoff Missile dropped from one of the wing hardpoints. The air-launched cruise missile seemed to float down from the BUFF. The stubby wings deployed into the slipstream as a puff of smoke signaled the start of the turbofan engine. Slowly, the missile started pulling ahead of the BUFF as the weapon continued its descent.

Across the span of sky, more AGM-158As and AGM-158Bs fell from the B-52s, rippling from the hardpoints. Wayne countered the aircraft's wanting to rise with each release of the two thousand-plus-pound weapons. With the weapons bay doors open, a sequence of the cruise missiles fell from the rotary launchers.

As the final projectile fell free, Wayne started a turn to the south, following the preplanned egress route. The intercom was all business as the crew went through the post-launch checklist.

"Weapon Control Panel LOCK/UNLOCK Switch?" the copilot read.

"LOCK," the radar navigator answered.

"Master Fault Light?"

"ON, said the radar navigator.

Munitions Consent Panel LOCK/UNLOCK Switch?"

"LOCK," Wayne replied.

"Master Fault Light?"

"OFF," the radar navigator stated.

"MISSILE LNCH MODE Switch?"

"Manual."

"Jettison Power & Jettison Control Circuit Breakers?"

"Out."

"FRMT-7?"

"Entered."

"Left Pylon and right pylon Location and ALL Station?"

"Selected"

"Classified Data Erase?"

"Entered."

The system erased the classified data associated with each missile, notifications appearing at the bottom of multiple displays when the data erasure was complete. Verifications came when each erasure was complete.

"Missile status?"

The displays were checked that the missile status had changed, and that the alignment and targeting status was blank.

"MIU Power Switches?"

"OFF."

"Post-strike checklist complete."

Crossing south over the island of Japan, Wayne then turned the B-52 to the southeast for the hours long flight back to Andersen Air Force Base.

Following in the footsteps of the B-52s, formations of B-1Bs soared across the clear skies, sunlight touching on sweptback wings. As each formation approached their launch point, doors under the fuselages swung open. Similar to a string of bombs falling free, twenty-four cruise missiles dropped from each aircraft. Descending, the carpet of cruise missiles flew east toward the shores of North Korea.

* * * * * *

Morning sunlight danced on a blanket of blue in a vibrant display of sparkling glitter. Across the East Sea, fishing vessels rode the undulating swells, the sun promising another day of sweltering work.

In the distance, a disturbance in the water drew the eyes of one such fishing vessel. Something rose from the depths, emerging into the sunlight with a roar. White smoke spread out across the surface, a cylindrical beast clawing its way free as if it had been trapped in an underwater dungeon.

A long jet of flame pushed the missile higher, a deep-throated roar reverberating across the water. An arcing trail of smoke marked the path as the Tomahawk cruise missile flattened its ascent, the rocket motor cutting out as the turbofan motor took over. Seconds later, another long-range land attack missile burst free, powering its way into the air. Over the next minutes, over one hundred Tomahawk missiles broke through the surface and raced eastward at nearly six hundred miles per hour.

"Missile away. That completes the launch sequence," the XO stated.

"Copy. Recover from launch. Right standard rudder to heading two zero zero, increase speed to fifteen knots. Make your depth three hundred," Commander Gambino ordered.

"Right standard rudder to two zero zero, speed fifteen knots. Ten degree-down bubble to three hundred," the executive officer repeated.

Off the east coast of North Korea, the USS *Ohio* slid into deeper waters after firing most of the cruise missiles in her inventory. Escorting the SSGN was an LA-Class fast attack submarine, the USS *Topeka*. The two boats silently crept to the southwest, looking to cross out of the Sea of Japan via the strait between South Korea and Japan. From there, the *Ohio* was scheduled to rendezvous with the USS *Frank Cable* to rearm.

* * * * * *

A wake trailed aft of the Najin-class frigate as the North Korean naval vessel sailed slowly up North Korea's eastern coast. To the west, a dark outline of land lay low on the horizon. On the opposite side of the warship, a watch officer squinted as he stared in the general direction of the rising sun. Looking through a powerful set of binoculars, the brightness made it difficult to focus for any length of time. Thinking the dark dots that suddenly appeared in his magnified vision were from looking into the glare, the officer took the binoculars away from his eyes to readjust.

Looking again in the same direction, the dots were larger and growing. With the warship only traveling at five knots, there wasn't much of a breeze flowing past the North Korean naval officer. That made it easier to hear the barely audible rumble coming from the objects racing toward him.

With each passing second, the objects grew larger. Almost as if the ship were a lone wrangler standing in the midst of a stampede, the flying objects flew north and south of the frigate, scarcely a hundred feet above the light swells. Raising the alarm, others had gathered to watch. Passing the vessel, the sound of the engines driving the thirty or more missiles faded until there was only the slap of waves against the hull. It was clear to all that cruise missiles were headed toward targets in North Korea.

The ship contacted the headquarters of the East Sea Fleet, which in turn passed word to Pyongyang. The alert from the frigate, and others sailing up and down the eastern seaboard, would come at nearly the same time as the one being passed up from the DMZ. The missiles, traveling at nearly six hundred miles an hour, would reach their targets in ten to fifteen minutes. Orders were slow to be issued from the centralized leadership due to communication difficulties, stemming from initial attacks conducted against North Korea.

* * * * * *

45,000 feet over the Sea of Japan
30 July, 2021

The sea eight miles below looked like a piece of blue wrapping paper that had been wadded up and spread flat again. Directly above the darkly-colored flying wing, the blue morning skies was darker. Some stars were even visible. Through the windscreen stretched a long north-south peninsula, the arbitrary lines that marked boundaries invisible from this height and distance.

Captain James Blackwood took his eyes from the distant shores of the Korean Peninsula, focusing on an alert sent by the pilot alert system. The LIDAR (Light Detection and Ranging) system had alerted to the detection of contrail formation and recommended a change in altitude. Blackwood pushed the twin throttles forward and initiated a climb to flight level 480 (48,000 feet).

James yawned, fighting off the tiredness from the long flight from Whiteman Air Force Base. Due to the requirement for specialized hangars, the flight from Missouri had to be accomplished in a single hop. With each pilot taking turns sleeping, the hours long flight from the middle of the Pacific Ocean had been a wearying one with nothing but the dark of the night for company. Now, with the target finally in sight, James was finding the weariness difficult to shake.

The protruding sections of land grew steadily closer in the windshield. James and the mission commander sitting in the right seat were the leading edge of the planned preemptive strike against North Korea; the first in. That meant that North Korea's layered air defenses would be fully intact.

However, James wasn't too worried about being picked up on radar. They had already "stealthed up," a secret maneuver meant to keep the aircraft off enemy radars. Even the lower frequency S and L band radars, those which had greater successes seeing fifth generation stealth fighters, had trouble locating the B-2 Spirit bomber. That was due to the continuous curvature design of the aircraft and lack of control surfaces. Stealth aircraft like the F-35 and F-22 weren't invisible like the B-2. Those fighters had only minimal signatures, which couldn't be picked up on higher frequency radars until within about twenty miles. But being nearly invisible to the radar systems of North Korea didn't mean that James could ignore the threat sensors.

James descended a few hundred feet when the aircraft system alerted him that the optimum light condition was there. That system analyzed the surrounding lighting conditions and offered recommended altitudes by which the aircraft would be nearly invisible from ground-based optics. The problem would come when the weapons bay doors opened and the aircraft suddenly became visible to radar systems, flaring on the screens like a beacon.

The plan for the high-altitude attack was to deliver the bombs tucked into the internal bay then stealth up again before surface-to-air missiles could be fired. Or, if any were launched, then the B-2s hoped to fade off of radar systems, causing the missiles to lose track. The aircraft also greatly reduced its heat signature by introducing frigid atmospheric air into the exhaust before it was expelled from the bomber.

The B-2 went "feet dry" as it crossed over the eastern shores of North Korea. Although he was unable to see any others, James knew that seventeen other Spirit bombers were spread out over the Sea of Japan. All were spaced apart so that they might arrive over their targets at the same time. That would minimize North Korea's response and hopefully confuse their air defenses by all eighteen bogeys appearing on their radars at once.

Passing high over North Korea's mountainous eastern side, James saw the metropolis of Pyongyang spread out on both sides of the Taedong River. Turning to a course heading northwest of the capital city, Blackwood spied their target lying on a long plateau cut into sharp ridges.

Having completed their checklist, there was nothing to do but sit back and monitor the systems as the B-2 flew along a plotted course. The system would calculate the drop point based on aircraft speed, altitude, ambient temperatures, and wind direction and velocity. His stomach tensed as he felt the drag tug at the aircraft as the weapons bay doors slid into their open positions. They were now visible to the search radars certain to be operating near North Korea's capital city.

Sure enough, seconds after feeling the soft clunk of the door locking open, threat sensors indicated that they were being painted by several search radars. It wouldn't take long for that information to be passed to fire control radars, and then missiles would streak skyward. James glanced nine miles down to see if he could pick out any white streamers coming from launching surface-to-air missiles.

Clunks, felt rather than heard, indicated that the B-2 had reached its drop point. Two GBU-57s fell from the weapons bay, the noses tipping downward as the massive ordinance penetrators fell through the thin atmosphere. Guided by lasers, the thirty-thousand-pound bunker busters dropped toward the Ryongsong Residence, the principal quarters and administrative buildings for the North Korean leader. Underneath was a suspected command and communications center. Although that would be the stated target if the subject came up on the world stage, the United States also hoped to remove the head, or several heads, of North Korea's leadership.

The heavy bombs fell through the clear skies, accelerating to their terminal velocity. Fins along the body altered the penetrators' courses as variable winds attempted to knock the MOPs off course. One bomb crashed through the roof of the residence, slammed through several floors, and vanished below the marbled first floor. Pieces of ceiling, pipes, and insulation fell from the holes created by the giant penetrator.

Designed to punch through two hundred feet of concrete, the GBU-57 plunged through the basement levels, entering the underground chambers beneath the primary residence. There, the five thousand-plus-pound warhead detonated.

Underground facilities collapsed under the pressure. Buried conduits containing electrical and environmental systems were ripped apart. The earth heaved upward, driven by the concussive wave following the massive explosion. Inside the central residence building, massive amounts of dirt blasted upward. Following in the wake of the upheaval, a giant fireball rose through the developing crater. Walls vanished from the extreme forces. Inestimable collections of rare and ancient art simply vanished.

Released from its confines, the fiery blast raced up and outward, devouring everything in its path. A gout of flame and smoke rolled out of what was left of the roof, racing into the morning skies. The palace, its foundations and load-bearing walls undermined by the monstrous blast, partially collapsed, trapping many of the staff in the ruins. Some managed to hang on until rescuers arrived, but many more succumbed to the poisonous smoke that filtered into every gap.

The second massive penetrator crashed into the Kangdong Residence situated just a few miles to the northwest of the Ryongsong Palace. This summer home and secondary residence of the North's leader was also thought to house an underground communications center. In a very similar set of sequences, the central building was left a smoldering ruin.

Although it seemed like a long time, the weapons bay doors were only open for a few seconds. The B-2, which briefly appeared on North Korean radars, abruptly vanished almost as soon as it appeared. Search radars scanned the areas, frantically attempting to locate the eighteen blips which had suddenly materialized, but the mysterious radar tracks were gone.

The massive ground penetrators struck targets scattered across the North Korean Peninsula. Centralized command, control, and communication centers were hit. The major chemical weapon storage centers at Anbyon and Masan-dong were obliterated, deadly sarin and VX gases seeping out of the ruins. Even if some of the weapons survived the hits, it would be some time before they could be excavated and used.

In addition, known nuclear storage and biological weapon facilities received their share of the massive bunker busters. The greatest fear of the United States was that the weapons of mass destruction horded by the North would be used by an unstable leader. It was imperative to remove that danger.

When the open bay door lights winked off and the B-2 returned to its stealth mode, the threat sensors went quiet. James turned the Spirit east. It wasn't long before the bomber reached the eastern coast and flew out over the Sea of Japan. The first strike against North Korea had ended, leaving behind a regime that would be slow to respond to any emergency, let alone control a widening battlefield. That was just one of the pitfalls of a dictatorship that demanded centralized control.

The initial attacks against North Korea's infrastructure were shortly followed by cruise missiles that were already in the air.

*   *   *   *   *   *

As the F-16s were flying sorties against North Korea's anti-aircraft defenses along the DMZ north of Seoul, cruise missiles fired from the bombers flying out of Guam began to arrive. Using terrain contour mapping, the numerous missiles attempted to avoid North Korea's radar defenses as they weaved through valleys that cut through the mountainous terrain.

Some of the weapons were picked up by search radars sitting atop ridge lines, the data sent back to targeting systems hidden in the rough landscape. Short-range missiles rose from clearings peppering the wrinkled landscape, arcing into the morning skies. The anti-air missiles turned as they sought out the threats racing along valley floors.

Small explosions marked successful intercepts, shrapnel raining down on remote villages or lost forever in the dense foliage covering steep hillsides. With each successful destruction of a Tomahawk, five more made it through the defenses. Missiles raced out of the ravines to streak over targets, their guidance systems analyzing the terrain and target before delivering their mixed warheads.

The problem that had faced planners was that much of North Korea's massed forces were holed up in tunnels cut into the mountains. One major North Korean underground endeavor was the construction of a series of troop bunkers near the DMZ. Each of the eight hundred-plus bunkers were built to conceal infantry brigades until the start of an invasion and were capable of housing up to two thousand fully armed combat soldiers.

As with every other country, underground facilities were built to shelter North Korea's leadership. The latest estimates were that six to eight thousand such shelters were scattered across the country, making it difficult to determine where the command structure might be located.

Equally alarming were the hardened artillery sites (HARTS) located just north of the DMZ. These bunkers were tunnels dug into the sides of the mountains to provide artillery support for an invasion of the south, or to provide direct fire into the city of Seoul. These HARTS made it possible for large caliber guns or rocket systems to be fired from the mouth of a cave and then withdrawn underground to reload. Due to the difficulty in locating these hardened sites, the exact number was unknown, but it was believed that there were up to five hundred.

Three of the north's military air bases also had underground hangars, with one even boasting a mile-long runway that ran underneath a mountain. North Korea's underground fortresses, including the sites where weapons of mass destruction were situated, were difficult to hit.

However, the number of forces that the north had sent south were too many for the caverns to hold. Many of the artillery units, tanks, and soldiers were massed in above-ground encampments. On the periphery of these bivouacs, missiles ignited and sped off rails, the glowing tracers streaking aloft as North Korean air defenses came alive.

Tomahawks flew through the anti-air curtain thrown up around the massed forces. Some of the weapons released canisters of cluster munitions, the mixed bag of anti-personnel and anti-armor bomblets falling among men and equipment. Considering the threat of chemical weapons being fired into Seoul and military centers, the artillery units were the focus of many attacks.

The air crackled with a series of sharp explosions as the cluster munitions detonated. Shrapnel cut through artillery units, turning many soldiers near the vehicles into bloodied pulps clothed in stained uniforms. Screams swept through the encampments as other cruise missiles arrived. Small craters formed throughout, the churned dirt mixing with the bodies of conscripts. Men and women ran in blind panic, many holding nearly severed limbs or clutching life-threatening wounds. With explosion after explosion peppering the area, some became shell-shocked and aimlessly wandered, their minds unable to process the slaughter around them.

Other cruise missiles arrived carrying unitary warheads. Those identified their individual targets through their guidance software packages. Giant fireballs formed above vehicles as thousand-pound warheads ignited. Thunderous blasts echoed throughout the encampments, the vehicles disappearing in a flash of fire and smoke.

As carnage rained down on military staging areas, other Tomahawks targeted North Korea's airfields. When the drones drove north toward the DMZ, North Korea sent an alert to their air bases, ordering their fighter attack aircraft into the air. Their primary mission was to engage any South Korean or American attack aircraft crossing the borders. The secondary mission was to move their airplanes to one of the three secure underground bases.

*   *   *   *   *   *

Wonsan, North Korea
30 July, 2021

The soft murmur of a gentle surf rolled against the long, curved sands of Kalma Beach, sunlight gracing the shoulders of the very few enjoying the shore. The cry of gulls occasionally pierced the calm of the morning, whether startled or defending some newfound discovery. The white outlines of their outstretched wings against the blue sky marked their search for the next meal.

Other seagulls, strutting along the wet sand next to the hissing waves as they rolled onto the shore, suddenly took flight. Carrying over the beachfront housing developments and a nearby resort, a piercing blare rose from the airport just inland from the serenity of water meeting shore.

Figures poured from buildings, urgently climbing aboard vehicles that began arriving to pick them up. The vans carrying the military pilots and crew members then tore off, some to the north and some to the south, heading to where lines of fighters were parked along taxiways. At the extreme north end of the joint international airport and military base, pilots ran from alert shacks. The sound of their boots pounding across the concrete ramp mixed with the alert siren sending its shrill tone echoing through the morning.

Pilots clambered up ladders and slid into the cockpits of the six Mig-29s parked next to a line of transport aircraft. Crew chiefs ran around the twin-engine fighters, checking for problems and pulling pins. Missiles attached to hardpoints were given a firm shake and red-flagged pins stuffed into pockets.

The whine of jet engines, loud as they were, could barely be heard above the cacophony of sound filling the air base. Puffs of smoke shot out from tailpipes as engines were started. The whines of turbines rotating changed to the powerful roars of engines igniting. Within minutes of the first blast of the alert sirens, the first Mig-29 Fulcrum rolled forward, the canopy closing as the aging fighter taxied briskly toward the runway just a few feet away.

One after another, the six Fulcrums sped out of their parking places. Just as quickly, the pilots turned onto runway 15R and ran the throttles up. Passing the detent, the rear nozzles opened up. Flames roared from the aft end as raw fuel was sprayed into the hot exhaust. Accelerating quickly, the Mig-29s lifted from the airfield and roared aloft, climbing steeply into the blue.

All along the taxiways, other jet aircraft were also in the process of preparing for flight as the Vietnam era fighters sought to escape the bonds of earth. Mig-21s and Su-25s vied with each other for space on the taxiway, with other idling jets waiting for their opportunity to inch forward. Toward the southern end of the airfield, Mig-23s joined in on the mass exodus, further crowding the single parallel taxiway serving the active runways.

The runways were scenes of intense activity as one jet after another raced down the surfaces and vaulted into the air. Tomahawk missiles, the same ones observed by the North Korean frigate, crossed over the silky sands. They rose over tall housing complexes and sped over the top of the base's security fencing. The first AGM-158s matched the terrain with that stored in their systems. Verifying the information, the cruise missile arced downward and dove into one of the concrete runways. Burrowing underneath, the warhead exploded. Earth heaved upward, showering the adjacent area with chunks of concrete, dirt, and stone.

Gaining speed, one Mig-21 ran straight into an explosion. In an instant, the aircraft was destroyed. The shock of the jet fuel exploding added another punch to the destruction. On the adjacent runway, another older Mig lifted off just as a JASSM dove underground. The upheaval threw debris into the tail end of the aircraft. Pieces fell from the engine and tail, the powerful roar of the engine taking on a concerning note of grinding. With a gout of flame shooting from the disintegrating engine, the canopy flew from the fighter, following by a dark object that was the pilot frantically ejecting. The vintage fighter nosed over and crashed into one of the high-rise apartment buildings, flames punching out the other side.

With the ALCMs cratering the runway, a Tomahawk cruise missile fired from the *Ohio* sped down the taxiway. Bomblets fell from the weapon and dropped into the midst of idling aircraft waiting for their turn to takeoff. Popping like a string of firecrackers, shrapnel ripped through wings and fuselages. Like tiny waterfalls, jet fuel ran from punctured tanks where it was quickly ignited by the exploding munitions.

More Tomahawks arrived. Frantically, pilots attempted to release their harnesses to drop from burning aircraft. Many jumped down only to find themselves in the midst of burning fuel, the flames rising higher as more fuel was added. Missiles flew out of the increasing conflagration as their propellants were ignited. Fires started raging through the densely packed fighters. Ammunition began exploding, their large caliber rounds adding to the destruction occurring throughout the air base.

The transport aircraft parked at the northern end didn't escape the onslaught. They too were caught in the fiery explosions rocking the airfield. Farther south, helicopters and transports sat astride the third runway that made up the airport. One Tomahawk flew over the row of military aircraft, leaving strings of explosions in its wake. With the siren still blaring its warning, thick pillars of smoke roared from the scenic peninsula.

All across the secretive nation, air bases were rocked as momentous explosions shook buildings. Huge balls of black smoke shot skyward, their interiors a roiling mass of orange flame as fuel farms were targeted. Trailing black smoke, flaming debris slowly arced across skies filling with columns of acrid smoke, landing among homes and buildings. Glass windows from unreinforced hangars blasted outward when missiles flew through their thin skins and blew up.

Those aircraft that managed to get airborne before the cruise missiles arrived came under the control of centralized air defense systems. Many of the Mig-29s headed south with orders to engage the bevy of American attack fighters striking at the southern air defenses. However, all semblance of control vanished due to the destruction from the bunker busters and from the air-launched cruise missiles targeting North Korea's communication network.

* * * * * *

Sohae Satellite Launching Station, North Korea
30 July, 2021

Shadows from the steel-girded gantry stretched long across the launch pad. Nestled in arms extending from the launch facility, a white-painted ballistic missile stood atop a massive railcar. With streamers of white vapor trailing down its sides, the deadly-looking missile appeared to be ready for launch. What was encased inside the top shroud was anyone's guess. It could be another earth observation satellite, a reentry vehicle containing a chemical agent, a nuclear warhead, or a conventional one.

Inside a hardened control room, technicians pored through checklists and systems, looking for the smallest indication that something was amiss. The glorious leader was known for his volatile retributions for failed launches and no one wanted to be in the path of one of his temper tantrums.

More nervous were the installation commanders, for they'd be the likely ones to incur the leader's wrath, should this launch go awry.

The North Korean leader had ordered the military to make some drastic improvements, but as was usual, the nebulous order didn't include details as to what he was expecting. Without much funding or the ability to procure materials available to most of the world's nations, improvement was a tall order. Much of the north's equipment was aging and part of the world's hand-me-downs. Submarines from the fifties and sixties were known to just sink, the archaic naval vessels had more rust than functionality. The air force was in equally bad shape, the few Mig-29 Fulcrums in the inventory unable to put up much of a fight against the modern equipment of South Korea and the United States.

So, many commanders fudged progress reports, sometimes outright lying as to the capabilities of the military. Some of the leaders in the rocket forces test-fired a ballistic missile which landed in the East Sea, prompting verbal threats from Japan and America. The leaders went on to mention that the test was for a hypersonic missile, similar to the one hyped by China. The glorious leader had been thrilled that the military was making such significant progress, aside from the nuclear program.

Of course, everyone within the rocket forces knew the statement, and many others, to be a falsehood. Those claims of military advancements were difficult to disprove. However easy it might be to fake test results; it was pretty hard to conceal a missile blowing up on the launch pad or coming apart in mid-flight.

The missile standing upright was presented on a large central screen, the time for the proposed launch counting down near the bottom right corner. Eyes turned from their consoles as the screen flashed brightly. A fireball was observed rolling away from the launch tower, filling the monitor. With another small flash, the screen went blank.

Dread filled those inside the control room, most thinking

they had done something wrong that had led to the missile's destruction. Heads would roll from the mistake. Those were the last thoughts many had as a cruise missile hammered through the reinforced roof and exploded deep inside the bunker. Sure enough, the operators were correct. Heads did indeed roll, but not in the manner they had meant.

The fireball and smoke raced away from the launch pad, revealing the twisted girders making up the tower leaning like a drunk leaving a bar late at night. With a squeal of tortured metal and loud reports as metal I-beams popped, the launch tower began a slow fall toward the concrete surface. Picking up speed, the tower, with the burnt remains of the missile embedded within, toppled. It slammed heavily onto the charred surface with a loud, ringing clang.

At a different launching site on the eastern side, another Tomahawk's unitary warhead exploded over the top of another missile waiting to be launched into orbit. The thousand-pound charge created a monstrous fireball, the compressed air crumpling the thin-shelled ballistic missile. A white-hot explosion blew away the roiling mass of smoke and flame as the highly volatile liquid hydrogen and liquid oxygen stored aboard the ballistic missile ignited. The concussive wave evaporated much of the missile and the launch tower. Secondary explosions from nearby fuel tanks added to the overall destruction. Additional missiles took out the support facilities associated with the Tonghae Satellite Launching Ground.

* * * * * *

The initial B-2 attack with massive ordinance penetrators went after North Korea's command and control infrastructure, communication centers, the chemical and nuclear weapons storage sites, and attempted to remove the political and military leadership. Following those attacks meant to limit the North's ability to organize their defenses, cruise missiles fell among air bases, fuel depots, ammunition storage, and anti-aircraft units.

They also struck artillery vehicles that were staged in the open. In addition, North Korea's rocket launch facilities were heavily targeted as the extent of their nuclear ballistic capability was largely unknown.

At the same time, F-16s sent missile after missile speeding across the DMZ as they initially focused on taking out ground-to-air systems. The North's response was slow to organize due to disrupted communications, either from missile attacks or from MC-130s conducting electronic jamming missions south of the demilitarized zone.

The initial attacks were thought to be mostly successful but would require thorough assessment before the full extent of the damage could be ascertained.

*   *   *   *   *   *

Sea of Japan
30 July, 2021

A hundred and fifty miles off the eastern coastline of North Korea, an E-3 out of Okinawa orbited at thirty-five thousand feet. While the E-8C flying to the southeast of Seoul was to manage the operations against ground targets, the Sentry was in place to control any air-to-air operations that might arise.

When the alert slowly propagated across North Korea, the operators in the E-3 fuselage observed aircraft coming onscreen as they took off from airfields scattered throughout the country. That was what they were waiting for. A flight of F-15s flew cover for the AWACs, but there were others loitering near two tankers flying off the western coast of Japan.

"Amber flight, Yukla One One. Turn left to heading two six zero. Climb to angels eight," the E-3 controller radioed. "These will be vectors to intercept."

Lieutenant Colonel William Gerber glanced to his left. One of his F-15Cs was still hooked to the KC-135's boom for refueling. The two aircraft bounced through the air in a synchronized dance and looked for the world like a grownup toting a child on a leash. A misty spray shot past the refueling F-

15C as the connection was severed, the boom raising to tuck underneath the tanker. Gerber's number four wingman pulled off the Stratotanker with a high-G turn away, joining up on the second element leader's wing.

"Copy Yukla One One. Left to two six zero. Out of angels minus two to angels eight," Gerber replied.

Pushing the throttles up, William eased back on the stick. The nose rose above the horizon and the altimeter wound upward. Knowing that combat was likely in the next few minutes, he sent his wingman to a chase position behind him and directed the second element to a tactical station a mile to the side. From there, the flight could cover each other no matter which direction the enemy chose to take.

However, William knew the chances of getting into a dogfight these days were fairly remote. Although they still practiced close-in dogfighting skills, most of the engagements in modern air warfare were fought at beyond visual ranges. Today's weapons strove to reach farther and be more resistant to jamming and countermeasures.

The problem of fifth generation stealth aircraft complicated matters as they weren't easily seen at those distances, thus the need for better radar systems. Lower frequency S or L band radars were able to track stealth aircraft that had multiple control surfaces by creating a resonance effect. But those same radars were highly susceptible to clutter and jamming. They were also lower precision radars, making their information dubious. Although faint or fleeting radar returns let controllers know that a stealth-type aircraft was in the area, the ambiguity of the readings made it difficult to manage effective intercepts. It was an eternal game that would continue for as long as Humanity walked the earth.

William prepped his aircraft for combat, arming the two AIM-120s and two AIM-9Xs nestled under the wings and the four AIM-120s tucked underneath the fuselage. Far below stretched a wide expanse of blue with the dark smudge of North Korea's coastline in the distance growing ever larger as the F-15C sliced through the thin atmosphere.

With some time before his flight came within range of the North Korean fighters taking off from their airfields, William spent a moment reminiscing about the changes he'd seen through his years in the Air Force. He missed the days when aerial combat included dogfighting. Sure, there had been long-range missiles such as the AIM-7 Sparrows and the early models of the AIM-120s, but those radar-guided missiles weren't as reliable as the ones manufactured today. They were mostly fired to provide a disruptive presence, allowing one side to perhaps gain a distinct advantage as the two sides closed.

Now, the aircraft were primarily launching platforms for a bevy of weapons. In fact, aircraft seldom operated their own radars and instead relied on replicated data handed down from combat management platforms. Even the words had changed. A battlefield wasn't really *fought in*, but *managed*. Missiles could be retargeted by an operator sitting miles to the rear. The F-22s could also function as airborne command posts, collecting data and disseminating it to other attack aircraft. Times had certainly changed, and the conduct of war had changed with them.

William stretched his legs as best he could. He loved the Eagle and was so glad he'd had the opportunity to fly it for his many years of service. It wouldn't be much longer before he would be contemplating his retirement. He wished he had been able to fly the F-22, or even the new F-15EX soon to enter the inventory, but in a way, he was glad that he'd spend his last days in the cockpit of the F-15. It just seemed right somehow.

One thing was certain, he'd miss flying such a magnificent machine. He'd also miss the people he flew with, the camaraderie, the Friday night beers, the flight or squadron BBQs. He wouldn't miss the politics that seemed to have become a larger part of his life since he'd made major, the competition to make the next rank, and the endless stream of paperwork that flowed across his desk. When the orders came down for this squadron deployment, there were papers left swirling in the air from his mad dash out of the office.

"Amber flight, turn left heading two four zero."

William double clicked the transmit button,

acknowledging the change in direction. Banking briefly, the Eagle rolled twenty degrees, the three other aircraft in the flight altering their speed and headings to maintain position.

"Four bandits at your twelve o'clock, heading one eight zero, range eighty miles, climbing through flight level two two zero."

Gerber again acknowledged the transmission and went to work. Four North Korean fast-movers were off his nose and heading south, to his left. The targets were eighteen thousand feet below but climbing. Their current course didn't indicate that they were aware of William's flight closing in on the coastline. Or if they were, they didn't care about it. The fortunate thing about heading toward North Korea was that they didn't have any fifth-generation stealth fighters. As a matter of fact, their air force was antiquated with the most advanced fighter in their inventory being the Mig-29, Russia's original counter to the F-15. But, whereas the Eagle had undergone many enhancements, the same couldn't be said of North Korea's Fulcrums.

Data was downloaded to two of the AMRAAMs, assigning them one of the bandits climbing into the morning skies. The weapons indicated that they received the information and were locked on to their targets. William pressed the trigger and one AIM-120 streaked off one of the wing rails. Trailing a line of white smoke, the missile leapt ahead of the aircraft, turning slightly as it continuously received guidance from the E-3. Traveling at over three thousand miles per hour, the weapon would close the eighty miles in about a minute and a half. Seconds later, Gerber pressed the trigger again, sending another weapon speeding toward the nearing coastline.

From four F-15Cs speeding at Mach point nine, eight white trails streaked away. The radar-guided weapons quickly faded from sight as they sped toward the four North Korean F-7 fighters racing south to engage the multitude of American F-16s firing missiles across the DMZ. The F-7 was an export variant of the Chinese J-7, which itself was a variant of the Russian Mig-21. The aircraft had very limited radar functionality and carried only short-range IR air-to-air missiles.

Climbing through twenty-eight thousand feet in a loose formation, the North Korean F-7s never fully understood their peril. The first long-range air-to-air missile made a minute course adjustment as it homed in on its target. Entering its terminal phase, the guidance software initiated the weapon's radar system. For the first time, the North Korean pilots recognized the threat and began defensive maneuvers.

The attempted high-G turn was too little and too late. The AIM-120 flew across the top of the lead aircraft near the tail. Fragments blew out from the dark puff of smoke and hammered into the fuselage. Pieces flew into the engine, tearing through the combustion chamber. A sheet of flame erupted from the back of the antiquated fighter, the engine coming apart. That further weakened the empennage.

A second after the AMRAAM exploded, the tail of the aircraft separated. With pieces flying off, the J-7 abruptly pitched up. Inside the cockpit, the North Korean pilot was thrown violently forward from the sudden deceleration. The control stick was forcefully punched out of his hand, slamming against the rear stops. Confused by the G-forces throwing his body against the straps, the pilot frantically clawed for the ejection handles. In a desperate grab, his fingers closed around one of the handles and he pulled.

Scratches in the canopy caught the sun's rays, emitting sparkles of light as it flew free of the mortally wounded aircraft and tumbled away. The pilot, still forced forward from the decrease in speed, felt a sharp pain in his back as the seat launched up the rails. Frigid air enfolded his body, the high-G ejection adding to the pilot's confusion. Thrown from his seat and relieved from violent forces, the pilot was able to garner a semblance of cognition. He saw the final throes of his aircraft as it continued to shed pieces. Trailing a thin line of smoke, the J-7 rolled over and plunged downward.

Free-falling through the heights, the pilot shivered from the cold, but adrenaline kept it from becoming his focus. Instead, he watched forested ridges slowly rise up to meet him.

A couple of seconds later, he wondered why his parachute hadn't opened. His limited training fled from the adrenaline-fueled freefall. Panic began to set in.

Grasping repeatedly for the manual ripcord, he was startled when he was suddenly jerked upward. The altitude sensitive setting had automatically deployed his parachute. The Gs imposed on his body aggravated the pain in his back he'd first felt when bailing out, the shock sending a white-hot electric jolt down his legs. The bolt of pain reawakened some of his meager training. In agony, the pilot looked up to verify that his parachute had properly deployed. The nylon panels fluttered in the wind, but the chute appeared to be fully inflated. With tremendous effort that sent additional waves of pain sizzling down his legs, he managed to release the steering handles.

He then looked for a decent place to land, but there was only mountainous terrain below. Off to one side, he saw a spiraling column of smoke rising from one hillside, the smoldering remains of his aircraft. Further in the distance, a fireball erupted, followed by a dark pall of rising smoke. Gazing skyward, he searched the blue for sign of another aircraft crashing to earth or for some indication that one or more of his flight members were descending under a canopy of nylon. He saw only faint, arcing smoke trails that were dark smudges marring the blue skies.

Focusing back on the ground, the pilot desperately searched for clear terrain to steer toward. With none in sight, he had to settle for the flattest stand of trees near the base of a steep ridge. At the mercy of the winds, the pilot slowly descended, making adjustments to his trajectory as best he could in order to land in the relatively flat treetops. The crests of the sharp ridges touched the horizon, the hillsides and valley floors combining into an endless carpet of green.

Descending into one of the many valleys, the winds shifted, flowing with the contours of the land. The pilot was blown off his planned course, drifting closer to the hillsides. Everything he attempted only resulted in an increased descent rate and more pain. The descent seemed to increase even more as he came closer to the treetops, the limbs rushing up to greet him. At the last moment, the pilot lifted his legs in an effort to delay his contact with the earth.

The soft roar of wind became sharp cracks and crunches as he crashed into the canopy. Branches whipped his body as he plummeted into their midst, limbs snapping as he collided with them. A confusing series of green and brown flashed by, and he heard himself grunt, although it seemed as if he was listening to someone else.

He felt himself hit a thick branch and he folded around it before sliding off to one side. Finally, he jerked to a stop. Gradually, the pilot fully opened his eyes. He was swinging slightly, hanging from his parachute straps about ten feet from the ground. Relieved that the pain that had ridden with him on his parachute ride down had vanished, he reached up for the releases on either side of his chest.

There was a coil of rope that he could use to ease himself down, but it was only ten feet to the ground and it looked flat and covered in a dense carpet of fir needles. Pulling the release wires, he started his final drop to earth. In what was a seemingly endless series of startlements, another occurred when he tried to bend his legs in anticipation of landing. He hit the ground awkwardly, falling forward to smack face first into a bed of needles.

Spitting dirt and debris out of his mouth, he managed to roll over. High overhead, streams of sunlight filtered through the limbs. There was a soft hiss of wind as it caressed the tops of the trees. One beam fell warmly across his face. In other streaks angling down from above, insects danced, darting from one place to another.

Struggling to rise to his elbows, the pilot attempted to roll over to stand, but his lower body didn't respond. Running one hand down his torso, the pilot could feel the touch of his fingers, right up until he reached his waist. In an odd assortment of sensations, he could feel his fingers touch the flight suit, but his legs couldn't feel his hand. It was as if he were touching another person's leg. He realized what had happened and what those earlier pain sensations had meant.

Remembering the rugged terrain he observed on his way down, he very much doubted he would be rescued anytime soon. If the Americans had indeed initiated attacks on his homeland, there was a good chance that attention would be focused elsewhere and rescue efforts much delayed, if ever even attempted.

Working as best as he could, he rifled through his survival pack, placing his scant resources of food and water within reach. Pulling out the flare pistol, he loaded it with one of the three flares and set it next to his food and water. Suddenly, he heard the faint whine of a jet engine, increasing in volume.

Thinking that one of his flight members had tracked his descent and was about to fly over his position, the pilot raised his flare gun toward one of the larger openings above. Pressing the trigger, the flare left the barrel with a *whoosh*. The explosive sailed through the canopy, into the clear, and ignited. Swinging under its own chute, the flare slowly settled back to earth. Something dark flashed overhead, the roar of the jet fading just as quickly as it had appeared. Thinking rescue would shortly be on its way, the pilot eased back to the ground, again feeling the warmth on his face.

* * * * * *

The radar returns from Gerber's flight's first targeted formations vanished from his screen. More enemy aircraft had lifted off from an airfield near Wonsan, situated on the eastern coast of North Korea. With the next set of targets passed down from the E-3, he selected two additional AIM-120s sitting under his fuselage.

A blue-gray missile with a white cone dropped from underneath the F-15. The rocket motor ignited and it accelerated away from the fighter. Nearing the North Korean coastline, William watched as the missile arced immediately downward, where North Korean aircraft were speeding south. Small puffs of dark smoke dotted the skies ahead, thinning in the higher speed winds aloft. Other F-15s scattered over the Sea of Japan were also making their presence known.

A second AMRAAM fell from the Eagle, chasing after the previous one. William had heard stories about the turkey shoots from Desert Storm, the first Gulf War. In that war, the Iraqi pilots had mostly fled toward Iran in the hopes of making it across the border. At first, the United States had lined up F-15s near the border and engaged those seeking to escape. That hadn't lasted long with orders coming down to let those who fit escape profiles make it across the border. The entire process seemed very much like shooting fish in a barrel.

In a way, this was a similar situation, although the North Koreans weren't exactly trying to escape. Some seemed to be hell-bent on making it to a different airfield. But for the most part, they were speeding toward the DMZ. And Gerber's flight was certainly within range of the north's long-range air defenses, yet the threat sensors remained quiet.

William watched as another missile raced ahead of his aircraft, plunging from the frigid heights to speed after North Korea's air force. The massed weapons struck. Planes fell from the sky with the North Korean pilots seeming to have little to no warning. One missile crossed over the back of a climbing Mig-19 and exploded just behind the cockpit. The Vietnam-era fighter came apart, the forward half of the aircraft separating and tumbling. In a violent flash, the Mig tore itself apart. Larger pieces fell away in streamers of white smoke.

Another AIM-120 hit near a wing root. The wing flashed brilliantly in the early morning light as it folded up and detached. The Mig-19 started a vicious roll before tumbling tail over nose. It too broke up, terminating in a bright explosion. Within seconds, a second flight of four North Korean fighters fell from the sky. A fifth and sixth AMRAAM sped away, tearing into a third flight lifting from the major air base. The rough terrain to the south and southwest of Wonsan was becoming pockmarked with rising tendrils of smoke from downed aircraft.

Having fired all of his long-range weapons into North Korea, William was left with only two shorter-range heat-seeking sidewinders. That limited any future engagement on this sortie to twenty miles or less.

"Amber flight, turn right heading two eight zero. Vectors for intercept," Yukla One One radioed.

Gerber eased the aircraft to the right a few degrees. The operators aboard the E-3 knew that he and his flight were out of long-range solutions, so they must be coming in for a closer-range shot with his AIM-9Xs.

"Amber flight, bandits at your one o'clock, forty miles, level at angels three. Heading one niner zero, speed five twenty."

That meant that there were four enemy aircraft just off to the right. As Williams was flying at flight level 400 (eight thousand feet above the designated angel's altitude), it also meant that the targets were five thousand feet below and on a southerly course. Forty miles from the coastline, the threat receiver lit up from search radars painting the F-15C.

William advanced the throttles past the mil power detent, the F-15C responding like a giant sportscar. The airspeed indicator increased up to, and then through, Mach 1. The transition to supersonic speed was barely felt. There was only a slight bump from the indicator from the compression of the leading-edge boundary layer.

Gerber knew that he needed to close in with the enemy aircraft before North Korea could fire their surface-to-air missiles. He figured if he could get near enough to them before the fire control radars pegged him, they wouldn't fire on him in such close proximity to their own aircraft. North Korea didn't possess modern weaponry, so it would be difficult for the ground operators to keep William's Eagle targeted when operating so close to their own aircraft.

"Amber flight, bandits turning to the east. They're at your twelve, heading two zero zero, range thirty miles. Climbing through angels six."

William took a deep breath and let it out. Taking the stick

in his left hand, he stretched the fingers of his right. Several times, he made a fist and then stretched to alleviate any tension or cramps. The show was about to change from a digital game to one of pilot skill. With a shrug of his shoulders, he replaced his hand and mentally readied himself for the upcoming engagement.

Onboard threat sensors warned of a fire control radar hitting the aircraft. Shortly thereafter, thin lines of white rose from the distant shore. Even though the missile launches looked far away, William knew that they'd be quickly upon him. Flares and bundles of chaff shot into the slipstream as he punched out countermeasures. Gerber had to multitask, keeping part of his focus on the enemy aircraft closing in at over twenty miles per minute. The other was reserved for the ground threat that was nearing even faster.

The lieutenant colonel felt his gut clench as he watched the surface-to-air missiles arc toward his flight. He ejected more countermeasures, filling the skies with foil and flares as he and the rest of his flight sought to evade the incoming projectiles. North Korea had archaic weapons with the S-200 semi-active radar homing missiles comprising their primary long-range air defense system. With the release of chaff bundles, the ground operators holding the link with the S-200s locked onto the larger radar presentations. When the tell-tale signs of the missile tracks deviated from their collision course and angled away from the F-15s, William breathed a small sigh of relief, expelling some of the held tension.

That relief didn't last very long as the threat warning system alerted him that additional fire control radars had targeted him. The indications were that the threat was coming from directly ahead. William assumed that the fighters closing the distance had lit up their radars. A quick glance verified his assumption; the passive sensors indicated that the enemy aircraft had indeed turned on their radars.

From thirty miles away, semi-active radar guided R-27 missiles raced away from the four North Korean Mig-29s climbing to meet the four F-15Cs. Bundle after bundle shot into the thin air, releasing strips of aluminum foil. The radar screens onboard the Migs showed an electronic cloud, from which it was difficult to pinpoint the single aircraft. The vintage air-to-air missiles, having lost their lock-on, latched onto the largest radar picture they could find. The Russian-derivative projectiles flew past the speeding Eagles to detonate within the tumbling foil strips.

Flying east with the sun in their eyes, the North Korean pilots weren't able to make out the dark shapes of the incoming American planes. In addition, the tight parameters of the ancient heat-seekers couldn't be fired because of the sun's position.

William eased back on the throttles, feeling the mil power detent as he brought the engines out of afterburner. The F-15C slowed, coming back down through the speed of sound. With updates coming from Yukla One One and visual clues depicting the target's location, William was able to glimpse the first dark shape when it materialized out of thin air.

The four enemy planes were flying closer together than were the F-15Cs, their spread barely wider than a finger-four formation. The dots quickly grew larger due to the twenty-mile-per-minute closure rate. The joint helmet-mounted cueing system, which was predominantly created just for the AIM-9 missiles, allowed William to target an opposing aircraft just by looking at it. With a sidewinder selected, the system alerted when it found a heat signature that fit within its parameters.

Locked on to one of the bandits, Gerber pressed the trigger. A missile streaked past the cockpit, the IR sensor aboard the weapon guiding toward the hot spot it registered. The high-offset oblique shot was a tough one for the missile to follow, especially when the opposing aircraft let loose a volley of flares. The AIM-9X slewed off course and headed directly toward the descending heat sources. It was too late for another shot, as the aircraft were now too close.

The North Korean fighters were flying in two elements, each comprised of two aircraft flying in close formation. With his second element off to his right, William selected the leftmost pair and maneuvered to take them down his left side. Knowing that the sun was directly behind him, he wondered if the North Korean pilots could even see him. Judging from the straight-on approach they were taking, without maneuvering for an advantageous position, William guessed they couldn't.

Just before the aircraft passed each other, William punched the throttles into full afterburner and pulled up sharply. The G-suit pressed against his legs and abdomen as the F-15C went vertical. Looking back over his shoulder, Gerber saw the two North Korean aircraft in a hard turn toward him. The pilots must have seen him at the last moment. However, William held a slight maneuvering advantage.

He was a little surprised to see that the two fighters in his field of vision had twin tails and the distinct shape of Fulcrums. They were the best North Korea had to offer and the Mig-29 and F-15C were once viewed as equals. That meant that this fight was going to come down to training and weapon systems, areas in which William was pretty certain that he held the advantage, though any mistake could prove disastrous.

Still looking over his shoulder while pulling nearly 9Gs, grunting under the strain and breathing in short, calculated pulls of air, Gerber kept his eyes on the turning Migs. With a slight change in course, William oriented his nose toward the opposing fighters using his rudders and pulled. Coming through the vertical, the Eagle began nosing toward the horizon. William felt the stick vibrate as he kept the aircraft on the edge of its optimal angle of attack.

The two Migs continued banking hard in an ascending turn, the lead pilot trying to get his nose around on Gerber's aircraft. However, William was on the inside of the turn and with him being nearly vertical, his turn radius was significantly shorter. Coming over the top, he kept pulling back on the stick, keeping his nose tracking toward the rear of the lead Fulcrum. It was an axiom from his early days of training, keep angling for a point just to the rear of the enemy aircraft.

The lead Mig had initiated a climbing roll toward William, negating some of the separation the Lieutenant

Colonel was hoping to achieve. By listening to the radio chatter, he knew that his other element was engaged with the two other Migs, so he wasn't overly worried about being sandwiched or having the opposing element maneuver behind him. His wingman's calls were also helpful, letting him know that his six was clear.

He came through the horizon partially inverted. Rolling upright, Gerber pushed forward, unloading the aircraft from a G perspective. Weightless, he quickly rolled the Eagle toward the aft end of the Mig-29, which was still turning for all it was worth. Pulling back on the stick again, William sought to edge around on the North Korean.

The enemy pilot seemed at a loss as to what the correct response should be. With the opposing American fighter maneuvering to get behind him, the North Korean only thought to pull harder to stop the F-15 from getting into a firing position. Bleeding airspeed during the high-G bank, the Mig shuddered as it edged toward a stall. The pilot was surprised when the stick in his hand started vibrating and then shaking hard.

Shoving the throttles to their stops, the Mig lurched ahead as raw fuel was pumped into the hot exhaust. Unloading the stick to less than 1G, the North Korean abruptly rolled in the opposite direction. He then dove toward the Sea of Japan miles below, accelerating quickly in its afterburner-fueled descent. The pilot was attempting to disengage from the aerial combat, extend, and escape.

William saw the Mig roll in the opposite direction, cutting directly in front.

"That, my friend, was a mistake," Gerber muttered as he turned inside of the fleeing aircraft.

The North Korean's maneuver away allowed William to slide behind. Sweat trickled from his brow under the Gs. Blinking once to clear his vision, Gerber eyed the enemy Mig gaining distance as the two aircraft raced out of the morning skies. A tone in his helmet let him know that his one remaining sidewinder had a lock on the Mig's exhaust.

A radio call from his wingman told him that the second

enemy fighter had exited his high-G turn and was coming after William. With a 3-Dimensional map of the fight playing in his head, William knew he only had seconds until he would be the one reacting to an enemy aircraft on his tail. Pulling the trigger, the last AIM-9X left the Eagle and sped toward the escaping Fulcrum.

Without looking to see how his shot went, William thumbed countermeasures from the aircraft and pulled out of the forty-five-degree dive.

"Amber Lead, come hard left," his wingman called.

Without hesitation, William rolled left and pulled. His flight suit was soaked from the G's pulling liquid from his body, but he didn't notice. Grunting with the effort, he looked back over his shoulder. The second Mig was coming around, but his nose was on the outside of the turn, which meant it would be difficult for the North Korean pilot to get around on him.

"Fox two."

With his eye still on the fighter attempting to get into a good firing position, William saw the flash of his wingman's missile explode near the turning Mig. The enemy aircraft seemed to almost halt in midair before the nose dropped. The canopy separated from the aircraft and a dark object was propelled from the cockpit. Trailing smoke, the Fulcrum spiraled toward the sea.

William came out of his turn and looked around. There was another faint smoke trail from where his last target had been, but he couldn't locate the aircraft or any sign of its demise. Throttling up and initiating a climb, William noted the lack of enemy radar signatures. A part of him had followed the radio calls, and he knew that the other two Migs had been shot down. Directed by the E-3, Amber flight turned east for the short hop back to base to refuel and rearm.

* * * * * *

Green flashed past the cockpit, the treetops just a few feet beyond the wingtip were a blur. Listening to his rear-seater grunt under the strain of the high-G turn, Captain David Miller pulled the Strike Eagle around one of the sharp bends that defined the narrow ravine. With cruise missiles slamming into targets all across North Korea, and with the single-seat 15s dealing with enemy aircraft lifting off from various air bases, David had come in from the Sea of Japan. Flying at wavetop level, he and his WSO had entered North Korea in a remote location.

Attempting to remain off radar, their route had taken them into the north's inhospitable mountainous region. Using ravines and crossing saddlebacks, David had made sure to keep the strike fighter below the level of the higher crests dominating the area.

A glimpse of brown water showed through the tree boughs as David whipped the aircraft from its sharp turn. Forested slopes dominated the view ahead, leading up to sharp, jagged crests. Rolling through level flight, Miller jammed the stick hard left, pulling back as the bank angle increased. In the recesses of his mind, he felt his G-suit compress, holding back the blood that was being forced toward his feet.

Wisps of moisture formed on the wingtips and curled behind the banking aircraft. Rolling out, the F-15E roared down a narrow valley. On the other side of the steep terrain, thin columns of dark smoke rose above the crests. David wasn't sure whether they were from the smoldering wreckage of aircraft shot down or from targets the cruise missiles struck. The pillars drifting skyward were reminders of the prevalent dangers.

The Strike Eagle whipped around another bend of the terrain. Rolling out, a black smear marred the otherwise solid green carpet. Parts of aircraft were spread around a slash of downed trees and churned dirt. One gray-painted wing displaying the red star roundel of North Korea lay among charred ashes, seemingly untouched by the intense heat which had burned most everything else. Remnants of an engine showed through a bed of white ash, and then it was gone, thrust behind the speeding aircraft.

"Oh shit!" David exclaimed, adrenaline coursing through

his system.

His thumb repeatedly hit the countermeasure button with flares streaming behind the F-15E. Higher up on the hillside, a red flare arced upward, clearing the treetops. At first appearance, David had been positive that it was a surface-to-air missile rising from a hidden position. He relaxed a touch once his senses calmed enough to identify that it was just a flare sailing into the air to then gently float under a parachute.

"I could use less of that," Captain Mark Foley stated from the backseat.

"Yeah, you ain't shittin'. I thought we were goners," David replied. "Mark the location of that flare. You never know, could be one of ours."

Mark quickly turned his radio to the emergency frequency to check if there was an emergency location beacon going off. He would normally be able to hear anything being transmitted over the emergency channel, but he double-checked just in case.

"I don't hear an ELT," Mark responded, "but I've marked it and sent the coordinates back to Yukla One One."

David whipped the aircraft around another turn. Ahead was the straightest path yet as the ravine ran between two tall mountain slopes. The trees opened up near the valley entrance where a small bridge crossed over a brown stream.

"All right, that's our IP," Mark said.

"Copy."

David maneuvered to the side of the clearing, taking the bridge down his left side.

"Ready, ready, mark," Foley declared as the bridge passed the cockpit.

David ran the throttles up. Both pilots were pressed back against their seats as the F-15E's response was instantaneous. The airspeed indicator climbed as the twin jet engines pushed the aircraft to five hundred and forty knots. Checking that the armament panel was set correctly, David briefly wondered who it was in the hills that had fired the flare. Was it the pilot of the crashed jet? Did he or she hear David's Strike Eagle and think it was one of theirs? Would they get rescued? What was North Korea's position on rescuing its pilots? A morbid thought occurred that his F-15E could be the last bit of hope that pilot ever saw.

The Strike Eagle raced through the ravine, the roar of its engines echoing along the wooded hillsides. Ahead, a ridgeline crossed the end of the valley.

"Terrain...pull up. Terrain...pull up," the terrain-following radar warned.

David pulled back on the stick, sending the sleek form of the Strike Eagle soaring skyward. The targeting system took the environmental conditions and aircraft parameters into consideration when determining a release point. Miller felt the *thunk* of release and the aircraft go light as the AGM-154 fell away from the climbing attack fighter.

The white-painted Joint Standoff Weapon soared over the top of the crest, the guidance package aboard the glide bomb made minute adjustments as it was lobbed toward its target. David noted the threat sensors come alive when he departed the low-level environment as the beams from search radars panned across his aircraft.

"Not to sound like Captain Obvious, but we're being painted," Foley stated over the intercom.

"I know."

"Perhaps we could try doing some of that pilot stuff," Foley added.

"Working on it."

In the adjacent valley with a city and the target, a search radar determined the track to be hostile and handed off its data to a nearby fire control radar. Within seconds, two short-range missiles flew from their rails. With white smoke trails, they accelerated and sped across the city. A few on the streets saw the streaks and wondered briefly what was happening, returning to their activities as the objects quickly flew out of sight.

Having locked onto the Strike Eagle's heat signature, both missiles turned with the aircraft and descended toward the distant ridges. Flying at Mach 4, the weapons rapidly closed the distance.

"That's a fire control radar," Foley said.

"Well, maybe try pressing some of those buttons you have back there," David replied.

"I'm not sure they actually do anything."

"Helluva time to share that information," Miller grunted.

Assured of a clean separation, Miller rolled the aircraft inverted and pulled. The G-meter pegged at just below 9Gs as David angled for a branching valley, seeking the comfort and safety of the rugged terrain.

The lead anti-aircraft missile tracked the heat source, clearing the top of a ridge by the span of its length. The trail of white bent sharply as the weapon attempted to turn with the descending heat signal.

"Ah, shit," Captain Foley remarked, catching sight of the missile giving chase.

The WSO grabbed one of the handles on the canopy bow, wrenching himself around in order to keep the weapon in sight. The missile tried to follow the aircraft, but slammed into the far hillside as it endeavored to make a course correction. Foley watched as the weapon vanished into the treetops, the lush foliage hiding any explosion.

The second missile, trailing the first by a couple of seconds, also arced down from the clear skies. It was a touch lower than its predecessor, as it tracked the heat exhaust. Continuing to make course corrections as the F-15E flew lower and passed below the line of ridges, the North Korean weapon suddenly lost its lock-on. A second later, the heat-seeking dart smashed into an escarpment. The explosion triggered a small avalanche of loose stone which clattered down one of the rock faces rising above the tree line.

Diving below the mountain crests, the threat sensors went silent as all signs of the radars vanished.

"Whatever button you just pushed there, keep that one in mind. Maybe press that one first next time," David commented.

"Um...okay. It was the one for the microwave, but we

can try it again if you think it'll work. On a side note, my soup is ready," Foley responded. "Want some?"

"What kind is it?"

"Today's treat is a creamy shrimp and crab bisque."

"Has anyone told you that you're weird?" David asked.

"On a daily basis."

"I'm going to have to get a new back-seater."

"Why?! You don't like soup? Fine! No soup for you!"

David and Mark kept their eyes peeled to the heavens, searching for any sign of enemy fighters. North Korea now knew where they were. There was a chance that some of their air force wasn't currently engaged and could be vectored against them. The two sidewinders hanging on pylons under the wings suddenly didn't seem like much protection.

The just-released JSOW arced into the morning skies, sailing over a line of ridges. Hitting its apogee, it began a gliding descent toward its target sixteen miles away. It passed over the wooded slopes that gave way to farms cut into the thick forests. Dirt roads appeared, widening as they grew closer to villages spaced along a wide river. Those villages grew into the outskirts of a city, the rutted country lanes turning into modern roads.

Not constrained by building walls, the eyes of some villagers glanced toward the rising smoke pillars, wondering if the army was training again. Some correctly guessed that the Americans were attacking and let their gazes linger on the overhead blue, dreading the thought of dark objects appearing. None saw the white glide bomb as it arced overhead like an avenging angel, descending toward the nearby city.

The AGM-154 swept over carts, swept over local vendors calling out over dusty streets, swept over municipal buildings flying the flag of North Korea. It saw its target, surrounded by squares comprised of statues, majestic figures striking heroic poses, and murals of the mighty leader painted on buildings. Thick wires led to and from a large, fenced area filled with a multitude of transformers and insulators.

Flying over the electrical substation, the AGM-154

discharged cluster munitions. Those fell inside the fencing and exploded. Showers of sparks rained across the installation as transformers blew. Separated from their insulators, live wires snaked across the ground like deadly serpents, angrily striking and hissing. The citizens hardly noticed when the electricity went out, being used to the fragile nature of the electrical grid. However, a nearby military communication center certainly noticed when its rooms went dark and the equipment failed. The radar screens of yet another air defense unit abruptly went offline.

Departing its first target, the F-15E sliced into a wider valley, lowering to near treetop level. The route to the next target showed on the navigation instruments. Banking around yet another tight corner, David guided the Strike Eagle toward its next victim.

* * * * * *

Other F-15Es came in over the Sea of Japan and crossed into North Korea. Individually, they flew across hostile beaches and vanished into the rugged interior of the north's eastern section of the country. Flying through radar gaps, the Strike Eagles pressed their attacks against power plants, electrical substations, and communication centers. One by one, AGM-154 glide bombs were lobbed into the clear summer skies covering North Korea.

Many of the targeted facilities had backup generators to provide their power. But with the annihilation of the North's power grid, those would only function for as long as diesel could be supplied. With follow-on attacks against fuel depots, North Korea would be forced to prioritize their distribution. Additional attacks targeted major bridges, in particular focusing on those along the Pyongyang-Kaesong highway. Several fell on the bridge across the Ryesong River, dropping two sections of the large concrete span into the wide waterway.

* * * * * *

The radar screen presented a completely different depiction than did the previous engagements. Replicated from the E-3 managing the intercepts, the four North Korean aircraft were laterally spread in a tactical formation, as compared to the bunched formations William had previously observed. It was more like what he was used to seeing during the many exercises he'd attended. Although it was a familiar situation, he felt a touch of anxiety.

Seeing the formation implied a higher level of competence in the pilots, or at least with the flight leader. The turkey shoot he had been involved so far with appeared to be coming to an end. The four enemy planes turned in unison toward Gerber's flight, the second element crossing behind the leader to arrive in the same position once they rolled out. The two formations, one American and the other North Korean, were a hundred miles apart and speeding toward each other at nearly twenty miles per minute.

William watched the mileage count down. He had two AMRAAMs armed and ready, just waiting for the enemy aircraft to come within range. Knowing that the North Korean's longer distance missiles still had a lesser range than what he was carrying, William relaxed a touch. The enemy weapons were old and had proven to be easily defeated by countermeasures. Still, something lingered in the back of the Lieutenant Colonel's mind that gave him a sense of unease.

The turnaround at Misawa Air Base had been a quick one, the F-15 returning with a fresh load of weapons and fuel. Once the flight had checked in with Yukla One One, they were immediately given an intercept heading and sent into the fray.

A flash of fire raced past the cockpit and zoomed into the distance. Seconds later, another missile sped away. White contrails flew from the other Eagles as AIM-120s were fired. William selected another of the long-range weapons nestled underneath in case the need for another volley arose.

Oh shit! William thought.

The startled response was due to the threat receivers that told of a launch coming from the four enemy aircraft eighty miles ahead. According to the latest intel, North Korea didn't possess weapons that could reach that far. William thought that pretty much par for the course. Intel had a lot of things right, but they also missed plenty that were discovered the hard way.

"Like this tidbit," Gerber breathed, readying the countermeasures.

William's flight was given a different heading when the four opposing aircraft made a turn to the southeast. However, as soon as he rolled out on the new course, it was time to focus on the incoming threats.

In the far distance, William glimpsed the contrails forming behind the enemy missiles. The multiple streaks tearing across the firmament presented an ominous picture. At each end of those white lines was the possibility of death. And that danger was closing in at nearly three thousand miles per hour.

Gerber banked the aircraft to present an oblique angle to the inbound missiles. When the projectiles neared, William pulled back on the stick. The F-15C nosed sharply upward, the sun glinting off the curvature of the canopy. He continued the climb while rolling the fighter into a barrel roll. The maneuver presented the missile's guidance system movement in three-dimensions, which was more difficult to track.

Keeping an eye on the thin white trails, he saw the enemy missiles curve as his flight began to maneuver against the threats. Two of them arced toward his aircraft. He discharged chaff and watched as the enemy missiles veered slightly. However, they then recovered and continued homing in on his Eagle.

Finishing his maneuver, William rolled ninety degrees and pulled hard. The missiles jinked with him. Rolling back level, Gerber pulled back on the stick and again shot skyward. The lead missile shot past his tail, the white contrail bending sharply as the weapon circled to regain radar contact. He thumbed more chaff as he turned away, the G-meter hovering at 9Gs.

With the F-15C heading directly toward the second missile, the weapon's software determined the bright radar picture from the countermeasure to be the better target. Arching away from the hard-turning fighter, the deadly dart veered and exploded in the midst of the foil strips.

The first missile came around and found the F-15C, again homing in on the maneuvering aircraft. With his neck craned over his shoulder, William frantically jabbed at the countermeasure button. The weapon looked like it was going to take the bait, but then veered back. It turned a third time, and this time remained focused on the countermeasure. It plowed into the bundle and detonated.

Although still tracked by a fire control radar, the immediate threat to William was gone. He yanked the Eagle around to recover his flight and found his wingman several thousand feet below. Contrails formed off the wingtips as the aircraft was banking hard to the left. William watched as the aircraft rolled upright and then went into a sharp right turn in the opposite direction. Flashing into his vision, he saw a white streak cross behind his wingman. A bright flash left a dark smudge hanging in the air.

A thin trail of smoke formed behind his wingman's fighter. A puff of white shot out of the rear, effectively eliminating the smoke trail. William looked around, searching for his other element. With the help of the E-3s data, he found them reforming a mile away.

"Amber two, status," William radioed.

"Engine two out," his wingman replied.

Looking again to his radar, there were only two of the opposing aircraft showing on the screen. His wingman was out of the fight, presenting William with a quandary. Protocol dictated that he should send one of his flight to accompany his number two home. However, he currently had a three-to-two advantage and would like to keep that. The opposing pilots were better trained than those he had run into so far, so any advantage he could garner could very well determine the outcome of the fight. He had only seconds to make a decision.

"Amber four, escort two home," William called.

"Negative lead. I'm good," Amber Two replied.

William hesitated a moment. It wasn't like he would be putting his flight member out there alone. There was the E-3 that could keep track of his damaged wingman.

"Very well. You're cleared off. See you at home," William said.

The two remaining enemy aircraft had turned and were again heading toward William's flight. The aggressiveness was also something that had been lacking from their previous opponents. For a brief moment, he wondered if he was actually fighting North Koreans. They were able to fire their missiles from a longer distance, and...William interrupted his train of thought down that path. There would be time to reflect and report on what he saw later. First though, he had to make it through the next few minutes.

The two flights were too close for another volley of long-range weapons. William saw two dark shapes appear out of the blue, the two aircraft spread slightly apart in order to support each other. That told William a lot about their training and the confidence levels of the pilots. As the dots rapidly grew in his windscreen, he saw the wingman cross over to the outside of their head-on meeting. That maneuver would allow the wingman to keep the second element of William's flight in sight and keep the wingman from being sandwiched between the two. Another tactically sound maneuver. William knew he had to bring his best game to the table.

As with the previous dogfight, William pulled up sharply just before the two opposing flights passed each other. Going vertical, he looked back over his shoulder. He expected to see the other aircraft in a sharp turn below him and was therefore startled to see another darkly-visored helmet peering at him from only a few feet away. The other pilot had also pulled up prior to crossing. William felt lucky that the two hadn't actually collided. He couldn't really fathom how the two of them had ended up like they were without hitting each other. But that was also for a later time. Right now, he was canopy to canopy with an enemy combatant.

Even though he was half expecting a missile to fly up his

tailpipe, William couldn't worry about what the enemy's wingman was doing. He had to trust that his second element was handling the other aircraft. Or at the very least, keeping his six clear. The two aircraft, the F-15C and the Mig-29, hung next to each other as the altimeters wound crazily upward.

Knowing that he had a slight advantage in thrust to weight ratio if needed, William eased off the throttles in an attempt to slide in behind the enemy combatant. The Mig momentarily pulled ahead as the two aircraft soared through flight level 450. The Fulcrum pulled toward William, shooting across his front. This forced the F-15C to overshoot.

With the airspeed bleeding off, William nudged the throttles forward and pulled back on the stick, attempting to follow the Mig. As the nose of the Eagle tracked back toward the Mig, the enemy pilot turned again, again crossing close in front of William. This caused another overshoot with the nose of the F-15C forced to the outside of the Mig's turn. As the two aircraft flew past fifty thousand feet, they were now engaged in a vertical rolling scissors: two aircraft continually turning into each other, each seeking to gain an edge and slip behind the other combatant.

The airspeed continued to bleed off with William applying enough thrust to keep from stalling while simultaneously preventing the aircraft from accelerating ahead of the North Korean Mig. Passing fifty-five thousand feet, the Mig made another pull into William. This time, instead of maintaining the rolling scissors, the enemy pilot nosed his aircraft down and went to afterburner. The Mig separated from the F-15C and accelerated as the enemy pilot dove toward the sea, eleven miles below.

William saw the Mig disengage from the maneuver. Knowing that they were approaching the altitude limits of the Mig, he had been expecting something similar. Using bottom rudder, William eased the Eagle over and slid the throttles into afterburner. With the increase in thrust, the aircraft surged forward as the nose passed through the horizon. The Mig was now growing smaller as the speed differential between the two was steadily increasing.

The F-15C nosed over and William began chasing the Mig. Seeing William commit to a nose down attitude, the enemy pilot pulled up into a high-G climb. Gerber followed the maneuver, but the foreign pilot had timed it perfectly and William again found himself on the outside of the vertical maneuver. With his lower airspeed, but higher altitude, the Mig shot past the nose of the F-15, just enough offset that William couldn't get a clean "guns" shot.

Keeping an eye on the climbing Mig, William wasn't able to get a sidewinder to lock-on. He was just inside the lower range parameter for the missile. Again, the two climbed straight up, the enemy pilot constantly maneuvering to keep William's aircraft from gaining a firing position. William was doing all he could just to maintain the slight advantage he currently held, knowing that positions could flip in an instant.

Nearing fifty thousand feet, William could see the darkness of space ahead of the Mig. The two twin-engine fighters were again engaged in a vertical rolling scissors maneuver. Each time the Fulcrum passed in front of the F-15C, William could clearly see his opponent's helmet swivel as the pilot turned to keep William in sight.

Taking a risk, William eased his throttles back and fanned the speed brake. He meant to gain a little separation, but with the slow airspeed and thin air, he ran the risk of stalling the aircraft. If that happened, the aircraft would fall, placing William at an extreme disadvantage as he plunged down to recover his airspeed.

When William turned to stay with the Mig, and the pilot turned into William's turn, Gerber selected guns and fired a short burst. Even though the pipper stayed on the enemy aircraft for a split second, William didn't witness any strikes, with most of the tracers trailing aft of the aircraft.

The enemy pilot continued to let his nose fall through the horizon, attempting the same escape maneuver as before. William nudged the afterburners and hung for a moment longer before turning hard to chase the fleeing Mig. When the F-15C's nose fell and William again committed to a nose down attitude, the Mig initiated another climb.

William's delay allowed him a little more separation. When he looked at the climbing Mig, the tone in his headset warbled to let him know that the sidewinder had a good signal on a heat source. Without hesitation, William fired. The AIM-9X roared off the wing pylon and streaked for the Mig's tailpipe. Flares shot out from the Fulcrum. The sidewinder turned to stay with the Mig, but the angle was too acute, and it flew right past the tail.

With the vertical maneuver and William's subsequent one to stay with the enemy aircraft, Gerber was once again inside the heat-seeker's parameters. Instead of remaining vertical, the Fulcrum continued over the top and pulled toward William's F-15C. William noted that each time he thought he had the Mig, the enemy pilot was able to put William on the outside of the maneuver and thus remain outside a good firing position.

Listening in on his flight's radio calls to stay aware of the overall fight, it was clear that they had their hands full with the wingman.

Whoever these guys are, they're good, William thought, banking to stay with the maneuvering Mig.

Pressed down in his seat from the Gs, barely noticing the pressure of the G-suit, William wondered just how this engagement was going to end. No matter what he did, he couldn't quite get into a good firing position.

"Splash one," the radio chimed.

William knew that the enemy wingman had finally been downed. Now he could get some help with this guy. However, the pilot seemed to have other plans. Knowing that he'd lost his wingman and that he was now at a huge disadvantage, the Mig crossed in front of William and hit his afterburners as he nosed down.

William used his rudders to edge his nose down and nudged his afterburners to keep from stalling. Coming through the horizon, he saw the Mig racing for all he was worth toward the expanse of sea below. Given William's slow airspeed over the top and the Mig's acceleration, the aircraft was miles away by the time William was able to get his nose pointed the right direction.

Having fired most of his AMRAAMs prior to this engagement, William was down to his last missile, a shorter-range AIM-9X. A tone warbled in his headset and he fired. The missile flew downward, appearing to head straight for the Fulcrum. At the last moment, the weapon veered toward a stream of flares that shot out from the Mig.

His number four wingman had two sidewinders available, but the second element was still some distance away. They could still give chase to the fleeing Fulcrum, though with little-to-no hope of catching the aircraft, which was now accelerating through Mach 2. William pulled up and eased back on the throttles. With another glance in the direction of the distant shore, he turned back to the east and set a course for Japan.

With one downed enemy combatant, he had joined an elite set of aviators. In two sorties, he had become an ace, an honor he shared with three others in his flight. When they landed, they were showered with cheers by those of the squadron who weren't out flying. The first to shake his hand was his number four wingman, who had four kills to his credit. They had maintained the F-15C's perfect record for aerial combat.

*   *   *   *   *   *

The post-flight briefing and video from the encounter made its way up the chain of command. It was generally known that North Korean pilots didn't receive a lot of training, the limits placed on them due to the heavy sanctions, which meant a shortage of parts and fuel. The encounter brought to light the rumors concerning Chinese or possible Russian pilots flying for the North, either to give the North Korean air force a boost, or to provide priceless experience for those foreign pilots. It could have been that the foreign pilots were there to provide training for North Korea. The rumors were much the same as those that had circulated during the Vietnam War, but the accusations proved difficult to substantiate.

The video from William's flight of F-15Cs, from the E-3, and the voice recordings taken from electronic intelligence aircraft that had been flying in the area couldn't prove anything one way or the other. The language heard from the combatant pilots during the encounter was definitely Korean, even using the North Korean standard form, but the accents were difficult to determine.

Also unknown was the weaponry used by the North Korean Migs. The long-range encounters couldn't have used standard North Korean missiles, as they were fired from longer ranges than had previously been known. That either meant that the North had engineered a new missile, enhanced one, or that it wasn't one of theirs to begin with. Analyzing all of the day's encounters showed that other North Korean missiles fired were from within expected ranges. There was also the fact that all other long-range air-to-air weapons were easily countered with chaff expenditures. This had not been the case in William's engagement. Rumors continued circulating about Russian involvement for years afterward, without any proof materializing to authenticate those claims.

*   *   *   *   *   *

Air-to-air missiles came raining down out of the heavens, catching many of North Korea's fighters as they either raced south to combat the F-16s or headed to one of the three runways with underground shelters. The crystal-clear skies over North Korea became marred with the dark smudge trails from burning aircraft plummeting out of the heights. The whines of damaged planes spiraling down ended with sharp explosions, which rang off steep hillsides and echoed down ravines. Palls of ascending smoke pockmarked the countryside.

Any North Korean fighter surviving the attacks of F-15Cs

flying over the Sea of Japan found that they were unable to land at any of the three designated airfields. The cruise missiles had been effective in cratering the runways. Most of the surviving planes diverted to special strips of highway that had been widened and subsequently denoted as emergency or alternate use runways. There they sat until fuel and ammunition trucks could be brought to their location.

Some of the fighters stationed at airfields with underground hangars never left the ground as they were designated as "secondary strike" aircraft. The plan was to have a semi-viable air force ready for when American and South Korean air bases were overrun, thereby limiting their air superiority. The plan looked good on paper, however, most of the North Korean Air Force was made of up Mig-23s and Mig-21s, both of which had a very short life span in modern engagements. The American attacks had effectively removed the North Korea air force as a viable battle entity.

* * * * * *

Cameras aboard a KH-11 satellite passing over North Korea peered through smoke rising from several target sites. Analysts associated with the Indo-Pacific Command reviewed the imagery, conducting damage assessments on primary targets. Many were marked as destroyed and received a line-through. Others made it to secondary target lists, the priorities altering depending on the type of facility in question. Two hours after the photos started coming in, orders were sent to units stationed in Japan, South Korea, and the Sea of Japan.

Chapter Seven

East China Sea
30 July, 2021

The USS *Louisville* was a large dark shape gliding slowly, a hundred feet below the surface of the East China Sea. The Ohio-class submarine had previously been part of the sea-based nuclear triad, supporting deterrence by carrying twenty-four nuclear ballistic missiles. After undergoing a conversion, the ballistic submarine became a guided missile boat, carrying one hundred and fifty-four Tomahawk cruise missiles, with the ability to fire Harpoon anti-ship missiles from the torpedo tubes. The firepower of a single SSGN could destroy an entire nation.

Twenty-two doors along the aft dorsal section eased open. Light from the surface filtered down to reveal domed objects recessed in compartments. Electronic commands from within the massive vessel signaled one of the cylindrical objects to be forcefully expelled from its chamber. Rippling light touched upon the Tomahawk as it surged from its tube, striking for the surface.

With an upheaval of water, the cruise missile broke free. The roar of the rocket motor echoed for miles, turning the seawater to steam and pushing the weapon clear of its watery confines. Accelerating, the SLCM pushed further into the morning skies. Winglets swung into position, wedges holding the aft control surfaces falling free. The solid-propellant rocket motor cut out, the missile continuing forward when the turbofan engine took over.

More followed, breaking free of the sea to race toward distant North Korean shores. They followed separate paths toward their individual targets. The main priority was to take out the ballistic missile launch facilities which survived the initial attacks. Next on the list were storage bunkers known to house North Korea's chemical, biological, and nuclear weapons. Third was the North's artillery.

North Korea had eight thousand artillery pieces capable of leveling Seoul within hours. The chief concern was that those could also deliver stockpiles of chemical or biological weapons. The United States considered North Korea's leader to be unstable and completely capable of ordering weapons of mass destruction to be used at the outset of hostilities rather than preserved as a last resort measure.

The problem facing target planners was that much of the North's massed equipment was hidden in underground bunkers. Bunker busters had hit some of the known cave systems but with unknown results. The majority of the cruise missiles fired from the *Louisville* again targeted artillery units, focusing on those massed aboveground.

With North Korean air defenses demolished by the initial F-16 attacks, there was little to stop the missiles from arriving over their targets. In some places, chaos still reigned from previous attacks. Explosions again echoed throughout encampments. Armor-piercing bomblets crashed through vehicles, punching into engine compartments and ammunition storages. Some exploded in sheets of flame while others belched dark, acrid smoke. Screams joined the chorus of explosions as anti-personnel submunitions tore into soldiers called to duty.

* * * * * *

Keeping up the pressure on North Korean forces gathered near the DMZ, waves of F-16s continued hammering at the air defenses. Falcons armed with Advanced Antiradiation Guided Missiles patrolled the DMZ, passively probing for search-and-fire control radars coming online. The doctrine was to establish and maintain air supremacy. With North Korea's aging air force all but eliminated, the greatest threat to that dominance was the surface-to-air missiles that could directly support the battlefield.

With the United States and South Korea's strategy of holding on to the peninsula through a series of defensive lines and strategic withdrawals, air supremacy on the battlefield was an absolute necessity.

Armed with AGM-65 Maverick missiles, a third wave of F-16s approached the DMZ boundaries. Firing from twelve miles away, the pilots targeted the massed armored formations that sat inside bivouacs surrounded by razor wire. The older precision weapons hammered into the top of the tanks and self-propelled artillery pieces. Burning armored vehicles added their funeral pyres to the many columns of fire and smoke drifting across North Korea.

*   *   *   *   *   *

Leaving the Han River to the rear, the F-16 coasted south. Captain Dave Lowry stared west, looking over the metropolis cities of Seoul and Incheon. Traffic jammed the freeways heading out of the cities, both lanes clogged with luggage-strapped vehicles. Dave could see armored vehicles on both sides of the roads, probably attempting to maintain some semblance of control or to clear avenues through which the army could proceed.

Returning to Osan after expending his contingent of antiradiation missiles, Dave knew that it wouldn't be long until the North Korean forces began to march south. The Army units would need clear lanes of travel in order to stem the coming tide, but good luck stopping ten million people when they decided it was time to move. In the distance to the south, lines of dust rose into the morning skies, signs that many fleeing the capital city and the surrounding area were also filling the backroads.

For the South Koreans on the ground, staring at the waves of aircraft that had been flying across the DMZ since near dawn, the look in their eyes said everything. After seventy years of relative peace, war was again coming to South Korea.

*   *   *   *   *   *

Beijing, China

30 July, 2021

Defense Minister Zhou Yang read the early reports coming out from North Korea. It appeared that the United States had opted to preempt an invasion of the South, attacking targets throughout the North. He didn't have preliminary damage assessments, but he could guess at the results. The number of aircraft and missiles the Americans had sent against the North Korean regime, coupled with the antique equipment the north possessed, could only have one possible outcome. North Korea's ability to wage a protracted campaign would be in jeopardy.

Zhou had been fairly certain that North Korea wouldn't be able to unify the peninsula unless they had moved quickly once they started their mobilization. The ploy of waiting for China's attack in order to give them a better chance was backfiring. Time was America's friend, and it gave them the opportunity for reinforcement and, as could be seen from the attacks, a chance to substantially damage the northern country with little fanfare.

Studying the attacks made Zhou nervous. Granted, China was in a far better position militarily than North Korea, but he was also aware of the sophisticated firepower available to the United States. While China had been able to keep America out of the East and South China Seas with its missile threat, that may not be the case much longer. The National Defense Minister had withheld information on the actual number of casualties China had suffered in order to push for the continuance of the invasion plans. But there was no hiding the fact that a startling number of anti-ship missiles had been expended destroying the Taiwanese naval fleet.

There was also the issue of the aircraft shot down or damaged in the engagements with the island nation, aside from those destroyed by the Americans during the battles for the Spratly Islands. China still had a large inventory of aircraft and missiles at its disposal, but Zhou was experiencing his first doubts as to whether that inventory would be sufficient. If they could just get enough soldiers established ashore in Taiwan, and supply them long enough, then it wouldn't matter. China would own Taiwan by occupation, and there would be little any country could do to evict them. Once Taipei and the government there was overrun, then Zhou thought that the war would effectively end. America would back off once Taiwan came under China's control. Zhou felt this in his bones.

The problem was getting there. America's carriers had to be kept out of the fight, or at least their involvement limited. The annihilation of the submarine force was a blow that Zhou was finding difficult to come to terms with. It had been so perfect. There hadn't been anything wrong with his strategy. It should have worked. Sure, war had variables that couldn't be wholly anticipated, chance encounters, lucky shots, but those anomalies shouldn't have led to the destruction of almost his entire undersea fleet.

The preemptive attacks from Taiwan had hurt; they had caught the military unprepared. It had been embarrassing to see how much damage the island had inflicted. Many of the systems placed near the eastern shores, anti-ship, cruise missiles, and anti-air, had been greatly reduced by Taiwan's missile attacks. Even some of the mobile ballistic platforms had been hit. Zhou was clever enough to figure out those had to have been targeted at the request of Washington, DC.

One major issue was that there weren't many hypersonic missiles remaining in the inventory. China had publicly declared the missiles to be operational, but Zhou knew the real status. Although the anti-ship weapon could fly and track a target through its terminal phase, the accuracy was still a problem. Reentering the atmosphere caused ionization, which hampered the missile's ability to locate its target until it reached a lower altitude. However, the latest computer tests did reflect advances in this area; it was entirely possible that the reentry glide vehicle could now find and hit a moving target at sea.

Another issue holding Zhou back from issuing firing orders was a review conducted some time ago and still thought to be valid. The current theory among some of the geo-political think-tanks was that use of a hypersonic anti-ship missile might actually cause the conflict to escalate to a nuclear exchange. There was also the possibility that it could start a regional arms race with Japan and India, perhaps even restarting a nuclear arms race.

Something had to shift the balance…something had to be done about keeping American carrier groups away from Taiwan. Taiwan had to be the priority. If the island fell, then China would hold the edge in the South China Sea. The military could be rebuilt, and the consequences of China's actions dealt with once they had achieved their aims. Minister Zhou lifted the phone to his ear and dialed.

* * * * * *

Eastern China
30 July, 2021

Dust trails rose into the afternoon sky. At their head were several heavy, olive drab trucks. Each of the ten-wheeled military vehicles carried a single missile strapped to the back of the transporter erector launchers. Since receiving orders, they had hastily driven throughout the afternoon, finally arriving in a desolate area near the eastern coast. With a hiss of brakes, the huge launchers stopped and began the process of setting up the battery of medium-range ballistic missiles. Mounted atop each of the DF-17 launchers was a DF-ZF maneuverable glide vehicle.

Dust settled to the ground amid shouts that reverberated across the area. Crews clambered over the trucks as the vehicles were prepped for launch. Steel arms extended from the sides, anchoring the large vehicles to provide stability. With a whine of hydraulics, the powerful-looking missiles slowly raised upward, brackets holding the weapons tight. A *clunk* of finality locked the long ballistic missiles into their upright positions.

A military satellite located and marked the position of the American carrier task force steaming in the North Pacific several hundred miles east of Japan. That data was relayed to a ground station which then processed the information and sent it along to the battery of DongFeng-17s. It was imperative that the missile guidance systems were continually updated with the correct targeting information, thus requiring a very specific kill chain.

A wall of dirt mushroomed outward from each of the TELs. Flames shot through the rolling clouds as the main engines ignited. With rumbling roars that were internally felt, the rockets lifted from their platforms. The transitions to flight seemed to be hesitant ones as the missiles slowly clawed into the air. They accelerated, but their vast size made it appear as if the entire process was a struggle.

Trailing fire and white smoke, the delivery systems forced their way into the afternoon skies.

*   *   *   *   *   *

The ballistic launches alerted the North American Aerospace Defense Command at Petersen Air Force Base, in addition to those of the Indo-Pacific Command. The ballistic trajectories were tracked as high-resolution photos of the launch sites were analyzed. It was quickly determined that the missiles were medium-range and therefore not a direct threat to the United States. Further analysis showed that the weapon launches were likely China's DF-ZF maneuverable glide vehicles, sitting atop DF-17 missiles that were specifically designed for the hypersonic anti-ship warheads. In addition to increasing the DEFCON level, warnings were distributed to all US installations within range of the ballistic missiles. According to the analysis however, with the type of weapon deployed, there were only four targets China could be looking at.

*   *   *   *   *   *

Rear Admiral Chip Calhoun lifted the handset.

"Bridge," a voice answered.

"Admiral Calhoun. Put Captain Kelley on," Calhoun ordered.

"Aye, sir."

"Kelley here, sir."

"Tyson. I suppose you saw the alert. Do you have any recoveries inbound?"

"I did see it, sir. And yes, we have four inbound 18s coming off patrol," Captain Tyson Kelley answered.

"Can they be pushed off to a tanker?" Calhoun asked.

"Aye, sir. They're being redirected as we speak."

"Very well. Halt all launches and recoveries. The task force will be turning east and accelerating to flank speed. The anticipated time to again begin recoveries should be thirty minutes."

"Aye, sir."

The coordination was done quickly. Task Force 70, with its two carrier strike groups, turned away from the site of China's launches and increased its speed to thirty knots. Weapons were released, and every ship brought to battle stations. The destroyers moved a little farther out to establish a wider radar picket in order to capture the missiles as far away as possible.

Even though initial indications showed a trajectory toward either Japan or the task force, similar actions were conducted with the southern task force comprised of another two carrier strike groups. Those ships turned and were speeding away to the southeast at thirty knots.

*　*　*　*　*　*

The first stage rockets burned out and separated. A couple of seconds later, the second stage motors ignited and propelled the DF-17 missiles higher, eventually entering a low earth orbit. When the second stages fell away, shrouds peeled off and drifted behind the rockets. Winged shapes were then expelled from their mounts.

The glide vehicles descended and reentered the atmosphere where they pulled up in 25G maneuvers. This shot them back into space where they arced at accelerated speeds. The glide vehicles then began a series of random moves meant to confuse ground and space-based radars. Their small profile and advanced maneuvering made them more difficult to track. The twenty-one Maneuverable Glide Vehicles then began heating up for a second time as they re-entered the earth's atmosphere.

The reentry process disrupted the ability of the MaRVs to receive targeting information, something the weapons had been constantly getting during their transit. They came into the upper reaches of the atmosphere traveling at Mach 10, gliding toward the latest coordinates they were given prior to reentry.

In their terminal dive, onboard targeting systems came alive and searched the vast expanse of ocean for any sign of the targets they were given. Traveling at a hundred miles per minute, the thirty-mile glide paths didn't give the missiles much time to locate and track their targets. At the same time, they didn't give defenses much time to react, even if they were able to track the six thousand-mile-per-hour weapons.

Still maneuvering to throw off ship-based radar systems, eighteen of the twenty-one hypersonic glide vehicles were able to locate their flattop targets.

Aboard the ships of Task Force 70 speeding and maneuvering across the Northern Pacific, guidance systems picked up the first reentry from the generated heat, and then the subsequent reentries. Once the missiles were again in the atmosphere and descending at Mach 10, RIM-174 Standard Extended Range Active Missiles roared from the decks of Arleigh-Burke destroyers and Ticonderoga-class cruisers.

Designed as ballistic missile interceptors, the long-range anti-air missiles soared into the air, maneuvering as they attempted to track the hypersonic weapons. Many shot past the speeding projectiles, exploding far behind the gliding vehicles. With the speed of the incoming threats, reengaging misses just wasn't possible.

Due to the maneuvers conducted at such high speeds, seven MaRVs turned to drastic angles away from the carriers thrashing the waters. Using their own terminal guidance, the missiles lost track of the carriers and weren't able to relocate them in the short time it took from reentry to ground. Well beyond the task force ships, they crashed violently into the waves. The nearest impacted eleven miles outside of the escorting pickets.

Three Arleigh-Burke destroyers were specially equipped with laser systems of varying wattage. The USS *Kidd* and the USS *Benfold* had been modified and their Phalanx systems removed, replaced by a HELIOS laser system. These were 60-kilowatt high-energy lasers equipped with integrated optical dazzlers and surveillance systems. The USS *Barry* carried a lower watt (30-kilowatt) Optical Dazzler Interdictor, Navy (ODIN) meant to interrupt optical and infrared sensors aboard UAVs and missiles.

Moving as they were in the higher altitudes, the warheads were difficult to track on radar. They'd appear on the scopes in one place, altitude, and course only to be in a different location on the next sweep. When radar contact held, both high and low wattage lasers lashed out toward the glide vehicles.

Two of the weapons were on courses veering away from the task force, so the defenses focused on nine that were rapidly descending toward the carriers. The USS *Kidd* was able to get a 60-kilowatt laser locked onto one MaRV. The high temperature beam ablated the surface material of the glide vehicle, burning through the dense material designed to withstand reentry temperatures.

A thin line of smoke trailed from the Chinese weapon. Burning through the skin, the MaRV began veering to one side due to drag differential. The roll became more pronounced, and the hypersonic vehicle began tumbling, tearing itself apart from the high speeds.

The USS *Benfold* was able to get its laser locked on to another target. The ray burned through the outer layer and the high-temperature light beam melted through system wiring. Without guidance, the glide vehicle entered a wide turn to the south where it spiraled down, impacting the Pacific eighteen miles from the outer picket screen.

The lower wattage beam from the USS *Barry* painted

across a third vehicle, but the laser couldn't do anything to interfere with the targeting system or the missile itself. As the weapons were being guided by radar, the dazzler system had no effect.

A fourth laser shot out from an amphibious ship, the USS *Portland*. This solid state, hundred-and-fifty-kilowatt system was part of a test that was able to get a hard kill on an unmanned drone. The laser latched on to a fourth missile, the Chinese anti-ship glide vehicle rolling sharply to one side before disintegrating. In a period of seconds, following the misses of the sea-launched anti-air missiles, three maneuverable glide vehicles either came apart in the air or were tossed off course.

As the remaining six MaRVs descended and encountered denser air, they slowed during their thirty-second approach. They went from Mach 10 down to Mach 7, and then slowed even further to Mach 3 when they passed through fifteen thousand feet.

Decks became awash in smoke and fire as both long- and short-range missiles were fired toward the incoming high-speed threats. The two Ticonderoga escorting cruisers, the USS *Bunker Hill* and the USS *Shiloh*, both conducted electronic countermeasures against the missile threat. Part of the system took in radar waves and sent them back out, making the cruisers appear as targets larger than the carriers they were protecting. The system also attempted to confuse radar homing threats by making the enemy sensors perceive their targets as being in a different location. Two of the MaRVs were fooled by the false radar pictures and homed in on a section of the ocean a mile behind the USS *Nimitz*.

Missiles and close-in weapon systems put up a solid defensive barrier. As the Chinese anti-ship weapons fell through fifteen thousand feet, these systems were able to better track the missiles. Lasers from the three ships were able to lock on more readily, sending three more MaRVs spiraling down.

The two which had been thrown off course by the electronic countermeasures slammed into the Pacific, sending giant fountains of water geysering into the air. The kinetic energy caused the weapons to disintegrate upon impact, scattering pieces across a wide area.

The automated targeting systems, which were able to integrate with one another, failed to retarget the lone Chinese weapon that the USS *Barry* had failed to take down. The Mach 3 missile was one of the only Chinese DF-ZFs to correctly track its target all the way down. It flew through the dense defensive barricades the task force had layered around it.

The USS *Nimitz* shook, almost seeming to come to a stop from its thirty-knot dash, as the last Chinese missile slammed into the forward flight deck. The kinetic energy caused a powerful tremor to run through the entire ship as it tore through the flight deck and crashed through the bow, the thousand-pound warhead detonating just in front of the carrier.

Smoke roiled up from the strike and explosion, the blast rolling aft as the ship continued to plow forward. Pieces of metal shot across the flight deck, slicing through several deckhands. With the high-pitched screech of tortured metal, a section of the forward flight deck tore free, taking some of the bow with it. It hung on to the main ship for nearly thirty seconds before it finally ripped free and fell into the ocean.

Steam from ruptured lines hissed into the air, along with the smoke from fires that were started below deck. Several F-18 attack fighters were swept clear from the impact, though two rolled off into the Pacific when the forward section fell away. Although it wasn't what was expected by either side, China had proven that, when delivered en masse, their vaunted ship killers were indeed a deadly force to be reckoned with.

# # #

About the Author

John O'Brien is a former Air Force fighter instructor pilot who transitioned to Special Operations for the latter part of his career gathering his campaign ribbon for Desert Storm. Immediately following his military service, John became a firefighter/EMT with a local department. Along with becoming a firefighter, he fell into the Information Technology industry in corporate management. Currently, John is writing full-time.

As a former marathon runner, John lives in the beautiful Pacific Northwest and can now be found kayaking out in the waters of Puget Sound, mountain biking in the Capital Forest, hiking in the Olympic Peninsula, or pedaling his road bike along the many scenic roads.

Connect with me online

Facebook:
https://Facebook.com/AuthorJohnWOBrien

Twitter:
https://Twitter.com/A_NewWorld

Web Site:
https://John-OBrien.com

Email:
John@John-OBrien.com